He held his breath, waiting for another blast from the automatic weapon. From his position in the thick brush he could still see the car. The day had turned still. Quiet as death, he thought. He lifted his head an inch or so. The car had maybe two dozen holes ripped along the driver's side. Streaks of blood, still wet and oozing, marred the blue surface.

That's when he heard the voice. "You're gonna die, kid. Might as well show yourself. You can't hide forever."

B.&E.

Dave Pedneau

BALLANTINE BOOKS • NEW YORK

Library of Congress Catalog Card Number: 90-93467

ISBN 0-345-36420-1

Manufactured in the United States of America

First Edition: March 1991

For Elaine, again,
and in memory of Christopher Cox

B.&E.
In police jargon B.&E. means
the "breaking and entering" of
a residence or place of commerce

PROLOGUE

THE SINGLE-EDGED RAZOR BLADE glided with swift and silent ease through the strands of plastic filament that formed the window screen. The assault on the screen had started in the lower left corner and had proceeded upward and then across the top, its course kept parallel and tightly adjacent to the tarnished aluminum frame. As the blade carved downward on the third and final leg of its journey, the flimsy screen collapsed into the house.

From the home's interior came a dull roar. The intruders were counting on the sound, produced—they knew—by several electric fans, to muffle any noises they might make. The small gloved hand that had controlled the blade tossed it aside. It made a slight ping as it bounced away from a natural-gas meter positioned close to the home's foundation. Other hands, also protected by gloves but much larger, hoisted the petite body upward and through the open window. The figure disappeared into the darkness of the house.

The others—there were two of them, both bigger than the one lifted into the house—moved through the muggy August night toward the back porch. They said nothing to each other. There was no need; their strategy was well practiced by now. The only sound came from their feet as they made a slight swishing sound in the dew-damp grass.

The atmosphere itself sweated a moist haze in the unseasonable heat parching the central Appalachians. At midnight the region had entered its eighth day of the late summer swelter. The newspeople and meteorologists were calling it the worst on record, at least in southern West Virginia. Mid-day temperatures had challenged the 100-degree mark on six of the past eight days. Such summer weather commonly afflicted the big eastern cities and the southern coastal plain, but the people in the mountains to the west weren't accustomed to such tropical assaults. Typically, a mountain "hot spell" translated to daytime temperatures in the mid-eighties. During the current unpleasantness the nighttime low seldom dropped below that. By the fifth day of the heat wave the feverish demand for air conditioners had depleted the local supply. Electric fans remained available, but at twice the pre–hot-spell price.

The residents did what they could to cope with the swelter, and for most that translated to high-priced fans and open windows. It had made the felonious work of those breaking into the small frame house almost too easy. By the time the two outside men reached the rear porch, an open back door awaited them. Dressed in zippered black coveralls, they melted into the dark, tepid interior of the home.

Margaret Trent watched from the open second-story window of the house next door. The short hedge, maybe thirty inches high, that separated her property from the Bennings' did not obstruct her view. In one hand she cradled a small telephone. With the other she wiped the perspiration from her forehead. She dropped the hand from her forehead and started to press the buttons in the dark—just the simple emergency number of 911. Her sweat-dampened fingers were trembling.

On her first attempt a woman answered. "We're sorry. Your call did not go through. Please hang up—"

"Oh my," Mrs. Trent said. "Can't you help me?"

The voice droned on. "—and call again. If you need help—"

"I need the police!"

"Dial your operator. This is a recording."

"A recording?"

Mrs. Trent, widowed now for five years, pushed more buttons, trying to get the dial tone back. Instead, she got the recording again. She hated the newfangled phones with their little soft buttons and their sensitive electronic natures.

"Damnation." It was the harshest word she ever used. She set the phone down on the telephone stand, took a deep breath, and picked it up. The dial tone had returned. She tried 911 again.

This time a man answered. "Milbrook Emergency Dispatch."

"People are breaking into the house next door." Her voice quavered as she relayed the information.

"Your address, ma'am?"

"They're not breaking into my house."

"Please, ma'am. Your address."

"One thousand and eight White Oak Lane, but—"

"Your name?"

"Margaret Trent. Look, young man, I don't think you understand—"

"I'm sorry, Mrs. Trent, but I need this information. What's your phone number?"

She gave it. "Young man, they are already inside the house."

"It's next door to you?"

"Yes!"

"On the same side of the street?"

"Yes. It's 1006 White Oak. Please, you must hurry. The people who live in the house are home."

"Please hold on, Mrs. Trent. I'll dispatch a unit right now."

The phone clicked.

Mrs. Trent looked back out the window at the darkened house of her neighbors. *Please, God . . . let them hurry.*

The phone came alive again. "I have someone in the neighborhood, Mrs. Trent. Please stay on the phone with me. You indicated there were more than one. How many?"

"I saw three. One went in the window. The other two went to the back of the house. I guess the one inside let them in."

"So there's no one outside now."

"No, I don't see anybody. The house belongs to—"

He placed her on hold again. She hung up.

Patrolman Jim Mayberry wheeled his cruiser around in the parking lot of an all-night convenience store. He hit the blue lights and siren just as soon as he bounced back onto Milbrook's main street.

His radio crackled on again. "Dispatch to Car Two."

"Go ahead, dispatch."

There was a moment's pause. "Are you running code three?"

"Ten four," Mayberry answered. Code three meant that he had both emergency lights and sirens activated.

"You might oughta nix that," the dispatcher said. "If there are burglars in the house, they'll hear you coming."

Jim Mayberry didn't say so, but that was exactly why he was heading to the complaint under code three. He wanted to announce his arrival. The only other officer working that evening was tied up at the county courthouse conducting a breath test on a suspected drunk driver. Without someone to back him up, he hoped to give the assholes in the house plenty of chance to get away. He'd been a cop too long—was too close to collecting on his pension—to be a one-man SWAT team.

"Any other info?" Mayberry asked.

"The lady next door says there are at least three, and all have gained entry into the home."

"Ask her if she saw any weapons."

"Ten four." Thirty seconds later the dispatcher was back on the air. "The caller's hung up, Car Two. She didn't mention any weapons."

But that doesn't mean they don't have any.

The dispatcher came back. "She gave her street address

as 1008 Oak White Lane. The address for the complaint is 1006.''

''I should be there in five minutes.''

He waited for an acknowledgment. It didn't come for a minute or so. ''County to Car Two.''

''Go ahead, County.''

''The chief has been monitoring the transmission. He advises that you should not—I repeat, not—run with lights and siren.''

Mayberry cursed, after which he flipped off both emergency signals. He keyed the mike. ''They're turned off, County. Call up to the courthouse and see how long before I'm gonna have some backup. I don't wanna have to kill anybody.''

Again the delay in the dispatcher's response was abnormal. A gentle fog mellowed the glare of the car's lights as he turned onto Folks Street, the most direct access to the exclusive section of the small city known as North Milbrook. Located on the city side of the subdivision, White Oak Lane wasn't exactly ritzy, but for all practical purposes its residents considered themselves a car model or two above middle class.

The dispatcher finally got back to him. ''County to Car Two, be advised that the chief himself is responding to provide backup. He said he was leaving his home immediately. He advises that you proceed with caution.''

''Well, shit,'' Mayberry said, but not into the mike. Just what he needed—Milbrook's new police chief looking over his shoulder. *Probably thinks I'm a gawdamn coward or something.*

When Officer Mayberry did respond to the police station, he said an unenthusiastic, ''Ten four.'' Then he tossed the mike into the seat beside him and gunned the cruiser toward the breaking and entering in progress.

In the master bedroom of the Benning home a large floor fan sat atop a dressing table, its outflow directed toward a queen-size bed that filled the center of the room. The woman slept under the thin cover of a sheet. Fred Benning, bloated by his love of food and naked except for white jockey shorts, rested on top of the sheet. He drifted in and out of sleep. The rush of hot air from the fan offered little comfort. Cursing, he lifted his head from the pillow and flipped it over, hoping that its cool underside would refresh him. It didn't. His wife, unbothered by the stagnant atmosphere, snored lightly.

"Dammit," he muttered, pushing himself up from the bed. "I can't stand this. I'm suffocating."

Damp and sticky with sweat, and itching, too, he tried to inhale deeply. It seemed as if his lungs had to work double time to provide his large body with oxygen. Christ, he had to do something. Maybe if he stood right in front of the fan.

He was just about to rise to go to the fan when he noticed the odd silhouette at the dresser next to the bed.

"Janice?" he said, thinking for an instant that it was his fifteen-year-old daughter. After all, she was the only other person in the house. Or the only other person who was *supposed* to be in the house.

He started to yank the sheet over his exposed body, but the sudden realization that it wasn't Janice made him suck viciously for a complete breath. His heart convulsed, ballooned inside his chest.

He tried to jump from the bed. "Who the hell—"

The trespasser lunged just as Fred Benning's bare feet hit the hardwood floor. A searing pain shocked the left side of his torso. At first he didn't know what it was, not until his hand went to the point of the pain. A warm flow covered his hand.

"Dear God." He collapsed to the floor, more a casualty of mental shock—the thought of it—than a victim of the effect of the wound itself.

"Alice!" he cried.

His wife was already waking up, her hand feeling for him on his side of the bed.

"Fred?"

"Run, Alice!"

"Where are you?"

"Janice! You gotta get Janice!"

"For God's sakes, Fred. Are you dreaming?"

"Get Janice!"

She continued to grope for him. "Where are you?"

"For Chrissakes, woman!"

The light came on.

His wife peered over the side of the bed. She frowned at her husband, flat on his stomach, crawling toward the door. "Fred? What on earth are you—"

"Burglars!" he managed to say, rolling over.

That's when Alice Benning saw the smear of blood on the soft white paunch of her husband. She screamed.

Margaret Trent, still standing at the open window of her bedroom, watched the police cruiser pull to a slow stop in front of the Benning house. The door opened, and a tall figure got out. He paused long enough to adjust his hat and his belt. Then he pulled his gun.

A light flashed on in a window she knew was the Bennings' master bedroom. She stepped forward a little, secure in the belief that no one could see her in the darkened room.

Mrs. Trent didn't hear Alice Benning's scream. Jim Mayberry, much closer to its source, did. He was moving up through the yard, his face already glistening with sweat. The sound made him drop into a crouch. He clicked back the stiff hammer on the .357.

That's when the phone in Mrs. Trent's hand screeched. Startled by the raw electronic warbling, she dropped it to the floor. The police officer down in the yard must have heard the shrill sound, too; he looked toward her house.

She bent down to retrieve it.

"Hello? Hello?" It was a male voice.

"Hello," Mrs. Trent said.

"This is the dispatcher at the city police department. I asked you to stay on the phone."

"Oh, I'm sorry. I thought—"

He wasn't interested in what she had thought. "Are you still monitoring the situation next door?"

"Yes," she whispered. "Your officer is here, and the Bennings' lights just came on."

"Do you see—"

"Ohmigod," the woman said, her fading eyesight barely able to pick out the movement of the three figures at the rear of the house.

"What is it?"

"They've come out."

Mrs. Trent then heard the screaming. More lights came on in the house next door. The officer was out of his crouch, inching alongside the house toward the back corner where the three figures in black were—

"They're going to ambush him," she said, her chest heaving.

"Do something!" the dispatcher said suddenly, passion overwhelming the control in his voice.

"They're just standing there . . . waiting."

"For Chrissakes, lady—"

The Bennings' front door opened, and Alice, still screaming, spilled out onto her front porch. The cop, hearing the commotion, glanced back toward the front of the house. At that moment the tallest of the three figures stepped around the back corner.

"I'm afraid," Mrs. Trent whined. "They'll see me."

"Lady!"

Jim Mayberry, apparently warned by some small sound, whirled just in time to see a shadowy face. Something sharp jabbed against his rib cage, and he started to bring around his gun. The second wave of pain was fleeting, just an intense but momentary agony in his chest. Then his head started to spin. His vision faded. Somewhere in the recesses of his dissolving consciousness he heard the gunshot. It meant nothing to him.

* * *

The gun's explosion made Mrs. Trent yelp. She squeezed her eyes closed as Jim Mayberry's body slumped to the ground.

"What happened?" the dispatcher was screaming. "For God's sake, lady! Answer me!"

Margaret Trent was trying to, but she couldn't stop crying.

ONE

"WHY CAN'T YOU get horny when it's cold and snowy?" Anna Tyree asked.

Whit Pynchon, in bed beside her, nuzzled her bare breast with the side of his face. "You know that old saying, some like it hot? I like it hot."

She laughed. "That was the name of a movie."

"Whatever."

In truth she hadn't minded his attention a bit, although it had been a surprise. As editor of the *Milbrook Daily Journal*, she always stayed at the newspaper until it was put to bed, which meant that the editorial work was done and the paper was ready to be printed. So she hadn't gotten to the house she shared with the special investigator for Raven County's prosecuting attorney until well after eleven. On most nights she found Whit in front of the television watching Ted Koppel's *Nightline*. On this night he stood just inside the door, holding a glass of white wine for her. That had been one hour and two climaxes earlier.

"I mean it, Whit. I think it's romantic to cuddle up in front of a fireplace on a cold winter's night, feeling the heat from the fire on your naked skin."

His hand caressed the soft swell just below her stomach. "Then you're out of luck. We don't have a fireplace."

"We could get one. Have one installed."

"I don't plan on staying here in Milbrook that much longer."

She just smiled. That was Whit Pynchon's perpetual re-

frain—how he intended to retire from his job and move to
the South Carolina coast. Earlier in their relationship the
prospect had worried her. She enjoyed being editor of the
Daily Journal. As a woman in her early thirties, Anna knew
she wasn't likely to find a job of equal responsibility in South
Carolina or anyplace else. In recent months Whit hadn't
mentioned his desire to relocate quite so often. On those few
occasions when he did, it was with a somewhat diminished
passion. Anna liked to believe that she was at least partially
responsible for the change.

If anything dwarfed Whit Pynchon's obstinacy, it was his
pride. She had concluded that he continued to mention his
desire to relocate simply so he wouldn't have to admit that
maybe—just maybe—things weren't so bad right here in
Raven County.

"Even if we do move," she said, "a fireplace would increase the value of this place."

Whit eased his face away from her breast but kept his hand
on the gentle swell of her tummy. "I'd scorch my ass if I
made love in front of a fireplace."

She elbowed him. "That's better than grunting around in
all this perspiration."

"Sweat is sexy. Besides, since you made me put in the air-
conditioning, there isn't all that much sweat."

She rolled over to him, nestling the front of her body against
his side. "There was plenty of sweat tonight," she said.

"Not enough. I like it when it pools in your belly button."

"Yuck."

"Well, I do."

"I believe it," she said, smiling up at him. "You know,
maybe we really should move to a warmer climate—if you'll
promise to stay like this all the time."

"I'm getting too old to stay like this all the time. Besides,
I'd have to get up once and awhile to go to the john."

"You know what I mean, Whit."

"Okay, I'm ready to go tomorrow."

She just shook her head and kept silent. Her finger toyed

with the sparse strands of hair on his broad chest. They were mostly gray, just like those on his head, but he didn't look like an old man. In spite of the premature graying, he had a face that looked younger than his forty-two years.

When she said nothing, he chuckled. "I know you don't really want to go. You like being a big fish in a little pond."

Anna jerked away from him. "Whit! What a terrible thing to say."

He was smiling. "It's true, isn't it?"

She reached over to turn on the lamp on the nightstand. In its glow, streaks of deep red highlighted her long auburn hair. "I like being editor of the newspaper," she said.

He rolled over to face her, the humor now absent from his eyes. "Seriously, Anna, I'm fed up with the job, and I don't want to spend another winter here."

"Whit, it's the middle of August. There's no way we could sell the house and be out of here before winter, not the way real estate is moving around here."

"I might not sell the house."

"What?"

"With Tressa going to the college here, she could keep living here."

Tressa was Whit's daughter by a previous marriage, a relationship that had dissolved many years earlier. After the recent death of Whit's ex-wife, his daughter had moved in with Anna and Whit.

"You would leave Tressa here in Milbrook alone?"

"She could come with us if she wants, but I don't think she wants to leave."

Anna sighed. "Whit, she just lost her mother this year. Do you think it's the right time to do this? She hasn't shaken that initial load of grief yet."

"I know," Whit sighed. "You're right." He flipped the covers back and got out of bed.

"Are you mad?" she asked.

He slipped on his robe. "Naw, I just dread the thought of another winter. I really do."

"Where are you going?"

"It's a beautiful night. I'm going out on the deck and enjoy it."

"The mosquitoes will eat you alive."

He patted the pocket of his robe. "I'm gonna smoke a cigarette. That keeps them away."

"Which should tell you something about cigarettes," she said.

"It does. In malarial areas they're good for your health."

"Sure. Did you hear from Tressa today?"

Whit nodded. "They saw some bears today."

His daughter was vacationing with a friend and her parents in the Great Smoky Mountains a few hours south of Milbrook. After that they were driving over to Nashville for a trip to the Grand Ole Opry.

"Is she having a good time?"

"Sounded like it to me. Wanna come outside with me?"

"No thanks. It's still in the eighties out there."

"It might be fun. There's that nice thick pad on the chaise. We could work up a real sweat."

"Thanks, but no thanks. You can give me a good-night kiss."

He shrugged. "Better than nothing, I guess."

He leaned over the bed. Their lips were about to touch when a coarse voice shattered their bedroom's silence.

"Dammit, Whit! I know you're there."

Anna wrenched herself away, fumbling to cover herself. Whit was laughing. "It's the answering machine, for God's sake. I turned the phone off."

"Shit," she said, embarrassed by her reaction.

The angry voice intruding into the privacy of their bedroom belonged to Tony Danton, Whit's boss and the prosecuting attorney of Raven County. "Christ almighty, Whit. Answer the damned phone!"

Whit stared at the machine. "But I forgot to turn the friggin' volume down."

"So answer it." She was up, searching the room for her robe.

"The hell with him," Whit said. "I didn't want to be bothered by calls. That's why I turned off the phone."

Tony Danton wasn't giving up. "Jesus H. Christ, Whit. This is an emergency!"

Whit lit a cigarette.

Anna headed for the phone. "If you don't answer it, I will. The tape keeps playing as long as he keeps talking."

But Tony solved the problem when he said, "We've just had an officer killed, Whit."

The special investigator snatched up the handset. Anna settled down on the bed to monitor Whit's side of the conversation. Whatever else she was, she remained a good reporter.

Whit didn't bother saying hello. He simply asked of the prosecuting attorney, "Who?"

"Jimmy Mayberry. Dammit, man! Get rid of that answering machine."

"The hell I will. What happened to Mayberry?"

"He got to the scene of a B&E in progress. The bastards gunned him down on their way out. They also stabbed one of the people in the house."

"It had to happen sooner or later, Tony. Is the stabbing victim dead?"

"He's at the hospital. That's all I know."

"Gimme the address. I'm on my way."

He jotted it down on a notepad kept beside the phone. Anna was peeking over his shoulder.

"One thing," the prosecutor said. "The new Milbrook chief of police is on the scene. Fact is, he was the first on the scene. He was monitoring the evening's radio traffic and heard the call."

"I haven't met him yet."

"I have," Tony said. "Just make damned sure you take charge of the crime scene and the investigation. I don't know anything about the guy, but I have a gut feeling he isn't gonna be easy to get along with."

"I get along with everybody."

"Oh, sure," Anna said aloud.

Tony wasn't amused, either. "Just get your ass over there. Oh, and I mean it about that damned answering machine."

"Like I always say, boss, I pay for this phone, and it's here for my convenience, not yours."

"Christ, Whit—"

"Hey, if you can't live with that, then tough shit." Whit hung up.

Anna glared at him. "He's your best friend, Whit. That's a helluva way to treat him."

Whit was heading for his closet. "He's a big boy. He can take it."

"Who was killed?"

Whit started to say "no comment." Then he remembered that Anna had heard Tony's admission on the answering machine. "Jimmy Mayberry. He's one of the older cops with the Milbrook PD. I'd bet he was damned close to retiring. Isn't that the way it always is."

"How did it happen?"

"He got to the scene of a crime a little too soon." Whit pulled a shirt from his closet and a pair of jeans from a dresser drawer.

"What does that mean?" Anna asked.

"He got to a housebreaking before the intruders got away. Apparently they shot him on the way out." He continued to rummage through the dresser drawer. "Christ, I can't find a pair of socks that match."

Anna shrugged. "Sorry, laundry's not my thing. Tressa's the homemaker around here."

He settled for two blue ones that would look about the same color in the gloom of the night.

Anna, though, was looking at him with open suspicion. "How come you're telling me so much? Usually I have to play hell even getting you to say 'no comment.' Are you misleading me?"

Whit was sitting on the bed, pulling on the socks that

almost matched. "I guess I've just got to the point where I don't give a fuck anymore. Why should I care what the hell you print? I won't be reading it."

Anna settled beside him. "What happened to your good mood?"

"Some bastards killed a cop. How the hell do you expect me to behave?"

"I expect you to be yourself. That's all."

"Okay," he said, standing to hoist up his jeans, "then I got no more comments for the press."

He headed for the bathroom.

"Whit?"

But he slammed the door shut.

She went into the living room and picked up the phone. She dialed a number. A sleepy male voice answered.

"Barney, Anna here. Get hold of one of the photographers and head over to White Oak Lane. There's been a police officer killed in one of those B&Es."

The reporter asked a question.

"Christ almighty, I don't know. Go find out."

Just as she hung up, Whit emerged from the bathroom. He opened a closet in the home's entryway and pulled his small .357 from the top shelf.

She kept silent.

"I guess you just called one of your bloodhounds," Whit said, sticking the gun inside his belt.

She shrugged. "It's my job."

He started for the door.

"Whit—"

He stopped.

She was smiling. "I did enjoy tonight."

"I planned to enjoy it some more, Anna, but the bad stuff always seems to happen in the middle of the night. That's why I hate this damn job." He slammed the door on his way out.

Two

NOTHING WAS MORE sacred to Whit Pynchon than the integrity of a crime scene. Street cops, only superficially trained in crime-scene investigations, had little enough respect for the sanctity of any evidence that might be present. When civilians had access to the hallowed realm of a crime scene, it became an investigator's worst nightmare.

The Bennings' daughter sat on the living room couch, her body quaking with fear. Alice Benning, her mother, paced the room. "This shouldn't have happened to us," she kept repeating, as if it were some mystic chant that would put things right again. Another man, tall and bulky, walked with her, trying to comfort her. Whit had no idea who he was. He wasn't the man of the house, who had been transported to the hospital.

Terry Watkins, the head of Milbrook's small detective division, rushed forward to intercept Whit. "I know what you're gonna say, but things just got out of control."

Whit pulled Watkins back into the small hallway that led into the Bennings' living room. "Why in the hell didn't you send those people with the husband? If he's hurt, they should be at the hospital."

Watkins shrugged. "He only got a flesh wound. The paramedics were here before me. They had him patched up pretty quickly. He just went to the hospital as a matter of procedure."

"I thought your new chief was here first."

17

Watkins nodded. "He was, but he was outside with Mayberry."

"I guess his body has already been moved."

The apprehensive look on Watkins's face confirmed Whit's suspicion.

"Jesus Christ," Whit said.

"There was a witness to the shooting," Watkins offered, hoping that might quell the investigator's rising anger.

"Who?" Whit asked.

"An old woman. She lives next door. The chief's over there getting a statement from her now."

"Did you tell the chief that I would be taking over the investigation?"

"Yeah, for what good it did."

Whit jerked his head toward the living room. "They see anything?"

"No. Benning—the guy that was stabbed—didn't see much, either. He described the guy who stabbed him as very small. In fact, he said he was stabbed by a midget."

"A midget?"

"Look, that's what the guy said."

Uniformed officers continued to parade in and out of the house. None of them appeared to be doing anything but milling around.

"Who's the big guy walking the floor with the woman?" Whit asked.

"Father Gabe. I figured you knew him."

"Father who?"

"Father Peter Gabriel."

"A priest?"

For the first time Watkins smiled. "No, actually he's the Baptist minister, but he's Italian and—"

Whit held up his hand. "Stop there. I don't wanna hear any more. Let's go outside."

He and the sergeant were heading for the front door when a deep, resonant voice said, "Please wait a moment."

Whit turned. The man Watkins had identified as the minister stood in the hallway. "Are you the investigator?" the preacher asked.

"One of them," Whit said.

The man rolled forward, his hand outstretched. "I'm Peter Gabriel, minister of the Milbrook Baptist Assembly. Some people call me Father Gabe."

Whit shook the hand as Watkins introduced him to the minister.

"Mrs. Benning would like some update on the progress of the investigation," Gabriel said. "I'm sure you understand her concern and—"

"Tell her I just got here," Whit said. "I haven't even started the investigation."

"Perhaps you might—"

Whit's jaws rippled as he clenched them. "Listen, Reverend. I know she's upset, but we had an officer shot down outside. Before I do anything else, I'm gonna examine the scene of the shooting. Then I plan to interview any witnesses to the shooting. I'll get to the Benning family in due course."

The minister's face was swarthy to start with, but it seemed to darken a few shades as Whit spoke. His bushy brows met just above his eyes. When he knitted them, they seemed to spring forward like an anatomic defense mechanism. "I don't think you understand, sir. This family has suffered—"

Whit stepped forward. "Let's get one thing straight, Gabriel. You attend to the affairs of your church; I'll attend to the investigation. This family has suffered, but not nearly so much as the family of Officer Mayberry. Right now his murder is my first concern."

The minister didn't yield an inch to Whit's reproach. "Tony Danton is a friend of mine, and you can rest assured your lack of compassion, not to mention your rudeness, will be reported."

"He won't be surprised," Whit said, wheeling back toward the front door.

Watkins didn't immediately follow him, pausing instead

to say something to the preacher. Whit glanced back. "Dammit, Terry. I need you out here now."

Watkins shrugged and hurried out to catch Whit. "Jesus, Whit. You shoulda been a little more diplomatic. Father Gabe's made a lotta friends around Milbrook. He's the one that got that teen center going and—"

"He shouldn't even have been allowed in the house," Whit snapped. "And the family should have been sent to the hospital with the victim, Watkins. You know that. This isn't just a house burglary. It's the scene of a homicide, Terry. There might have been evidence in that house that'll help us convict a cop killer."

"I tried, Whit."

"Not gawdamn hard enough. You oughta know better. Cops are always the first to bellyache because their cases fall apart. They're also usually the first to fuck up a crime scene, and let me tell you something, Terry. You really let this one get fucked up but good."

"The chief got here first, Whit. I'm not about to start telling him how to do his job. I need my own too much to do that."

"If your new chief doesn't understand the need to maintain a crime scene's integrity, then it's your job to tell him."

"Easier said than done."

Whit was in the front yard. "Where was Mayberry shot?"

"Around there," Watkins said, pointing toward the eastern side of the house. "That's the same side of the house that they entered."

Whit headed in the direction the detective sergeant had indicated. "You haven't even roped it off," he said as he rounded the corner.

This time Watkins didn't reply.

Whit let it go at that. "Does this fit the MO for the other burglaries?"

"The same," Watkins said. "They used a razor blade to slash open the window screen. The woman in that house—" He nodded to the adjacent structure. "—she saw it all. The small one was lifted into the window by the other two. Then they went around back. I guess the little one let them in.''

"Christ, it's dark around here. How did you search the area?''

"Flashlights,'' Watkins said. "We found this.'' He pulled a plastic pouch from the pocket of his sports coat.

"What is it?'' Whit asked, reaching for it.

"Careful. It's a new single-edged razor blade. It was in the grass at the base of that natural-gas meter. Mayberry was laying right there, too.''

"You think they used it to cut open the screen?''

"Fits their pattern. Whenever screens have been sliced, we've always found one of these. They use it, then toss it away.''

"Fingerprints?''

Watkins shook his head. "Not on any of the others. That's one reason we didn't see much sense in fingerprinting the house. It's obvious this crew always wears gloves.''

"I swear to God, Terry. You've been a cop long enough to know that we catch a lot of these bastards when they make that one single mistake. You don't leave any stone unturned. You don't assume anything.''

The city detective pulled a white handkerchief from his hip pocket and dabbed at the sweat on his face. "So we'll fingerprint the house.''

"Doncha think it's a little late?''

"I guess maybe it is. Damn, Whit, don't you ever sweat? It's muggy as hell tonight.''

"Enjoy it while it lasts. Cordon off this area. We can search it more thoroughly at daylight. What about the witness? Did she see them escape the scene?''

Slowly the Milbrook officer shook his head. "She went all to pieces after the shooting. Besides, she can't even describe them except to say that one was small.''

Whit sighed.

"We've got nothing,'' Watkins said.

Whit looked up. "Wrong, Terry. We've got the body of Jimmy Mayberry. We've got a homicide. The killing of a police officer. Trouble is, we've treated it as if it were a minor misdemeanor."

The interior of the widow's home was even more oppressive than the night air. Even Whit wilted a little as he entered the woman's kitchen. Milbrook's new chief of police sat at the kitchen table, trying to comfort Margaret Trent.

"I should have tried to warn him . . . shouted at him," the woman was saying, dabbing tears from her eyes. She was short, a little bent, with hair so richly gray that it had to have been artificially colored.

"You're not a trained offisuh, ma'am. You called us. You did what you could," the chief was saying, his voice laden with a pronounced southern drawl. He glanced up at Watkins, who entered the kitchen ahead of Whit.

"Chief, sorry to interrupt," Watkins said, "but Investigator Pynchon is here."

Whit stepped into the chief's view.

"Whit Pynchon," Watkins said, "this is Hayden Wallace, Chief Wallace."

Whit managed a quick glance at Watkins. A slight tension made Watkins's smile lopsided.

"Nice to meet you," Whit said, offering a hand.

Wallace took it. "Likewise, I think. I gotta tell you, Pynchon. The feelings about you among my officers are . . . well, you might say they're mixed."

Watkins flinched and took a step back.

But Whit, still amused by the thick accent, just smiled as he finished the handshake. "I'm not overly fond of some of your folks, either, except Terry here. I have a great deal of regard for him, even if he did let things get out of hand tonight."

The chief of police rocked back a little on his heels. "I took charge tonight. You got some complaints?"

The woman was staring at them, assimilating every word of the conversation.

"Let's go outside," Whit said. He smiled at the woman. "Please excuse the chief for a few minutes."

She nodded.

The chief continued talking as the three men moved back toward the front of the house and out onto the porch. "Watkins here said that the DA—"

"Prosecuting attorney," Whit said.

The interruption flustered the chief. "What's that?"

"He's called the prosecuting attorney here."

"Be that as it may," Wallace said, "down in Georgia we do things a little different. Each department hauled its own load, so to speak."

Whit stood an inch or so over six feet. The new chief went a couple of inches taller than that. He dwarfed the short and stocky frame of his detective sergeant. As tall as Wallace was, though, he didn't appear gawky. He carried his height and weight with the coiled tension of an athlete, reminding Whit more of a collegiate football player with the name of Bubba than a former big-city cop. His dark black hair was immaculately cut and worn rather long on the sides and top. However, in the back it was wedged well above the collar of the pale blue shirt that he wore beneath the expensive suit. His badge case, flipped open, dangled from the front pocket of the coat.

"Tell me, Chief. In Georgia isn't it standard practice to secure a crime scene?"

" 'Course it is."

"Then why wasn't this crime scene secured? It's a three-ring circus in that house over there."

The chief cocked his head. "Are you raggin' me, Pynchon?"

"Just asking a question, Wallace."

"The scene was secured," the chief said.

Whit threw up his hands. "I give up!"

Watkins tried to forestall the coming confrontation. Beads

of sweat dotted his forehead. He brushed them away, saying, "Christ, this heat is something."

The chief shrugged. "I've been telling a lot of the men that this is typical Atlanta weather—Hotlanta, they call it down home. It doesn't bother me 'cause I'm accustomed to it. I was hoping for somethin' more tolerable when I came here, though."

Whit saw no use in pushing the point with Wallace, and he knew Watkins wasn't anxious to play referee. "I like this weather, but sit tight, Chief. There's one thing about nice West Virginia weather. It never lasts long."

The chief wasn't finished talking about the crime scene. "Let's get back to what you were saying, Pynchon. I gotta admit I never was much of a detective. I was assigned to the SWAT team in Atlanta early on and stayed with it until I got into police administration."

"We all find our special little niches, Chief."

"I got no problems admitting that I was a little out of my depth here tonight. I lost an officer. Kinda frazzles you, ya know. I've lost them before, but it ain't ever easy. Nonetheless, I think Watkins here and his CID boys oughta handle this case. I want my department to carry its load, and that includes the big cases as well as the little ones."

Whit nodded. "I understand that, Chief. However, here in Raven County the prosecutor has decided that its office will supervise most major investigations and all homicides. If you want that policy changed, you'll have to talk to Tony Danton."

"I will, Pynchon. First thing in the morning."

From the corner of his eye he saw Father Peter Gabriel heading across the lawn toward them. "Chances are, Chief, you'll have to get in line."

THREE

ANNA TYREE SAT behind her desk at the *Milbrook Daily Journal*, examining the day's hefty delivery of letters to the editor. Most of them were addressed simply to "Editor." Anna's title was executive editor, but only a few of the letter writers bothered with either her name or her formal title. Usually the editorial page editor handled the mail from the paper's readers, especially those generically addressed to "Editor." Two weeks earlier Anna had changed that procedure. All obvious "letters to the editor," those expressions of opinion by Milbrook's citizens, now came directly to her desk.

The editorial page editor wasn't being punished. That had nothing to do with it at all. Rather, the volume of mail had increased geometrically in recent weeks as the paper, in its news columns, continued to report on a rash of residential and commercial break-ins. Hardly a day now passed when there wasn't news of a new intrusion or a follow-up on the efforts of the Milbrook city police to stop the crime wave.

Wave . . .

These days that word dominated the *Journal*'s headlines. Sometimes it appeared twice on a single edition's front page, once concerning the series of breaking and enterings—B&Es in the cops' lingo—and a second time in the continuing headlines about the incredible dome of muggy, tropical air under which the central Appalachians were sweltering. In a way one wave facilitated the other. According to the investigators for the city police, the intruders often gained entry by slashing window screens. In an edition several days earlier Anna's lead editorial had suggested that the residents of Milbrook might be well advised to leave easily accessible ground-floor windows closed. Not surprisingly, many of the letters she had in front of her castigated both her editorial and the police for their inability to apprehend the burglars. She wouldn't be surprised to find several of the missives blaming the same parties for the incredibly warm temperatures.

"How can we sleep with windows shut in this heat?" a woman had written in the letter she had in her hand. "It's the police's job to protect us. Maybe we need some *knew* police?"

Anna shook her head at the woman's spelling of "knew." In spite of that, the letter succinctly summed up the consensus of that morning's letter writers. It reminded Anna of the public's reaction to a different series of crimes on the other side of the country—the "Night Stalker" killings in Los Angeles. During the many months of that killer's reign of terror residents had also been advised to increase their attention to the security of their homes. Nobody in Milbrook had thought much about the Night Stalker. Things like that happened in places like LA. They didn't happen in small rural communities like Milbrook. In a way, they didn't. Sure, somebody, probably more than a single individual, was breaking into homes while folks slept in their beds, but no one had been killed, at least not until last night. They were stealing stereos, VCRs, even money from wallets resting on furniture within a few feet of the victims' beds while they slept. However, the objects most often stolen were guns—handguns, rifles, shotguns. It didn't matter. The burglars had a passion for firearms. To be fair, she still wasn't certain that the incident of the previous night was related to the series of B&Es. Her reporter hadn't yet returned from covering the story.

A knock sounded on her door.

"Come in."

The visitor was Katherine Binder, the publisher of the paper. "You're here awfully early."

It was true. Since most of Anna's work took place between

four and midnight, it was rare for her to show up before early afternoon. That morning she had arrived at her office not long after nine. "I couldn't sleep. Just reading another batch of letters to the editors."

"About the break-ins?" Kathy asked, taking a seat in front of Anna's desk.

Anna tossed the letter across to the publisher. "What else? This one lady's not happy with us, either. She says she shouldn't have to close her windows at night."

Kathy picked it up and started to read. The *Milbrook Daily Journal* was something of a joint effort between the two women. Kathy had taken over as publisher of the paper after the death of her husband. The paper had been in her husband's family for years, and she had inherited it. A West Coast native, Kathy had known little about the politics or culture of southern Appalachia. She had even known less about the newspaper business, especially the editorial side. Before the death of William Binder, Anna had been a reporter. When Kathy had taken over the paper, she had promoted Anna to the position of editor. The actual management of the paper had become a partnership between the two women. They shared a common philosophy as to the function of the paper.

They were as different in appearance as they were alike in belief. Anna was a darkly complected redhead, well endowed, who used very little makeup and spent only a small amount of time enhancing her appearance. Kathy was blond, fair-skinned—featureless, the publisher said of herself. She spent at least an hour each day painting on the features nature had denied her. She was thin, too, but her personal wealth made it possible for her to dress in such a way as to transform her bony frame into the sleek figure of a high-fashion model.

"The lady has a point," Kathy said, putting the letter back on Anna's desk. "Was the killing of that officer last night related to the break-ins?"

"Barney's still out on the story, so I don't know yet. If so, then it puts things in a new light."

"I'll say. Is it time for us to start giving the city police some editorial hell?"

"Not according to Whit. He says they're doing their best. The culprits simply haven't left any clues, and not a single stolen item has turned up. Of course I haven't talked to him yet this morning, either."

"Is Whit's opinion all that objective?" Kathy asked.

"He hasn't been in on the cases," Anna said, "so if anything, he would be more inclined to give the city cops a hard time if they weren't doing a good job."

"Knowing Whit, you're right," Kathy said.

When the publisher had entered Anna's office, she had left the door open. Barney Williams, the reporter Anna had phoned the night before, peeked inside.

Anna noticed him. "Hi, Barney. I've been waiting to see you."

He stepped into the office. "I just came from city hall. They say our resident burglary squad were definitely last night's killers."

Anna frowned. "It had to happen sooner or later."

Kathy had twisted around in the chair. "How's the man who was stabbed?"

"Just a flesh wound, actually. He ended up with a couple of stitches."

"Who was it?" Anna asked.

The reporter pulled a small notepad from the pocket of the limp sports coat he wore. "His name is Fred Benning. He lives in North Milbrook."

"Naturally," Kathy said. North Milbrook was the upscale part of town. It was where Kathy lived and had been the area most frequently victimized by the intruders.

"Do you know him?" Anna asked of Kathy.

The publisher shook her head. "I don't think so."

Barney flipped a page in his notebook. "He's an assistant administrator at the hospital."

"I wouldn't know him," Kathy said. "They come and go about as fast as you reporters."

Barney smiled. "So pay us more."

"Why?" Kathy countered. "So you can eat better when you go for your next job interview?"

The reporter shrugged. "Can't blame me for trying. Anyway, they treated the victim at the hospital and released him. I've been putting together background on the cop. I also managed to talk with an eyewitness to the killing."

Anna surged forward in her chair. "They've got an eyewitness?"

Barney settled into a chair beside the publisher. "Sorta. In fact, she saw the burglars enter the house, and she was the one who called the police. She saw the cop arrive and the killers ambush him. Her word . . . ambush. Not mine."

"Could she describe them?"

"Two tall men and a short one, all three dressed in black."

"That's it?" Anna asked.

"That's it. She's an old lady, scared to death."

"How did you manage to talk to her?" Kathy asked.

"I got to the scene, talked to a couple of the cops I get information from, and they told me about her. Her light was still on, so I just went over and knocked. She was so upset that I couldn't stop her from talking."

"Where were the cops? Whit?"

"They'd already interviewed her. Oddly enough, if the woman hadn't seen the break-in, Mayberry would probably still be alive. They would have fled the scene before the police arrived. For some reason I find that rather ironic."

"What about the man who was stabbed?" Kathy asked. "Could he give a description?"

"As soon as he saw the guy's silhouette, the intruder stabbed him. When he got his wife awake and the lights on, there was no sign of the burglar."

"Did they have a chance to steal anything?" Kathy asked.

Barney didn't need to refer to his notes. He remembered the answer. "This time just a VCR. That's all. They probably didn't have time to take much else."

"So the police still don't have any leads?" Anna asked.

The reporter shrugged. "If they do, they're not telling me. But I don't think they have any. They're pretty frustrated."

"Stay on it," Anna said.

"One last thing before I go, Miss Tyree. I hear the new chief isn't happy about Pynchon taking over the investigation."

"What's new?" Anna asked.

Barney chuckled. "My sources—and I have some good ones in the city department—tell me Chief Wallace is really gonna make a stir about it."

"I almost hope he wins," Anna said.

"I gotta go try to find a photo of the dead officer," Barney said.

"Keep me posted," Anna said as he left.

Kathy studied the face of her friend. "I get the impression that you had a bad night. Don't you want Whit involved in the case?"

"I have mixed emotions. He's the best cop in Raven County . . . maybe even in West Virginia. On the other hand, once he gets involved in the case, we will no longer be able to get answers to any of our questions. Besides, it doesn't matter what I want or what the new chief wants. If the prosecutor wants Whit involved in the case, he'll be involved."

A wry smile crossed Kathy's face. "Can't you get him to talk in his sleep or something? For God's sake, Anna, you and Whit are cohabiting."

Anna chuckled. "You know him almost as well as I do, Kathy. We've been together for almost a year, and his opinion of the press is no higher now than it was when we first met. Besides, with this godawful weather we've been having, he's been in a good mood, if you can believe that. I'd like to keep him that way."

"Only Whit would like this unbearable heat. It wasn't this miserable in California when the Santa Anas were blowing, but, we didn't have this humidity."

"Whit likes the humidity."

"Whit's weird. Nonetheless, I think it's high time they got

him in on these cases. It's obvious the city police need some help.''

Anna seemed lost in a sudden thought. ''Tell me, Kathy, have you met this new chief of police?''

''Not yet. All I know about him is what I read a few weeks ago when Barney did that piece about him.''

''First chance I get, I'll pay him a visit. If Whit does take over these cases, perhaps I can keep our flow of information coming from the new chief.''

Kathy shook her head at the suggestion. ''Here we go again. Another tug-of-war between you and Whit.''

''If this new chief is cooperative, I can avoid another head-on with dear old Whit. It's certainly worth a try.''

Kathy rose to leave. ''If the chief starts leaking news about the investigation to you, then both you and he are liable to have a head-on with Whit.''

Anna lifted the next letter to the editor from the pile. ''The new chief came from a big city. Maybe he can outflank Whit.''

Kathy smiled. ''My dear, a battalion of Marines couldn't outflank Whitley Francis Pynchon. You of all people should know that.''

FOUR

WHIT PYNCHON WAS flailing away at the keyboard of an old manual typewriter when Raven County's prosecuting attorney peered into his office. Tony Danton watched for a moment as his investigator hammered away at the keys. When one jammed, Whit reached up quickly and flicked the key arm back down into the machine.

"Why don't you go buy a new one?" Tony said. "I told you six months ago that we had a little extra money in the budget."

Whit looked up from the cherished relic. "This one's just as good as its operator. No sense buying a fancy machine when I'm such a klutz."

"What are you typing?"

"The grand jury report for the Dunn case."

"You about have it wrapped up?" The prosecutor settled down into the slumping plastic couch that filled one corner of the office.

Whit leaned back and stretched. "All except the lab reports. We probably won't get those until after the grand jury meets, but the lab guys gave me a verbal summary of their findings."

A month before, in a secluded hollow in extreme western Raven County, Isaac Raymond Dunn, a retired coal miner, had walked into his trailer and found a young boy in bed with his daughter. He had become enraged and had attempted to grab the kid. Somehow, even in the narrow confines of the trailer, the young boy had eluded the old man. Once he was out in the yard, the kid, who had just turned eighteen, didn't do the smart thing and flee the scene. Instead, he got into his car, pulled a small .22-caliber handgun from the glove compartment, and went back inside. Old man Dunn was busy giving his daughter a tongue-lashing and didn't even see the boy until after the first shot had smacked into the back of his skull.

Somehow, even with three slugs in him, the old man had managed to take the gun away from his assailant, pistol-whip him, and then drive the boy's car into Tipple Town, where he collapsed in front of the town cop's office. He had died three days later. The kid had been arrested immediately after the incident for A.D.W., assault with a deadly weapon. The charge was amended to first-degree murder after the old man's death.

"I'm gonna offer the kid a plea to second degree," Tony said.

Whit frowned. "That's mighty damned generous of you."

"You know how juries react to these sorts of killings, Whit."

"How would you know, Tony? When's the last time you tried one? Seems to me like you always make some kind of deal."

"Not 'some kind of deal,' Whit. I make good deals."

"I'm sure the bottom feeders think so. Their lawyers, too."

Tony laughed. "Christ, Whit, I expect this shit from the cops but not from you."

Whit shrugged. "I just think this kid's actions were pretty damned cold-blooded. I mean, he coulda hopped in that car and made tracks. He had the chance."

"His lawyer is going to claim that he went back in to stop the old man from beating his daughter."

"He wasn't beating her," Whit said.

"But the kid didn't know that. Even the daughter's a little wishy-washy on what the old man was doing to her. The kid heard the old man shouting and—"

Whit interrupted him. "So when he got inside, he saw that she wasn't being beaten."

"It'll still be a bitch to try. Even if I do try it, I don't think I can do better than second degree. The jury might even decide it was involuntary manslaughter."

"No way," Whit said.

His boss was incredulous. "Whadaya mean, no way?"

Whit was waving off the attorney's objection. "I meant, no way will they come back with involuntary. I think second degree is the most lenient verdict you'll get if you try it. So why not let a jury decide?"

Tony rolled his eyes. "If you want the truth, Whit, I honestly think it's a second-degree murder. The kid did it in the heat of passion. He didn't go there planning to kill Dunn. The old man tried to whip up on him, and he got mad."

"Christ, Tony, the punk was pumping his sixteen-year-old daughter! If it'd been me, I would have wrung his horny little neck."

"In which case I would have offered you second-degree murder, also. Besides, the daughter's a little slow mentally. I don't think there's anything to be gained by putting her through the trial."

Whit jerked the paper out of the typewriter. "Well, offer them the damned deal before I do all this paperwork. I've got better things to do than whip dead horses."

"The offer's already been made," Tony said. "Actually, I came in here to see what you did to Reverend Gabriel last night. He called this morning demanding your head on a pike."

"I told him to mind his own business."

"Whit, the man is a very prominent minister. I know you don't care much for preachers."

"I like some of them just fine—the ones that keep their religion in their churches."

Tony just shook his head. "He was the family's minister."

"And the minute I got to the scene he wanted to know the progress of the investigation. Damn, Tony. The owner of the house got a minor flesh wound. Jim Mayberry took a small-caliber bullet right in the ticker. Mayberry deserved precedence, doncha think?''

"Can't you just learn to be a little diplomatic?"

Whit shook his head. "No reason to be. You pay me to investigate. If you want a diplomat or a public relations man, then fire me and hire one. 'Course, I doubt you'll get many cases closed that way."

Tony dropped his head in frustration. "Chief Wallace also phoned first thing this morning."

"Before or after the preacher?"

"What difference does that make?"

"I'm just curious."

"Before," Tony said. "He's not happy, either."

"You were emphatic last night that I was to take control of the investigation. I did my best to do that without stepping on Wallace's toes."

"I'm not criticizing you about your actions with regard to Wallace. I'm just warning you. He's displeased with my policy, not with you."

Whit managed a smile. "Are you making the mistake of assuming I give a damn?"

Tony laughed. "Hell, no. I quit making that mistake years ago. So, what's the story on last night?"

Whit stood up behind his desk and stretched. "Wallace corrupted the whole gawdamn crime scene. He let the family remain in the house. When I got there, the preacher was prowling through the house. No one even bothered to cordon off the area outside the house where Jimmy was killed."

Tony closed his eyes and massaged them with the heels of his palms. "Jesus, didn't Wallace know better?"

"I reminded him about the importance of maintaining integrity at the crime scene. Believe it or not, he had the gall to tell me that he had never been much of a detective. He spent most of his time with the Atlanta SWAT team."

Tony sighed. "That's gonna be real useful here in Raven County."

"After telling us that," Whit continued, "he then launched into a mild tirade about me handling the investigation. I just let him talk."

"Did you find anything last night?"

Whit, who was still standing, bent down and pulled open his center desk drawer. He withdrew a plastic bag containing a small gold object and handed it to the prosecutor. "I found this at daylight, close to the spot where Jimmy's body was. It had been stepped on and pushed down into the ground."

Tony examined the object. It was a brass bullet casing. "A .22-caliber?"

"No, a .25-caliber. I talked to the local coroner just before he shipped the body up to Charleston. Both Jimmy's uniform and the area around the wound showed marked evidence of powder residue. It looks like the killer came right up to Jimmy, jammed the gun against his chest, and fired. The heart must have stopped almost at once. There was very little external bleeding. The bullet didn't even exit the body. The doc says he died instantaneously."

"Do any of the city guys wear body armor?" Tony asked.

"The ones that can afford to buy it themselves. The city doesn't provide it. Jimmy never wore it. If he had, well, it would have stopped that bullet, anyway."

"What about the alleged eyewitness?"

"Oh, she saw everything from a second-story window, but all she can tell us is that two of the suspects were tall and the third was very small. Fred Benning, the guy that was stabbed, just saw the one intruder—the midget, as he calls him."

"And we're sure these are the same guys that have been pulling these B&Es?"

Whit shrugged. "Watkins says so. We did a find a discarded razor blade near their point of entry. That fits their MO. Oh, and they took guns, just as in the other break-ins."

"I didn't think they had time to steal anything. That was the coffee-table scuttlebutt this morning at Ketchum's Diner."

"The town grapevine is running slow today. We didn't

know about the guns until Benning got home. Seems as if the two full-grown intruders went right to the closet where he kept them. The small one went into the bedroom, probably looking for a wallet."

"Was one of the stolen guns the murder weapon?"

Whit shook his head. "They took a deer rifle and two shotguns from Benning's closet. His handgun was in a drawer by the bed. It was still there."

"Oh, shit," Tony said. "That means they're going into these houses armed."

"Yeah. Scary, isn't it?"

"Maybe we oughta release that to the press. Whadaya think?"

Whit made a face. "Then we'll have the good people of Milbrook taking shots at anything that moves after dark."

"That might start happening, anyway."

Whit had settled down on the corner of his desk. "Don't you think it's unusual that the burglars seemed to know exactly where to go for the guns? I pieced the sequence of events together. Given the timing of the witness's call to the emergency dispatcher, they didn't have more than a few minutes."

"You've had more time to think about it than I have," Tony said.

"I talked with Watkins about it after Benning discovered the guns gone. That's been an aspect of the other cases that's been bothering him. In several of the break-ins, it appears that the thieves had some inside information."

"But how?"

"There was a teenager in each of those particular homes."

"There are teenagers in a lot of homes."

"I know, but so far it's the only common denominator."

"Benning have a teenager?"

"A fifteen-year-old daughter."

"Have you talked to her?"

"She was all to pieces last night. I'll get around to her. I'm certainly going to follow it up. We've got a lot more to

work with if we follow up the burglary angle rather than
Mayberry's murder. He was just in the wrong place at the
worst possible time.''

FIVE

ON NIGHTS and weekends the teenagers of Milbrook gathered in one of two places. Either they managed to find rides out to the Blackbird Mall west of Milbrook or they filtered down to the recently opened teen center in the heart of town. The center's popularity was beginning to overshadow that of the mall, a trend of some note since the sponsor's center was Peter Gabriel's Baptist church. The center came to be known as the PU, pronounced *pee-you*. An old abandoned bowling alley, the building didn't smell all that bad, at least not quite bad enough to justify the nickname. Rather, the Baptist effort to provide Milbrook's young people with a constructive outlet for their gregarious natures had named itself Project Uplift, abbreviated to PU.

The development of a teen center represented but one facet of an overall youth program envisioned by Father Gabe. It sought to address the increasing problem of drug and alcohol abuse among Milbrook's kids. At first he had dubbed the effort Project Teen Uplift, but when folks started calling it PTU, that sounded too much like PTL to suit Father Gabe's fund-raising efforts. He dropped the word "teen," and the project became PU. Even that, in Father Gabe's mind, was preferable to the connotation that attached itself to PTU.

As it turned out, the kids loved to talk about the "pee-youuu" center, and each time they said its name they held their noses and drawled out the "u." It attracted both attention and money to the project. The largest single contribution had come from the corporate management of the Blackbird

Mall, which was growing weary of the invasion of rowdy teenagers on Friday nights and weekends. The kids still went to the mall, especially when some hot new movie premiered, but with each passing day more and more of those who wanted simply to socialize and sip soda pop showed up at Milbrook's PU.

Janice Benning arrived at the center shortly before seven. The old bowling lanes had been ripped up. One corner had been marked off as a dance floor. A modern jukebox provided a selection of reasonably current top forty hits. A couple of Ping-Pong tables, several out-of-fashion arcade games, and even a pool table filled another corner.

Some of the more conservative members of Father Gabe's congregation lifted their eyebrows at the dance floor and the pool table, but the preacher was nothing if not a practical man. "If we want kids to come here, then we must respect their culture," he would say when asked about the dancing or pool shooting.

At the same time he was quick to add that a platoon of chaperons—composed of members of several congregations, parents, a few off-duty cops, and schoolteachers—were on hand to insure that the kids stayed away from drugs, from each other in an intimate sense, and from any gambling. Father Gabe himself spent nearly every evening at the center.

The restaurant area of the bowling alley had been renovated and was once again serving hamburgers and hot dogs as well as microwave pizza. Janice Benning first went to the game area in search of Mickey Moses. Several high school boys surrounded the pool table, but Mickey wasn't among them. She then headed back toward the restaurant area. A group of her girlfriends was seated at one of the large round tables. They waved and shouted to her, and she hurried over to them.

"Have any of you seen Mickey?" she asked.

One of the girls—her name was Marie—giggled. "I hear you got the hots for him."

Janice put her hands on her hips. "That's not why I want to see him, Miss Know-It-All."

Susie Watkins, one of Janice's best friends, pointed toward the rear of the restaurant area. "I think he's over there. In one of the booths."

"You really shouldn't be so obvious," Marie said, winking at Janice.

"And you should mind your own business."

"How's your father?" Susie asked.

Janice shrugged. "He's okay. Shook up, though. We're all shook up."

"Mickey'll protect you," one of the other girls said.

Janice gave her the finger and left them to their giggling. She hurried toward the maze of booths at the very rear of the old bowling alley. The older kids—the juniors and seniors in high school—claimed that section of the restaurant for themselves. The PU's chaperons kept an even closer watch on the booth area than they did on the game corner. The lighting in the rear of the building wasn't so good, and the old wooden booths were separated by high plywood panels that provided each booth with a certain degree of privacy. If kids were going to make out or do drugs, it would happen in that area.

Janice moved by the booths, trying not to be too conspicuous in her search for Mickey. As it happened, he found her, coming up from behind and putting a hand on her shoulder.

She turned. "There you are."

"What's up, Janey?" Mickey was the only who called her that. It had started when they had first met two years earlier, when he had thought her name was Jane.

"Let's talk," she said, nodding toward a vacant booth.

He seemed surprised. "Sure, just let me tell the guys."

Mickey ambled over to the booth in the deepest corner of the building. Janice squinted into the shadows and saw Zeke Morton and Bert Ringwald. The sight of them made her shiver.

"So what's so important?" Mickey said as he came back.

She guided him to the empty booth. "You sure have lousy taste in friends."

He eased down into the seat beside her. "Zeke and Bert?"

"They're creeps."

Mickey stopped. "Is that what you want to talk to me about? You gonna ride me about my friends? If that's it—"

"No," she said. "You remember last week when we were talking about hunting?"

Mickey frowned. "Hunting?"

"You know . . . when you were talking about how wrong you thought hunting was?"

Mickey shrugged. "Kinda. Why?"

"And you asked me if my dad had any guns?"

Mickey's face darkened. "Yeah, I remember. Why are you asking me about this?"

"Last night somebody broke into our house and stole those guns. Whoever it was stabbed Daddy. They killed a policeman, too."

Mickey's mouth dropped open. "You're shittin' me. I heard about the cop, but I didn't know it was your place."

"It was."

"Is your dad okay?"

Tears dampened her hazel eyes. "Yes, it just cut the skin on his side. You remember, though . . . when we were talking about hunting? I told you where he kept his guns. You remember?"

"I guess. Why?"

"You didn't mention it to anyone, did you?"

Mickey was sixteen, a year older than Janice. At that stage in life even a year represented a significant generation gap. In spite of that, he liked the girl. With her slim figure, ash-blond hair, and hazel eyes, she was a real looker. "C'mon, Janey. You know I wouldn't do anything like that."

"Maybe you did it without even thinking about it. Just kinda offhand. You know?"

"I didn't talk to anybody about it."

"Whoever it was knew right where to go, Mickey."

"Hell, maybe your dad told somebody. Maybe your mother did. Why you comin' down on me?"

Janice leaned out from her booth and glanced back toward the booth housing Mickey's two friends. "Daddy says the person who stabbed him was a midget. Bert Ringwald's almost a midget."

Mickey threw up his hands. "Christ, Janey, grow up. Stop playing like a cop. Bert's not gonna break into somebody's house. He sure as hell isn't gonna stab nobody. God knows he's not gonna waste some cop. You're paranoid."

She had returned her attention to Mickey. "I've heard stories about that Zeke guy and Bert."

"They're just stories, Janey. They're good guys."

"Is that why Zeke's on some kinda probation, Mickey?"

Mickey's face turned serious. "Where did you hear that?"

"From Susie. Her dad's a cop."

"Susie's got a big mouth. Zeke had a run-in with a city cop. The guy was hassling him."

"But Bert's so little. That's exactly how Dad described him—little like a midget or something."

Mickey stood. "What time did it happen?"

"A little after midnight."

"Well, they were with me last night. We played cards until two in the morning. So much for your dee-tective work, Janey."

Her eyes continued to glisten with emotion. "I didn't mean to make you mad."

He glared down at her. "Well, you did. That's the damned trouble with this town. Everyone—"

At that moment Mrs. Boone, one of the evening's chaperons, ambled by them. Mickey stopped speaking.

"Good evening," she said.

Janice said, "Hi."

Mickey didn't say anything until she was out of earshot. "Like I said, Janey, they were with me last night."

"I didn't mean—"

He put a hand up to stop her. "It's okay. I gotta get back there. I'll see you later."

Mickey slipped onto the empty seat across from Zeke Morton and Bert Ringwald.

"What'd she want?" Zeke asked.

Mickey's eyes locked onto those of little Bert Ringwald. "She accused you of stabbing her old man."

Bert's face drained of color. "How the fuck did she know?"

"Forget it," Mickey said. "I took care of it."

Zeke Morton was the oldest and the biggest of the three boys. He reached across and wrapped his fingers around Mickey's wrist. "I wanna know the answer, too. How did the bitch know?"

Mickey ripped his hand away. "Don't ever do that again, Morton."

Zeke's jaws were clenched. "How did the gawdamn bitch know, Moses?"

"She remembered us talking about her old man's guns, and her old man said that whoever stabbed him was little." He looked at Bert. "Since you were little, she figured I might have said something about the guns to you."

Zeke's fist slammed down on the tabletop. On the other side of the booth area the chaperon, Mrs. Boone, cast a suspicious glance toward the trio in the distant booth. Mickey smiled at her until she looked away.

"I told you," Mickey said. "We shouldn't have pulled that job last night. It was too soon. We shoulda waited a few weeks."

"Aw fuck, Moses. The girl just made a lucky guess."

"She knew something about you, too, Zeke."

"Me?"

"She knows you're on probation. Her friend's daddy is Watkins, the cop."

"Shit," Zeke said. "So I guess she knows you're on probation, too."

"She didn't say nothin' about me."

"How did you take care of it?" Bert asked.

"I told her you guys were with me, playing cards, until way after the break-in. She believed me, but I'm telling you now, Zeke. Next time we're not cutting it this close."

Zeke leaned across the table. "The man was getting antsy. He wanted to see some more goods."

"Fuck the man," Mickey said. "How come you're the only one who talks to the man?"

"That's the way he wants it. You get your share, don't you? You don't think you been cheated or somethin', do you?"

"I'd just feel a fuckin' lot better if I knew who this mystery man was."

Zeke's face reddened. "You knew the deal, Moses. You agreed to it. So did Bert. Right, Bert?"

The smallest of the three boys was trembling. "I didn't mean to cut the guy. I don't know what happened. I coulda turned and run. I just got scared. Then you go and shoot that cop, Zeke."

"We all shot that cop. Just like we all cut the bitch's father. Like I said, forget it. Too gawdamn bad you didn't gut her old man."

But Bert was shaking his head. "She fingered me, man. Just like that. She figgered it was me. I'm scared, man. I don't wanna go to the pen for the rest of my life."

Zeke smiled. "You friggin' pussy. Look, if she gets curious one more time, I'll take care of her. Chill out."

Bert's face turned an even more sickly shade of white. "Christ, Zeke, you mean kill her?"

The tallest of the three nodded.

Bert was shaking his head. "You're sick, man."

Mickey reached across the table. Zeke was still glaring at Bert. Mickey caught the larger boy off guard when he reached across the table, dug his fingers into the front of his shirt, and jerked him forward. The action pulled Zeke's rib cage tight against the tabletop. "What the fuck—"

Mickey stuck his face close to Zeke's. "You lay one gaw-damn hand on Janey and I'll pull your balls outa your ass-hole."

"Look out, guys," Bert said. "We got company."

A huge man dressed in a shiny silver suit was approaching the table. Mickey released Zeke's arm. The boys settled back onto the benches of the booth.

The man came right up to the table. "You guys know we don't suffer any kind of trouble in here."

Zeke looked up, shrugging. "No big deal, Preacherman. We was just blowin' off a little steam."

Peter Gabriel tensed at the boy's word. "You can call me Reverend Gabriel, or Father Gabe, if that's easier for you. However, I am not Preacherman."

"He didn't mean anything by it," Mickey said.

Zeke laughed. "No, sir. I didn't mean nothing at all, Fa-ther Gabe. We were just getting ready to go over and play some Ping-Pong."

The Baptist minister pointed a finger at Zeke. "One more disturbance, young man, and you'll be banned from the cen-ter." He turned and headed back toward the center's office.

Zeke gave the finger to the minister's back.

SIX

IN THE PITCH BLACKNESS of their bedroom Anna watched the tip of Whit's cigarette as he inhaled. For the second consecutive night they had made love when she had arrived home.

She snuggled against him. "This is the only time I think it might be enjoyable to smoke a cigarette."

"Want a drag?"

"No, thanks. I might like it. I've got enough vices without adding that one to the list."

They lay on top of the bed covers, allowing the cool rush from the window air conditioner to evaporate the perspiration from their bodies. "Will you get mad if I talk a little shop?" she asked.

She felt his body stiffen.

Before he could reply to her question, she said, "Forget it. I don't want to ruin a very pleasant evening."

He reached over to stub out the cigarette in an ashtray on the nightstand and then rolled to face her. "I was going to ask what you wanted to talk about."

"The break-ins and the killing last night."

"I don't know anything that you would consider newsworthy."

"Why don't I believe you?" she said, stroking his thigh.

"Because you're a suspicious and cynical reporter."

She had to laugh. "You're calling me a cynic?"

Whit laughed, too. "Yeah, coming from me, I guess that did sound a little funny."

"Actually, I was going to pass some information along to you."

Whit worked his arm under her neck and shoulder and pulled her tightly against him. "That'll be a pleasant change."

"Reverend Gabriel called me today. Do you know him?"

Again she sensed the sudden surge of tension in his body. "I met him at the murder scene. He was the Bennings' minister. I didn't exactly make a good impression."

"He didn't mention that," she said, "but that might explain the call."

"What did he want?"

"He wants to organize some kind of community watch group to help the police."

"Oh, shit," Whit said. He pulled his arm from her and sat up on the side of the bed. "That's all we need. A bunch of citizen vigilantes roaming the streets after dark."

As Anna sat up, Whit switched on the light and started searching for his robe. Anna, comfortable with her nudity, made no effort to cover herself. "He addressed that concern, Whit. In fact, he said that was the one thing he didn't want."

"So what did he want from you?"

"He just wanted us to print a notice about an organizational meeting he's planning for next week."

Whit pulled on his wine-colored robe. "And I guess you're going to oblige him?"

"Of course," Anna said. "Give the man credit where credit's due. The reverend's done a very good job with the teen center. His community watch program might be just as good."

"I won't hold my breath," Whit said. "I never did get to sit out on the deck last night. I'm going to try it tonight. Wanna join me? I promise to smoke enough cigarettes to keep the mosquitoes off us both."

A humid calm greeted them as they stepped out onto the rear deck.

"It hasn't cooled off much," Anna said. She had donned

a full-length robe as protection against the mosquitoes that usually invaded in droves from the woods behind the house.

"I love this kind of night," Whit said, settling down into a chair beneath the new awning he had recently installed over a portion of the deck.

"I could use a cold drink, maybe a Coke," she said. "You want one?"

"Sure."

When she returned, Whit was smoking another cigarette. "The mosquitoes?" she asked, settling down beside him.

"No, I just wanted a smoke. I don't think the mosquitoes will bother us tonight. It's been dry for a while. They won't get stirred up until it rains."

"I hear the chief of police isn't happy with you."

Whit glanced at her. "How do you know that?"

She put a finger to her lips. "I always keep my sources confidential."

He shook his head. "You've never offered to keep anything I say confidential."

"That's different," she said, smiling. "About the chief, Barney picked that up from some city cops he knows."

"He's an odd duck," Whit said.

"Some people say the same thing about you."

"Who?" Whit asked, feigning shock.

"Confidential sources," she quipped.

"Then you misheard them. What they actually said was 'good fuck.' It just sounded like 'odd duck.' "

"Oh, sure," she said, laughing.

"Seriously, he reminds me of some dumb jock. You know the type. They graduate from college with letters in several sports but don't recognize a single one of them."

"There you go again, tossing around stereotypes."

He smiled. "Stereotypes have a place. They're efficient. Besides, you know exactly the type I mean."

"Well, I'll reserve judgment. I haven't met him yet. Are you going to share any information with me about this case?"

"Right now there's nothing to share. I was serious when I told you that earlier."

"Barney got an interview with your eyewitness, the old woman who lives next door."

Whit sighed. "And I guess you're gonna print what she said in the paper."

She nodded. "Front page, tomorrow morning. That shouldn't bother you. She didn't see very much, did she?"

"That's the trouble with eyewitnesses, and as the days pass, their memories can become even more selective than their eyesight was. She told us that there were three of them, two tall guys and a short one. I hope to God the description she gave your reporter wasn't any more specific."

Anna smiled. "It wasn't. That's all she told Barney, too."

"If this case ever gets to a trial, she will do one of two things," Whit said. "Either she will forget even that vague description, or she will have embellished it to the point that it perfectly describes the defendants sitting in front of her."

"Just because she's old?" Anna asked, incredulous at the suggestion.

Whit shook his head. "No, just because she's human. I'd rather have an airtight case of circumstantial evidence any day. Eyewitnesses are about as unreliable as confessions."

In another part of Milbrook the headlights of a musty black Dodge van shot two visible bands of milky light through the warm night's haze. The vehicle turned into the parking area of a bankrupt mine supply company. Its wheels crunched on the sparse layer of gravel that covered the lot as it eased into the dark shadows behind the abandoned building. Its lights illuminated another vehicle, a rusted old Chevrolet Malibu. Zeke Morton, smoking a cigarette, lounged on the hood of the Malibu's trunk.

The van pulled up beside the Chevy and killed its lights. Zeke jumped down from the car and walked around to the driver's side. The window rolled down.

"What the fuck happened last night?" the man inside the

van asked. His face was little more than a featureless silhouette.

Zeke shook his head. "That gawdamn cop showed up just as we came outta the house."

"It was a stupid thing to do. We aren't happy."

"Fuck you, then, all of you. If I hadn't shot him, we'd be in jail right now."

"Who stabbed the man inside the house?"

"Bert panicked. No big deal. The guy wasn't hurt bad. If it'd been me instead of Bert, the guy would be at the undertaker's right now."

"I've warned you about being too aggressive. Stay the hell outta people's bedrooms."

"Who says we were in the bedroom?"

"I have my sources."

Zeke couldn't see the man's eyes, but he could feel them. "Whatever you say."

"What did you get?"

"A VCR and a couple of guns. One of 'em looks really good. It's a 20-gauge pump. Oughta fetch a good price."

"I thought you said the place was loaded with merchandise."

"The guy woke up, man. Somebody called the cops. We got what we could and made tracks."

"We need to concentrate on bigger jobs. We're not making enough to cover expenses."

"Bullshit," Zeke said. "I know you get top dollar for these guns."

The hand shot out of the van's window. Fingers grasped Zeke's Metallica shirt and jerked him toward the window. The boy's forehead cracked against the top of the window frame. "Don't get smart with me, Morton. I don't put up with that kind of crap."

"Hey, man, c'mon. That hurts."

The hand released the boy. "Here's the next job. There's this doctor in town who's a real gun nut. I hear he's got a roomful. Some of them are exotic automatics."

Zeke was rubbing his forehead. "They're illegal, ain't they?"

"The doctor has a federal gun collector's license."

"No shit."

"That's right, kid. No shit. His name is Peter Lewis."

"Lewis? I don't know no Lewis kids."

"He has no children. Besides, you won't need that kind of help on this one. The doctor has the guns in a special room in his basement."

"It might have alarms," Zeke said.

"It does. What I want you to do is stake out the guy's house for a few nights. Get a handle on his schedule and movements. I'll figure out a way for you to disable the alarm and get back to you."

"I don't know, boss. I don't like the idea of messin' around with a place like that."

"From what I'm told, that gun collection of his is worth thirty grand. That can mean at least ten grand for each of you. Or twenty for you and five for the other two. That's up to you as long as you keep the other guys in the dark."

Zeke whistled. "Not fuckin' bad."

"It's time we moved up. Better to do a few good-paying jobs than a bunch of little ones. There's less risk that way."

"You gotta come up with something good, then, on the alarm."

"And you'd better get a leash on Bert. I don't want a repeat of last night."

"I will. By the way, the daughter of the guy that got stabbed fingered Bert."

There was a sharp hissing intake of air from the man in the front. "You mean she told the police—"

"Naw, man. Don't blow a gasket. She told Moses. It was Moses who got the information 'bout the guns from her. They're kinda sweet for each other. She remembered talking to him about the guns, and she knows he hangs around with Bert. Her old man said the man who stabbed him was little, so she came up with Bert."

"Jesus fucking Christ."

"Like I said, she's hot for Moses. He took care of it."

"How the hell did he do that?"

"He said we were with him playing cards last night. She believed him."

"She still might say something."

Zeke grinned. "I'll take care of her if you want. I'd like that. I bet she's got a nice little pair of tits."

"Forget it," the man said. "You're not good enough to handle that kind of thing. Just move that stuff into the back of the van. I gotta get out of here."

"You're s'posed to have some money for us."

"Don't worry. I've got it, but this is your first and last warning. One more fuck-up like last night and you won't need money where you'll be going."

SEVEN

THE DIGITAL DISPLAY on the bank sign alternately flashed the time and the temperature. At eight twenty-seven in the morning it was already eighty-four degrees. The steady throng of people who walked under the display toward jobs in the various stores and governmental complexes nearby paid the heat no mind. Unlike the residents of Milbrook, who lived in the traditionally cool mountains several hundred miles away, the people of Raleigh, North Carolina, expected hot summers. This summer had been no worse than most.

Besides serving as the location for North Carolina's capitol, downtown Raleigh also was home to the Wake County courthouse as well as a massive federal complex. Many of the county and federal offices were located in modern, dark gray structures that circled a wide pedestrian garden. The garden area had once been a city street, but the city fathers had decided to close the street to create the square. At that time of the morning, workers in the various federal, state, and county offices in and around the square hurried toward their jobs.

One man, dressed in a light blue seersucker suit, stood out from the bustling workers. He moved much less quickly. The others had to be at their various desks very soon. He didn't. In fact, he didn't work in Raleigh. He had driven up from Fayetteville the night before to meet with FBI and state law-enforcement officials at nine that morning. By that afternoon he might well be testifying in front of a federal grand jury. The closer he came to the federal building, the more slowly he walked.

When he was within thirty yards of the building, he came to a complete stop. Sweat glistened on his tanned face. His stomach grumbled, and he yawned. Not that he was bored. The yawning resulted from his anxiety, an effort by the body to provide more oxygen for his brain.

A woman carrying a thick briefcase bumped him. She didn't slow down to apologize. He watched as the people bustled by him.

"The hell with this," he said. He was just starting to turn around when something hard jabbed against his spine.

"Jesus," he said just before his stomach erupted in an explosion of blood and guts.

The gunshot echoed between the tall buildings.

A man behind him cried, *"Get down!"*

But the man in the blue seersucker was already going down, the light of life gone from his eyes.

Women shrieked.

Most people ran. A few dropped to the concrete.

For a few moments no one noticed the man in the blue seersucker. He rested facedown on the brick surface. By the time someone did see the single victim of the gunshot, the digital clock on the bank sign read eight thirty-five. The temperature had climbed to eighty-seven. Steam rose from the bloody gore that was blossoming in a pool on the hot sidewalk. The stench from the man's ruptured intestines drifted through the warm morning air.

"Anything new on the murder?" Tony asked as he entered Whit's office.

"Not much," Whit said. "I'm gonna try to see—"

At that point Whit noticed that Tony wasn't alone. A young man dressed in an off-white suit came in behind the prosecutor.

"What were you going to say?" Tony asked.

"Nothing worth mentioning," Whit said, eyeing the stranger.

"Have you met Sloan Keating?" Tony asked.

The man stepped in front of Tony to offer his hand. "I've heard a lot about you, Whit."

Whit shook his hand, still baffled by his presence.

"Sloan's a relatively new attorney in town," Tony said. "He's opened his own practice."

"That's being optimistic," Whit said.

Keating laughed. "I managed to strike a deal with some of the bigger firms. They're farming out their juvenile cases and mental health appointments."

Whit made a face. "That's a hell of a way to make a living."

Tony and the attorney sat down.

Keating reminded Whit of most new attorneys. He wore his shirts just a little too big, and his tie was badly knotted. "You just out of school?"

"Oh, no. I've been out for about three years."

"Keating moved up here from Virginia," Tony said. "The court has appointed him to represent Isaac Dunn's daughter."

"What the hell does she need a lawyer for?"

Keating grinned. "Well, at the time I was appointed she was being viewed as a possible accessory to the murder."

"Not by me," Whit said.

"The state police were making noises about charging her," Tony said. "She wasn't cooperating with them."

"Well, shit," Whit said. "There's no way we would have let that happen, counselor."

"That resolved itself as soon as you took over the case," Keating said. "As it turned out, though, she needed a guardian ad litem anyway."

Whit was looking at Tony. "So what's all this got to do with me?"

"I was telling Sloan here about the plea agreement I've offered in the case. He's talked to the daughter. She's not exactly retarded, but she apparently does have some learning disabilities.''

Whit was shaking his head. ''So what?''

Keating answered. ''I've gone over the plea agreement with her. She understands it, and it's acceptable to her.''

Whit's gaze shot back to Tony. ''Is that what this is all about, Tony? Are you trying to convince me that second-degree murder is an acceptable plea?''

''I just wanted you to hear what Sloan had to say. Dunn's daughter more or less speaks for the victim's side.''

Whit threw up his hands. ''Hell, Tony, you don't need to impress me. Do what you want with the case. You're the prosecutor.''

''It does sound like a just disposition to me,'' Keating said.

Whit chuckled. ''Do you lawyers have a course in law school called Let's Make a Deal?''

Keating's face reddened.

Tony just laughed. ''You'll have to excuse Whit. He's no diplomat.''

Keating, though, appeared offended. ''It makes no difference to me what kind of plea is accepted. My client—Dunn's daughter—is satisfied with second degree. From what she tells me, her father was no inspiring specimen of humanity.''

Tony stood. ''The defendant's lawyer is going to present the plea agreement to his client this afternoon. I'll let you know if he agrees.''

Keating also rose. ''I look forward to hearing from you.''

''Of course,'' Tony said, ''it won't be a done deal until after the kid enters the plea in front of the judge. Sometimes these plea bargains can fall apart at the last minute. The judge himself has refused to accept one or two this past year.''

''I'm sure he'll accept this one,'' Keating said, casting a displeased look at Whit. He then left the office.

Whit had a smile on his face. ''I didn't mean to make him mad. The comment about the deal was aimed at you.''

Tony sat back down. ''You know how sensitive young lawyers can be. He's a real go-getter. From what I gather, he's handling about two-thirds of the juvenile cases and almost all the mental health hearings. It's a good way to get a practice started. It certainly will make him friends among the other lawyers.''

Whit, though, had something else on his mind. ''What did you hope to accomplish by bringing him in here?''

''I just wanted you to see that this plea bargain makes sense.''

''To who?'' Whit countered.

''To me. To the defendant's lawyer. To the daughter of the victim.''

''Too bad we can't ask Isaac Dunn how he feels about it.''

Tony's brow furrowed. ''Don't pull that on me.''

''Look, Tony, I'm on your side. I don't approve of letting this pond scum plead to second, but that's your bailiwick, not mine. You don't have to justify it to me.''

Tony shrugged. ''You seemed devoutly opposed yesterday, and it is your case.''

''And you seem awful damned anxious to have me like this arrangement. Is it possible you don't feel too proud of accepting a plea to second degree?''

''Bullshit,'' the prosecutor said.

Whit glanced down at the legal pad on his desk. ''Let's change the subject before one of us gets bent out of shape.''

''Suit yourself.''

''About the B&Es,'' Whit said.

''You do have something?''

''Not anything to get excited about. I'm going to try to talk to Benning's daughter. So far, the presence of teenagers in several of the target homes is the only thing we have to go on. The state medical examiner called with his report on Mayberry. The bullet, as small as it was, destroyed the heart. One thing the ME did say. Mayberry wasn't long for this world even before he answered that complaint.''

''Whadaya mean?''

''The medical examiner said he had one hell of an aortic

aneurysm just above the heart. He was surprised it hadn't burst already.''

Tony grimaced. "Frightening, isn't it? At my age I go to bed every night wondering if I'll wake up in the morning.''

"You're not much older than I am," Whit said.

Tony eyed the overflowing ashtray on Whit's desk. "I don't smoke, either, but still—just like Mayberry—you don't know what kind of time bombs are ticking away inside you.''

Whit shrugged. "When I do go, I just hope it's like that.'' He snapped his fingers.

"When are you gonna stop smoking?''

Whit rolled his eyes. "Jesus, Tony. Probably never. What's the big deal? I guaran-damn-tee you one thing. I won't wanna die any more at eighty than at sixty.''

"What kinda sense does that make?''

"To me one hell of a lot.'' He defiantly lit a cigarette, then changed the subject. "As I was saying, I'm gonna start with the Benning girl and work backwards. I'll take each case in which there was a teenager in the house.''

"You think they're pinpointing the property for someone?''

"Maybe other teenagers," Whit said. "For drugs.''

"It's a theory," Tony said.

"I'm also going to work an insurance angle. Maybe it's some form of insurance fraud. Watkins is getting his case files together. We're gonna go over them this afternoon.''

"It may just be coincidence, Whit.''

"Well, let's hope not. We need to find some common denominator.''

"Have there been any break-ins out in the country?''

"Oh, sure. The sheriff's department has had a few. So have the state police, but the modus operandi in those doesn't jibe with these in the city.''

Tony started to leave, but he stopped at the door. "Did you see the paper this morning?''

Whit shook his head. "No, but she told me about it last night. I guess you mean that story on the eyewitness.''

"Not so much that," Tony said. "There were at least eight letters to the editor raising hell about these B&Es and the inability of the local law-enforcement agencies to apprehend the culprits. Now that a cop's been killed, I bet there will be even more—only now it's your investigation."

Whit shrugged. "You know how I feel about that, Tony. What I don't read can't hurt me . . . or upset me."

Something was awry. Anna knew as much when she received the summons to Kathy Binder's office. It wasn't SOP—standard operating procedure. If Kathy had something to say to Anna, even if that something was criticism, she visited Anna's office. It worked the other way, too. When Anna wanted to talk to Kathy, she went to the publisher's office on the other side of the building. The protocol of their working relationship had remained very informal. So when the paper's teenage gofer stuck her head in Anna's office and said that Mrs. Binder needed to see her, that simple signal set off alarms. She had been on the phone with a member of the county's legislative delegation at the time. She had ended the conversation as quickly as she could.

As she walked through the newsroom toward the administrative suite of offices, she cataloged recent editorials and features. Nothing out of the ordinary, nothing even vaguely controversial came to mind. If anyone's toes had been tromped, she wasn't aware of it.

But Kathy's spinsterish secretary smiled as Anna stepped into the office.

"Trouble?" Anna asked.

The question surprised the secretary. "I don't think so. I haven't heard any shouting. Mrs. Binder buzzed me a few moments ago and asked me to call you. Your line was busy. So I sent Amy."

It made no sense to Anna. "Is she alone?"

"Oh, no. Didn't Amy tell you?"

"I was on the phone. What didn't she tell me?"

"The new chief of police is with her."

That news brought a smile to Anna's face. "Okay. I get the picture now."

But Kathy's secretary was puzzled. "Did I miss something?"

"No. Mrs. Binder was simply trying to give me a little advance warning, a chance to be prepared."

"For what?"

"Well, since you haven't heard any raised voices, probably just some subtle pressure."

"Pressure?"

"Arm-twisting," Anna said. "I'd wager that he isn't happy over the letters to the editor. You have been reading them, I hope."

The secretary blushed. "Well, to be honest—"

Anna had to laugh. "You mean you don't read the paper?"

"Oh, yes. I scan the front page. I read the society—oops! I mean life-style—pages. Oh, and the comics."

Anna just shook her head. It reaffirmed her belief that journalists gave the public too much credit for caring. "Buzz Kathy and tell her I'm here."

"She said for you to come straight in."

Anna took a deep breath. At such times she was thankful for her relationship with Whit Pynchon. If she could handle him, then she could handle anyone. She opened the door to Kathy's office and stepped inside.

EIGHT

AS MICKEY MOSES pulled into the parking lot of the PU, he saw Bert Ringwald standing out front. A thin blanket of milky clouds did nothing to moderate the sun's intensity, and curling heat phantoms rising from the broad asphalt parking area distorted the boy's small frame. The boy hurried across the lot to meet Mickey, who didn't even notice the damp sweat stains that darkened the back and underarms of Bert's blue T-shirt. The ugly bruise on the side of the boy's left cheek snagged his attention first.

"What the hell happened to you?"

"My old man," Bert said. "The bastard knocked hell outta me last night."

Mickey jammed the manual transmission into LOW and eased out of the parking area. "What for?"

"No reason. He don't need no reason. He was drunk, and I guess he just felt like it."

"Shit, Bert. People don't beat you for no reason."

"My old man does. I don't wanna talk about it no more."

They rode in silence as Mickey navigated the late afternoon traffic in Milbrook's downtown area. Once they were on the residential streets south of Milbrook's business district, Bert said, "You and Zeke are lucky. You ain't got no old man fuckin' with you."

"I thought you didn't want to talk about it," Mickey said.

"I don't. I just wanted you to know you're lucky your old man's not around."

"Just leave my old man out of it, then." Mickey's father

was a sore point with the boy. A Marine, John Moses had been surprised by a Vietcong ambush just outside Saigon a few months after Mickey had been born and just one month before the big U.S. pullout from South Vietnam in March 1973.

"Sure. Whatever you say."

Mickey had rolled down the windows of the Pinto just as soon as he had gotten in the car, but the rush of hot air did little to relieve the swelter.

"I hate this friggin' heat," Bert said, leaning forward to allow the air to circulate between his back and the torn plastic seat. "We shoulda met Zeke at the PU. It's air-conditioned."

"I suggested it. Zeke didn't wanna meet at the PU."

"Fuck Zeke," Bert said. "Who died and made him the top dog, anyway?"

"I guess the man made him top dog."

"That's something else. I think he oughta tell us who the man is. Christ, how do we know we're gettin' our fair share? Maybe Zeke and the man are ripping you and me off. Maybe the man is ripping all three of us off. How the fuck do we know?"

Mickey sighed. He didn't really like Bert much. The kid whined all the time. If he acted that way at home, no wonder his old man whipped hell out of him now and then. "You're probably gettin' what you're worth."

"What the hell does that mean?"

"Forget it."

Mickey wheeled the Pinto into the driveway of the trailer. Zeke and his mother—his father had abandoned them six years earlier—lived in area known as the Bottom. Mackey's Run, a small creek that divided the Bottom, marked the southernmost boundary of Milbrook. The Mortons' trailer was on the south bank, so it wasn't in the city limits. In fact, a city ordinance banned trailers within Milbrook proper. As a result, the southern plain of Mackey's Run hosted an amalgamation of small trailer parks, most of which sat on high foundations of cinder blocks to escape the creek's frequent spring flooding.

Zeke sat on the mobile home's metal steps, bare-chested, a beer in his hand. As the other two exited the car, he reached into an ice-filled cooler and withdrew two cans. He tossed one to each as they approached. "Your mom home?" Bert asked.

Zeke rolled his eyes. "You see the gawdamn car here, Bert?"

Bert shook his head.

"Then she ain't gawdamn home, is she?"

Only then did Bert pop the top off the beer. He took a sip, frowning at the taste. He didn't really like beer, but it was easier to drink the yeasty brew than to listen to Zeke's bitching.

"You got our money?" Mickey asked.

Zeke grinned. He already had had several beers before they had arrived, and a telltale rosy flush highlighted his cheeks. "Sure, but I deducted a few expenses."

The muscles in Mickey's jaws rippled. "What expenses?"

Zeke held up the can of beer. "The refreshments."

"I'll buy my own gawdamned beer," Mickey said. "I don't like your brand."

Zeke laughed. "Don't get bent out of shape. I was just kidding." He reached down into the pocket of the grimy jeans he was wearing and withdrew two rolls of bills secured by rubber bands. As he had done with the cans of beer, he tossed them at the two boys.

Bert set his beer down and fumbled to remove the rubber band.

"There's three hundred there," Zeke said.

Bert's eyes widened as the rubber band flew off. "You're shittin' me?"

"Not enough for ya?"

"God, it's plenty, Zeke."

Mickey was surprised, too, but he didn't allow it to show. "How many jobs is this from?"

"Just one—that big two-story house we did last week."

"The Jacksons," Mickey said.

Zeke shrugged. "I don't wanna remember the names."

Bert thumbed through the twenties and fifties. "Hey, man, this is great."

For the first time Zeke noticed the smaller boy's battered cheek. "Who the fuck got a piece of you?"

Bert jammed the money into his pocket. "My old man."

"You oughta kill 'im."

"Maybe I will someday. If we keep making money like this, maybe I can hire a hit man." He giggled at that thought.

Zeke leaned back on the small porch. "How about a job that'll pay up in the thousands?"

"The thousands?" Bert said.

Zeke nodded.

Mickey was smiling. "Who we gotta kill?"

Zeke sprang to his feet. "It's just a break-in, man."

"Better not be a bank," Bert said. "I don't wanna get in trouble with the FBI."

Zeke crushed his beer can in his hand and hoisted it into the yard next door. "You're a dumb asshole, Ringwald."

"Christ, Zeke—"

"Just hear what I gotta say." Then Zeke told them about the doctor's house, except he left out the part about the alarm system.

"The Chief came to assure us that his department is doing all that it can to end this crime spree," Kathy said after she had introduced Anna to Chief Hayden Wallace.

The chief's soft but firm handshake lingered for a moment as he smiled at Anna. "I can understand the public's concern, Miss Tyree. I'd like to at least let them know that we're doing our best."

Anna had to pull her hand away. It bothered her a little that she really didn't want to. "Do you have any suspects?" She knew the answer to the question, but it was the first one that came to mind.

"A passel of 'em," Wallace said, his southern dialect thick and heavy. "Anybody who ever committed a B&E in or around Raven County is a suspect. Like I've told my boys, you can just about bet this year's harvest that these perps will have prior records."

"Perps?" Kathy asked.

"Short for perpetrators, ma'am. You know us cops. We got a lingo all our own."

Anna kept thinking about Whit's description of Wallace—a dumb jock with a southern accent. She could see where Whit would have come up with that description. To her, though, he looked like the reincarnation of Clark Gable's Rhett Butler, absent the mustache. "You do understand, Chief—"

"Please, ma'am. Call me Hayden."

"Well, please understand, Hayden, that we're bound to print the responsible letters to the editor that we receive. Sometimes we may shorten them somewhat, and we certainly wouldn't print anything irresponsible or libelous, but—"

"Miss Tyree—"

"Call me Anna."

He smiled. "Awright, Anna. I didn't come here to raise a ruckus about the letters. If I was in these folks' shoes, I'd be sittin' up all night with a shotgun on my lap. They got a right to be upset. I just wanna assure them that we're not dawdlin'. We know we got a real grievous situation here, and come hell or high water, we're gonna apprehend these punks. It was bad enough when they were violating the sanctity of people's homes. Last night they took a life."

Kathy couldn't help but notice the eye contact between her editor and the new police chief. Surely, she thought, in so short a time Anna wasn't becoming a little smitten with the new chief. "Chief, I understand that your department has enlisted the assistance of the investigator for the prosecuting attorney."

The question produced a glare from Anna, but the chief

didn't lose a beat in answering it. "Oh, yes, ma'am. If I learned one thing down in Atlanta, it was the importance of interdepartmental cooperation. I was working down there when we had the Atlanta child murders. I'm sure both of you remember that dark time."

"Certainly," Anna said.

Kathy nodded that she remembered as well.

"That was one of the shortfalls in that investigation. The various departments and even the divisions within the department didn't have good enough communication. We plan to enlist the help of all the local law-enforcement agencies."

Kathy wasn't ready to let go of the issue. "Will Whit Pynchon be taking charge of the investigation, Chief?"

"Officially, yes, but in actual fact we'll be jointly working the case. I've been told that Pynchon is one hell of an investigator."

Anna attempted to divert the conversation. "You mentioned those series of killings in Atlanta—"

Kathy, though, wasn't finished. She interrupted her editor. "Just a minute, Anna. Have you heard anything else about Pynchon, Chief?"

Anna's face reflected her mounting frustration with Kathy. The publisher kept her gaze on the chief.

Wallace was shrugging. "Sure, some of my men aren't too fond of Pynchon. I gather he kinda serves as the internal affairs investigator for the county departments. Down in Atlanta we had an internal affairs division. As much as the officers resent them, you gotta have 'em."

"I don't understand the point of your question," Anna said, no longer able to keep silent.

Kathy leaned forward. "If I remember, Anna, the reporter who handles our police beat told us that the chief here wasn't pleased when he found out that Whit would be handling the case. Wasn't that the information we received?"

"Uh, yes," Anna said, somewhat taken aback by her publisher's sudden and uncharacteristic journalistic interest. "We were told you didn't want Pynchon called into the case."

The chief maintained his pleasant smile. "Up until that point, Mrs. Binder, I had only heard of Pynchon in the context of police misconduct. For the life of me, I couldn't see any basis for his involvement in these series of break-ins. Later, Watkins enlightened me as to Pynchon's investigative abilities. Once I knew that, I had absolutely no objections to seeking his input."

"You do know," Kathy said, "that Pynchon investigates all homicides?"

"I do now. Watkins told me. It's a bit unusual, but we can live with that. We just want to apprehend the person or persons who killed Officer Mayberry. We do have reason to believe that more than one individual was present. Since they were jointly involved in the commission of a felony at the time of the shooting, that makes them all susceptible to the felony murder rule. I discussed that with Tony Danton this mornin'."

"I thought all murders were felonies," Kathy said.

Anna provided the explanation. "When several people are committing a felony, like a burglary, and one of them kills somebody, then it makes them all guilty of first-degree murder."

"Makes sense," Kathy said.

The chief had a wistful smile on his face. "I kinda thought I'd be coming to a quiet little town when I left Atlanta."

"Why did you leave?" Anna asked.

"I just got tired of the big-city hubbub, ma'am. Besides, I had my twenty years in."

"So you're semiretired?" Kathy asked.

For the first time Wallace's face lost some of its good humor. His deep blue eyes settled on the publisher. "Mrs. Binder, I get the impression you've got some kinda crow to pick with me."

Kathy shrugged. "Why would you think that?"

"Because you're kinda cross-examining me. I'm not semiretired. I can't draw that Atlanta pension until I reach fifty-five. As for Investigator Pynchon's involvement in the case,

I did question it at first, until I got a handle on Pynchon's skill as an investigator. I'm serious, ma'am, when I tell you we are doin' our damnedest to catch these people."

Kathy managed a smile. "Welcome to Milbrook, then, Chief Wallace. I can only tell you that I came here from California several years ago, and I've found it a warm and wonderful place to live."

She then stood. "I don't mean to be brusque, but I have a dental appointment."

The chief rose to his feet and offered his hand to the publisher. "If you ever have any questions about this case or any other, or if my office can help you in any way, please let me know."

"I'll show you out," Anna said.

The chief turned toward the door. Anna followed, but as she did, she glared back over her shoulder at her friend and employer. Kathy was shaking her head.

Once they were outside Kathy Binder's office, Anna said, "I'd like to do a story on your involvement in the child murder case."

"How about now? Over a cup of coffee and a piece of apple pie?" the chief said. "I've fallen in love with that little restaurant down on the corner."

"You mean Ketchum's Diner?"

"Absolutely. It reminds me of somethin' straight out of a Norman Rockwell painting."

"It is," Anna said, "but I'm afraid we call Ketchum's place 'The Greasy Spoon.' "

"Not to his face, I hope."

"Of course not, but his menu would hardly receive the endorsement of the American Heart Association."

"I believe in the American way, Miss Tyree, and that includes Mom and apple pie. Cholesterol be damned." He lowered his voice to a whisper. "All that health stuff is dirty communist propaganda, anyway."

Anna had to laugh. "Sort of like fluoridation of the water. And please, don't call me Miss Tyree."

"I can't help myself. It's such a traditional southern name. How 'bout it? Coffee and a piece of pie."

"Certainly, why not? But it's Dutch treat."

"You don't think I'd try to influence your good offices with a bribe of so piddlin' a consequence?"

Anna laughed again. "We just want to avoid the appearance of impropriety, Chief."

He offered her his arm. "Fine, you call me Chief, and I'll call you Miss Tyree, and everybody'll think we're as proper as prayer on a Sunday."

NINE

THE SHERIFF OF RAVEN COUNTY, Gil Dickerson, intercepted Whit just as he exited the prosecuting attorney's suite of offices. "Where the hell do you think you're going?"

"Home," Whit said. He pointed up to the clock in the hall of the courthouse. "The county's gotten their pound of flesh from me today."

Gil brandished a sheet of paper. "Think again, pal. This teletype just arrived. It's for Watkins at the city, but he gets to keep better hours than you. He's already left the station."

Whit took the flimsy piece of paper from his close friend. "What the hell is it?"

"A hit on a gun stolen in one of the city's burglaries. One hell of a hit."

Whit scanned the numbers and jargon. "I never could make heads or tails outta these things."

"It says that the Raleigh, North Carolina, police department has recovered a weapon that Watkins entered in NCIC as stolen."

"Does it say where they got it?" Whit asked, still frowning at the abbreviated data on the sheet of paper.

"No, but I took the liberty of calling down to Raleigh. The city boys down there referred me to the local FBI office. The gun was used in a homicide."

Whit's gaze left the paper and came up to meet Gil Dickerson's. "A homicide?"

"They're calling it a termination in Raleigh."

"A termination?"

71

"Seems as if this guy was on his way to talk to the local boys and the feds about some kind of terrorist group. He was terminated—that's the word the fed's used—practically on the steps to the federal building."

"With a gun from here?"

"That's what the FBI claims." Gil produced a white piece of paper from the shirt pocket of his uniform. "Here's the agent's name. He wanted you or Watkins to call him. He said he would be in his office until eight tonight."

Whit looked again at the clock. "Damn, Gil. This really isn't my case. The weapon wasn't stolen during last night's incident. Did the folks at the city know where they could reach Watkins?"

Gil shook his head, still offering Whit the note. "They gave me his home phone number. I called there, and no one answered."

"Gimme the damned thing. You know how thrilled I get when I have to deal with the feds."

"C'mon, Whit," the sheriff said, smiling. "Haven't you got any respect for the real cops?"

Whit made a face and turned to return to the prosecutor's office.

"Mind if I tag along?" Gil asked.

Whit slowly nodded. "Fact is, if you're that interested, you're more than welcome to handle it."

"No way. The break-ins have all happened in the city."

"So far," Whit said.

Whit and the sheriff moved back to Whit's office. Dickerson walked with a pronounced limp, the result of a gunshot wound to the knee, but he had no trouble keeping pace with Whit. The investigator dialed the number on the piece of paper Gil had given him. He flipped the phone on to the speaker so Gil could monitor the conversation.

"Federal Bureau of Investigation," a male voice answered. "Agent Kerns speaking."

"Agent—" Whit checked the paper. "Agent Noble, please."

"Who's calling?"

"Investigator Pynchon. I'm with the prosecuting attorney's office in Raven County, West Virginia."

"What are you calling in reference to?"

Whit rolled his eyes. "Look, friend, I've got a note here asking me to call Agent Noble. It was your ox that got gored down there—or maybe I should say witness—not mine. If Noble wants to talk to me, put him on. If he's not there, otherwise tied up, or doesn't need to talk to me now, then I'll hang up and go on home."

"Just a minute," the voice said.

The agent placed the call on hold.

"Jesus," Whit said. "These guys get under my skin."

"Everyone gets under your skin," Gil said. "And you'd better watch what you say. They're probably taping the call. You know the feds. They love that kinda thing."

"And there's probably some crime in the federal code making it a conspiracy to bad-mouth the FBI," Whit said, meaning it.

The phone clicked again. "Agent Noble here."

"Investigator Pynchon. I have a note to call you."

"You're from Raven County?" the agent asked.

"Yes, sir."

"Are you with the city department?"

"No, sir. I'm a special investigator with the prosecutor's office. You guys recovered a gun that was stolen in a residential burglary here in Milbrook. That's the county seat of Raven County."

"I know," the agent said. "Actually, I'm from West Virginia myself, the Huntington area."

"You were smart enough to get out," Whit said.

The agent laughed. "Well, I don't know about that."

"Then you haven't been back here for a while."

"That's true. Are you assisting in the city's investigation?"

"Last night we had an officer killed in a B&E by the same gang. Our office handles all homicide investigations."

"I bet that isn't a very popular policy."

Whit laughed. "You must have our phone line tapped. Either that or you've been reading my mail." He winked at the sheriff.

"No, Investigator Pynchon, but I can just imagine the other departments' attitude toward that kind of policy."

That was enough small talk. Whit got to the point. "What do you need to know about the gun?"

"Not a lot," the agent said. "It's what you people need to know. According to the county sheriff—"

"He's here with me now," Whit said, "listening on the speaker."

"Hi again, Sheriff."

"Greetings," Gil said.

"The sheriff told me that Milbrook had suffered a series of business and residential burglaries in which the primary target was weapons."

"He told you right," Whit said.

"I'm assigned to a special-investigation unit dealing with domestic security and internal terrorism, Investigator Pynchon. Several communities, especially in the south and the northwest, have been victimized by similar burglary rings, and we believe it's part of a nationwide campaign to arm certain extremist organizations. The gun that was recovered this morning confirms that your community may now be targeted by one of these groups."

Gil was frowning. Whit was shaking his head. "Hold it a second, Noble. Are you telling me that we've got Arabs or Iranians or whatever breaking into our houses just to get weapons? Christ, they can buy all they need."

"Oh, no. That wasn't what I said."

"You said terrorists," Whit countered.

"These are the home-grown kind. Right-wing groups. Groups with the same political leanings as the Posse Comitatus and Bruders Schweigen."

"Bruders what?"

"We call it The Order for short. This group and similar

groups were involved in political assassinations, the murder of police officers, bank robberies, armored-car robberies, counterfeiting, and bombings. The Order has been put out of commission, but there are plenty of other similar fringe groups. The most violent of them consider themselves to be in a state of war with the U.S. government. We've managed to disrupt some of their traditional supply lines, so in recent months they've been encouraging and financing widespread B&E rings in order to secure a huge cache of safe weapons.''

"You're kidding me," Whit said.

"I wish we were. These people are dangerous terrorists, and it looks like you have a local infestation.''

"I'm afraid I lured you here under false pretenses," Hayden Wallace said.

Anna sat with a glass of cola. The chief sipped his coffee. She had passed on a slice of pie, and the plate containing his was already clean.

"What do you mean?" she asked.

"Well, I was with the Atlanta department during the Atlanta child murders, but I'm afraid I wasn't involved in the investigations.''

"But you said—"

He smiled. "I said that a lack of communication between and within departments hampered the investigation. That was true. You inferred that I was an investigator.''

"I see.''

"However, I did let you operate under that false assumption.''

"Why?" Anna asked.

"For the continued pleasure of your company, Miss Tyree.''

"You're flattering me, Chief.''

"I can't help myself. Would you think me forward if I told you that I'm somewhat taken with you?''

"Taken with me?''

"I guess that's a southern phrase. It means—''

"I know what it means," Anna said. "I should tell you, Chief, that I am involved with someone."

"Investigator Pynchon," he said.

"So you know about that?"

"Of course. I figure that was why Mrs. Binder was giving me such a rough time. She obviously noted my interest in you."

"She's the protective type."

"That's what good friends should do."

"Are you married?" she asked.

"Divorced. Goin' on five years now. It's mighty difficult for a woman to live with a cop, especially during the early years of his career. I think divorce is an occupational hazard."

Anna sipped her cola. "Exactly what did you do in Atlanta?"

"For a long time I was a patrolman. There was an opening in the department's SWAT team—that stands for Special Weapons and Tactics. I applied, and I guess that was my thing. I started to move up in the ranks and ended up being the head of that group for a few years."

"Did you like it?"

"Yeah, I gotta admit I did. We managed to escape most of the dull routine of police work. When we got a call, it usually meant some real action. I loved it."

"So why did you give it up?"

Wallace's blue eyes twinkled as he said, "I chickened out."

"You what?"

"I chickened out," he said again.

"Somehow I find that hard to believe."

He grinned. "I don't mean to imply that I was guilty of cowardice in the field or while under fire. I just figured the law of averages was no longer on my side. You can only dodge so many bullets. It was time to get out before I was killed or wounded."

"I wouldn't call that chickening out, Chief."

"I also got tired of the big-city crap. The drugs, the courts that plea-bargained anything and everything, the ten-year-old kids with guns in their pockets and a hard-on for the cops. Pardon my language again, Miss Tyree."

"Don't worry about it."

"So I decided to try to finish my career in a small town. I saw Milbrook's ad for a chief, and I applied. Here I am."

"Do you like it?"

"So far. I like it even better after today."

She lowered her eyes. "I don't think you should get your hopes up, Chief. I care a lot for Whit Pynchon."

"But you're not married to him."

"No, that's true."

"Are you engaged?"

Anna laughed. "Do people still get engaged in this day and age?"

"They do where I come from."

"We're not engaged. We do, however, live together."

"I don't mean to get personal, but how does that go over in a small town like this?"

"Frankly, Chief, neither one of us really cares how it goes over."

He lifted his coffee cup in a toast. "Here's to your spunk. I like it."

She lifted her glass and clinked it against the cup.

"Well, then," he said, "maybe we could just have lunch one day . . . or, better yet, dinner."

"Not a good idea," she said.

"That, Miss Tyree, depends on your point of view."

TEN

"CAN YOU TELL ME exactly what happened in Raleigh?" Whit asked.

"Hold one moment," the FBI man said. The phone was placed back on hold.

"Do you buy this?" Gil asked.

"I dunno. It sounds wild to me, a little frightening, too. I've heard of these groups out in the west, but—"

The speaker came alive again. "Investigator Pynchon?"

"Still here."

"I had to get some clearance from the special agent in charge before revealing too many details. Procedure, you know."

"I understand."

"Here's the situation. A businessman from Fayetteville—it's about an hour south of here—contacted a resident agent in Raleigh a week or so ago. He claimed to be a longstanding member of a group calling itself The Aryan Front—TAF for short. They have dubbed themselves taffers. This subject said that he had been raised inside the group, so to speak, that he had attended youth camps that it sponsored. These fanatics believe in teaching their kids to hate at an early age. Anyway, he told the agent here that he wanted to talk to us about the group and its illegal activities, and he even said that he would provide us with names."

"Why?" Whit asked. "When a fellow wants to do that, it's because he's got some kind of chip on his shoulder."

"We never had a chance to find out. We were skeptical.

78

To be honest, others like him have come forward before. Most of the time they proved to be double agents. We were even more skeptical when he refused any kind of protection, at least until after he met us. That meeting was scheduled for today—this morning, in fact, around nine. I came in from Washington just for the meeting.''

"But your stool pigeon didn't make it," Whit said.

"No, sir. He was just outside the courthouse, on his way inside, we presume. It was the morning rush hour, and there were people all around. Witnesses report a single gunshot. When the confusion ended, our subject was dead. The local police handled the initial investigation, and they found a handgun—a .357 Smith & Wesson—under a blood-spattered coat. It appears that the killer came up behind our subject . . . that he had the gun concealed under a coat draped over his arm. He jammed it right up against the subject's backbone. The bullet was a steel-jacketed hollow point. I don't have to tell you the result.''

Gil grimaced.

"No," Whit said. "You don't."

"Of course, no one really saw anything. It's a typical mode of operation. These people have established a pattern of abandoning the gun at the crime scene. It's always clean of prints, and on many occasions the gun's serial number turns up in the national computer system. In other cases it doesn't.''

Whit was nodding. "Probably all stolen, though. The owners just didn't have the serial numbers.''

"Right," Noble said.

"Agent Noble, this is Sheriff Gil Dickerson again.''

"Yes, Sheriff.''

"Are you saying we have a band of these people here in Raven County?''

"I couldn't say, Sheriff. It isn't likely that you have a group there, but I'd bet my pension that you have at least one individual. Usually they recruit local talent—street criminals—to commit the B&Es, and they pay top dollar for the guns. If the locals happen to be addicts, these groups aren't above offering payment in the form of drugs. They also fence other stolen items simply to finance their operations. All too often you'll find that those committing your intrusions have no idea who they are dealing with. In those few instances when the police have managed to nail a theft ring, the contact person, the intermediary between the locals and the taffers, has always ended up dead. We're dealing with incredibly ruthless people here. Last year we managed to work an agent into the group. He survived two weeks before they discovered his identity. He was brutally tortured and then murdered. Three months later we found what was left of his body down in the Green Swamp. It's located—''

"I'm familiar with that area," Whit said. "Southeastern North Carolina, right?"

"That's right."

"Is there anything you need from us?" Gil asked.

"Not really," the federal agent said. "Not much we're going be able to do on this one. We didn't even get to meet with the subject. You might check the background of the gun's owner, but I suspect you'll discover nothing. That's one reason this group uses stolen weapons."

"In how many other places has this gone on?" Whit asked.

"Almost fifty communities across the country. Usually, after several months, the break-ins stop. The Aryan Front, or whichever group might be operating in that region, moves its actions on to the next town. We don't know if the principals remain or not. It's possible that those behind the B&Es are residents of the community, and that's how the locations are chosen. We just don't know. The pattern of the crime fits with the groups' areas of geographic strength."

"Have you ever nailed the organizers? The behind-the-scenes people."

There was a moment's hesitation, then Noble said, "Not a single time."

Whit looked at Gil. "Well, Noble, maybe Milbrook will be your first."

* * *

Dark purple-blue clouds covered the sky, and thunder grumbled as Janice Benning hurried into the PU. No one, including Janice, believed that the storm would do much to alleviate the devastating heat. More than likely, once the storm passed, its residue of moisture would only intensify the humidity. She sighed with relief at the cool crispness inside the center and began to search for Mickey Moses. He wasn't there, but Susie Watkins was sitting at the same table she had occupied the night before. Most of the same girls were with her.

" 'Lo, Janice," Susie said.

"Skinny Janice," one of the other girls quipped.

"Can I talk to you a sec?" Janice asked of her friend, ignoring the comments from the others.

Susie nodded, her face suddenly pinched with concern. She stood.

"Oooh, secrets," cooed the girl who had called her skinny.

"Not really," Janice said.

"I bet it's about that Mickey Moses," another said.

"He doesn't even know you exist," the first said.

"C'mon," Janice said to Susie. "Let's go over here."

"Is it raining yet?"

"No, but soon." She guided Susie to a vacant table well out of earshot of any of the other kids.

"What's wrong, Janice?"

"I don't know what to do."

"Are you in trouble or something? You're not pregnant or anything?"

"Don't be silly."

"You've been actin' weird lately."

"You know that break-in at my house?"

"My dad's working on it."

"Well, my dad . . . he got a sort of a look at one of them, not really so he would know him, but enough so he told the police—your father, I guess—that the one that cut him was real little."

"So?" Susie asked.

Janice leaned even closer to her friend. "I think it was Bert Ringwald."

"Bert Ringwald? The dwarf that runs around with Mickey Moses?"

Janice nodded, but she also said, "He's not exactly a dwarf. He's just little."

Susie glanced around the center. "There are lots of little people, Janice."

"I know that."

"Well—"

"Well, do you think maybe I oughta tell your dad or something?"

Susie vigorously shook her head. "No way, girl. I know my dad. He'll yank Bert up right then. What'll that look like? Think about it, Janice. Just because he's little and all, that's no reason—"

"There's something else," Janice said. She scooted her chair around the table until she was closer to her friend.

"Secrets! Shame, shame," a female voice cried. It came from the table where Susie had been sitting and was audible all over the center.

"How can you stand them?" Janice asked.

Susie just shrugged. "They're okay. You're just kinda standoffish. They think you're a snob."

"They're wrong."

"What else were you going to tell me?"

"A couple of weeks ago Mickey and me were talking, right here in the center, in fact. Somehow we got on the subject of hunting, and he asked me if my dad hunted. I said he did. We talked some more. Then he asked me if my dad kept his guns where no one could get to them. I told him where they were, Susie."

"That's not enough to get all stirred up about." The look on Susie's face belied her effort to sound unimpressed.

"Susie, the burglars went right to the place where he kept his guns."

"C'mon, Janice. You don't think Mickey's a housebreaker or whatever it is they call them."

"No, not Mickey, but maybe he accidentally, without thinking, like sorta mentioned it to Bert . . . or maybe to that Zeke character he hangs around with."

"Have you asked him?"

Janice nodded. "Last night."

"And?"

"He got really upset."

"I don't blame him."

"And he said that Bert and Zeke had been with him when my dad was cut."

Susie leaned back. "There you go. If you believe Mickey, then you're wrong."

Janice didn't say anything.

"You do believe Mickey, don't you?"

"Yeah, I guess, but I just wonder if I'm doing the wrong thing by not telling somebody—somebody like your father. I mean, that poor policeman was killed in my yard."

"By Bert Ringwald?"

"Maybe."

"He's just a little stain, Janice."

"I just have this feeling."

Susie threw up her hands. "So tell my father, but don't forget I warned you not to. It'll get things all in an uproar."

"Maybe he wouldn't—"

Susie put a hand on Janice's. "I love my dad, Janice, but I learned a long time ago not to tell him too much. He's a cop, Janice. He thinks like a cop. God, when I really start dating, I bet you he'll run a make or whatever on my boyfriends. Either that or he'll frisk 'em looking for drugs or something. He comes home now wanting to know if I ever see any drugs around here or around the school."

"What do you tell him?"

Neither of the girls used drugs, but they knew kids who did. A lot of their classmates, even in junior high, smoked dope, and a few bragged about using crack and cocaine and

Tylox. Some even showed white powder around, claiming it was heroin. More than a few drank, mostly beer, but sometimes they came to the center or even to school smelling like real booze.

"I tell him I haven't seen any," Susie said. "If I told him the truth, he'd make me give him names and dates. You'd best just keep your mouth shut."

"If you think so," Janice said, still not convinced.

Susie stood. "Tell me, Janice, do you really think Mickey Moses would be into something like that?"

"I wouldn't think so."

"See, you even think you're wrong. C'mon, let's go get something to drink."

Janice glanced toward the door. "I oughta get home before it storms."

"Too late," Susie said.

It started suddenly, a dull roar from above them. Rain cascaded down on the roof of the PU. Lightning cracked outside, and the lights in the center flickered, then died.

A boy shouted, "Gotcha." A girl screamed.

The emergency lights, powered by batteries, blinked on, but they did little to erase the deep shadows in the center. It promised to be a busy night for the center's chaperons.

ELEVEN

A KEROSENE LANTERN cast a dim dancing light over the Bennings' living room. An old Sam Cooke song blared from a battery-powered radio sitting on the coffee table.

"Christ, I wish they would get the power back on," Fred Benning said.

"You heard the radio," Alice, his wife, said from her place on the couch. "The storm knocked out something at the generator plant. It might be several more hours. Besides, I think it's romantic. If you're worrying about the hospital—"

"I don't give a damn about the hospital. It has a big generator. I'm gonna miss that movie."

Alice sat across the room on the couch. "How many times have you seen that same movie?"

"It's one of my favorites."

"TBS broadcasts it three or four times a year. You'll get to see it again."

Benning slapped his hand down on the recliner. "This weather's ridiculous. It's time for Janice to be home, too."

"She's at the center, Fred. You wouldn't want her walking home in the storm, anyway."

"It's late."

"Not really. It just seems that way because of the storm. It made it seem dark earlier than usual. It's not even nine yet."

He pushed himself out of his recliner and whimpered slightly at the pain in his injured side.

85

"Are you all right?" his wife asked.

"I'm gonna go open some windows. I can't stand this."

"But the rain—"

"I'll open them in back. The rain's not coming from that direction. We've gotta get some circulation in here."

"Do you think that's wise?"

"Christ, Alice, they won't come back here a second time. They got what they wanted."

Benning was almost to the kitchen when the phone rang. Alice yelped. "For God's sakes," he said, hurrying back to answer.

"It scared me. I thought the phones were off."

"The phone company has a generator, too. It switches on when the power goes off."

He answered it.

"Daddy?"

"Where are you?" Benning demanded.

"At the center. I can't find a ride home, and they're going to close early because of the power failure. Can you come get me?"

"Uh, sure, babe. I'll be there in a few minutes."

"I hate to ask, but I don't want to walk home in the storm."

"You stay put. I'll be down to get you."

His wife was listening to the conversation. "Can you drive? You haven't tried yet."

"Of course I can drive," he said as he hung up the phone.

He went to the closet and pulled out a plastic raincoat. "I won't be long. You want me to open those back windows before I leave?"

Alice Benning thought about it for a moment. The flashes of lightning were less frequent now, the booming cracks of thunder not so loud. Still, she said, "I'd rather wait until you get back."

"Suit yourself."

He moved slowly out the door and onto the front porch. Rain continued to fall in a fashion that weathermen described as moderate. The downpour, though, had ended, or at least it had traveled toward the northeast. He moved gingerly down the steps. That's when his side hurt him the most, going up and down steps. The motion seemed to pull at the stitches that kept the wound closed.

His wife stood on the front porch, savoring the rain-cooled air as her husband backed the family station wagon out into the street. Once he was out of sight, she shivered a little and stepped back into the sticky warmth of the house. Neither she nor Fred Benning had noticed a van, painted the same color as the thunderclouds that had rolled over Milbrook, parked across and about fifty feet down White Oak Lane.

Water dripped off the narrow awning that covered a portion of the deck. Whit sat beneath it, watching the powerful flashes of lightning off to the northeast. With the power still off, the brilliant electrical discharges provided the only illumination in or around Whit's house. The chill brought by the violent winds within the storm was easing. Whit inhaled deeply, smelling the musty odor of ozone left in the storm's wake. A single firefly blinked. It was the time of summer when they began to disappear. The small incandescent insects fascinated Whit. They loved to congregate in the vicinity of the stand of lush rhododendrons that lined the backyard.

He heard Anna's footsteps even before she stepped out onto the back porch.

"Damn storm," she said. "I wouldn't mind if it would break this heat."

"For Chrissakes, Anna. To hear you tell it, the weather around here suits you all year long. Let me have a few days of enjoyment. Besides, we needed the rain," he said. "My rhododendrons were beginning to droop."

"I thought you liked it hot *and dry*." She checked the porch chair to make sure it was dry before sitting down.

"I like it hot and tropical," he countered. "That includes an occasional storm. You're home early. I didn't even hear your car."

"I parked out on the street, and I do have to go back to

work. The power outage has us shut down. If they don't get it back on soon, we might not be able to get a paper out tomorrow.''

Whit chuckled. ''Believe it or not, the world would keep turning.''

''The paper has never missed an edition.''

''There's a first for everything, but they'll have the power on before long.''

''The electrical surge might have zapped some of our computers,'' she said. ''We won't really know until they get it fixed. Anything new on the murder?''

He didn't say anything. He just shook his head.

She frowned. ''C'mon, Whit. I know you. You appear to be in your 'no comment' mode. Did you uncover something today?''

''A gun stolen in one of our burglaries turned up in North Carolina. That's all. It just confirms my suspicion that the contraband is being fenced down there.''

''Can you trace it?''

Whit shook his head. ''Not too likely.''

''I met the new Milbrook chief today.''

A flash of lightning momentarily delineated the twin summits of Tabernacle Mountain, the mountain towering to the north of the small city. In its sudden brilliance, Whit glanced at Anna. ''So what'd you think?''

''I wouldn't call him a dumb jock, Whit. For someone who wants to relocate in South Carolina, you have a strange prejudice against southerners.''

''I do not,'' Whit said.

''Oh, sure.''

''I mean it, Anna.''

''Well, I was impressed with Chief Wallace. I think he might be an asset to Milbrook.''

Whit sighed. ''So I guess we'll be reading a lot about Chief Bubba?''

''If we can get a paper out tomorrow, I have a story in which he assures the people of Milbrook that his department is doing all it can to catch the killers. He even talks about the importance of cooperation between the different departments. Did you know he was with the Atlanta police during the investigation of the child murders?''

''So were a lot of cops, and they still aren't really sure if they got the right guy. Or if one guy was responsible for all of the killings.''

She threw up her hands. ''Sometimes you're brutal. Do you form opinions about everyone so quickly?''

''Yeah. I can't help it. They just spring to mind.''

''Are you ever wrong?''

He nodded. ''Once in a while. I do try to keep an open mind. If he shows me something, you'll be the first to know.''

''Jesus, you're something else.''

The porch light flashed on.

''Voilà!'' Whit said.

Anna sagged. ''I'd better head on back to the paper and see if our equipment was fried.''

''I guess you'll be late getting back.''

''Probably just an hour or so later than usual. We were pretty close to having things wrapped up when the storm hit. It's a small paper tomorrow, but if the computer system is down, then God knows.'' She got up and started for the door into the house, stopping before going through it to her car. ''I get the feeling you're not telling me something.''

''I'm not telling you a lot of things. What exactly did you have in mind?''

The bright glare from the porch light had already started to attract night bugs. She swatted at a mosquito. ''Forget it. I don't have time to play games tonight.''

''Too bad. I can think of a couple of really fun games.''

That made her smile. ''Like playing doctor in sweat puddles.''

''For a start.'' Since she was leaving, he saw no reason to tell her that he was heading out the door right behind her.

* * *

Fred Benning and his daughter stood at the entrance to the teen center. Janice shifted her weight impatiently from one foot to the other while her father chatted with Father Gabriel.

"I was lucky," Benning was saying. "The knife didn't do any real damage."

"Praise God," the preacher said softly. "I tell you, Fred, all of this crime is related to drugs and alcohol. They're bringing our society down to its knees."

"You'd think the cops could catch these—" Benning had started to say "bastards," but he remembered that he was talking with a preacher.

"I've been discussing the issue with some members of my congregation, especially those who live in your part of town. We've been thinking about organizing our own community-watch program. We're planning an organizational meeting next week. If the police don't have enough men to properly patrol our city, then maybe we can help them."

"I'd be for that," Benning said. "If this keeps up, somebody else's gonna get killed. I gotta be honest with you, Father. I get a little weak in the knees thinking about how close I came to dying last night."

"Why don't you attend church with your wife?" the preacher asked.

Benning shrugged. "Just not my kinda thing, Father."

Father Gabe smiled. "I wonder what God thinks about that kind of answer."

"I know I should do better."

"Maybe God tapped you on the shoulder last night, a little reminder of your earthly mortality."

"Maybe," Benning said. The conversation had taken a turn that made him uncomfortable. "Well, the wife's home alone, so Janice and I had better be moving on."

Janice sagged with relief.

Father Gabe, though, wasn't finished. "I didn't mean to be nosy, Fred. One thing before you go. Would you have a night or two a month that you might be able to give to us?"

"For the community-watch program?"

"Well, maybe that, if we can get it organized. I was thinking about the center. We need chaperons here."

Janice withered. That was all she needed, her own father chaperoning at the center.

"Uh, sure," Benning said. "We're real proud of what you've done here. Janice spends a lot of time here. It's saved me some money, too. She always managed to find something to buy when she was spending all her time out at the mall."

The preacher grinned. "If we've saved you some money, we could always use a donation, too. However, your participation as a chaperon is what we need most."

"I guess I should heal up a little first, Father. It kinda hurts when I move too much."

"Certainly," the preacher said. "If you think that you and your wife might be able to give us a night or two a month, then call the center and ask for me. I'm here most every night."

"Will do," Benning said. "And if you get that community watch thing on track, let me know. I'll help in that, too. I still have one gun the burglars didn't get."

"Oh, I don't think the police would want us doing it armed," Peter Gabriel was quick to say.

"What they don't know won't hurt them."

That's when the lights came on inside the center.

"Praise the Lord," Gabriel declared.

Benning was relieved, too. With any luck, he might not miss much of the movie. Then he noticed that the lights on the other side of the street remained unlit. "That's odd. The lights over there aren't on."

The minister hadn't noticed. "They're probably bringing them back on line in stages."

The man pulled the small cardboard box from the satchel he had brought with him from the van. He had hoped to complete his task before power was restored, but the street lamp twenty yards up the street, just across from the Benning residence, flickered to life just as he placed the box beneath

the shelter of the gas meter. The lights inside the house
flashed on for a moment, then went out. He also heard the
sound of an approaching vehicle.

The street lamp's glare made it a little easier for him to
activate the delicate electronic receiver installed in the unit.
He depressed the button and was just starting to turn when
the car came into sight. He dropped to the wet ground, waiting for it to pass.

It didn't. The vehicle pulled to a stop in front of the house.

Alice Benning had blinked when she had seen the figure
in the gentle flicker of the distant lightning. She was sitting
in her living room, waiting for her husband to return with
their daughter. The vision of the human silhouette had appeared for only an instant, briefly enough that she wasn't
certain it had really been there—just a quick man-size shadow
in the window frame. Then she heard a soft bump against
the side of the house.

She covered her mouth with her hand to squelch a scream.
They've come back!

The thought made her start to tremble. With her heart
racing, she stood and carefully eased her way through the
living room to the hall, where the phone was.

Another flash from the disappearing storm revealed nothing in the window. She picked up the phone and then remembered the back door. *Is it locked?* She replaced the phone
and started back toward the kitchen. That's when light
flooded the house. At the same time the refrigerator motor
kicked on with a noisy rattle. Alice did scream this time.

The power stayed on only for an instant. Almost immediately the house was plunged into darkness again. The only
light came from the three kerosene lanterns positioned around
the living room and hallway. The woman glanced toward the
front door and saw that the street lamp on the other side of
White Oak Lane was burning brightly. She started back toward the phone just as someone started to hammer on the
door.

* * *

From his position midway down the side of the house the man could see only the rear end of the vehicle, but he had gotten a glimpse of it as it had rolled passed. It wasn't Benning's station wagon.

He had heard the car door shut and had continued to listen as the visitor walked up the front sidewalk and onto the porch. At that point he slithered through the soaked grass to the thigh-high hedge that separated the property from that of its neighbor. He heard the visitor knock on the door. The man quickly stood and hopped over the hedge, dropping down behind it to wait.

TWELVE

THE BENNINGS' principal phone rested on a small table just inside the front door, so close to it—and the threat on the other side—that Alice had no intention of using it. She looked back toward the kitchen, where there was a second phone. It was pitch black. The only other phone in the house was upstairs, and the bottom of the steps was almost as close to the front door as it was to the phone.

"For God's sakes, Fred, where are you?" she said in a whisper.

The knocking started again. She backed toward the dark kitchen and then remembered that she hadn't checked the back door yet. For all she knew it was still unlocked.

"Just go away," she said, a little louder this time.

The pounding became more persistent.

"Go away!" she screamed.

A man responded. He shouted a single word that she thought sounded like "police." Alice moved closer to the door.

"Who are you?" she shouted.

He answered, but once again she didn't understand his words. He started knocking again.

"I can't hear you."

She pressed her ear to the door and heard the word "identification."

"Get hold of yourself," she said to herself. "Answer the door."

The knocking stopped. The man shouted something again.

He knew she was home, and he obviously wasn't going to leave until she opened the door. She managed to force herself to put her hand on the dead bolt's latch. In the glow from the street lamp across the street she could see the man's outline. She took a deep breath and quietly slipped the chain lock into place. Then she flipped the latch to open the door.

"How come there aren't any lights on at our house?" Janice asked as her father slowed the car to make the turn into the driveway.

Considering that all the other homes around them had power, her father was wondering the same thing. "I dunno. Whose car is that in front of the house?"

"Look!" his daughter cried. "Someone's at this side of the house. He's got a flashlight."

For the second time in as many nights Fred Benning's heart hitched and then started to pound away inside his chest. "Jesus, I saw him."

He pulled into the driveway on the opposite side of the house and swung open the door. "You stay put."

"But Daddy—"

"Dammit, keep your ass in the car."

He forgot all about the painful stitches as he circled around behind the house. Behind him he heard the car door open. Janice was getting out, doing exactly what he had told her not to do.

"Freeze!"

The sharp command stopped Fred Benning in his tracks.

"Hands high," the voice said.

Fred obeyed.

"Don't make a move." The man appeared from the deep shadows immediately behind the house. Even in the muggy gloom, Fred could see that a gun was pointed at him this time. The sight did nothing to quell the pounding in his chest.

"Who . . . who are you?" Fred asked.

"Keep your hands high and turn away from me," the man said.

Fred's knees were trembling as he followed the man's orders. "Just don't hurt my family, mister. Take whatever you want and leave. I won't give you any trouble."

The man's hands touched him, and he felt a few drops of urine seep from the head of his penis.

"What's your name?" the man asked as he patted him down.

"Benning . . . Fred Benning. I—"

The man spun him around. The glare of a flashlight exploded in his face.

"Jesus Christ," the man said, "what the hell are you doing prowling around your own backyard?"

"Daddy?" It was his daughter's voice.

"Run, Janice!"

"Slow down," the man said. "My name's Pynchon. I'm investigating your break-in last night."

"Your wife thought she saw a prowler, Mr. Benning. I was checking the perimeter of the house."

Benning tried to compose himself. "Damn, I swear to God I almost wet myself. We saw the flashlight and you sneaking around as we pulled up."

The wife, who had been summoned by her daughter, came out on the small back porch. "Are you all right, Fred?"

"I dunno. Gimme a moment." He took a couple of deep breaths, then looked toward his wife. "What's wrong with the lights?"

"They went back out," she said. "They came on and then went right back out."

"I saw that," Whit said. "It happened just as I pulled up in front of your house. You probably had a circuit breaker blow when the lights came back on. If you had a lot of lights on and your appliances, that happens as everything kicks back on."

Benning was nodding. "Yeah, the breaker box is down in the basement. I'll go check it."

"Take this," Whit said, offering him the flashlight.

Benning accepted it. "Jesus, my legs are still wobbly."

"Did you see anyone, Mr. Pynchon?" his wife asked.

Whit shook his head. "Just Mr. Benning here."

"What happened?" The question came from Janice, who had exited the house behind her mother.

"I thought I saw someone prowling around the house. It was just before Mr. Pynchon arrived."

Her husband eyed the officer. "It wasn't you, was it?"

"I was about to ask you the same thing, Benning."

"You got here before I did."

Whit just shook his head. "The whole town's getting jumpy. Go on down and take care of the breaker. I need to talk to you and your wife."

Benning wiped a copious sheen of sweat from his face. "I feel a little queasy. Maybe you'll come with me."

"Glad to," Whit said. "Mrs. Benning, you and your daughter should go through the house and turn off as many of the electrical appliances as you can. Otherwise, it might just blow another breaker again."

Once down in the basement, Benning directed Whit to the breaker box and held the flashlight while he checked the various switches. He found one that felt loose. When he flipped it, light flooded down from the open basement door.

"Got it," Whit said.

"I hate to sound like such a wimp, but I need to go lay down."

Whit felt a little guilty. "I didn't mean to scare you like that, but your wife was rather adamant about the prowler."

"It's not just that. I'm over the scare. I think maybe I mighta pulled a stitch or two loose or something. My side's burning like hell."

Whit could see the sweat glistening on the man's face, the absence of color around his lips. "You don't have chest pains or anything like that, do you?"

Benning shook his head. "It's just my side. I think it's opened up a little. To be honest, I'm sweating like a stuck pig. I think maybe the sweat's getting into the wound."

"Come on, I'll help you up the steps."

"I can make it," Benning said. "Just come behind me in case."

Benning's wife waited at the top of the steps. "My God, Fred, you're white as a sheet."

"I'm just woozy. That's all."

Whit had a hand on the man's arm, supporting him. "He needs to lie down, Mrs. Benning."

"This way," she said. Then she shook her head at herself. "But you know the way, don't you? You were here last night."

When they reached the bedroom, Whit said, "You might also check his wound if you can. He thinks he's pulled some stitches loose. While you're doing that, I'd like to have a few words with your daughter."

As bad as he was feeling, Benning hesitated before sitting down on the bed. "Why do you want to talk to Janice?"

"I'll explain," his wife said. "You go ahead."

But Benning stiffened. "Just a minute—"

"Get on the bed," his wife said, not too gently, "before you pass out. I told you I would explain."

The man wasn't in any shape to argue. His wife was helping him onto the bed as Whit left the room.

He found the daughter in the living room. She was using a remote control to flip through the channels. "Is Daddy all right?"

"I think so. He's had a couple of rough nights."

"I saw you first when we pulled up. I thought the burglars had come back."

"I'm sorry. I didn't mean to frighten you or your father. Actually, I came here tonight to talk to you."

The young girl reminded Whit of his own daughter a few years earlier. Janice Benning was just at that age when she was beginning the transformation from a girl into a woman. That period hadn't been an easy time for Tressa. He hadn't known Anna then, and he really hadn't been able to communicate with Tressa for a year or so. Perhaps for that reason, he suspected that he wasn't going to have much luck with Janice.

Her face had become tense, almost frightened. "Why do you want to talk to me?"

"I didn't have an opportunity to do so last night, Miss Benning."

"I didn't see anything."

"That's not what I want to ask you. The people who broke in had a pretty good idea where your father kept his weapons. Do you have an explanation for that?"

It seemed to be his night for rattling the members of the Benning family. First there had been the girl's mother, then her father. Now she started to shake.

"Of course not."

"Maybe you told some of your friends at school where he kept his guns?"

Her expression changed from one of fear to one of confusion. "Do you know Mr. Watkins?"

Whit nodded. "If you mean Detective Watkins, the answer is yes. Why?"

"His daughter Susie? She's a friend of mine."

Whit frowned. "Does she have something to do with this?"

"Oh, no! I didn't mean that. I mean—"

"Listen, Janice. That's your name, isn't it?"

She lowered her head. "Yes."

"I have the feeling that you want to tell me something."

"I don't," she said, her gaze riveted to the floor.

"You mean you don't want to tell me, or you don't have anything to tell me?"

This time she raised her eyes to meet his. "I don't have anything to tell you. I really don't."

Her mother came into the living room.

Janice jumped at the opportunity to redirect the conversation. "How's Daddy?"

Her mother, though, spoke to Whit. "He was right, Mr.

Pynchon. I loosened the bandage enough to check the wound. It is bleeding again.''

"How much?" Whit asked.

"Not a lot," she said. "Should I take him to the emergency room?"

Whit shrugged. "I'm afraid that's a little out of my department, Mrs. Benning. Right now I'm not sure he could make it without quite a bit of help. If you want, I'll phone an ambulance."

"No, Fred works at the hospital. I'll call the emergency room and ask their opinion."

Janice was on her feet. "I'll go sit with him."

Her mother stopped the girl and looked at Whit. "Are you through with her?"

He wasn't, but he lied. "For tonight I am."

Janice Benning hurried out of the living room.

"I seem to batting a thousand tonight," Whit said. "I've upset all of you."

She settled down in the chair Janice had been occupying. "Did she know anything?"

"She said she didn't, but I think otherwise."

Alice Benning's face flushed. "My daughter's not a liar, Mr. Pynchon."

"No, but she's a teenager. I have a daughter not much older than Janice. I don't think your daughter was involved in or responsible for what happened last night. She's not the type. On the other hand, I have a pretty good built-in polygraph. She's not telling me the whole truth, but we'll let it go tonight. I've caused enough trouble."

"To the contrary, Mr. Pynchon, I'm thankful you came. I did see and hear a prowler."

Outside, the van remained parked on the street. The man was in the rear, stripping away the sopping black coveralls. Only moments before, he had managed to slip back to the vehicle. He had been on the other side of the hedge, wedged tightly against its dense base, and he had heard the woman telling the visitor that she suspected that there was a prowler. As that visitor had come around the house to investigate, he had quietly pulled a small lightweight revolver from the ankle holster he wore. If Benning had not returned at that moment, he might have had to use it. As it turned out, he had managed to slip across the street during the altercation between the two men.

He quickly wiped the mud and grass clippings from his face and went to the van's back window. The lights in the Benning home were burning now. From the same satchel that he had lugged across the street, he withdrew a palm-sized transmitter. Two small buttons and a tiny unlit bulb decorated its otherwise nondescript casing. Using the light from the street lamp, he placed a finger on the one that would initiate a simple communication sequence with the activated receiver in the cardboard box. The other button was useless until the two units were talking to each other. Once that simple task was accomplished, the bulb would glow bright red. At that point, the second button would become deadly.

He pressed the first button.

THIRTEEN

THE PLEASANT VALLEY section of North Milbrook housed Milbrook's social and economic elite. If the people who lived in North Milbrook were upper class, then those who lived in its subdivision of Pleasant Valley must have considered themselves high class. That particular portion of North Milbrook wasn't even in the city limits. Those who lived there had the money to keep the subdivision's streets paved. They could even afford the high insurance payments that went along with the speed bumps they had had placed at frequent intervals on their street. The most common occupation among Pleasant Valley residents was the practice of medicine, but a few lawyers, usually those who defended the doctors' insurance companies, also managed to earn enough money to afford the high-priced real estate.

Zeke Morton hated the speed bumps. "Gawdamn rich idiots," he said as he bounced over another one.

Mickey sat in the front seat with him. Bert Ringwald was in the back. When the three of them were together, Bert usually ended up in the backseat. That was the trio's pecking order.

"You'd better slow down," Mickey said. "You're liable to break a shock absorber."

"Rich fucking assholes," the driver said again. "Who the hell puts bumps into streets?"

As the car rolled over the next strip of raised asphalt, Bert's body actually bounced. His head clunked against the roof of the car. "Jesus, Zeke. Take it easy."

The driver glanced in the rearview mirror. "Screw you, Ringwald."

The houses in Pleasant Valley each occupied a lot of no less than an acre, as required by the subdivision's restrictive covenants. Many of them sat on pieces of property much more generous than that. None of the homes looked alike. Some of them, usually those which resembled chalets, were nestled back into woodsy glades. The one-story brick ranch styles sprawled over open, virtually treeless lots. The house the three boys sought was a white two-story structure that looked like a small replica of a southern plantation house.

The street remained wet from the earlier storm, and they hadn't seen a single car since entering the exclusive subdivision.

"We're gonna stick out like a sore thumb," Mickey said. "What the hell's the good of this?"

This time Zeke braked for one of the speed bumps. "The man wants us to watch the house for a few nights before we pull the job."

"Why?" Mickey asked.

"Just to see what the guy does at night, I guess."

From the backseat Bert said, "Maybe he thinks this guy's got his own security or something."

Zeke shook his head. "That's bullshit."

But Mickey didn't think so. "It makes sense to me, Zeke. These people got the money for that kinda thing."

"Okay," the driver said, "so we'll look for security. First we gotta find the gawdamn house."

Mickey used a small flashlight to illuminate a slip of paper clutched in his hand. "We need to find the street first. The address is 1001 Blue Spruce Way."

They were on the subdivision's main road and had already passed several intersecting streets. "Here comes another," Zeke said. "See what it says."

As they neared the small street sign, Mickey squinted at it. "Blue Spruce Way. That's it."

They saw the plantation house as soon as the car made the

turn. It sat on a huge corner lot dotted with drooping weeping willows. Zeke eased the car to a stop on the other side of the street.

"What a house," Bert said.

Mickey was staring at it, too. "I think maybe we should tell the man to forget this job. I bet most of these houses have some kind of alarm systems."

Zeke hadn't told them that he knew the house had an alarm system. He still kept it to himself. "Looks like cherry pickin' to me, Moses. You gettin' cold feet?"

"I just got a bad feeling, Zeke."

"There's maybe five grand in it for each of us," Zeke said.

Mickey wasn't impressed. "You can't spend it in jail, Zeke."

Just as Whit was preparing to leave, Fred Benning came into the living room. Much of the color had returned to his face. He gingerly patted his side. "I think this'll keep until tomorrow," he said.

"How's the pain?" his wife asked.

"Just about gone. I think it must have been the sweat."

"But there is a stitch loose," his wife said.

Benning shrugged and turned to Whit. "Why are you questioning my daughter?"

Whit glanced at Benning's wife.

"I haven't really had a chance to explain it all to him," she said.

"I want to hear it from you," the girl's father said, pointing at Whit.

Whit thought about it a moment before he answered. As a rule he didn't share the product of an investigation with civilians, but in this case it seemed like a good idea. "I'm going to ask that you keep what I'm about to tell you confidential."

"Of course," Benning said.

His wife nodded, indicating that she would also.

Whit tried to condense the explanation. "In most B&Es

the intruders tear apart a house searching for the kind of items they like to steal, but in several of the recent burglaries the intruders seemed to know exactly where to go to recover certain items, usually weapons.''

''Meaning?'' Benning asked.

''It indicates to us that they have some source of inside information.''

The man's face darkened. ''Janice!''

The sharpness of his voice startled both Whit and his wife.

His wife became immediately angry. ''Fred! Not tonight!''

But the man wasn't listening. ''Janice! Come in here! Now!''

''One moment, Mr. Benning,'' Whit said. ''If you do talk with her, try not to back her into a corner where she has to lie. Actually, it might be better to let me talk to her again tomorrow, when everyone feels better.''

''She's my daughter, Pynchon.''

''I know that, but I don't think she's an accomplice. I don't think that at all. If I talk to her alone, after things have settled down from tonight, she might open up to me.''

''And she won't open up to me?'' Benning said.

Whit tried to adopt a joking attitude. ''My daughter never would, Benning, especially once I backed her into a corner. I have to be leaving.''

Janice eased into the room.

Benning, though, was glaring at Whit. ''You started this. I think you should stay.''

''I've told you my opinion,'' Whit said, the good humor quickly vanishing. ''It's your call now.''

''Damn right it is,'' Benning said. He turned his angry face to his daughter. There were tears in her eyes, but Benning wasn't paying any attention to them. ''Pynchon here says the burglars knew where to look for my guns. What do you know about it?''

''Nothing, Daddy.''

''Janice, don't lie to me.''

Alice Benning stepped between her daughter and her husband. "We'll talk about this tomorrow, Fred."

Something in her voice told Whit that the issue had just been settled. He nodded to the woman and slipped out the door.

In the van the man cursed as he struggled to replace the battery cover. When he had pressed the first button, the light hadn't come on. He had pressed it repeatedly, each time in vain. Finally, he had prized open the battery compartment. It was empty.

"Damn!" he muttered, searching the interior of the van for the battery. He had bought a brand-new one, but somehow he had forgotten to put it in the transmitter. Once he found it, he fumbled to get into the package. Finally, it was installed. He replaced the cover that completed the device's circuit.

Just as it snapped into place, the front door to the Benning home opened. The visitor came bounding down the steps. In his rush to activate the device, the man dropped it to the carpeted floor of the van. By the time he found it in the van's darkened interior, the visitor had reached his car.

No matter. He pressed the first button. The light came on much more brightly than he had anticipated, brightly enough so that he had no difficulty jamming down the second button.

In the house next door Margaret Trent had decided to go to bed early. After all, she hadn't gotten a wink of sleep the night before, and she had been too keyed up to nap that afternoon. Now her lack of sleep had caught up with her. The newspaper had been reporting on the burglaries for days, and Margaret's nephew had come over at her request and moved the television to a spare bedroom on the second floor. Margaret kept her downstairs shut up tight, and she spent most of her time in the converted TV room upstairs, where she could keep the windows open.

That night she didn't even bother coming back downstairs.

She had no reason to. She went to her bathroom and put on her pajamas and a robe. Then she returned to the spare bedroom and turned off the television. Her own bedroom was across the hall.

When she stepped into it, the stuffiness made her wince. When she had heard the first grumblings of thunder, she had closed the windows on the west side of her house. Those were the ones in which it always seemed to rain. After the violent storm and the loss of electricity, she had forgotten to reopen the window in her bedroom.

She went to it. As she was lifting it, she saw a man step down from the Benning porch. He walked toward a car that was parked on the street. She remembered the man from the night before. He was one of the police. He hadn't talked with her, but he had been in her home. For most of the day she had wrestled with the memories of the other policeman's killing. In the light of hindsight she realized that there hadn't been much she could have done. That new police chief, he had assured her of that. Still, she grieved for the dead police officer. She planned to send flowers to the funeral home.

Before turning away from the window, she reached up to adjust one of the curtain hooks. The blast caught her in that position—on her tiptoes, her hand reaching up. The concussion preceded the heat. It drove her across the room and slammed her into the wall on the opposite side. Margaret Trent was just barely conscious when the combination of fire and debris inundated that side of her house.

Down in the street Whit was opening the door to his car. He didn't hear or see anything. An unseen hand, almost gentle at its first touch, lifted him up and over his car and sent him soaring across the street. The concussion came a nanosecond later. He had lost consciousness even before he landed in the middle of the street.

The dark van was screeching away from the scene of the cataclysm as the flaming debris started to fall to the ground. A plume of fire soared high into the sky.

* * *

Bert Ringwald, sitting in the backseat of the car, glanced back to look out the rear window when the column of fire shot skyward. "Holy shit." He wrenched himself around to get a better view.

Mickey jumped out of the car. "Jesus, look at that."

In spite of its name, Pleasant Valley's elevation enhanced the boys' view of the fiery exhibit, but the conflagration was visible from just about anyplace within Milbrook.

The pillar of fire burned with a bluish tint. The night sky, still damp from the storm, glowed a dull red. Where the two met, a purple halo formed. Within a few minutes most of the residents of Milbrook were standing on their porches or outside their places of business gaping at the sight. Screaming sirens shattered the night's silence.

FOURTEEN

THE POLICE SCANNER in the *Daily Journal*'s newsroom started going berserk at 9:11 P.M. It was just about the only piece of electronic equipment on the premises that hadn't been toasted by the electrical storm. Barney Williams summoned Anna at once. She had just started to monitor the sudden bursts of emergency messages when a female employee from the composing room rushed in from one of the building's back doors. "My God, it looks like the whole town's in flames."

"Round up the photographer," Anna said to Barney.

The desk editor looked up from his work. "What about tomorrow's edition?"

Unless they managed to strong-arm the computer service people into making a service call that night, it looked as if the *Daily Journal* was going to establish an unfortunate precedent: It wasn't going to publish an edition the next morning. To Anna, that prospect was unacceptable. She viewed it as a potentially personal defeat.

"Call Mrs. Binder. Explain the situation to her and ask her to try to get those jerks down here."

The young desk editor's face was flushed with frustration. "I just talked to the dumb bastard. His team's on their way to the bank. Their data-processing system was zapped, too. I guess the bank gets priority. Isn't that typical?"

Anna didn't have time for this right now. "Screw the bank," she said. "Just call Kathy—Mrs. Binder. Tell her to put the pressure on them somehow."

"Do you think the lightning caused the fire, Miss Tyree?"

"Jesus, if you'll let me get out of here, I'll try to find out. Call Mrs. Binder—now!"

By the time she got out to the car, Barney was waiting with the photographer. "Damnedest thing I've ever seen," Barney said, gazing northwestward toward the shooting fountain of fire.

Anna had her back to the source of the excitement. When she turned, she gasped. "It looks like an oil-well fire or something."

"I thought the same thing," Barney said.

Anna managed to tear her gaze away from the hellish vision and looked at the young photographer. "I'd love to get a good color shot of that. We could run it on the front page, assuming we have a front page. Is there any way to do it? Get the photo, I mean."

The photographer made a face. "I could try a time exposure, Miss Tyree, but I'm still not too good at that kinda stuff."

"So try it," she ordered.

The photographer stared at the blaze for a moment. "I'd sure like to get a better perspective."

"What if we drove a little way up Tabernacle Mountain?" Barney suggested.

"Good idea," Anna said. "Tell you what, Barney. You take the kid up there. I'm going on over to the fire. Don't take all night. I suspect we can get plenty of good shots at the scene, too."

They could still hear the wailing of the sirens, one of which was drawing closer. "Let's move it," Anna said.

But Barney was pointing down the street in the direction of the blaze. "It's an ambulance," he said, "coming this way. Musta been some injuries."

"Time for that later," Anna said. "Remember. Get to the scene as fast as you can."

For the first few blocks Anna encountered no difficulties. Then she came to a standstill in the traffic. The fire appeared to originate in the North Milbrook area, which remained a good half mile from her present location. Even so far away, sightseers were starting to park their cars so they could walk to the scene of the fiery display. Anna cursed and tried to navigate her way through the morass of vehicles. What the hell were the emergency vehicles going to do when they had to get through? She mentally filed the issue as a good topic for a future editorial: the lack of consideration by the public.

At that instant a hole opened in the traffic, and Anna saw an opportunity to cut onto a side street. Maybe she could get through that way. Glancing over her shoulder, she saw a car coming up quickly to fill the hole. She cut the steering wheel of the small Nissan Stanza to the right, swerving in front of the closing vehicle. The driver of the other vehicle laid on his horn. Anna ignored him. The effort turned into a fruitless one. Almost immediately she found herself bogged down once more.

The column of bluish flame loomed above her. It reminded her of some special effect from a big-budget movie—so tall, so overpowering, it just couldn't be real.

The vehicles in front of her came to a complete stop.

''Jesus Christ,'' she said, her teeth clenched. Up ahead she eyed a place where she could get the car off the street. If she could just get to that spot, she would abandon the damned car, but she wasn't moving at all. She waited five minutes, and still the traffic showed no sign of budging.

The first sign of trouble came when the car hiccuped. At least that's what it felt like. Anna frowned and glanced in her rearview mirror, thinking that maybe the car behind her had bumped her lightly. Its headlights were a reasonable distance away.

She forgot about it for a few moments—until it happened again. The engine jerked, then seemed to cough. She looked at her instrument panel and at once groaned. The gas gauge read ''empty.'' It wasn't the first time Anna had allowed herself to run out of gas. Twice in the past few months Whit had had to rescue her. Now rescue wasn't even possible.

"Screw it," she said. She switched off the motor, pulled the keys from the ignition, and climbed out.

The door to the vehicle behind her opened. A man got out. "Hey, lady, what the hell you doing?"

She made certain that the large sign that read PRESS was clearly visible before she looked back at him. "Parking the car."

"You can't do that!"

"Screw you," Anna said, slamming the door shut.

"I'll call a tow truck."

Anna had to laugh. What made the dumb son of a bitch think even a tow truck could get through? She ignored him and started trotting toward the source of the blaze.

"Had to be a damned bomb," Terry Watkins said.

Tony Danton, like Anna, had been forced to abandon his vehicle several blocks from the scene of the excitement, but he had managed to get his out of the street. He had just arrived and was only beginning to assimilate the full extent of the tragedy. The Benning home was nothing more than a foundation. The homes on either side of it were burning out of control. Fire fighters weren't even bothering with them. They were concentrating on the structures on either side of them, trying to keep them from catching fire. When the Milbrook fire department had first arrived at the scene, it had been confronted with two burning automobiles. Because of the gas tanks inside each car, the vehicle fires had been doused first.

The towering column of fire came from a ruptured natural-gas line in the Bennings' front yard. It didn't give the slightest indication of going out.

"Can't they shut the gas off?" the prosecutor asked.

Watkins nodded. "Yeah, if they can get to the damn shut-off points. This whole end of town is one big traffic jam."

Tony glanced around at the chaos. Fire trucks clogged the street. Their hoses ran across the pavement and nearby lawns. Two ambulances waited. "Where's Chief Wallace?"

"I raised him on the radio a few minutes ago. He's going to try to clear out the traffic."

Tony nodded. "Good. Where did they find Whit?"

Watkins pointed to the street. "He was on the pavement almost on the other side."

"What was his condition?" Tony had yet to ask that question. Watkins had intercepted the county attorney as soon as he had appeared on the scene to tell him that the only known victim so far was Whit. Tony hadn't had the nerve to ask exactly what the city police sergeant had meant. It was time to know.

"Alive, sir. That's about all I can tell you."

"They've already got him out of here?"

"Luckily an ambulance had just completed a run and was down on Main Street. They saw the explosion and radioed in the initial report. When they got here, Whit was laying in the street. They had transported him by the time I arrived. I think they managed to get out before the traffic jam."

"But he was alive?" Tony asked.

Watkins nodded and then added, "When he left here."

"Other casualties?"

Watkins grimaced. "We can't say for sure, but there's not much doubt that there will be." He nodded toward the foundation. "The Bennings lived there, the ones who were burglarized last night."

Tony's eyes, illuminated by the false daylight created by the tower of flames, widened. "Jesus, what do you make of that?"

"Dunno, but there were three family members. The daughter is a friend of my daughter." He pointed to the burning skeleton of a house to his right of the Bennings. "Our elderly witness lived there by herself. On the other side there was a family of four. Whoever was home is probably dead, and we're afraid that they all were home."

"Eight people?" Tony said.

"Not counting Whit."

"But Whit *was* alive?" Tony said, needing to hear that again.

"Yes, sir."

"Has anyone notified the sheriff?"

"I had the city dispatcher call his department. They said they would call him. I checked back, and he's en route, too."

"Damn this traffic," Tony said.

"It happens any time you have something like this. This was just so . . . so visible, so spectacular that things got out of hand almost immediately."

"That's an understatement."

"Tony!" a female voice shouted. The prosecutor knew who it was before he saw her. He glanced at Watkins. "That's Anna Tyree. Does she know?"

Watkins was shaking his head as she rushed toward them. "Not as far as I know," he said quickly.

Her face was red, and she was breathless. "Christ, what happened here? I had to park six blocks away."

Watkins eased away, leaving Tony to answer. "We don't know for sure, Anna."

"Is that gas burning?"

Tony nodded. "They're trying to shut down this part of the system, but traffic's so bad—"

"The idiots," Anna said.

Tony sensed that Anna didn't know about Whit. "This is off the record for now, Anna, but we think there might have been a bomb involved."

"A bomb? You mean like a bombing? Here in Milbrook?"

"That's what it looks like."

"Why, for God's sake?"

"The house in the center? It was the scene of the burglary last night and the murder of Jim Mayberry."

"We *are* on White Oak," Anna said, suddenly making the connection. She studied the devastated foundation. "But why bomb it?"

Tony shook his head. "I have no idea."

"I guess Whit will be here, then."

Tony turned to her. "Whit was here, Anna."

She glanced around. "I don't see him."

"He was here when the bomb went off."

Anna was looking at the tower of flaming gas when he said it. The awesome display seemed to quiver for a moment, then consumed itself from the bottom upward. From somewhere came the sound of brief cheering, but the flames from the burning houses continued to cast a bright glow over the residential landscape.

When Anna spoke, her voice was soft but firm. "Is he dead, Tony?"

"He was alive. An ambulance crew found him lying on the street. They've taken him to the hospital. So far he's the only casualty we've found."

Anna dropped her head. "Thank God he's alive."

"I don't know anything else to tell you, Anna."

"I've got to get to the hospital."

Tony looked around. "Maybe I can find—" He saw Gil Dickerson walking toward them. "There's Gil."

The sheriff nodded to Tony and went straight to Anna. "Watkins just told me. Do you want to go to the hospital?"

"If I can," Anna said, fighting back her tears.

Gil looked at Tony. "Do you want to go?"

"I want to, but I had better stay here. If there was a bomb, I want to be sure we don't let the criminal investigation get away from us. Try to get back in touch, though, and let me know his condition."

"Will do. Let's go, then. The city boys and some guys from my department are managing to clear a couple of the streets."

He put an arm around Anna and started to guide her toward his cruiser, which was parked a half block away. A second thought stopped him. He turned back to the attorney. "Have you talked to Whit this evening? I mean, since you left work."

"Not since I left the office. I had to have my car inspected, so I left early."

"So you don't know about his conversation with the feds?"

Tony frowned. "What conversation?"

"I'll get back in touch with you, Tony."

The prosecutor went after him. "Just a damned minute, Gil. Maybe you should tell me now."

"Later," the sheriff said. "I'll get back here as soon as—"

Anna put her hand on Gil's arm. "If it's something you don't want me to hear, I'll go on to your car."

"It might be best," Gil said.

Anna's face sagged a little. It wasn't really the response she had expected. Nonetheless, she turned to walk away.

"It's halfway down the block on your left," Gil told her.

Once she was out of earshot, Gil told Tony about the call from the FBI agent in Raleigh.

"Whit should have called me," Tony said. "Damn him, he should have called me."

"Would that have changed things?"

The prosecutor shrugged. "No, I guess not. Maybe I had better get in touch with Charleston and ask them to send down that forensics laboratory on wheels."

"What about the feds?" Gil asked.

"I hate working with them. All they do is muddy the waters."

"Suit yourself."

Tony stared at the smoking ruins of the Benning house. "But why a bomb?"

"Either to kill Whit or the Bennings," Gil said. "They may have accomplished both."

FIFTEEN

ONE MINUTE the purplish red column of fire filled the boys' vision; the next it was gone.

"What the hell?" Zeke said.

Mickey gaped. Bert said, "Shit."

A glow still painted the quickly dissipating clouds blood-red, but the spectacle itself had vanished in the blink of an eye. Zeke had been bullying his way through traffic, trying to reach the scene of the fire. From what they could tell, they were still several blocks away. All of them had been nearly hypnotized by the sight, and it had remained visible above the residential skyline of Milbrook until just then. The throng of cars also appeared to be ebbing.

"Look up there," Mickey said.

Ahead of them a city patrol car was directing traffic onto streets that led away from the scene.

"Motherfuck," Zeke said.

"Can't we somehow turn around?" Bert asked.

Zeke glanced into the rearview mirror. "Turn around? Jesus, I wanna see what the hell's goin' on."

The cops—there were two of them—were saying something to the drivers before routing them onto the side streets. "Just play it cool," Mickey said.

Zeke laughed. "What the hell's the matter with you two? You worried about something?"

"Cops make me nervous," Bert said.

Zeke shook his head. "Ringwald, you're a real pussy. Ya know that?"

117

The cop directed them to the right, then leaned down to the window. "You're advised to remain out of this area."

"Or what?" Zeke said.

The cop, expecting the car to move on just as the others had done, wasn't certain he had heard what he thought he had heard. He leaned closer. "What did you say?"

"It's a free country," Zeke said.

"Look, asshole, get the car outta this area and keep it out. You understand me?"

"My aunt lives up there," Zeke said. "I wanna check on her."

The cop eyed him for a moment, trying to decide if he was being conned. He took a second look at the old car. Then he said, "Check on her tomorrow, pal. Now, move it along."

"Just go," Mickey whispered.

Zeke's hands choked the steering wheel as he made a squealing right turn. "Fuckin' pigs! Always telling you what to do. I hate 'em."

Mickey was holding on to the dash. "Jesus, they're gonna come after you for reckless driving."

"Fuck them and their mothers," the driver said, gunning the engine as he rushed to catch up with the line of exiting traffic.

Gil, his aching knee giving him fits, had to quicken his pace to keep up with Anna as she trotted down the hall of the hospital toward the emergency room.

She rounded a corner and found herself at the entrance to the ER. A hospital employee, dressed as if she were a nurse, stepped in front of her. "May I help you?"

"I want to see Whit Pynchon."

"Are you a relative?"

"Well, he's my—" She didn't exactly know what to say.

At that moment Gil Dickerson hobbled into view. "She's his fiancée," he said.

The nurse recognized the sheriff. She said, "I see, Sheriff. Let me check with the head nurse."

"Dammit," Anna said.

The sheriff shrugged. "Sorry, I thought I did some pretty quick thinking."

She looked at him. "I'm sorry, Gil. I wasn't . . . I mean, I didn't mean that I was mad at you. I'm beginning to see why Whit has such a prejudice toward hospitals."

The nurse reappeared. "Actually, Sheriff, we're glad someone is here."

"How is he?" Anna asked.

"Hard to get along with," the nurse said. "Perhaps you two can talk some sense into him. He wants to leave."

Anna started to laugh. It was inappropriate, she knew, but the woman's complaint about Whit told her that he was probably OK. "Then he must be all right," she said, to explain her jovial reaction.

"He has no apparent life-threatening injuries, but the ER doctor wants to admit him for observation, just for overnight. He took a pretty nasty blow to the head, and we'd like to monitor him."

Gil smiled. "I doubt we're gonna be able to change his mind."

The nurse's frustration was obvious. "He's one of the most cantankerous persons, not to be a drunk, that I've met. Please try to explain to him that we just want to help."

"Can we see him now?" Anna asked.

The nurse nodded. "Follow me."

They heard him as soon as they stepped into the emergency room area. He was in a cubicle near the main desk. A white curtain concealed him from their view. "There's not a thing wrong with me," he was saying. "I want my clothes, and I want to leave."

Anna eased the curtain back but remained outside the small cubicle. "Whit?"

He managed a smile. "Hi there. Don't worry. I'm fine."

A woman stood by his bed. "I'm Doctor Blair. If you're

friends of his, will you please try to convince him to remain with us just for tonight.''

"No way," Whit said. "No damned way. I've got a knot on my head, and that's all."

It wasn't quite true. A two-inch-wide streak of skin had been scraped from the left side of his face. It had been painted a dull orange with whatever medicine they had applied. His left arm was in a sling, the wrist wrapped in ice.

"You don't look fine," Anna said.

He lifted the injured arm. "This is nothing. I pulled a muscle."

The female doctor rolled her eyes. "And we want you to keep it immobilized, Mr. Pynchon."

"Fine, I can do that at home."

"But it isn't your intention to go home, is it?"

"Probably not, Doc, but that's my business."

Anna stepped into the cramped space.

Gil followed her. "You look like hell," he said as a greeting.

"But I feel fine."

The doctor tried to plead her case. "He received a rather serious blow to the head."

"It didn't even break the skin," Whit countered.

The doctor ignored him. "I'm surprised he's even lucid. There's a good chance he has a concussion, a small chance that he might develop some form of subdural or intracranial hematoma. We simply want to monitor him and perhaps do some additional testing in the morning."

"You've x-rayed me," Whit said. "You said there was no fracture."

"That was your shoulder and wrist," the doctor snapped. She looked at Anna. "We need to run certain more elaborate tests to rule out head injury. I'm not going to argue with him any longer. If you can't talk some sense into him, then he's certainly free to go once he signs a release."

"Like hell I will," Whit said. "I'll sign whatever I need

to sign assuming financial responsibility for my treatment, but I don't have to sign a release to leave here.''

The doctor pushed past Anna and Gil. Before exiting, though, she paused. "Let me ask this. You're his friends. Is this behavior typical, or—"

"It's typical," Anna said.

"God help you," the doctor said as she walked out.

Immediately Whit sat up on the side of the bed and tried to bend down to peer beneath it. He was wearing a flimsy white hospital gown that was open all the way down the back. Anna rushed forward. "Take it easy."

"Are my clothes under there?"

Anna didn't even bother to look. "Please, Whit, do what the doctor asks."

He looked her straight in the eye. "Save your breath, Anna. I have no intention of staying here."

"But what if—"

"I'm okay," he said, then looked to the sheriff. "What the hell happened?"

"You don't know?"

Whit shook his head. "The last thing I remember is walking out of the Benning house."

"It was a bomb, Whit."

The investigator rocked back in shock. "A bomb? Where? In my car?"

"No. In or around the house," Gil said.

Whit closed his eyes. "I had just walked out of the house."

"Were all three members of the family there?" Gil asked.

"Yeah."

Anna had kept silent until that point. "I know it's probably a waste of time for me to ask, but what on earth is going on here? Who would want to bomb a house in Milbrook?"

Whit slid down off the cot. "I'll fill you in later. Right now I want to get back there."

But as soon as he tried to right himself, he staggered. He grabbed his head. "Jesus."

Gil eased him back on the cot. "Listen, old friend, maybe you had better listen to reason this time."

Anna peeked out of the cubicle and called for the doctor.

Whit was rubbing his forehead. "It was just a dizzy spell."

The doctor wedged her way into the small work space. "What happened?"

"Nothing serious," Whit said.

"He got dizzy when he stood," Anna said, glaring at the stubborn investigator.

The doctor pulled a small flashlight from the pocket of the white smock she wore and pointed the beam of light into Whit's eyes. "That's not unusual after a severe blow to the head. It's also symptomatic of a concussion."

Whit finally pushed the light away. "I'm not staying here. You're all wasting your breath. I am light-headed, and I won't try to drive. I'll ride with Gil."

"As I said, I don't have time to argue with you, sir." The doctor walked out.

"What's the situation out there now?" Whit asked. This time he eased off the bed more slowly. The pain in his shoulder and wrist made him flinch a little.

"The Benning house is totaled, nothing much left but a foundation. The homes on either side of it are burning out of control. If there were people in them, they're dead."

"I guess I'm lucky to even be here," Whit said.

"From what Watkins told me, the initial explosion tossed you up and over your car, and your car shielded you from the full blast. Of course, you need a new car."

Whit took a deep breath. "Would one of you get my clothes from under this thing. I don't think I should bend over."

Anna crossed her arms. "Not me. If you plan to kill yourself, you won't get any help from me."

"I'll do it," Gil said, "but only because I don't want you passing out in this cracker box."

Whit started to strip off the hospital gown. Anna stepped out of the cubicle.

"She's pissed off," Gil whispered.

"She'll get over it." They continued to talk as Gil helped Whit dress.

"That must have been one hell of a bomb," Whit said.

"Think it's tied in with that story we heard from the FBI?"

"The Benning daughter knew something, but I couldn't get it out of her. What could she have known that was so important that these assholes wiped out a city block?" Whit was easing his arm out of the sling as he spoke.

Gil started to unfold Whit's shirt. "Christ, Whit, I don't think you want to wear this."

He held it up. It hung in tatters from his hands.

"Did the explosion do that?" Whit asked.

"Looks like the ambulance crew cut it off of you. To be honest, we expected to find you in critical condition from what we heard."

Whit managed to smile. "If you listen to that doctor, I am. Just slip my sports coat on. We'll stop by the house on the way so I can change clothes."

"What about Anna? She rode with me."

"Where's her car?" Whit asked as he slipped his trousers on without help.

Gil chuckled. "Probably at some tow service somewhere. The explosion drew a lot of onlookers, and there was one hell of a traffic jam. Anna ran out of gas while stalled in traffic. She just left her car parked in the middle of the street somewhere."

"Good," Whit said. "We'll leave her at the house."

"Like hell you will," Anna said, swinging the curtain open.

"You were eavesdropping?" Whit asked.

"No, I was just coming in to tell you that I need to get my car. It's the only transportation either one of us has now."

"And then?"

"I've got to get back to the paper to see if we're going to be able to get an edition out tomorrow. The storm did fry most of our equipment."

"You mean you don't want to go back to the—"

"I hope I have a reporter and photographer there," Anna said.

"Let's get outta here." Whit hadn't bothered to put on his socks. He stepped barefoot into the scuffed loafers he had been wearing and started out toward the ER exit.

The doctor intercepted him. "I need you to sign this, Mr. Pynchon." She offered him a clipboard.

Whit read the form on it and handed it back. "Like I said, I'll sign whatever form you have assuming responsibility for the treatment, but I don't have to sign that."

"Mr. Pynchon, it's policy to—"

Whit fished around in his coat pockets until he found his cigarettes. "Listen, Doc, I don't have any problems signing that piece of paper. It just irks me that you think I have to sign it before I can leave, and I'm going to prove to you that I don't. This isn't a jail. This time I don't have time to argue with you."

He pulled a cigarette from the pack. The doctor's eyes widened. "You can't smoke that in here," she said.

"That's why I'm leaving," Whit said.

The doctor threw up her hands. "Leave! Go!" Then she turned to Anna. "If he has any really serious dizzy spells or if you have trouble waking him, try to bring him back."

Whit and Gil were already on their way out. "Do you really think he might have some serious damage?" Anna asked.

"If that's his normal personality, I doubt it. He's too damn hardheaded to have been seriously injured."

SIXTEEN

WEDNESDAY MORNING dawned sunny and hot. The previous night's thunderstorm had done little to ease the temperature inversion over the lower Ohio valley, but its moisture had refreshed the landscape. The grass and tree leaves seemed a more healthy shade of green. The layers of summer dust had been washed away. On White Oak, though, the pungent stench from the gutted houses dimmed the morning's beauty. Firemen prowled among the remains of the two homes on either side of the Benning property, searching for bodies and in the process dealing with any burning hot spots remaining in the rubble.

Whit, his battered, iodine-stained face streaked by black ash, stood beside the foundation of the Benning home. His shoulder ached, and his head sometimes threatened to go into another spin, but he ignored the discomfort. City officers and technicians assigned to the state police's mobile forensics laboratory probed through the debris-filled basement. To his right, firemen and ambulance personnel lifted a chunk of greasy charcoal from the blackened timbers of Margaret Trent's house. Someone had gone out on a limb to identify the broiled mass as Margaret Trent. They had located her purported remains not long after sunup.

The bodies of the Benning family were spread over a gruesome radius. A team of Gil Dickerson's men, assisted by the local medical examiner and a forensics specialist, was conducting a pattern search, recovering pieces of the mother, father, and daughter as well as any other evidence that appeared relevant. In truth, the neighbors were likely to be mowing and raking over debris, including human remains, for weeks to come. The remains Gil's team had found were being placed in a single body bag. The state medical examiner would have the grisly task of trying to put the pieces back together.

Chief Wallace came up behind Whit. In the furor of the night before they hadn't had any contact.

"Glad to see you're in one piece, Pynchon."

Whit grimaced. "A bad pun, Chief."

"Sorry. No pun intended. Down in Atlanta, we'da called this kinda thing overkill."

"I don't think I've ever seen so much destruction," Whit said. " 'Course, I was lucky. I didn't go to Vietnam. I guess this is about as bad as it gets short of war."

"We're gettin' reports of windows being shattered a half mile away."

"Any other injuries?" Whit asked.

"None I heard of, just the poor folks in these three houses. The fire boys did a gawdamn admirable job keepin' the other houses from goin' up."

Wallace, glancing down, noticed the sunshine glimmering off a metal object at his feet. He bent down and retrieved it. "A fork," he said, turning the utensil over in his hand. "The scientific types found anything yet?"

Whit just shook his head.

Wallace looked back at the mobile laboratory. On the outside it looked like an oversized ambulance painted in the state colors of blue, white, and gold and decorated with the state seal. "We had several of those in Atlanta," he said. "We had one just for fire and arson investigation, another for crime-scene investigation, and a third one for the SWAT team."

Whit really wasn't interested in a conversation, but he said almost absentmindedly, "The Atlanta department's budget is probably bigger than our state police's."

"I wasn't braggin'," the chief said. "Fact is, that Dodge van there has as much in it as all three of ours did. They got fingerprinting equipment, blood- and body-fluid testing, evidence-collection kits, even a small arson lab. One of the guys gave me the tour.''

"Trouble is," Whit said, "it has to service the entire state. We were lucky to get it. I suspect it's a waste of time. Other than the bomb's own traces, I doubt we'll find much of anything useful. At least they're helping with the remains.''

"Where's Watkins?" the chief asked, changing the subject. "I've been lookin' all over for him.''

"He went home for a few minutes," Whit said.

The chief's face darkened. "Home?''

For the first time Whit looked back at the chief. "Don't get your bowels in an uproar. He's coming right back. His daughter and the Benning girl were good friends. He just wanted to tell her before she heard about it from some other source.''

"Didn't know that," Wallace said. "I'm gonna head back on to city hall. I reckon you can keep things under control until Watkins gets back.''

"Reckon so, Chief.''

Wallace started to walk away, but he stopped and turned back to Whit. "You know, maybe we oughta see if the sheriff's department, our department, and your office could get together and buy one of those vans. Make a hell of an addition to our crime-fightin' capability.''

"Right now I'd be happy with a few guys who could just secure a crime scene," Whit quipped.

Before waking his daughter, Terry Watkins opened her bedroom curtains to allow the bright summer sunlight to flood the room. The glare settled squarely on her sleeping face. She made a face and covered eyes with her hands.

"Golly, Mom—''

He went to her bed. "It's Dad, Susan. We need to talk.''

She shielded her eyes so she could see him. "Dad? Gosh, what time is it?''

"A little after seven.''

She moaned.

"C'mon, babe. Wake up. I've got some bad news."

She sat up in bed and tried to straighten her coal-black hair. "Mom?"

"She's fine, Susie. It's Janice Benning."

"Janice? Did she talk to you?"

Watkins hiked his eyebrows. "No. Was she supposed to?"

"Uh, no. I don't know why I asked that. What about Janice?"

"I don't know any easy way to tell you this, Susan. She died last night."

Her mouth dropped open.

"In fact, Susan, she was murdered—she and her mother and father."

"Oh, no, Daddy." She just stared at him as the tears filled each eye. As soon as they poured over the rims, she fell against him. He hugged her tight.

Her mother stepped into the bedroom and sat on the other side of her daughter. "I'm sorry, Susan."

Her daughter continued to cry. Watkins eased her away and toward her mother. Melody Watkins, still clad in a robe, pulled her daughter's face to her chest.

"It was that explosion and fire that we heard last night," he explained. "It looks like someone planted a bomb just outside their house. Several other people died, too."

Her daughter pulled away from her mother. "You're sure it wasn't an accident?"

Watkins slowly shook his head. "It was a bomb. The forensics folks have already recovered a small fragment that proves it. Whoever did it put the device right below the gas meter. That was what caused the fireworks last night, that column of fire. Look, I've got to get back—"

"I know who did it." Susie Watkins blurted it out between sobs.

Mickey Moses heard the news on the radio that morning. He didn't usually get up so early, but the fact was that he hadn't even been to bed yet. He was just getting ready to undress and lie down when the seven-thirty news came on.

"At least eight people are dead this morning as a result of a mysterious explosion last night in North Milbrook." Mickey turned the volume up.

"The police are withholding the names of five of the victims," the announcer said, "pending notification of family, but they have released the identity of three of the dead, all of whom were members of the same family."

"C'mon," Mickey said. "Who the hell was it?"

"According to a police official, dead are Fred Benning, forty, his wife, Alice, thirty-nine, and his daughter, Janice, a fifteen-year-old student at—"

Mickey threw the radio across the room. "That son of a bitch!"

He heard footsteps outside his door. His mother stuck her head in. "What on earth was that?"

"I knocked the radio off the nightstand."

"It looks to me like you threw it. What time did you get in last night?"

Mickey was heading toward the door. "I gotta go out, Ma. Can I borrow the car?"

"I have to be at work by one. I'll need the car back by noon."

"I'll have it back by then," he said.

"You haven't answered me, young man. What time did you get in last night? I went to bed at midnight, and you still weren't here."

"Around one," he lied. "I'll be back as soon as I can."

"What about this mess?"

He tromped out of the room. "I'll clean it up when I get back."

She hurried to catch up with him. Mickey was getting the car keys from her purse.

"Where are you going this early?" she asked.

He looked up at her. "You don't wanna know."

* * *

Watkins looked to his wife, then back at his daughter. "What do you mean?"

Susie took several deep breaths. "I mean, she came to me last night. She wanted to talk to you, but I talked her out of it, Daddy. I killed her!"

The young girl started to cry again, this time almost hysterically. Watkins sat back down on the bed and wrenched her away from her mother. "Get hold of yourself. Tell me what she wanted to talk to me about."

"But I killed her . . . I killed her . . . I—"

Terry Watkins slapped his daughter, something he had never done before. It wasn't too hard, but the sound of it was harsh and brutal. Melody Watkins gasped. Susan stopped crying instantly.

"I'm sorry, Susan, but you need to get control and tell me what she told you."

"I should have listened to her last—"

"Don't start it," Watkins warned. "Just tell me what she said. Tell me now."

Half sobbing, snuffling, Susan tried to put the story into some coherent form. "Janice has . . . Janice had this thing for a boy named Mickey Moses. He's kinda wild, and he runs with some bad dudes."

Watkins was rolling his finger, motioning for Susan to hurry up.

"I'm trying, Daddy."

"Give her a minute," his wife said.

Watkins nodded. "I'm really trying to be patient. Is this the boy who you think killed her?"

"I don't know, Daddy. I mean—"

"You said you know who—"

"Let me tell it my way," his daughter snapped, her grief replaced by a sudden anger.

Watkins shrugged. "Okay, tell it your way. Just tell it."

"A couple of weeks ago she said that Mickey and her were talking about hunting, and she told him that her daddy did some hunting. He wanted to know where her dad kept his guns.''

Watkins pulled a small notebook from his jacket pocket. ''What was the boy's name again?''

''Mickey Moses. But there's more. He hangs around with Zeke Morton and—''

''I know Zeke Morton,'' Watkins said.

''Bert Ringwald, too, Daddy. Bert's real little, almost like a midget.''

Watkins's jaws were clamped. ''That fits the description of the person who stabbed her father. Why didn't you want her to come to me?''

''Because she had talked to Mickey about it, and Mickey told her that it couldn't have been Bert because Bert and Zeke had been with him when her father was stabbed.''

''And she believed him?''

''She had a thing for him, Daddy. I know Mickey and Bert both, not real well, but they don't seem like the type to—''

He sprang up from the bed. ''You should have brought her to me, Susan.''

''I know that, Daddy.'' The tears started to flow again. ''I killed her, didn't I?''

Watkins started to say something, but he saw the look of reproach in his wife's eyes. ''No, you didn't, but maybe these three boys did. What were their names again?''

She wiped the wetness from her cheeks. ''Mickey Moses.''

''I got that one.''

''Zeke Morton and Bert Ringwald.''

''Do you know where they live?''

She shook her head. ''I don't hang around with them.''

''I hope not,'' her father said. ''I have to go.''

''I'm sorry, Daddy. I knew she believed Mickey, so I—''

He walked out of her bedroom and closed the door behind him.

She started to bawl. ''I swear to God, I'm sorry. I'm sorry. I'm sorry.''

SEVENTEEN

WHIT EYED the three boys' names on the slip of paper. "I could tell the girl knew something."

He and Chief Wallace stood with Terry Watkins beside the city detective's cruiser. The technicians with the mobile laboratory continued to probe through the debris, bagging and tagging anything that even remotely resembled evidence or human remains.

"What was the basis for the Benning girl's suspicion?" Wallace asked.

"My daughter was pretty upset. She wasn't making a lot of sense, but apparently this one—" He pointed to the name of Mickey Moses. "—was asking about her father's guns recently. Then her father had said that the one that stabbed him was little. The Ringwald kid is short. The Benning girl put two and two together."

"Kinda shaky," the chief said.

Watkins and Whit exchanged glances. "It might be shaky," Whit said, "but at least we have some names. Besides, the girl thought she knew something. Someone else agreed with her, and they were scared enough to waste a city block, not giving a tinker's damn about who got killed in the process."

The chief smiled. "Like I said, I never was much of a detective. Guess I keep provin' that."

"At least you listen to reason," Whit said.

"Only when it makes sense, Pynchon."

"That's why it's called reason, Chief."

"Where can we find these kids?" Wallace then asked of his detective sergeant.

"Susan didn't know. I know Morton there. He had a run-in with one of the guys on the evening shift, and he's on probation. I'd say the juvenile office can give us an address if they will."

Whit checked his watch. It seemed as if it should have been noon, but it wasn't even eight-thirty yet. "Let's grab some coffee, Terry. After that we'll go to the courthouse and get an address for Morton."

"I'll head on back to city hall and see if we got a file on Morton. Who was the officer who—"

Terry was shaking his head. "Don't waste your time, Chief."

Wallace frowned. "Whadaya mean?"

"We don't keep reports on the juvie cases. As soon as they're cleared through the courts, we turn everything over to the juvie office. They seal it in the kids' files."

"Seal it?" Wallace asked.

Watkins nodded. "Orders from the circuit judge."

"That's gawdamn ridiculous."

Whit smiled. "Welcome to West Virginia. In this state juveniles get kid-glove treatment."

"So what?" Wallace said. "Why don't you just keep a copy of the damned reports in a secure place? What the judge don't know won't hurt him."

"We did that," Watkins said. "One of the younger officers showed up in court with one of our secret files. Somebody forgot to tell him that was a no-no. The judge just about put the poor kid under the jail. Since then we've lived at the foot of the Cross."

"Gawd almighty," Wallace drawled. "Deliver me from fuckin' bleeding-heart liberals."

"You're welcome to join us for some coffee," Whit said.

But Wallace shook his head. "No thanks. Reckon I'll just go on back and see what kinda flak I caught in this mornin's newspaper. By the way, Pynchon, I met the editor the other day.''

Whit glanced at him. "So?"

"Mighty fine-lookin' woman."

"That she is," Whit said, "but never forget that she's also a dyed-in-the-wool reporter. Oh, and you might get a break today. That storm last night knocked out the paper's computer system. Last I heard, they weren't even certain they could get an edition out today."

In fact, that morning's edition of the *Journal* had rolled off the press at 5:30 A.M. On a normal morning the route men already would have completed their deliveries by that time. No matter. At least they had managed to print a paper.

At eight-thirty Kathy and Anna, both exhausted, sat in the newspaper's lounge. The morning paper rested in front of them. Kathy lifted it. "It's lightweight."

Anna chuckled. "Eight measly pages, but at least we didn't miss an edition."

Kathy's gaze settled on the massive four-column-by-full photo on the front page. "That makes it worthwhile. The color is exceptional."

The live-color photo displayed the pillar of fire that had towered above Milbrook the night before. Above it, in bold sixty-point type, the headline announced, BOMB CLAIMS EIGHT LIVES.

"We had plenty of time to get it right while the computers were down, and the photographer did a magnificent job getting the shot."

"It makes up for the small paper," Kathy said.

Barney ambled into the lounge, a smile on his face. He had been at the paper most of the night, too, staying on top of the story about the bombing.

"The kid did a pretty good job with the shot, didn't he?" the reporter said.

Anna nodded. "A hell of a job. You did a pretty good job at the scene."

"Did you ever find your car?" he asked.

"Yeah, at Harry's Wrecker Service. It cost the paper thirty bucks to get it out of custody."

Kathy laughed. "I'm not sure that qualifies as a legitimate business expense. Have you talked to Whit this morning?"

Anna shook her head. "I've called the house and his office. He wasn't at either place. I guess he's still at the scene. I'm going to head over there in a few minutes."

Barney snapped his fingers. "Jeez, I almost forgot why I came in here. You have someone waiting to see you, Anna."

"This early?"

"Oh, yes. It's Father Gabe, and he's in one of his righteous moods."

Anna slumped. "Dear God, what did I do to him?"

"Nothing," the reporter said. "He's fired up at the police department. The Bennings were members of his congregation. He's calling a community meeting for tonight at his church."

"What for?" Kathy asked.

The reporter shrugged. "He really wouldn't tell me, Mrs. Binder. He wants to see Anna."

Anna stood, placing a hand on Barney's shoulder as she did. "You come, too. If he wants us to write something, you can do the honors."

"But I was going home to grab a few hours of sleep."

"That's right, you were—and still can. Right after we see what the good preacher wants."

Kathy got up, too. "Well, I am leaving. If you need me, Anna, I'll be at home. You need to get a little rest, too."

"I want to see if they've come up with anything on the bombing. After that I'll go home. See you later."

The Baptist minister was waiting in her office. He rose as she and Barney entered.

"Sorry to keep you waiting, Reverend. It's been a rather hectic night."

"I understand, Miss Tyree. I wanted to extend a personal invitation for you to attend the meeting that I've called for tonight. As editor of the paper, I think it's very important for you to be there.''

Anna sat down behind her desk. Barney leaned against a filing cabinet off to the side of the small office. "What's the purpose of the meeting, Reverend?''

"It's something I've been considering since this crime wave struck Milbrook, Miss Tyree. Last night's tragedy has convinced me to forge ahead. The Milbrook police need the assistance of their citizens. To that end, I want to organize a citywide community-watch program. Private citizens can augment the city police in patrolling the community.''

The minister had not resumed his seat and had moved around the desk closer to Anna. She nodded toward the chair. "Please, Reverend Gabriel, take a seat. You make me nervous looming over me like that.''

"My apologies,'' he said. "I'm distraught this morning. The Bennings were members of my congregation. So, too, was Mrs. Trent, their next-door neighbor.'' He eased back to the chair in front of Anna's desk and lowered his massive body into it. "Milbrook lost some fine citizens last night.''

"Have you discussed this with Chief Wallace?'' she asked.

He shook his head. "No, ma'am, but I plan to do so this morning. In fact, I intend to invite him to the meeting also.''

"What if he objects to a community-watch program?'' Barney asked.

The preacher gave the reporter a look of disdain. "Why on earth should he be opposed to some assistance? God knows he needs it. This town has become an unfit place in which to live in recent weeks.''

Barney looked at Anna and saw no indication on her part that she wanted him to ease up. He pressed ahead. "Some people view an active community-watch program as something of a vigilante organization, Reverend Gabriel.''

"Nonsense,'' the preacher declared. "Our program would simply increase the number of eyes watching the community. Throughout the nation, citizens are banding together to assist local police efforts. I can tell you this. Until the courts start treating criminals like criminals, decent folk won't be able to sleep safe and sound in their homes.''

Anna decided to continue where Barney had left off. "Do you anticipate that some of your volunteers will be armed?"

"Of course not," he said. "I mean to say, it certainly won't be the policy of the program to arm its volunteers. Some may feel more comfortable with some sort of protection."

"That's what concerns me," Anna said.

The preacher used the chair's arm to push himself to his feet. "I came to invite you to the meeting, Miss Tyree. I don't need your consent to do this. For that matter, we don't need the consent of the police chief. We would, however, hope for your cooperation and support as well as the cooperation of the authorities."

Anna smiled. "We'll see, Reverend Gabriel. Barney will be attending your meeting on my behalf, and—"

"Isn't it worth your time?" the minister countered.

The smile slipped from Anna's face. "I have a paper to edit, Reverend Gabriel. We do most of our work in the evening, so it's not that your meeting isn't worth my time. Barney will be attending strictly as an observer. If the paper decides to take a stand on your program, it will do so on the editorial page."

The minister's eyes narrowed. For a moment Anna thought he was going to lose his temper. He didn't. Instead, he asked, "Is Mrs. Binder here?"

"She just left," Anna said.

Gabriel nodded and then left.

"He's a horse's ass," Barney said.

"But he can stir things up."

Mickey pounded on the door of the Mortons' mobile home. Mrs. Morton's car occupied its customary place in the driveway, so he knew that someone was home.

"Who is it?" a female voice shouted from inside.

"Mickey Moses. I wanna see Zeke."

The door opened. Zeke's mother, a once beautiful woman gone to fat, peeked out. She wore a ratty robe. "He's still asleep, Mickey."

"I gotta see him, Mrs. Morton."

Her eyes reflected her uncertainty. "I dunno. He gets awful mad if—"

"It's important!" Mickey repeated, this time almost shouting.

One of the woman's pudgy hands gathered the robe tightly about her neck. "I don't want him mad at me," she said, easing open the door.

"Don't worry," Mickey said. "He won't be mad at you."

"You gotta look over the mess. I ain't had time yet this morning to—"

But Mickey brushed by her and headed for Zeke's bedroom. As it turned out, the boy was already awake. Dressed in a pair of drooping jockey shorts and nothing else, he leaned against the door frame. "What the hell you want this early?"

Mickey didn't bother to answer. He threw a straight right that exploded against Zeke's nose and mouth. The boy, unprepared for the blow, staggered back into his bedroom and sprawled on the bed.

"Mickey!" Zeke's mother shouted.

He ignored her and lunged toward the bed. Zeke gaped at him, his hand wiping at the blood oozing from his split lip. When he saw his friend coming at him again, he kicked out with his bare feet. The left foot caught Mickey in the balls, doubling him over.

"You boys stop!" Zeke's mother cried. "Stop right now!"

Zeke flung himself from the bed and drove Mickey against a cheap dresser. "You son of a bitch," he screamed, trying to pummel Mickey with a hail of blows to the head.

Mickey drove a single left uppercut into the bottom of Zeke's chin. The larger boy lurched back, howling at the pain. The cry shocked Mickey, who didn't think he had hit Zeke that hard.

The trickle of blood from Zeke's mouth turned to a copious flow. It poured over his chin and onto the grimy carpet.

"God in heaven," his mother wailed. "He's bleeding to death."

Zeke tried to catch the blood in his hand. "I bit my tongue," he managed to say.

In the living room, the Mortons' phone started to ring.

EIGHTEEN

TONY DANTON SUFFERED from a case of conflicting emotions. He was pleased that his friend and investigator hadn't been killed by the explosion. On the other hand, he remained furious with Whit for leaving him in the dark about the existence of some neo-Nazi conspiracy in his backyard. Tony waylaid Whit as soon as the investigator walked into the office that morning.

Whit didn't even make it to his office. Tony accosted him in the lobby. ''Why the hell didn't you tell me about your conversation with the FBI yesterday?''

''I'm fine, thank you,'' Whit said, smiling into the angry face of his boss.

''How the hell do you know?'' Tony countered. ''I went by the hospital early this morning expecting to find you. They told me what a jerk you had been, how you refused treatment.''

''I didn't refuse treatment, Tony. I just refused to allow them to admit me. My shoulder's sore, my head hurts, and my face got a little skinned up. Otherwise, I'm okay.''

''You look like hell.''

Terry Watkins had come into the office with Whit so they could go to the juvenile office together. ''I tried to get him to go home, but he's like a junkyard dog this morning.''

''Who told you about the FBI?'' Whit asked.

''Gil did. I was at the scene of the bombing. You might have taken the time last night to call me.''

"I planned to," Whit said, "just as soon as I finished talking to the Benning girl."

"I gather she didn't tell you anything."

Whit shook his head. "I sensed she was withholding information. As it turned out, we found out about it anyway."

The prosecutor's look changed from one of indignation to one of sudden curiosity. "What?"

Whit nodded back toward the city officer. "The Benning girl was a friend of Terry's daughter. They had seen each other at that teen center last night, and she had told Terry's daughter about her suspicions."

Watkins provided the county attorney with the details.

"Where do we find these kids?" Tony then asked.

"Zeke Morton's on juvenile probation," Whit said. "Terry and I were on our way up there to get an address from the probation office."

"So what's holding you up?" Tony said.

Whit smiled. "Up until now, you have been."

"So go," the prosecutor said.

Watkins, though, was worried about his daughter. "You can handle it," he said to Whit. "I'm going to call home. If Susan's settled down some, she might have some more information."

"Good idea. I'll be back shortly."

Under West Virginia law it was illegal to process a juvenile as if he were an adult, so no department could legally maintain case files on juvenile offenders. No mug shots. No fingerprints. No handwriting samples. No biographical data. Legally, they weren't criminals. They were delinquents, a temporal and fleeting state under the law existing only until a kid could go through some degree of rehabilitation. No matter how sullied their juvenile criminal record, they entered the adult world of law enforcement as virgins white as a newborn's behind. There were exceptions, of course—the meager handful of instances in which a juvenile committed a crime serious enough to warrant trial as an adult. Since the three suspects he sought hadn't previously incinerated eight people, their records would still be confidential. If they had had anything to do with the prior night's madness, they might lose their virginity a little sooner than they expected.

The juvenile office was a part of the court's overall probation department, located on the second floor of the courthouse. It had been several months since Whit had had any cause to deal with the juvenile authorities, and there had been recent changes in the offices. The most noteworthy had been the retirement of Irvin Skeens, the chief juvenile officer. Skeens, something of a political hack when he had first been appointed way back in the sixties, had developed into a first-rate bureaucrat. He had been replaced by a youthful native of Charleston whom Whit had yet to meet.

Mary Washington, the department's secretary, had been with the office for as long as Whit could remember. She was the first black to be hired for a job in the courthouse.

"Morning, Mary."

The woman, still slim and attractive in spite of the fact that she was approaching retirement, didn't even glance up from the screen of a computer. "I hate these things," she said, nodding toward the monitor.

"I said good morning, Mary."

She laughed. "I apologize, Whit. It's just this darned computer. It never does what I want it to."

"Might as well get used to them. You and I will be gone before they are."

"Don't remind me. What brings you up here?" She finally looked up at him. "My God, Whit, what happened to you?"

"I got too close to a bomb."

"That one last night?" Mary asked.

" 'Fraid so."

"Is your arm broken?"

He shook his head. "My shoulder's wrenched. Nothing serious. I need to see the head honcho. Is he in?"

"Oh, yeah. He's always in, but he has someone with him."

Whit hiked his eyebrows. When he spoke, he lowered his voice. "Do I detect some dissatisfaction?"

Mary glanced over her shoulder at the door to an office that was situated behind her desk. She motioned for Whit to move closer.

"He's a nut," she whispered.

Whit nodded toward the door. "The man that's visiting—"

"Him, too," she said emphatically but still in a whisper. "But I was actually referring to Mr. Bainbridge, the new chief."

It startled Whit. In all the years he had known Mary Washington, he had never heard her make a disparaging comment about anyone, not even some of the wretched teenage misanthropes whose behavior the office presumably supervised.

"Why do you say that?" Whit asked.

"Because it's true. That's why. He makes me say a short prayer with him every morning."

Whit frowned. "You're kidding."

"Nosiree. Now, I'm as God-fearin' as the next . . . more so than most, but this guy lives and breathes it. He preaches to the kids, too. You know how that goes over."

"I can imagine. I do need to see him. It's something of an emergency."

She threw up her hands. "Sorry, Whit. He's in there with this preacher buddy of his, and I got my orders. Don't disturb him. They're probably on their knees together, prayin' as if there wasn't going to be a tomorrow."

Whit had to laugh. "He couldn't be that bad."

"You don't think so? Shows what you know, Whit Pynchon. I walked in the other day, and he was on his knees with some poor fourteen-year-old boy, praying for his soul. You know what I think?"

"What's that?"

She lowered her voice even more. "I think the supreme court sent him down here to us just to get rid of him from up there."

"What's the judge say?"

"He doesn't care. All that's on his mind is his retirement."

The door latch to the JO's office clicked.

"Quick, Mary," Whit said, "what's the new man's name?"

"Bainbridge, just like I said. Pete Bainbridge. I call him Prayin' Pete."

The office door opened. Whit immediately recognized the hefty figure who came out of the door.

"Well, well, Mr. Pynchon," said Peter Gabriel, "I'm glad to see you're on your feet. I pray your injuries aren't too serious or painful. I'm on my way down to see your boss."

"I'm sure he'll be thrilled," Whit said. "More complaints to register?"

"Not this morning, sir. I want to inform him about the community meeting scheduled at my church this evening. After last night's tragedy, it's time that the citizens of Milbrook take a more active role in their own defense."

"How so?" Whit asked, and was at once sorry that he had. What the hell did he care what this Baptist buffoon did?

"A massive community-watch program, Mr. Pynchon. You're more than welcome to attend, and—"

Whit held up his hand. "Save the speech, Gabriel. I won't be there."

Whit glanced to the much smaller man standing behind the minister. He was slim, very young, and wore a three-piece pinstripe. "Mr. Bainbridge, may I have a few words with you?"

Sensing that Whit was dismissing him, Father Gabe turned to the new juvenile officer. "God be with you, Pete. I count on your attendance tonight.

"I'll be there, Brother Gabriel."

The minister smiled at Whit. "You really should attend, Brother Pynchon. You might be impressed."

Whit thought of many things he wanted to say. He settled for the least offensive. "I'm not your brother, Gabriel."

The minister just shook his head. "For a public servant, you have a very poor attitude."

Whit chose to remain silent. The Baptist preacher nodded to Bainbridge and didn't even give Mary Washington a look as he marched from the office.

The man whom Whit presumed to be Pete Bainbridge came out into the outer office, a friendly smile on his face in spite of Whit's encounter with the minister. Before Mary could say anything, he offered Whit his hand. "Pete Bainbridge, I don't think we've met."

"Whit Pynchon, Pete."

Mary Washington was rising. "He's the—"

"No need to tell me, Mary. Mr. Pynchon's reputation has preceded him. Can this office be of some assistance to you, Whit?"

"I hope so," Whit said. "We had more than half a dozen people killed in a bombing last night. According to information we have received, we suspect juveniles may have been involved. We're trying to locate them."

A cloud seemed to pass over the JO's face. "Please come inside, Whit."

Bainbridge moved ahead of Whit, who winked at Mary as he passed her. He didn't know a thing about the new JO, and perhaps it was Mary's opinion that had prejudiced him, but already Whit didn't like the man. He reminded Whit of one of those chatty types who spent their lives attending courses on how to win friends and influence people. Usually, you found them selling magazine subscriptions door to door, not supervising juvenile delinquents. Anna, of course, would accuse him of stereotyping. The juvenile officer closed the door behind them.

As Whit settled into a chair offered to him by Bainbridge, he noticed the change in the office. Under the previous administrator the floor had been bare. The walls, like most of those in the courthouse, had been painted institutional green. The furniture remained unchanged, typical metal issue, but the walls were now a pale blue, and a brightly decorated carpet covered the floor.

"I see you've made some improvements," Whit said.

"Oh, yes." The man gracefully lowered himself into his chair. "I believe that we need to put our best foot forward when dealing with troubled children. They see adult life as drab and unpromising. We need to give them a more positive image."

Whit also noted the small pictures on the walls, each one of them a different re-creation of Jesus of Nazareth. Bainbridge's desk was clear except for a phone, an address book, and a small silver cross mounted on a marble base.

"Father Gabe was telling me about the tragedy. I haven't read the newspaper reports yet, but it sounded incredible."

"It was. I was there, but I don't really remember it."

"I can understand. How can I help?"

"We have the names of three individuals whom we believe to be juveniles, one of whom is on probation with your department. I was hoping you might give us his address and the addresses of the others if you happen to have them."

Bainbridge suddenly stood. "I don't mean to be uncooperative, Whit, but that wouldn't be at all proper."

Whit flinched, not certain he had heard the man's words correctly. "What did you say?"

"We're an arm of the judicial branch, Mr. Pynchon. It's not our place to involve ourselves in this type of investigatory activity. In addition, it can undermine the faith that the young people place in us."

"Look, Bainbridge, I know what your damned job is. I'm not trying to influence your neutrality. I just want to catch the little bastards that did this. Once I get them, I'm sure you'll have a chance at them."

Bainbridge's face flushed. "We don't condone that sort of language in this office."

"Oh, Jesus," Whit said.

"Nor do we countenance blasphemy."

Whit stood. "On the other hand, you don't seem to be too

offended by the mass murder of eight people, including several juveniles. I'd say, Bainbridge, that your religion is a bit fucked up.''

The juvenile officer tensed. ''You can be certain, sir, that Prosecutor Danton will hear of this.''

A look of sudden fear crossed Bainbridge's face as Whit moved around the desk. Whit would have loved to drive a fist into the asshole's face. He settled for jabbing a finger against the man's chest. ''And you can be just as sure that I'm walking across the hall to the judge's office.''

Whit turned and started toward the door.

''He's not in today,'' Bainbridge said, an immediate smugness to his voice. ''He's home ill with the flu.''

''Fine,'' Whit said, ''I'll talk to him there.''

''I wouldn't advise it.''

After opening the door, Whit wheeled. ''You know where you can put your advice.'' He slammed the door.

Mary Washington was smiling. ''See what I mean?''

''I need to talk with you,'' Whit said. ''Can I call you at home?''

''I have a break in ten minutes,'' she said. ''I'll come down to your office. I wanna hear about this.''

''You're right about him,'' Whit said.

The door to Bainbridge's office opened. He didn't come out. Instead, he stood there. ''I hope you aren't trying to elicit information from Mrs. Washington.''

''What if I am?'' Whit said.

The man blinked. ''Uh, in that case I would instruct Mrs. Washington as to her obligations as an employee of the judicial branch.''

''After which,'' Whit said, ''you would probably pray for both our souls, right?''

Mary couldn't help it. She giggled.

Bainbridge said something else, but Whit didn't hear it. He was on his way out the door of the probation office.

NINETEEN

ON THE OTHER side of town Zeke Morton sat in a chair in the living room of his mother's mobile home. He held a hand mirror and was using it to examine his tongue. "Jesus," he mumbled, his speech still slurred, "I hope I don't need stitches."

Mickey sat across the room. "They blew her fuckin' house up, man. Don't you understand?"

Zeke lowered the mirror. "I done told you. I didn't have nothing to do with it."

Zeke's mother, after having made certain that the two boys were finished fighting, had hurriedly dressed and gone out. The phone call that had come at the conclusion of the altercation had been for Zeke.

"Look, like I said, the man wants to see us today at noon," Zeke said, grimacing with pain as he spoke. The jagged wound on the tip of his tongue continued to seep blood, and he used a piece of toilet tissue to absorb it.

"Screw him," Mickey said. "I'm through with it. I'm through with him. He didn't have to kill her. Christ, Zeke, not just her. He killed her family and other people, too."

"I don't know for sure it was him. He didn't say so."

"You told him about Janey, didn't you?"

"Yeah, sure. I done told you that, but I told him, too, that you had her under control."

"The bastard," Mickey said, getting to his feet.

"He wants to see us, all three of us," Zeke repeated.

148

"You guys been wantin' to know who he is. Now's your chance if you ain't chicken."

"So tell me now," Mickey said. "I might just go pay him a visit."

Zeke shook his head. "No way, man. You wanna know? You go with me today. He wants to meet at Rock Crusher Quarry."

"I'm out," Mickey said. "I'm not goin'. This guy is crazy. Maybe he's gonna kill us now."

"Shit," Zeke said too loudly. He flinched in pain. "The damn thing's swellin' now. Jesus, man, you didn't have to beat hell outta me."

"And you shouldn't have told him about Janey, asshole." Mickey had been pacing the small living room. He stopped in front of the chair in which Zeke was seated. "If you don't tell me who he is now, I might start on you again."

Mickey didn't even see where the small gun had come from. In hindsight, he figured it must have been stuffed down in the chair.

"You ain't gonna hit me again, Mickey. I don't wanna hurt you, but I will."

Mickey knew that. He stepped back. "Okay, Zeke, I'll go with you, but just to see what the guy has to say and who he is."

"Fine by me," Zeke said. "The man said he has details on that doctor's house. That's all he wants. He said it would be our last job."

"I've pulled my last job, Zeke."

The other boy lowered the gun. "Christ, I better put some ice on this. Otherwise it's gonna swell up so big, it'll choke me."

"I'll get Bert," Mickey said. "Then I'll come back after you."

"You ain't gonna do nothing stupid, are you?"

Mickey was at the mobile home's front door. He paused before going out. "I've done that already. It's about time I did somethin' smart."

* * *

Tony Danton emerged from his office as soon as he heard Whit's voice from the lobby.

"Let me guess," Whit said as Tony came down the hall. "You just got off the phone with that nitwit from upstairs."

Tony wasn't smiling. "My God, Whit. What in the hell did you do to the man? He was livid."

"I didn't do anything to him. I thought about shoving that big cross he had on his desk right up his—" Whit didn't finish the sentence in deference to the office's secretary, who was within earshot. "Anyway, he's gonna be a real winner."

Tony followed Whit into his office. "You must have done something. He's going to file a formal complaint with the judge."

Whit dropped into the battered chair behind his desk. "What the hell's that?"

"What?" Tony asked.

"A formal complaint."

Tony had to think about it. "Come to think of it, I don't know. I guess he means he's going to put it in writing."

"I don't work for the judge, do I?" Whit said.

"You work for me, and I have to keep peace with the judge."

"I took those names up to him to see if he or Mary would give us their addresses. He told me that it wouldn't be proper for him, as an official of the judiciary, to lower himself to participate in an investigation."

"To which you responded?"

Whit shrugged. "I was polite—at first. I attempted to change his mind. At some point in the conversation I used a word to which he took offense. You have to know one thing, Tony. The guy is one of these holier-than-thou types."

"In other words, you two exchanged pleasantries."

Whit smiled. "Yeah, you might say that."

"I thought you must have shoved him around or something."

The good humor left Whit's face. "Did he say that?"

"No, but he said your actions were violent and unprofessional."

"That son of a bitch." Whit pushed himself to his feet. "I think I'm gonna go back up there and—"

Tony was shaking his head. "Oh, no, you don't." The prosecutor stepped in to block Whit's way.

It brought the smile back to Whit's face. "I wasn't really going. I just wanted to see if you would have let me. Actually, I came down to call Judge O'Brien. According to that pompous Holy Roller, the judge is home with the flu. Maybe he can talk some sense into Bainbridge."

"Let's just let it lay for right now," Tony said.

Watkins, accompanied by Gil Dickerson, entered Whit's office. "I talked to Susan. I guess she told me all she knew this morning."

Both Tony and the detective dropped into the chairs facing Whit's desk. Dickerson leaned against the door frame. The prosecutor was shaking his head. "I've always said that there's nothing more dangerous than a kid gone bad. When you find one like that, they've got absolutely no conscience."

"Did you get the addresses?"

Whit shook his head. "That idiot upstairs refused to help us."

The sheriff cocked his head. "What idiot upstairs?"

"Bainbridge," Whit said.

At the mention of the name the sheriff cringed. "I shoulda known. He hadn't been here hardly a week before he was in my office wanting to start some kind of cockamamy religious program in the jail. I told him that we already had one, and he said that he wanted to review it. He then proceeded to start preaching to me about the need to be certain that an appropriate form of 'Christian belief'—his words—was available to the inmates."

"What did you tell him?" Tony asked.

"I gave him the name of the minister who handles it for us and suggested that he contact him."

"You shoulda kicked his ass out of your office," Whit said.

Gil nodded. "Yeah, I should have."

Whit looked back to Tony. "What about that call to the judge?"

"I'll do it," Tony said. "Maybe Bainbridge is going to wait for the judge to get back. I think maybe I'd better get to O'Brien first."

Just as the prosecutor was about to leave Whit's office, Mary Washington appeared.

"You came," Whit said.

"Told you I would. What did you need?"

Tony directed her to the seat he had vacated.

Whit handed her the names. "Take a look at these, Mary. See if they remind you of any of the little darlings that have been through your office of late."

Mary accepted the piece of paper. "Is that what that ruckus was about with Mr. Bainbridge?"

Whit nodded.

"After you left, he gave me this long-winded lecture about the impartiality of the judicial system and how it was a violation of that impartiality to share information with police agencies. I didn't know what the hell he was talking about."

"Me," Whit said.

The woman studied the names. When she reached the final one, her face tightened. "We've got files on two of the three, Ezekiel Morton and Mickey Moses."

"Can you get us their addresses?" Tony asked. "That's all we want."

"First," she said, "what did they do?"

"We think they have information on last night's bombing," Whit said.

Mary Washington shook her head. "Did you tell Bainbridge that?"

Whit said that he had, adding, "Not that he gave a damn. Whatever you tell us will remain confidential, Mary. I don't want to get you in trouble with your boss."

"He shoulda helped you," she said. "I can get the addresses and call them down to you."

"You don't happen to remember what kinda trouble they were into, do you?"

The black woman pondered for a moment. "Morton was arrested for creating a disturbance. He was drunk outta his mind. The officer was going to just take him home, but Morton wanted to fight. He ended up being charged with obstructing an officer. That wasn't too long ago."

"That was my department's case," Watkins said.

"Mickey Moses got into some sort of fight at the high school. About that same time he got a ticket for reckless driving. Mr. Skeens just counseled him. He's technically still on probation, but we've pretty much closed his file."

"What about Ringwald?" Whit asked.

She shook her head. "His name doesn't ring a bell. If he'd been through our office, I'd probably remember."

"Can you check?" Whit asked.

Mary was looking at her watch. "I'll take a look. I best be getting back upstairs. If you need anything else, you just let me know. I'll give you a ring back with the addresses. 'Course, I'll have to wait until Prayin' Pete can't hear me."

Tony put an arm around her shoulder as she walked out. "We really appreciate it, and we'll keep your name out of it."

"Do what you have to do," Mary said.

Hayden Wallace came out of his office to greet Anna. "You look like the rest of us," he said. "Don't guess you got much shut-eye last night, either."

She laughed. "Not a wink, but we did manage to get a paper on the streets."

He guided her into his office. "Whit told me you had computer troubles last night."

She took the chair he offered. He moved around behind his desk. It was covered with paperwork and reports, and he waved a big hand over the chaos. "You'd think I'd been here all my life with all this mess on my desk. I'm not too organized.''

"Join the crowd," Anna said. "Your desk looks just like mine.''

"So to what do I owe this unexpected but welcome visit?" he asked.

"I don't need to tell you, Chief, that the bombing last night is one of the biggest things to happen in Milbrook in a long time. I thought maybe I should stop by to see if you had any leads.''

"Why don't you check with Pynchon?" he asked.

She grinned. "I can't seem to catch up with him. Besides, Whit doesn't tend to cooperate with the press. It's a prejudice he hasn't overcome.''

"He is a colorful character, Miss Tyree." Wallace got to his feet and went to a window that overlooked the lawn of the city hall. "I don't want to steal his thunder, but I think I can tell you that we have isolated some suspects.''

Anna was looking at his back. "Already?"

"Yes, ma'am. I can't give you any more details than that." He turned back around. "However, the people of Milbrook do need to know that we are not sitting around twiddlin' our collective thumbs.''

Anna really hadn't expected to get much information, so she was fumbling for the small notebook she carried in her purse. "Do you expect arrests soon?"

"I wouldn't be surprised, but I can't give you any exact timetables.''

Anna jotted down the quote. "Was the bombing connected to the burglaries?"

Wallace resumed his seat. "We think so, but again, I'm not prepared to go into details.''

"What about a motive for the bombing?" Anna asked.

"I'd rather not comment on that right now, Miss Tyree."

"My reporter told me that he heard rumors from some of the officers that the daughter of the Bennings might have had some information about the burglaries. He said there was speculation she was killed to keep her quiet."

The chief shrugged. "Well, we can't say that for sure, so it's best that we don't say anything yet about motive."

"But that is a theory?" Anna asked.

"It's a theory."

Anna scribbled as fast as she could. "Whit was at the Bennings' house last night. Did he manage to elicit any information from the girl?"

"Maybe you'd better ask Whit about that," Wallace said. "How about dinner tonight, Miss Tyree?"

The question, coming in the context of the rapid-fire interview, caught Anna off guard. "Dinner?"

"I'd like to take you to dinner."

Anna actually felt her cheeks glow. "Chief, I've told you I'm involved. Besides, I wouldn't be much company. I'd probably fall asleep."

"Then how 'bout tomorrow night?"

She shook her head. "Not a good idea. Have you heard about the meeting at Father Gabriel's church tonight?"

Wallace said that he hadn't.

"Reverend Gabriel wants to organize a citywide community-watch program," Anna said, hoping the change in subject would work. "He thinks that local citizens can help the police keep an eye on the city."

"I've always been a supporter of community-watch programs, Miss Tyree. We need all the help we can get. I welcome the good minister's efforts."

"Will you attend?"

He knitted his brows. "Are you going?"

"I'm sending a reporter," Anna said.

"Too bad. Since I haven't been invited yet, I don't have plans at this time to attend."

"Some people have suggested that this kind of community-watch program often leads to citizens taking the law into their own hands. Is that a concern of yours, Chief?"

He formed a steeple with his fingers and leaned back in

his chair. ''We live in a democracy, Miss Tyree. So long as the people involved in community-watch do just that—watch, I mean—then I have no problem with it. As I said, I welcome it. Besides, I think there's a good chance we might be bringing some of our problems to an end pretty soon.''

TWENTY

NONE OF THE FOUR men gathered in Whit Pynchon's office that Wednesday morning had slept a wink the night before. Only Tony Danton had even managed to refresh himself after the bombing of the Benning residence. Whit had stopped by his residence long enough to change out of the clothing that had been decimated by the blast. Besides the ugly scab on his cheek, his forehead was still smudged by soot. The pain in his head had eased, but the stiffness in his shoulder had worsened. When he reached for the phone book, a sharp pain shot from his shoulder to his neck. He moaned at the discomfort.

Gil, more than any of the others, knew what it meant to move in pain. Since the gunshot wound to his knee, he had lived with it on a daily basis. "I've got some extra-strength aspirin in my office," he told his friend.

"I doubt it will help much," Whit said.

"It helps me," the sheriff countered. "In cold and damp weather, it's all that keeps me going."

"I'll try it," Whit said as he started to thumb through the phone book. Gil went after the medication.

"What are you doing?" Tony asked.

"I think we're all so exhausted that we're overlooking the obvious," Whit said. "We might be able to get these kids' addresses out of here."

Terry Watkins, sitting on the couch, had almost dozed off. The conversation made him sit up. "That's an idea."

Whit reached the right page and scanned it. "We've got about four families named Morton here."

"We can check each one," Watkins said.

Whit moved on to the next page. "And three by the name of Moses."

The investigator checked the name of the third suspect and flipped through several pages. "Bingo! There's just one Ringwald listed."

Watkins reached over for the book. "I'll write that one down for you."

"Go back and get the others, too," Whit said. "If we don't hear from Mary pretty quickly, we'll start checking each one of them."

Tony appeared thoughtful. "A question, Whit. Do you really think three juveniles could design that kind of bomb? The guys in the mobile forensics lab figured it was triggered by a radio transmitter, pretty sophisticated for kids. They also found evidence that it was some form of plastic explosive."

His investigator shook his head. "I've been thinking about that, too. Somebody else—probably someone from this political outfit—designed it. The boys could have planted it, though."

"We need some more information on this group," the attorney said. "Is this a typical tactic of theirs? To use bombs?"

"They assassinate witnesses," Whit said. "I wouldn't put it past them."

Gil reappeared with the medication and a glass of water. As Whit was downing the pills, the phone on his desk rang. Tony answered it.

He mouthed the words. "It's Mary." Then he started jotting down information.

Whit was getting to his feet. "Gil, you wanna go with Watkins and me?"

The sheriff smiled. "I was hoping you would ask."

The prosecutor hung up the phone and handed the addresses to Whit. "Are you going to bring them in?"

"I'll play it by ear," Whit said.

"Your probable cause is a little shaky, and they are juveniles," Tony reminded his investigator.

Whit was on his way out the door. "Don't worry, boss. I promise not to screw up the case."

Tony followed the three officers into the hallway. "One of them might roll over," he was saying. "It sure would be nice to nab the creeps behind them."

Whit looked back over his shoulder. "Let's not start playing Let's Make a Deal just yet."

Just as the three men were leaving the courthouse, Mickey was picking up Bert Ringwald at his house. "The bastards killed Janice Benning," he said to the diminutive boy who climbed into his car.

"I heard that's who it was," Ringwald said, "but how do you know it was the man?"

"It was him . . . or them . . . or whoever."

"So how come we gonna go meet them?"

The heat wave had continued. The morning sky was a cloudless blue, and already the burning sun was starting to send the temperature above the ninety-degree mark. The windows in Mickey's car were down, and the air rushed in as he headed over toward Morton's house.

"I wanna see who the man is," Mickey said. "Once I know that, then he's gonna pay."

Ringwald, the bruise around his eye now a yellowish purple, shook his head. "C'mon, Mickey, we got a damn good thing going here."

"The bastard blew up a gawdamn city block, Bert. He's crazy, man, but don't say a word to Zeke. You understand?"

Ringwald's face dripped sweat. "Yeah, Mickey, but what about us, man? That cop got killed the other night. I stabbed Benning. If we ain't careful, the cops'll get us, too."

"So we'll be careful," Mickey said.

"What's Zeke say?"

"Fuck Zeke."

"Where we s'posed to meet the man?"

"Rock Crusher Quarry."

Ringwald frowned. "Where?"

"It's down below the cliffs. Haven't you ever been down there?"

Ringwald shook his head. "No, guess not. I never heard of the place."

"It's not too far from town, but it's really isolated," Mickey said. "We'll get Zeke and go on down. I wanna be there when the son of a bitch gets there."

Ringwald saw the furious determination on Mickey's face. "Are you carryin', Mickey?"

The driver glanced at him. "Huh?"

"You got some heat? A gun?"

"Christ, Bert, you sound like some cheap movie hoodlum."

"Well, are ya?"

Mickey shook his head. "No, I'm not gonna do nothing now. I just wanna see who this guy is."

"Why's he wanna see us?"

"Zeke talked to him. He said he wants us to hit that doctor's house and needs to go over the plans with us."

Whit decided to check out the residence of Mickey Moses first. For one thing, it was the closest to the courthouse. The house was in the eastern part of the small city in a neighborhood that once had been populated by the town's elite. Most of the bigger homes in the area had been converted into small rental units, the residents of which depended on welfare subsidies to pay the rent. It wasn't the most poverty-stricken part of town, and its neat residential appearance belied the circumstances of the inhabitants.

They rode in the sheriff's unmarked cruiser with the city detective driving. The sheriff sat in the front seat with the city detective. Whit had opted to sit in the back. He was checking the house numbers as the cruiser eased its way down the street.

"We should be a block or so away," he said. "Go pretty slow, Terry. If the kid's home, we don't want to spook him."

"Ten four, Whit."

The cruiser came to a four-way stop sign. "Hold it here a second," Whit said. He was leaning forward, squinting across the front seat and out the windshield into the summer glare.

"Which one is it?" Gil asked.

Whit pointed. "From here, I'd bet it's that small single-level brick house two houses back from the corner."

The other two men's eyes settled on the house. "On the left?" Watkins asked.

"If the house numbers run true, then that's it," Whit said.

Watkins had been a cop with the city of Milbrook for almost as long as Whit had been with the prosecutor's office. He knew Milbrook well. "An alley runs behind those houses," he said. "Maybe we oughta park here. You and Gil go to the front door. I'll go down the alley and cover the back, just in case he tries to rabbit."

Whit nodded in agreement. "Just remember that we don't have enough evidence to make an arrest."

Watkins looked back. "What if he runs?"

"Accidentally trip him," Whit said.

At that moment Zeke Morton was ordering Ringwald out of the front seat of Mickey's car.

"How come I always gotta ride in the back?" Bert said. Nonetheless, he was exiting the two-door sedan.

" 'Cause I like to ride shotgun." The injury to Zeke's tongue continued to muffle his speech.

Bert shoved the seat forward and started to wedge himself into the tight confines of the backseat. His body reeked of soured sweat, and Zeke made a face. In one swift motion he put his booted foot against the smaller boy's rear end and shoved. Bert was rocketed into the backseat.

"Jesus," he gasped, trying to right himself. "Gawdamn, Zeke. I almost cracked my head on the door handle."

Zeke was getting into the car. "You stink, Ringwald. Don't you never take a bath?"

"I can't help it," the boy whined. "It's hot, and I sweat."

Zeke lowered himself into the front seat. "We all sweat. You just plain stink."

"How come you're talking funny? You sound like a hare-lip or something?"

"I bit my tongue." Zeke didn't embellish the tale. No way did he want Ringwald to know that Mickey had whipped him.

Mickey didn't say anything, either. Once Zeke was in the car, he peeled out from the curb and headed toward a narrow, twisting country road that led down from the plateau on which Milbrook was located to the remote location known as Rock Crusher Quarry.

As Gil and Whit moved toward the Moses house, they could look between the houses and see Watkins moving par-allel to them in the alley. All three of the men were dressed in plain clothes, but given the manner of their movement, it wasn't hard to tell that two of them—Whit and Watkins—were cops. Gil Dickerson, with his halting gait, looked any-thing but.

"There's no car in the drive," Gil said.

Whit kept his eyes on the small house. "I noticed."

"Maybe we shoulda rounded up some other units and hit all three addresses at the same time," the sheriff said.

"Couldn't do it, Gil. It's not like we've got enough evi-dence to take them into custody. Maybe if we confront one of them, he'll say or do something to give us grounds, but I'd rather handle each myself."

"I haven't had much dealings with juveniles," Gil said.

"Nor have I, and I was hoping to keep it that way."

They had reached the edge of the property. Whit slowed to take stock of the house. He couldn't see the rear, of course, but the driveway led to a small covered carport on the left side of the house. A side door opened into the carport. If there was a back door, that meant there were three exits to the residence. The windows were open, and so, too, was the front door, the entrance protected only by a screen door.

"It looks like someone's home," Gil said.

"You hang back and keep your eye on the side door," Whit said. "I'll go to the front door."

"Can you handle yourself with that arm in a sling?"

Whit made a face. "Who the hell knows? I hope I don't have to find out, but we've got to make our move now. Terry's already in position around back."

Whit's weapon was jammed in a holster on his left side. If he had to draw it, he would be forced either to use his incapacitated right arm or to try to do it left-handed. In either case he probably wouldn't make it. On top of that, he needed to display his badge. He pulled out his wallet with his left hand and flipped it open. He decided not to think about the gun and moved quickly up the three steps to a small concrete stoop that provided access to the front door. He rang the bell.

"Coming," a woman's voice cried.

Seconds later he could see her walking toward the front door. She stopped at the screen and didn't open it. Whit wasn't surprised. A stranger stood at her front door, his arm in a sling, his face scraped and dirty, unshaven.

"What is it you want?" she was asking.

Whit showed his badge. "I'm with the office of the prosecuting attorney. Is Mickey Moses here?"

"Mickey?"

"Is he here, ma'am?"

"Uh, no. He isn't. Who did you say you were with?"

Something made her wheel from the door. Whit, fumbling with his badge case, grabbed the screen door just as she screamed. He flung it open. She was staring at Terry Watkins, who had come in through the back door. He had his gun in one hand and was showing the badge in the other.

"What right do you have to barge into my house?" she said, turning back to Whit.

"We need to see your son."

"What's he done?"

"Where is he, Mrs. Moses?"

"Not here," she said.

Gil had come up the front steps and eased open the door.

The woman appeared to be in her forties. She had been a knockout in her youth, and even now she wasn't hard to look at. She wore white tennis shoes and a figure-hugging white uniform that flattered her full figure. Whit concluded that she worked either in the medical profession or as a waitress.

At that moment she was incensed. "You people just can't come in here like this. Don't you have to have a warrant or something like that?"

"I apologize," Whit said, "but, Mrs. Moses, your son may be in a great deal of trouble. We just want to know where we can find him."

She glanced at a clock above the television. "He should be home any minute. He knows I have to be at work at one o'clock."

TWENTY-ONE

"TERRORISTS?" Anna eyed her reporter with obvious disbelief. "What kind of terrorists?"

Barney shook his head. "All my source told me was that they suspect the bombing was the work of a group of terrorists."

Kathy had been in Anna's office when Barney had come in to tell them about the rumor. The news shocked her, too. "Why in God's name would terrorists want to blow up a house in a residential section of Milbrook, West Virginia? It sounds to me like the authorities are getting desperate for an explanation."

"My source has been right on target several times before," the reporter insisted. "In fact, he has never given me any bad information. He did tell me that it was just a rumor circulating around the department, but he knew for a fact that some local officials have already had discussions with the feds."

Anna's face continued to reflect her open skepticism. "Kathy's right. Why would we be of interest to terrorists?"

Barney's normally composed demeanor began to deteriorate. "Jesus, Anna, I'm just telling you what I was told by a good source. I don't care whether you believe it or not."

The staff at the *Milbrook Daily Journal* was about as wasted as the police team now pursuing their juvenile suspects. Besides the chaos created by the bombing, they had spent most of the night trying to produce a newspaper on equipment that remained glitchy and unpredictable.

Anna was probably more tired than most. She didn't react well to Barney's brief flare of temper. "Dammit, Barney. I'm not personally criticizing you for bringing the report to me. I just can't accept it as anything but a wild rumor. Who talked to the feds? Did your source tell you that?"

Barney took a deep breath. "Yes, ma'am. He did, in fact. It was Whit Pynchon and the sheriff."

The mention of Gil's name sparked Kathy's interest. "I didn't even know Gil was involved in the investigation." She and the sheriff were almost as deeply involved as Whit and Anna were. In the case of the former couple, both of them had lost their spouses, and both remained somewhat hesitant about becoming too deeply involved.

"Every law officer in the county is involved," Barney said. "Maybe not directly, but it's the only thing on their mind. A cop was killed Monday night, and then last night the bombing."

Anna had her phone in hand and was dialing. "By God, we'll find out what's going on."

"Who are you calling?" Kathy asked.

"Whitley Francis Pynchon."

The phone in the office of the prosecutor rang eight times. Anna was just about to slam the handset down when someone answered. The voice was that of Tony Danton.

"Tony, this is Anna. I was beginning to think that no one was there."

"Sorry, Anna. The secretary stepped out for a few minutes, and I was on the other line. If you're calling for Whit, he's out in the field."

"Looking for terrorists?" Anna asked.

The long pause on the other end of the line spoke volumes. Before Tony could even respond, Anna went on to say, "Look, Tony, what the devil is going on? My reporter tells me that you people suspect some type of terrorist involvement in last night's bombing. I thought it was a crock, but you were speechless when I mentioned it."

"Anna, there's nothing that I can say right now. Believe me, just as soon as we can comment—"

"Do you suspect that the bombing was an act of terrorism?"

"Anna, I've told you that I can't comment."

"Jesus, Tony, I'm as interested personally as I am professionally. Was Whit the target? Or was it the Benning family?"

"Can we talk off the record?" he asked.

Anna took a deep breath. "I don't know. You might tell me something I can't in good conscience withhold."

"You're right," the prosecutor said. "It's best if I don't say anything at all."

Both Kathy and Barney had moved forward in their seats. Obviously, the rumor that the reporter had heard wasn't as ridiculous as it had sounded. "Ask him about the feds," Barney whispered.

"On the record, Tony, have you all had conversations with federal officials regarding the bombing?"

"I haven't," Tony said.

"Has anyone?"

"No comment, Anna."

She decided to try another approach. "I interviewed Chief Wallace this morning, and he indicated that you have suspects. That's going to be in tomorrow's paper for certain. Do you have any comment on that?"

"Wallace told you that?" Tony asked.

"This very morning, Mr. Prosecutor. He implied that arrests were imminent."

She didn't have to see the county attorney to know that he was fuming. When he did speak, all he said was, "No comment."

"The public has a right to know if their safety is in danger, Tony. Christ, you had eight people killed last night—a police officer the night before. You can't just stonewall this thing. Do you expect more such incidents?"

"Any comment I might make could jeopardize the outcome of the investigation, Anna. I certainly hope to be able to give you some information before your paper publishes tomorrow, but even if I can't, I hope you don't print that rumor about terrorists.''

"I don't see how I can withhold it." She slammed the phone down.

Barney was actually smiling. "My source was right, wasn't he?''

Anna pushed herself up from her desk and started to pace behind it. She hadn't even heard the reporter's question.

Barney glanced at Kathy, who said to her friend, "What did he say, Anna?''

Anna was shaking her head. "He wouldn't comment, but from the way he acted, it's true, Kathy. He didn't confirm it, but at the mention of the word 'terrorist' there was this pregnant silence. It's true. Or Tony Danton thinks it's true.''

Barney rose to leave. "I'll check with a few other guys who might know something.''

"Fine," Anna said, not paying all that much attention to what he said.

Barney shrugged at the publisher and walked out.

"What's wrong, Anna?''

The editor looked at her friend and employer. "This is one time they're really out of line. They had best let us know what's going on. Christ, if Barney's hearing rumors, then you know other people in town are also. Imagine the panic if the tales get out of hand.''

"Why wouldn't they panic if we reported it in the paper?''

Kathy had a point, but Anna tried to frame an answer. "If we report it the right way, then people will at least know that there's a danger, but perhaps not a general danger. Maybe they will panic. Maybe they've got a right to panic a little.''

"That sounded like a crock of crap, Anna.''

"I know," she sighed. "I'm just baffled at the idea. Why here in Milbrook?''

"It has to be a wild rumor," Kathy said.

"I don't think so, Kathy. Tony was thrown for a real loop

when I asked him about the terrorist theory. He was downright evasive when I asked about the feds.''

"Want me to try to talk to Gil?" Kathy asked.

"If you can find him." She settled back down at the desk and again picked up the phone.

"What are you going to do?"

Anna was dialing the number. "I'm going to invite a man out on a luncheon date.''

No one answered the door at the Morton residence. In fact, when Whit rapped on the frail metal door, it opened a few inches by itself. Gil stood down in the yard of the mobile home; Watkins had gone around to cover the back.

"Whadaya think?" Whit asked.

Gil smiled. "Let's take a look inside. We could always say we got a prowler call and went there to check on it.''

Whit cringed. "Christ, I doubt we could get away with that. I'd hate to walk in and find some blockbuster piece of evidence which we couldn't use because of an illegal search.''

"Always by the book," Gil said, shaking his head at Whit's reticence. "At least take a peek inside. It's suspicious that the door's been left open.''

Whit used his foot to push it open. The day had grown noonday hot by that time, and the temperature in the metal-wrapped mobile home was even warmer. It rolled out to greet Whit. "Jesus, it's a wonder the place doesn't burn up from spontaneous combustion." He was peering into the gloomy living room.

Watkins came around from the back. "What the hell's goin' on here?"

"The door was open," Gil explained.

"Sure," Watkins said, smiling.

"It was. I mean, it wasn't even latched. When Whit knocked on it, it opened by itself.''

Watkins's smile turned into a chuckle. "Just like on TV.''

Whit stepped inside.

It surprised Gil, but before he could respond, the prosecutor's investigator reappeared. He was displaying a darkly stained paper towel. ''Looks like somebody got themselves hurt,'' he said.

''You wanna search the place?'' Watkins asked.

Whit shook his head. ''No, I guess we might as well try the address for Ringwald, the one we got from the phone book. I'm going to pull the door closed.''

Watkins was shocked. ''Christ, man, we might find some of the contraband from some of those burglaries in there. I think we at least ought to do a plain view-type search.''

Whit clicked the door closed. ''Too late,'' he said.

''Jesus fucking Christ, Whit.''

Whit came down the rickety steps. ''What the hell do you mean by a plain-view search?''

''Walk through just to see if there's anything out in the open. I think that'd be okay.''

But Whit was adamant. ''Like hell it would. We've got no search warrant and no grounds for a warrantless search. You go in there and find something, and it'll be useless to us. I'd just as soon come back later, when we can take the place apart—legally.''

Zeke glanced at the clock on the dash of Mickey's car. It read five o'clock. ''Your fuckin' clock don't work.''

Mickey held out his wristwatch for Zeke.

''It's only twenty till twelve. We oughta run around a few minutes first,'' Zeke said. ''No sense just goin' down there and just sittin', not in this gawdamn heat.''

''I wanna be there first,'' Mickey said.

''You ain't gonna pull nothing, are you? I mean, you said you weren't.''

Mickey shook his head. ''I just don't trust this sonuva-bitch. Maybe if we're there first, we can see trouble coming.''

''He ain't gonna mess with us,'' Zeke said. ''He wants the haul from that doctor's house. Imagine, guys. Maybe five grand apiece.''

"Shit," Mickey said. "No way he's gonna give us that much."

"If we steal it, he will," Zeke said.

From the backseat Bert said, "How do you know he ain't been holdin' back on us already, Zeke?"

The boy on the passenger side wrenched around in his seat. "You gotta whine all the time? I didn't notice you bitching the other day when I gave you that wad of green."

"I just meant—"

"Fuck what you meant."

A maze of low hills rested below the plateau on which Milbrook had developed. They were separated by hollows, some of which were inhabited and others of which remained about as remote as they had been when the eastern Indian nations had used the region as a sacred and common hunting ground. Rock Crusher Hollow wasn't populated, but a narrow surface-treated road wound its way about two and a half miles up the valley, coming to an abrupt end just beyond Rock Crusher Quarry. In years past it had been a major source for commercial gravel, but more than two decades earlier its owners had abandoned it for more productive and accessible sites.

Isolated as it was, the rocky terrain around the quarry had become a favorite breeding ground for the northern copperhead, a pit viper with a venom that, while rarely fatal, produced a great deal of discomfort. Occasionally kids still hiked to the quarry to examine the fossilized seashells that were visible in the exposed strata of rock. Over the years, though, the weeds had taken over to such a degree that few people braved the risk of snakebite to look at the imprints of small seashells.

The quarry was so overgrown that Mickey almost drove by it.

"Stop here," Zeke shouted. "This is the quarry."

Mickey started to argue until he saw the walls of shaved rock peeking through the tall vegetation. "Jesus, this place has changed," he said as he eased the car into what remained of a parking area.

Bumblebees flitted about the car as Mickey exited it. From that vantage point the place looked more like he remembered. He could see the high back ridge of the excavation. Zeke climbed out, too, and Ringwald followed.

"This place is creepy," Bert said.

The only sounds came from the ticking of the engine as it started to cool and the buzzing of the fat bees.

"Look there," Zeke cried.

Mickey, still on the driver's side, couldn't see what Zeke was pointing to, but Bert saw it. His eyes widened. "It's a gawdamn snake."

Mickey hurried around the car.

"Too late," Zeke said. "It crawled into the brush. Looked like a copperhead to me. Musta been sunning itself."

Bert shivered. "This place gives me the creeps. I hate snakes."

"Just stay out of the brush," Mickey said. He checked his watch. "It's ten till twelve. My old lady's probably biting her nails right now."

"Why?" Zeke asked.

"She's s'posed to go to work, and I got the car."

"What'll she do?" Bert asked.

Mickey shrugged. "Call a taxi, I guess."

The three of them were leaning against the passenger side of Mickey's car. Bert kept his eyes to the ground while his hands stayed busy swatting at the bees buzzing around them.

"Christ, it's hot," Zeke said, wiping the sweat from his brow.

Mickey glanced up at the ridge. He frowned. "I saw something shine up there." He pointed.

Zeke shielded his eyes and looked.

Mickey looked to his friend. "You see it?"

The left side of Zeke's skull exploded in Mickey's face. The blood and bits of skull blinded him. The noise hammered his eardrums. Bert and Zeke crumpled to the ground at the same time. Mickey, his eyes stinging, dived headfirst into the snake-infested brush.

TWENTY-TWO

"WHAT A DUMP," Watkins said.

His words also summed up the opinions of Whit and Gil Dickerson as the three men approached the residence of Wallace Ringwald. The house was on the eastern outskirts of Milbrook. A jungle of overgrown rosebushes and untrimmed pines concealed the bulk of the stucco structure. Broad-leaf weeds, some of them sporting intimidating spikes of thorns, had overtaken the small front yard.

"The place could use some landscaping," Gil said.

Whit was looking at the front door. It was open, and entry into the house was blocked only by a screen door with gaping holes torn in the mesh. They had parked the car about fifty yards down the road from the house and were approaching it on foot. As they drew closer, Whit could hear the sound of the television.

"Somebody's home," Whit said. "I guess we'd best use the same drill as before."

The city detective studied the thick vegetation surrounding the building. "I hope I can get around to the back."

"Watch out for predators," the sheriff said. "God knows what's lurking in that jungle."

Whit laughed, then said, "We'll give you a few minutes before—"

The screen door opened at that moment, and a tall waddling figure emerged. It was a man dressed in limp work pants and a sweat-stained white T-shirt.

"Who the fuck are you?" he shouted, glaring at the trio.

"Forget the back," Whit said.

With Whit in the lead, the men moved slowly into the unkempt yard. In his left hand Whit held up his badge. "My name's Whit Pynchon. I'm an investigator with the prosecutor's office."

"A cop?" the man asked, his puffy red face twisting into a look of obvious distaste.

"Yes, sir," Whit said. "This is Sheriff Dickerson and Detective Watkins. Are you Wallace Ringwald?"

"You got a warrant to come on my property?"

Whit glanced back at Gil, then to the man. "Why should I need one, Mr. Wallace? We just want to talk to Bert. Is he your son?"

The look of defiance fell away for an instant. "Bert? You here to see Bert?"

"If he's home."

The man's body jiggled as he came down the steps. To Whit, Wallace Ringwald looked like a man who lived on booze and a bad attitude. As red-faced as the man was, his arms and shoulders, exposed by the undershirt, resembled white bread dough. A ring of fat drooped over the man's pants waist and was clearly visible beneath the thin cotton of the shirt.

"Well, he ain't home," the man was saying, "and you've already walked past your welcome. I got no use for cops, and I don't want 'em on my property."

"It's pretty important that we talk to your son," Watkins said.

The man's eyes narrowed. "Not to me, it ain't."

"Don't you care why we want to talk to him?" Whit asked.

"I don't need to ask, mister. You wanna fuck with him. That's the problem with you cops. All you wanna do is harass folks."

A thin, gray-haired woman pushed open the tattered screen and came out onto the porch. "What's goin' on, Wally?"

He looked back. "Fuckin' cops. They're lookin' for Bertie."

The woman's face knitted with concern. "Has he done somethin' wrong?"

"We just need to talk to him, ma'am. I was telling—" Whit started to ease past Wallace Ringwald.

The man's beefy hand latched on to Whit's arm. "Done tol' you, asshole. You're not welcome on my property."

Whit jerked away. "Look, friend, I'm trying to be civil about this, but you're getting on my nerves. Why don't you just back off and let me talk to the woman there?"

"Why don't you go fuck yourself, pig?"

The man's body tensed as he prepared to make a move, but the woman shouted at him. "Wallace, you shut up. I want to hear what the man's got to say."

"Don't matter what it is," Ringwald said. "I don't want cops on my property."

The woman had moved down in the yard. "Well, it's my house, too, and I'm inviting him to have a cup of coffee. Maybe a cold glass of water. The others, too. If he's got something to say about Bert, I wanna hear it."

"Well, shit," Ringwald muttered. He turned and vanished into a narrow gap between two sprawling pines.

"I apologize for him, mister. He ain't been fit for human company since he lost his job."

"A miner?" Gil asked.

The woman shook her head. "Naw, but he might as well have been. He was an armature winder. Worked at Nichols Manufacturing. They made parts for mining equipment. When times got hard, they had to go outta business. You gentlemen wanna come up on the porch and talk? That noonday sun is mighty hot. Never seen a summer like this one."

"Do you know where Bert is?" Whit asked as they started toward the porch. Gil and Watkins followed.

She stopped and looked at him. "Are you askin' because you wanna know? Or because you already know and you think I oughta?"

"I need to talk to him, Mrs. Ringwald. I was hoping he might be here."

She just nodded. "He ain't. Left about an hour or so ago and said he was going over to that teen place, the one run by the Baptists."

Watkins snapped his fingers. "I never thought about looking there."

They had reached the bottom of the sagging steps that led up to the cluttered front porch. The woman started up them, but Whit held back. "I don't think we have time to visit, Mrs. Ringwald. Can I ask you a few questions?"

"What kind of trouble is the boy in?"

"Does he know a Mickey Moses and Ezekiel Morton?"

The woman reacted to the names with a shake of the head.

"He doesn't know them?" Whit asked.

"Oh, he knows 'em, mister. I was just shaking my head. Just last night I was tellin' Bertie that those two—the Morton boy especially—weren't nothin' but trouble."

"So he hangs around with them a lot?" Gil asked.

"I guess you could say so." Until that point her face had remained stoic, as if she were a woman who had surrendered already and now simply accepted whatever misfortune life dealt her. When the tears welled up in her eyes, she wiped them away quickly with the back of her hand.

"What's wrong?" Whit asked.

She pressed the palms of her rough hands against her eyes. "Don't mean to get weepy on you, but Bertie takes the brunt of his daddy's misery. He drinks . . . Bertie's daddy. 'Fore he lost his job it was just on the weekends. Now it's almost ever' night. Seems like he takes all his spite out on the boy. He's a good man . . . was a good man. Never so much as lifted his hand to me, but he's been mighty hard on the boy."

Watkins, standing behind Whit, tugged on the investigator's arm. "We oughta head on down to the teen center."

Whit nodded. "I know."

The woman took a deep breath. "Didn't mean to burden you with my worries. I was just wantin' to ask you somethin'."

"I'll answer if I can," Whit said.

"I guess you ain't gonna tell me what Bertie's gone and done, but if he is in trouble and if there's any way you can, could you maybe see that he gets some help growin' up? Lord knows he needs it, and he surely isn't getting any around here."

Mickey held his breath, waiting for another blast from the automatic weapon. From his position in the thick brush he could still see his mother's car. The day had turned still. Quiet as death, he thought. All he could hear was the occasional buzzing of one of the thumb-size bumblebees that flourished among the late summer wildflowers.

The killer had been above them on the rim of the quarry. Hidden in the green thicket of bramble bushes and milkweed, Mickey didn't think he could be seen even from the bluff above.

He lifted his head an inch or so. The car had maybe two dozen holes ripped along the driver's side. Streaks of blood, still wet and oozing, marred the blue surface. A chunk of Zeke's head, frothy pink and bloody with some white mixed in, rested on top of the car. Already flies had started to buzz around it. Mickey could see them, too. Worst of all, he could see Zeke and Bert, crumpled to the ground beside the car. For an instant after they had fallen, they had twitched and jerked. Mickey thought maybe they were alive, but within seconds both of them were still.

Stomach acid crept up into his throat. Before he could stop it, the puke followed. It splashed out on the ground in front of him as he retched. He coughed and gagged, trying to snatch a breath between spasms.

That's when he heard the voice. "You're gonna die, kid. Might as well show yourself."

He tried to swallow the vomit, but it kept coming.

"You can't hide forever," the man shouted. The killer was still up on the rim, hoping to get a clean shot from there.

Finally, the convulsions from his stomach eased. He

started to back away from the rancid puddle just inches from his face. The first bullet struck a little behind him.

"Oh, dear God!" he cried, surprised by how much he meant the cry.

Still on his belly, he scrambled forward through his own vomit. His heart throbbed as he wallowed his way through the wild berry bushes and brambles. The thorns ripped at his face. Any moment he expected to feel the impact of a bullet in his back. When the sharp pain stabbed his right hand, he knew for certain that he had been shot. He started to pull back the hand, but something snagged it. Through his tears he saw the brown snake, its fangs still buried in the fleshy web between his thumb and forefinger. Its cat eyes looked back at him.

Anna met Chief Hayden Wallace at Ketchum's Diner. The restaurant, which was close to the courthouse and city hall, provided a lunchtime gathering place for Milbrook's power structure. A number of county officeholders sat at some of the smaller tables. The owner of the establishment had placed a long table in the center of the room. By tradition, most of the attorneys who had offices near the courthouse assembled at that table.

By the time she arrived, the chief was already there. He stood at the center table, joking with some of the attorneys. When Anna came in, he smiled. "There's my date, boys. Y'all eat hearty."

The lawyers looked around and laughed. Anna tried not to blush, but the looks on the faces of the attorneys embarrassed her.

"I reserved us a small table over here," the chief said, guiding Anna to a rear corner of the restaurant.

"I should have suggested we go somewhere else," she said, still eyeing the cluster of attorneys.

"Don't worry 'bout them, Miss Tyree. You just pull out your notebook or somethin'. They'll think we're talking business." He pulled out her seat for her.

"Thank you. I'm not accustomed to such southern gallantry."

After she was seated, she opened her purse and pulled out her notepad. Wallace had walked around and was taking his seat. "I was just jokin' about the notebook."

"Actually, Chief, I did want to talk business."

Wallace leaned back in his chair. "No fair, Miss Tyree. I thought we were havin' a date."

"Then we're even," Anna said. "The last time we were here, it was you, I think, who was apologizing for trapping me by false pretenses."

"Touché. A point to you, Miss Tyree."

"How can you say that and make it sound so flirtatious?"

He laughed. "It's the only French word I know."

"No, I mean my name."

"Oh, you mean Miss Ty-ree. It's just such a good southern name. I love the way it sounds."

"From now on call me Anna. Did anyone ever tell you that you look and even sound a little like Clark Gable's Rhett Butler?"

He lifted an eyebrow. "How long's it been since you've seen *Gone With the Wind*?"

"Years. Why?"

"That movie's kinda popular down in Atlanta. If memory serves, Mr. Butler didn't have a very pronounced southern accent, my dear. Nor was he a very loyal southerner."

"Come to think of it, you're right."

"No matter, Miss Tyree . . . uh, I mean, Anna. I take the comparison as a compliment."

A waitress appeared. Wallace ordered a piece of pie and coffee.

"Is that all you're going to eat?" Anna asked.

He grinned. "Actually, I was planning on a second piece of pie. I love apple pie."

Anna ordered a club sandwich.

"Let's get this business of yours out of the way, Anna. Fire away."

Anna opened her notebook. "I want to know about this terrorist bombing in Milbrook."

TWENTY-THREE

AT FIRST the pain hadn't been as bad as Mickey had expected, no worse than a bad bee sting. The sight of the reptile, its fangs still snagged in his skin, had brought on another wave of nausea, but Mickey had managed to hold it back until the snake let go. Then it started to coil. Mickey pulled back. The copperhead, concerned with nothing more than its survival, took the opportunity to slither away into the bush.

The man on the rim had stopped shouting, and in the moments after the snake's attack Mickey had heard him moving around the edge of the quarry and down toward the road. Afraid even to budge, he stayed on the ground, listening to the footsteps as they moved first away from and then back toward him. As he listened, he stared at the puncture marks on his hand. At first they had looked like pinpricks, but with each passing moment he could feel the discomfort intensifying. The area around the bite had started to swell and bruise. The pain, surprisingly mild at first, became a throb that radiated from his hand to his elbow.

Mickey, sprawled in the bush, reeking of his own vomit, started to cry softly.

The killer starting shouting again. "C'mon, kid. Show yourself. You know you're not gonna get away. I can't let that happen."

The boy scanned the dense stands of vegetation, looking for some way to work his way into deeper cover. At the same time he also looked for copperheads between the clumps of foliage. His stricken arm quivered, and the throbbing had already traveled up to his shoulder. At that moment it seemed as if the only choice he had was in the way he was going to die. Snakebite, though slow and maybe agonizing, seemed preferable to the certainty of the automatic weapon the killer was carrying.

He could hear the man's feet now as they crunched across the gravel berm of the road. Dragging his right arm, Mickey used his left to pull himself between two thick stands of grass.

The thunder from the automatic came at once. The bullets whirred above his head, some of them whining as they ricocheted off the quarry's rock face.

"Jesus," he cried, his voice muffled by the gun's roar.

The shooting ended. Mickey pressed himself tightly against the ground.

"You still alive?" the killer shouted.

When Mickey dared to lift his head, he saw it, not two feet in front of him. Another snake. Maybe the same snake? He froze. The snake, stretched out across the gap in the underbrush, was frozen, too.

The boy stared at it, then sagged in relief.

This time his snake proved to be a thick tree branch. He could hear the killer moving back and forth in the gravel. With his good hand he reached out and retrieved the stick. If nothing else, he could use it to probe his way deeper into the cover in the quarry's basin. The stems of the thicket started to sway as the afternoon breeze picked up.

Mickey realized it might be the only chance he would get. With the entire meadow moving this way and that in the gentle wind, his own movement would be concealed. The swelling, following the same pattern as the pain, had started to spread above his wrist, and he was beginning to feel dizzy. Best make a move while he still could. With the stick as his only defense, he managed to get to his knees, then to a squatting position. The breeze came and went, so he waited for it to come again. When it did, he made a crouched dash toward the rear of the quarry and the even denser cover it offered.

The killer must have seen or heard something. He unleashed another barrage of fire, this time strafing from one side of the quarry to the other.

"Where'd you hear that?" Wallace asked, the smile still on his face but the humor gone.

"Police officers are just like everyone else, Chief. They love to share inside information. If we do have terrorists operating in Milbrook, don't you think the public has a right to know?"

The chief's smile vanished. "It's just a theory. Not my theory, either. It's something Pynchon cooked up. I haven't seen any evidence that he's right, Miss Tyree."

"I thought we'd settled on Anna."

He shrugged. "Miss Tyree seems more appropriate right now."

"Will you give me the details off the record?" she asked.

Before he could answer, a familiar voice interrupted. "Since when did you ever go off the record? I thought it was against your policy."

Anna looked up and found Tony Danton standing three feet from the table. "Since when did you start sneaking up on people and eavesdropping?"

"I was just coming over to talk to Chief Wallace."

The chief stood. "I'm on my lunch break, Mr. Prosecutor."

"Me, too," Tony said, grinning. "Mind if I join you?"

Anna certainly minded, but what could she say? Given the look on the chief's face, he minded, too. Both of them, however, said that they did not.

"We've ordered already," Anna said.

The waitress brought Tony a glass of water and asked, "The usual?"

He nodded to her just as Anna said, "I was just asking the chief about some rather unsettling rumors I've heard."

Tony leaned back in his chair. "What would you newspaper people do without gossip? You should know by now that most rumors are just products of someone's imagination."

"Sort through enough rumors, Tony, and you usually find a few grains of truth. I was asking the chief about the rumors regarding the terrorists. I did come to you about them first, Tony. Remember? It was just a short time ago."

"And I told you no comment."

Anna looked to the chief. He was checking his watch. "I may have to pass on that piece of pie, Miss Tyree. I have another matter—"

"Just a minute," Anna said. "You indicated this morning that there will be arrests."

"I didn't say that," Wallace countered.

"Yes, you did. Or at least you implied it. If I remember correctly, you said that this whole mess might be cleared up pretty soon."

"But I didn't mention definite arrests, Miss Tyree."

Before Anna could unleash her frustration, the waitress appeared with their lunch. Wallace used it as an opportunity to escape. He pulled a handful of bills from his pocket and handed it to the waitress. "Sorry, hon, I gotta run. Take all three lunches outta this." He rose to leave.

"Want me to fix the pie so you can take it with you?"

"Naw, I forgot about my diet."

"Before you leave, Chief," Anna said, preparing to play her ace in the hole, "you should know that I'm planning to run a story tomorrow reporting the rumor about the terrorists."

Wallace's grin spread from ear to ear. "I don't think you're that stupid, Miss Tyree. I think you're just tryin' to bait me."

"That son of a bitch," Anna said once he was out of the restaurant.

Tony reached out and snagged the piece of pie. "Wanna share? No sense letting it go to waste."

Anna didn't even bother to respond to his offer. "Do you think I'm bluffing, Tony?"

The prosecutor took a bite of the pie before he answered. "I dunno, Anna. I've known you to do things that I wouldn't have thought you would do. All I can tell you is that we have things in hand. The chief may be right. We might settle this whole thing very soon. That's when you'll get your story."

"Where is Whit?"

"Working," Tony said before shoveling another generous portion of pie into his mouth.

A sturdy afternoon breeze, perhaps the harbinger of another spate of evening thunderstorms, provided a welcome relief from the stagnant heat. The temperature remained in the mid-nineties, but with the wind blowing it didn't quite seem so hot as Whit, Gil, and Terry Watkins exited the teen center.

"What now?" Watkins asked.

The trio moved slowly toward Gil's cruiser.

"We've got a description of the Moses vehicle," Whit said. "Let's issue a B.O.L.O. Maybe somebody will spot it. We need to get our hands on those kids."

Even before they reached the vehicle, they could hear the voice on the radio. The county dispatcher was trying to reach the sheriff.

"Unit One to county," Gil said into the mike. "Please repeat your traffic."

"Ten four, Unit One. Is Mr. Pynchon with you?"

"Ten four, County. Right here."

"Be advised that a Mrs. Ringwald has been trying to reach him. She wants to see him."

"Bingo," Whit exclaimed. "Maybe her son's home."

"Is there more to the message?" Gil asked of the dispatcher.

"Negative, Sheriff. That was all she said. I asked for her address, and she said that Mr. Pynchon knew where to find her."

Gil signed off. "Let's roll."

Whit, though, had other ideas. "I'm going alone. We'll drive back to the courthouse, and I'll get my car."

"But what if all three kids are there?" Watkins asked. "You oughta have some backup."

Whit was already climbing into the car. "I don't think the boys are back, Terry. I think she just wants to talk. Don't ask me why. It's just a feeling. I think I can get more out of her if I'm alone. You go on back with Gil and get that B.O.L.O. issued on the Moses car."

"What should I say to do if someone spots it?"

"Pull it over and notify one of us."

A few minutes later Whit was back at the home of Bert Ringwald. Bert's mother must have been watching for him. Just as soon as he pulled to a stop in front of the house, she stepped out on the porch.

"Is Bert home now?" Whit asked as he approached the porch.

"No, but after you left I got to thinking. The boy's been actin' mighty strange lately. I figured it was 'cause of his daddy."

Whit wondered about the whereabouts of Ringwald's father. "Is your husband still here?"

"He's gone to town. He needed some more cigarettes, he said. Like as not, he's gone to the likker store. Anyway, like I said before, I got to thinking, and I went to Bertie's room and kinda looked through it."

Whit was up on the porch now. The woman took a seat in a weathered wooden rocker. She motioned Whit to an old kitchen chair that sat beside it.

"I think kids has got as much right to their privacy as grown-ups," she was saying. "I ain't never prowled through Bertie's stuff before."

"Did you find anything?" Whit asked, hoping to move the woman along.

"Hold your horses, mister. Anyways, I didn't dig back

into the closets or nothin' like that, but I did kinda look through his bureau drawers.''

She reached into the large pocket of the apron she wore and withdrew a fistful of rolled-up money. "Found this, mister. My boy's got no legal way to get this much money. Fact is, there ain't been this much money in this whole family for a long time. Almost three hundred dollars here. He ain't been selling dope, has he?''

She still held the money in her hand.

"I have no evidence of that,'' Whit said. "That's about all I can tell you.''

She displayed the roll of currency again. "These here's new bills, crisp and crinkly. Where would Bertie get near three hundred in new money if he ain't selling drugs?''

Whit decided that he could use the woman's full cooperation, so he answered her question. "I think he's been breaking into houses, Mrs. Ringwald.''

The woman started to rock back and forth. Her eyes again glistened with tears. "I been hearing about all these break-ins on the TV news. Never thought much about 'em. Folks like us don't get robbed too often. Nothing much to take.''

"Has Bert been out a lot at night?''

She nodded. "Figured he was just staying out so he wouldn't cross his daddy.''

"Would you give me consent to search his room, Mrs. Ringwald?''

This time the woman firmly shook her head. "Can't do that, mister. Not without first talking to Bert. I've been doin' a lotta thinking. Bert's probably gonna need a lawyer. Reckon this money might be enough to hire one?''

Whit sighed. "Mrs. Ringwald, that money is more than likely evidence of a crime.''

"You prove that?'' she asked.

"Not at this time. However, you can rest assured that the court will appoint a lawyer for Bert if you and Mr. Ringwald can't afford one.''

She stuffed the money back into her apron. "Seems to me

like Bert's got enough money to afford his own. Besides, I've always been one to believe that you get what you pay for. A free lawyer couldn't be a good lawyer.''

''That's not always the case, Mrs. Ringwald. You might even get the same lawyer appointed that you planned to hire.''

For the very first time since he had met her, he saw her smile. She pushed herself up from the chair. ''Thanks for comin' back to talk to me.''

''Will you notify me when Bert comes home?'' he asked as he, too, rose.

''Gonna talk to a lawyer first. If he says call you, then I'll call you.''

''In that case, Mrs. Ringwald, I might be forced to have a unit maintain surveillance on your house.''

''You mean keep a watch on the place?''

''Yes, ma'am.''

''So be it,'' she said.

Whit started down the steps, but she kept talking. ''But Mr. Ringwald ain't gonna like that at all.''

TWENTY-FOUR

IN THE DEEPER recesses of the quarry the foliage had thinned somewhat as older, taller plants had shaded the ground from the sun. The quarry itself faced east, which meant that its back wall also shaded the ground just beneath it after the sun reached its midday zenith. Finally, the earth itself was more rocky in that area of the quarry floor, making it difficult for many plants to gain a roothold.

Mickey managed to get within ten yards of the carved rock face at the rear of the quarry before he was forced to stop. He found himself at the edge of a pool of black stagnant water. During the strafing of the quarry several rounds had struck so close to Mickey that they had showered him with sand and rock, but he hadn't been hit. For the last ten or so yards he had felt reasonably safe standing more upright. Looking back over his shoulder, Mickey couldn't see the car or the killer, but the man hadn't left. In fact, a few minutes earlier the killer had moved into the thicket in search of Mickey, telling the boy that he was coming in after him.

The pain in his arm continued to get worse. His other arm and both his feet were also tingling, and he was sweating buckets. His head reeled, and he needed something to drink. Not the dark water in the pool, though. He wasn't that thirsty yet. His entire right hand had turned dark blue. The skin around the fang marks actually looked black, and clear fluid oozed from the two punctures. The hand was about twice the size it had been, and the swelling was already up to his elbow.

He remembered a TV program he had seen once about snakebites. Copperhead bites usually weren't deadly, but that was because people got treatment. Mickey saw no chance to get treatment. If the torment became much worse, he might reconsider his choice. Maybe it would be better to die from a bullet.

Behind him he could hear the man as he moved slowly through the undergrowth. Mickey's eyes scanned the rock wall behind the narrow pool of water. He saw no place to hide. If he couldn't find some way out of the quarry and into the woods, the killer would surely find him. The woods were closest on the same side the man was searching. He decided to try to move the other way.

"I hear you," the killer shouted. "I'm not gonna waste any more rounds until I've got you in my sights. Then you're one dead son of a bitch."

Mickey clenched his teeth against the spreading agony and moved away from the man's voice and toward the woods. They were a long way off, though. At least he could see the ground in front of him, and he had managed to hang on to the stick.

"Was it your girlfriend I blew to pieces last night?" the man shouted.

"Bastard," Mickey mumbled as he moved along the edge of the pool.

"Are you Mickey?"

If only he could get a chance to see him—and live, of course. The man seemed to be gaining ground on him. His words were clearer, the sound of him moving through the foliage louder.

"Might as well answer me, kid. I can hear your footsteps."

"Go to hell," Mickey cried, no longer able to tolerate the smug taunting.

The killer laughed. "I knew you were still alive. Maybe we can make a deal."

"Why did you kill them?" Mickey asked.

"The cops are on to you, kid. I couldn't have you talking."

Mickey continued to move as he talked. He also kept a close watch on the ground ahead of him. "But I can't tell them anything. I don't know who you are."

The man laughed. "Sure you don't."

"I swear to God, mister, I don't."

"Are you trying to tell me that Zeke never told you?"

"He didn't. I swear it. Bert or me didn't know."

"Wish I could believe that."

"It's true," Mickey said.

The automatic came to life again. The path of fire drove Mickey back into the pool. He sank to his knees in the stagnant pond as the large rounds kicked up sparks in the rocky earth where he had stood.

But the firing stopped abruptly. Immediately Mickey heard a strangled cry.

"Gawdamn," the killer bellowed.

Mickey kept quiet.

"Oh, sweet Jesus." The man sounded hurt, as if maybe he had somehow shot himself. Or twisted an ankle, maybe. Or—

The copperheads! Maybe the killer had been bitten.

"Did one of 'em get you?" Mickey shouted, almost gleeful.

"Fuck!" the man screamed. "Fuck! Fuck! Fuck!"

"You're gonna die, too, mister."

"I saw it," the man shouted. "I mean I saw the snake, but what kind is it, kid? I just saw it strike . . . just a blur."

"A fuckin' rattlesnake," Mickey lied. "This place is crawlin' with them."

He heard the man gasp, then say, "I didn't hear a rattle."

"You were firing that fuckin' cannon."

The man didn't say anything else. The next thing Mickey heard were footsteps moving away from him. He started to chase after the sounds to try to get a good look at the man, but his head started to spin as he waded out of the pond. The quarry wall, the tall vegetation . . . they were turning in circles. Then the world went black.

The last thing Whit expected to see as he entered his office was Anna Tyree. She was sitting on his couch, flipping through one of the Myrtle Beach real-estate magazines that Whit regularly received.

"To what do I owe the pleasure?" he said. He carried a handful of phone messages that he tossed onto the desk. Then he dropped down on the couch beside her.

"How's the arm?"

"Sore as hell."

"What happened to the sling?"

"It's in the car. God, I'm bushed." He leaned his head on the back of the plastic couch.

"I guess I would be wasting my breath to suggest that you go home and get a few hours sleep. You look like hell."

He smiled. "Gee, thanks."

"You still have smudges on your face from last night. Have you rested at all?"

"I haven't had time to rest, and if I sit here too long, I won't be able to get back up. Every muscle in my body is starting to stiffen up."

"I came here to harass you until you surrendered and gave me some background on that bombing." She reached over and took his hand. "But you look so pitiful."

"Couldn't tell you much, anyway," Whit said.

She stroked his hand. "You could tell me about the terrorists."

Whit opened one eye and looked at her. "What terrorists?"

"The ones who planted that bomb last night."

Whit sighed. "We don't know that the bomb was planted by terrorists. Besides, I'm not sure that's the right word to use, anyway. Fanatics might be more appropriate."

Anna decided to push a little harder. "So there is some truth to the rumors?"

"Some," Whit said. He sat up and started to massage his temples. The pain made him grimace as he attempted to move his right arm.

"Go over and get in your desk chair. I'll do it for you."

He pushed himself up from the couch and moved slowly around the desk.

"Jesus, Whit. You're walking like an old man."

"I feel like an old man. If I slow down at all, I get so damned stiff." He eased himself down into his chair.

Anna went behind him and started to massage his temples. "I don't want to make a habit of this."

He laughed. "I don't want to make a habit of getting blown across a street."

As she looked down at him, her gaze settled on the wide scab on his left cheek. "You don't know how lucky you are."

He had his eyes closed, savoring the relaxing action of Anna's hands. "Oh, yes, I do. I saw them putting the pieces of the Benning family in body bags. Jesus, Anna. I can't imagine people who care so little for human life. I thought I'd seen it all in this business, but when I think I've seen the worst, something comes along to top it. After this one's over with, I'm going to seriously consider getting out of this."

"Oh, Whit—"

"I know. I know. You've heard that song and dance before, but this time it's different. Even if I don't go south, I still might give up this job. After a while you get so damned cynical. When I pass the most innocent-looking person on the street, I find myself wondering who he or she brutalized the night before. Or what they might have stolen that day. I'm tired of living day in and day out with the dark side of life."

"You're just exhausted."

He eased away from her touch. "Thanks. That felt great, but I guess I'd better get to work."

"Can you tell me what's going on?" Anna said.

He nodded.

Anna blinked, certain that her eyes were deceiving her. "You mean it? You'll tell me?"

"I'm going to ask you to keep parts of it off the record, though."

The look of pleasant surprise vanished. "I don't think I can make any promises."

"I don't want promises," Whit said. "I'm going to tell you what I know. You and Kathy decide what should be printed."

She moved around and settled back down on the couch. "What's the gimmick?"

"No gimmick, Anna."

"Why so cooperative?"

He reached over and picked up the pieces of pink paper that he had tossed on his desk as he had entered his office. "These are phone messages, all of them from television stations. Reporters are on their way down here from Charleston, Beckley, and Bluefield."

"And you're going to give them the story, too."

Whit slowly shook his head.

Anna frowned. "You're not?"

"Fuck 'em," Whit said. "I cannot abide small-time TV newspeople."

"I know your opinion about them, but you know someone's bound to say that you're playing favorites because—"

"Save your breath, Anna. This might well be my swan song, and I just don't give a damn anymore. Let them bitch."

"I'm sure Tony or someone else will talk to them."

"Like I said, Anna, I don't give a damn. Tony can talk to them. Bubba Wallace can talk to them. Or they can read about it tomorrow in your paper. I do not care."

Basil Thompson counted heads. It was the second time in five minutes. Both times he came up with nine. The goats were gathered closely together, grazing in the shade of the tall oak. It was the only tree that he had left standing when he had cleared the steep hillside some fifteen years earlier.

The old man was standing on his back porch, looking up at the small herd. The sun, well past its midday high point, forced him to squint. For sure, two of his animals were missing, but from this distance, with the sun in his eyes, he couldn't tell which ones.

He turned back to the house and opened the screen door. "Ma, we're two goats short. I'm gonna go check on 'em."

His wife was in the living room, ensconced in front of the television, watching the afternoon soaps. Basil had always made fun of his wife in years past for her devotion to them, but since his retirement he, too, had become a fan.

"You're gonna miss the ending of the show," she called back.

"Gotta check on the goats." He crossed the living room and pulled a shotgun from its resting place against the stone fireplace. "I still say that was a damned coyote I saw the other day. Fellow from over in Monroe County says they're getting to be a real problem over his way. They just hired a professional hunter of some kind just over the border in Tazewell County."

"Don't go shootin' your foot off."

"I'll be careful."

"And be careful you don't shoot somebody's pet dog."

"If somebody's pet dog is killin' my goats, it oughta be shot."

Basil's property, nestled on both sides of the dirt road that split Thompson Hollow, had never been much good for real farming. He had stayed there because it was his home place. It had been in the family since the Civil War, and Basil wasn't going to be the one to break tradition. As it turned out, it hadn't mattered much. He and his wife had never had kids. Once they passed on, he planned to leave it to his wife's fifteen-year-old niece. She could do with it what she wanted.

His father had mined coal, and so, too, had Basil until he retired. There was room for a small garden on the field across the road, but the rest of the property was pretty much nothing but rock and steep hillside. Goats, surefooted if somewhat smelly, were about the only thing that would flourish on the terrain.

Though well past seventy, Basil had no problem ascending the steep, rocky slope. He hadn't yet spent a single day in a hospital and felt as good now as he had twenty years earlier. As he approached them, the goats lifted their heads and started wagging their short tails.

"How's my babies today?" He wandered among them, taking stock and speaking to each one.

When he was finished, a scowl formed on his face. His best stud ram was missing, along with a young female. He doubted they were off anywhere sparking. For one thing, the fenced area had been well cleared. What he hadn't cut down had been consumed by the ravenous goats. The vegetation that tried to reseed itself met the same quick demise.

Basil had discovered early on that goats had a sixth sense about getting out of fences. Most of the time they were content within their spacious confines, but every now and then one of them got headstrong and somehow managed to escape.

"They like to bamboozle you," Basil would say, loving to tell the story. "Never seen one of 'em escape with my own eyes, and only once have I figured out how it happened. They're almost spooky that way."

Basil, his jaw set, started toward the top of the ridge. The muggy afternoon heat brought sweat to his face, but he wasn't even breathing hard when he reached the top and looked down the other side into Rock Crusher Hollow. At first he didn't see anything. Then he lifted his eyes from the thick blanket of green vegetation that swept down toward the quarry itself.

"Damned coyotes. I knew it," he said aloud, his angry gaze now locked on the half dozen turkey buzzards that circled in the hazy white sky.

TWENTY-FIVE

"THIS ISN'T the first time these right-wing militaristic groups have shown up here," Anna said.

Whit, who had been telling Anna about his conversation with the FBI, looked surprised. "It's the first time I've heard about them."

"That's because you don't read the papers."

"Well, yeah, I guess that's true."

"One of these groups was talking about establishing a training camp in West Virginia. Senator Rockefeller sought passage of a bill in Congress that would have made paramilitary training camps illegal."

"Come to think of it, I do remember that," Whit said.

"They give me the chills. They like places such as West Virginia. They can find secluded sites where they can shoot their guns and teach their kids to hate."

"Well, there's no evidence they're doing that here," Whit said. "According to the FBI guy, it's probably just one person who came to organize the burglary ring. All they want from Milbrook is to add to their supply of untraceable weapons."

"But why bomb the Bennings' house? They haven't bombed any of the other houses they've burglarized."

Whit again flinched with pain as he leaned forward in his chair. "I do really want this off the record, Anna. People's lives may be endangered."

She held up her right hand. "Scout's honor."

"Were you in the Girl Scouts?"

"You've got to be kidding, but I promise anyway."

"They bombed the house to kill the Benning daughter. It looks like she managed to solve the case ahead of us."

"How?"

"A boy she knew, perhaps was even dating, had been asking her about her father's guns. If he had any. Where he kept them. That sort of thing. Her father got a good enough look at his assailant to say that he was a very small person. Apparently, based on those things, the Benning girl suspected that this boyfriend was involved. He and his friends aren't all-American boys, and one of his friends is a very small person."

"Did she tell her boyfriend about her suspicions?"

Whit nodded.

"Did she tell you?"

"Nope. I could tell she was withholding something, but she wouldn't talk to me. I don't know whether it was because of the boy. Maybe she was afraid. God knows, it appears she had reason to be."

Anna stood and started a slow pacing in his small office. "So how did you find out?"

"Janice Benning had confided her suspicions to a girl-friend, who just happens to be Terry Watkins's daughter."

"Watkins? The city detective?"

"We've been out all morning trying to find the boys. We have three names, but so far we've come up empty-handed."

"Is the Watkins girl safe?"

"As long as the boys don't find out that she knows. Actually, I think she'll be safe even then. They'll know we're after them if any of them go home. We've talked to the parents of two of them. Since the Watkins girl isn't a witness in any way, there's no reason for them to hurt her."

Anna settled on the corner of Whit's desk. "If these guys are tied up with one of these hate groups, they won't need a reason to kill. Are they juveniles?"

"Oh, yeah, and that makes it even more of a bitch."

"Are they skinheads?"

Whit frowned at the term. "What the hell is that?"

"Jesus, Whit. You know there are times when your distaste for news makes you downright ignorant."

He had to laugh. "And sometimes ignorance is a blessed state. What the hell is a skinhead?"

"Kids who have swastikas tattooed on their arms and who hate anyone who isn't a WASP—a white Anglo-Saxon Protestant."

"I know what a WASP is."

"They shave their heads as an obvious display of their political inclinations."

"I don't think these kids are anything but two-bit hooligans out to make a quick buck or maybe buy drugs."

"Do you think they planted the bomb?"

Whit pushed himself to his feet. "If they did, someone else was the mastermind."

Tony Danton came into Whit's office. "You still trying to dig out a story?" he said to Anna.

"Nope. I've got it," she said.

Tony looked from her to Whit, then back again. "What do you mean?"

"She means," Whit said, "that I've filled her in on it."

"You what?" Tony said.

"I gave her the story we got from the feds."

Anna gathered up her purse. "Well, guys, I have to run."

"Just a minute," Tony said.

"Got a story to write," she said. She paused at the door. "Seriously, Whit, if you don't get some rest, you're going to be totally useless. You might try some aspirin for those muscle aches."

Tony was still glaring at Whit. "I think you've already suffered some kind of breakdown. You of all people should have . . . I mean, Christ, you were the last person I thought would give this to the press. Do you know she had Wallace down at the diner at lunch, trying to charm it out of him? Even he had enough sense to keep his mouth shut."

"I did it on purpose, Tony."

The prosecutor threw up his hands. "So tell me something I don't know. I gather you did it on purpose. I just can't figure out why."

"To bring this to an end."

Tony threw up his hands for a second time, his frustration growing. "Pardon my ignorance! It's all crystal-clear to me now. God, how could I have been so stupid? Anna writes about it in the paper tomorrow, and everyone lives happily ever after."

"Ease up, Tony."

"You go to hell, Whit. Once, just once, I wish to God that you would consult with me before doing one of your outlandish tricks. After all, I am the prosecutor. I was the one elected. I'm the one that takes the heat."

"Get down off your high horse, Tony. I don't need any lectures."

"Just what the hell do you need, Whit?"

Whit dropped back into his chair. "A good night's sleep and a couple of aspirins."

"Oh, is that it? I guess you're pleading some form of diminished capacity."

Whit shook his head. "No, I'm not. You asked what I needed, and I told you. I could also use about a minute of your time to explain, but frankly I really don't give a damn whether you want to hear it or not."

Tony's face turned a bloody crimson. He started to say something, then decided against it. Instead, he went to the couch, dropped down on it, and then said, "So explain."

Basil Thompson fully expected to find the bloody, gutted carcasses of his goats beneath the flight pattern of the turkey buzzards. It wouldn't be the first time. Over the twenty years he had raised the animals, he had lost maybe a dozen or so. Three or four had simply vanished. Those, he figured, had been stolen by human rustlers. The remaining animals had been killed, usually by a dog. Folks lived both above him and below him in the hollow, and nearly all of them kept at least one dog. Human behavior continued to amaze Basil. Dogs had their place, and he certainly didn't hate them. On the other hand, he didn't let them sleep in his house, much less in his bed. The worst sheep-killing dog in his memory had been a big shaggy mutt of mixed breed called Doofus or something like that. It had belonged to the two kids who had grown up in the house about a quarter of a mile up the hollow. Basil had had all the evidence any reasonable person would want as to the dog's guilt, but the kids' father had refused to listen.

"That animal wouldn't kill a flea," the man had said. "He sleeps with my kids."

Basil had wanted to beat the daylights out of the fool. Instead, he had said, "Well, I hope it don't eat your kids."

He had been on the verge of going to the animal-control people, but Doofus had several nasty habits. Besides killing sheep, he also liked to chase cars. One day good ol' Doofus tangled with the front wheels of the mailman's car. It happened in sight of Basil's house, and he actually cheered when he saw the dog's skull flattened out in the dust of the road. In Basil's mind it proved the existence of a good and just God.

He had moved halfway down the hillside and still had not reached the site over which the buzzards continued to rotate. They were lower now, and two had vanished altogether. Those two, probably the youngest and most daring, were already on the ground pecking at the ravaged flesh of his goats. He didn't hurry, though. No reason to when buzzards circled. Besides, the forest was thick, and the ground was rocky. He carried the loaded gun at his side, avoiding the temptation to use it as a walking stick. That practice had killed many a man. More than that, a fellow walking along the ridges of this particular hollow stood a good chance of meeting a copperhead or even a timber rattler. Basil had blown the heads off more than two dozen, and he still felt the hackles on the back of his neck rise whenever he saw one on the forest floor.

He'd heard of dead ones that still managed to bite. In his book the only good snake was a headless one.

The quarry itself wasn't straight over the hill from Basil's place. In fact, it was about a half mile on the diagonal. As Basil paused to judge his progress, he came to the conclusion that the buzzards were just about plumb on top of the quarry itself.

"Damn coyotes," he muttered. Basil didn't like going to the old quarry. Some people claimed to have seen strange things around the place. Not that Basil believed much in ghosts, but a man who believed in God, as Basil did, certainly had to believe in Satan. If you believed in the devil, then ghosts and demons and such weren't beyond the realm of the possible. For a long time after it had ceased operations, the quarry itself had been a popular gathering place for kids who wanted to screw around. In those days it wasn't unusual to visit the quarry on a Saturday or Sunday morning and see a half dozen used prophylactics.

Over time, though, Mother Nature had regained her claim to the quarry. The snakes had taken it over, again mostly copperheads, but some of the biggest Basil had ever seen. When that many of the creeping, slithering bastards came together in one location, it was a place to avoid. Even that day he didn't plan to go down into the quarry itself. No damned way. He would go to the rim and look in. If his goats were down there, the buzzards could have them.

A single buzzard remained in the sky as Basil neared the abandoned excavation. The white haze had thickened into actual clouds, and a breeze carried the smell of rain. He quickened his pace as he neared the edge of the quarry. He didn't want to be caught that far from home in a rainstorm.

The gouged-out cavity of the quarry came slowly into his view as he worked his way through the thickening undergrowth along the rim. When he pushed his way out of the wall of weeds, Basil Thompson gasped. For the first time in his life he set the stock of the shotgun on the ground and used it to brace himself.

Two buzzards sat on the hood of a blue car. Their compatriots were on the ground, feeding. Basil's eyes hadn't fared as well as the rest of his body, but he didn't need his eyeglasses to see what they were eating. One of the coal-black birds pulled out a long rope of bloody intestine. Even at that distance it made Basil gag. He bent forward in case he vomited. There, some thirty feet below him, was another body. The buzzards hadn't found it yet. Either that or it wasn't—

Basil jumped when the body started to move.

TWENTY-SIX

"I WANT THOSE BOYS, Tony, but I want the person or persons behind them even more."

"And just how is the publicity going to accomplish that?" Tony asked of his investigator.

Whit could feel the muscles in his back tightening. He pushed himself up from his chair and leaned back as far as the pain would allow. "If these jerks—the ones in charge— know that we're on to them, then they'll go after the boys. From what the FBI told me, they don't leave witnesses behind."

Whit's words transformed Tony's anger into disbelief. "You don't mean you're going to use those boys as bait?"

"In a way, that's exactly what I have in mind."

"My God, Whit, they're juveniles, for God's sakes." Tony jumped to his feet. "I think you'd better go home and get some rest. No, on second thought maybe you'd better go back to the hospital. I think maybe you've got a screw or two loose."

"Dammit, Tony, we can protect those boys."

"Bullshit. It's a risk I'm not willing to take."

Whit had another card to play. "I bet the FBI wouldn't object."

"You may be my friend, Whit, but so help me, if you try to bring them in on any sort of plan that involves risking those boys, I'll fire you on the spot. I can't believe you would even suggest such a thing."

Until that point Whit had managed to control his anger.

For one thing, he knew just how unorthodox his idea was. He had expected Tony to resist. "Hear me out, Tony. I don't have all the details worked out, but—"

"No way, Whit. I don't even want to hear any more."

"Be sensible, Tony. If we get the boys, we can talk them into fingering the head man. You know that. I know that. Whoever the people behind this might be, they know that, also. If we do manage to get those boys in custody, then they will be targets automatically. I don't have to remind you that the juvenile detention center isn't Fort Knox. They'll be sitting ducks out there."

"We can stash them somewhere safe," Tony said. Whit's argument was beginning to make a sort of damnable sense to the attorney. "In this case, the judge might even allow us to use the jail."

"It doesn't matter. These right-wing nuts will still have to come after them, somehow or some way. They have no choice."

Tony was shaking his head, now not so much in denial as in exasperation. "I don't quite understand this, Whit. Surely these burglary rings have been busted before. I don't recall reading about too many jail sieges by these assholes."

"That's because the people who could identify them were killed before they were arrested. They do not leave witnesses behind. If we can get the kids into custody before Anna's story breaks, then we've got a chance to draw these bastards into a trap. You do want me to go after the boys, don't you?"

"Of course."

"Then I had better get busy. If we don't find them, they'll be sitting ducks come tomorrow morning."

"Thanks to you," Tony said, still infuriated with his friend.

"I'm counting on finding them, Tony."

"How do you know they haven't rabbited already?"

"I guarantee they haven't."

"You do?"

"Absolutely. Bert Ringwald left a three-hundred-dollar

bankroll at his house. If they were going on the lam, he would have taken the money. They're still around. Watkins has an officer watching Moses's house, and Gil's men are maintaining a discreet surveillance on the homes of the other two boys.''

"There are always telephones," Tony said. "One of them might call home and find out you've been there looking for him."

"We'll have to live with that chance. Besides, now that we know who these kids are, I bet we have them in custody by tonight. Maybe by that time I can come up with some kind of plan that you'll accept."

"Don't count on it, Whit."

When Anna returned to the *Daily Journal*, she bypassed the newsroom and went straight to Kathy Binder's office. The publisher was studying a new circulation report.

"I've got the story," Anna said.

"I hope you didn't have to go to bed with Wallace to get it," Kathy said, the tone of her voice clearly transmitting her displeasure.

"For your information, I didn't get it from Chief Wallace. He clammed up. I got it straight from the horse's mouth."

"From Whit?" Kathy said, dropping back into her chair.

"Absolutely, and it's going to shock you."

Kathy closed the report. "If Whit gave you a story, I'm already shocked."

Anna sat down to tell Kathy the story. "Yesterday a man was gunned down outside the federal building in Raleigh, North Carolina. The killer or killers abandoned the gun that was used. It turns out that the gun had been stolen in one of Milbrook's burglaries."

"You're kidding," Kathy said.

"Nope, the victim was going to talk to the feds about his longtime involvement in some ultraright political groups. At least that's what the FBI anticipated. Of course, the witness never made it to the meeting. Anyway, the FBI contacted

Whit and told him that the most violent of these groups had started organizing burglary rings in several areas in the nation. They need weapons that couldn't be traced."

"And that's what has been happening in Milbrook?"

Anna nodded. "So it seems."

"And the bombing?"

Anna went on to brief her employer on the complete story. When she ended, she said, "I did promise Whit that I wouldn't mention the three juvenile suspects, but we can do a story on the fanatical right's connection to the burglaries."

Kathy shivered. "It's chilling. Wasn't one of these groups responsible for gunning down some talk-show host in Denver a few years back?"

"Yep, same kind of people. White supremacists who hate blacks, Jews, and Mexicans and who have no hesitancy to use murder and assassination to accomplish their ends. Whit doesn't necessarily think there's an entire group here. He thinks one person has come here simply to benefit from the house burglaries."

Kathy seemed puzzled. "I didn't think these groups had any trouble at all getting weapons. Why resort to something as risky as multiple burglaries?"

"I asked the same thing. According to the FBI, they have managed to interdict some of the traffic in weapons. Besides, these nuts have it in mind to organize armies to carry out their plans. The FBI also thinks that they must be planning something big to need so many weapons. Lastly, they use some of the stolen property to finance their activities."

"As I said, it's chilling."

Kathy's phone rang. She answered it, said a few words, then glanced immediately at Anna. Cupping the receiver, she said, "It's Tony Danton. He wants to talk to both of us. I'll put him on the speaker."

Kathy clicked on the speaker. "Okay, Tony, Anna's here with me."

"Hi, Tony."

"I wanted you both to know that I'm worried about Whit." The prosecutor's voice sounded tense.

"Why?" Anna asked.

"Because he gave you that damned story. That's not like Whit, but there's more to it. He did it because he wants to use those kids as bait for whoever is behind all of this violence."

Kathy frowned. "I don't understand."

Tony went on to explain, then said, "Whit normally displays better judgment than this. He's exhausted. For all I know, that concussion is clouding his reasoning."

Anna couldn't help but smile. "C'mon Tony, he seemed fine to me."

"You just want to write a blockbuster story, Anna."

The editor's eyes narrowed. "That's not true, Tony. I agreed to withhold a great deal of information."

"I want you to hold the story completely," Tony said.

Anna lurched to her feet. "No way, Tony. The public has a right to know—"

"Christ, Anna. If Whit doesn't find those kids before your story runs, then we could be signing their death warrants."

Kathy jumped into the conversation. "Do you think he can find them?"

"I just don't think we can risk it if he doesn't locate them. Even if we do, I can't allow their lives to be placed in that degree of jeopardy."

"Look, Tony." This time it was Anna speaking. "As a journalist I can't see any reason not to report that some bizarre group of neo-Nazis is behind the rash of burglaries. The B&Es are the biggest news in Milbrook in a long time. This makes it an even bigger story."

"The hell with the story," Tony snapped. "If you print that, those kids may be killed. Do you want that on your conscience?"

"Why don't we wait to see if you locate those kids?" Kathy suggested.

Anna turned her glare from the phone to her friend and boss, but Kathy put a finger up to her mouth to shush her.

"I don't think you should run it regardless," Tony countered.

Anna started to say something, but the publisher reissued her command of silence. She spoke to Tony. "We're going to go ahead and write the story. If Whit finds the kids, then we go with it. If not, we'll give some thought to your request."

"Dammit, Kathy, I want a commitment."

"You have it, Tony. If the kids are caught, we run the story. If not, we'll talk again. That's my commitment." She pushed the button disconnecting the call.

Anna was furious. "We can't suppress this story, Kathy!"

"I didn't say we were going to. I have more faith in Whit than you or Tony. If he locates those kids, then the problem's solved. Once they're in custody, then I think they can protect them. So let's just wait and see."

"And if Whit doesn't find them?"

Kathy shrugged. "Then we'll talk, just as I said to Tony."

Raven County's prosecutor was just hanging up his phone when Whit entered his office. The harried look on the investigator's face spoke volumes. "What's happened?" Tony asked.

"We've found the kids, at least we think we have."

"Where?" Tony asked.

"Down at Rock Crusher Quarry. A farmer spotted the car. He says there are two bodies, maybe three. He said one of them was moving. He thinks one is still alive."

"Jesus fucking Christ," the prosecutor said. "When is this mayhem going to end?"

Whit knew the answer. "Not until we catch the bloody maniac who's behind it. We've already phoned for a meat wagon. Gil and I are on the way out there."

"What about the guy who found the bodies? Can't he tell you for sure whether one's still alive?"

Whit shook his head. "He saw them from up on a ridge and hurried back to call someone. You want to go with us?"

Tony rubbed his face with his hands. "No, not really, but I guess I should."

TWENTY-SEVEN

FIFTEEN MINUTES later a small convoy of emergency vehicles turned into Rock Crusher Hollow. In spite of the previous night's storm, the collection of tires created a choking dust storm as the vehicles bounced up the rutted, unpaved road that led to the quarry.

Gil's cruiser, driven by the sheriff and containing Whit and Tony, headed the procession. Second in line was the ambulance. It had fallen in behind the cruiser as it descended the curvy road to the rugged lowland hollows below Milbrook. The sheriff had radioed for his other two field units to come to the scene, and they had caught up with the sheriff and the ambulance just as the vehicles had turned into the isolated hollow.

"I haven't been here since I was a kid," Tony said.

Whit studied the landscape through which they were passing. The two gently sloping ridges that formed the valley came right down to the road. The timber that covered it looked to be second growth, mostly red oak. Wildflowers, brambles, and berry bushes filled the space between the straight trunks.

"I don't ever remember being here," Whit said.

"Didn't you used to bring your girl down here?" Gil asked.

Whit turned a questioning eye to the sheriff. "My girl wouldn't have come down here."

Gil smiled. "Are you implying that I dated girls with no morals?"

212

"We all tried to do that," Whit said.

Tony occupied the rear seat. He didn't join in the nervous banter. Instead, he, too, kept staring at the passing scenery. "How the hell did this farmer spy the bodies? I haven't seen the first sign of human habitation."

"He lives in the hollow on the other side of the ridge," Gil said. "He was looking for sheep or something that had gotten loose. He saw some vultures and figured they were having lunch compliments of his livestock."

It took a second for the implication to strike home. "Ohmigod," Tony said.

"How much farther?" Whit asked.

The sheriff checked his odometer. "If I remember, the quarry is about two miles from the main road. We've come a mile."

"What a godforsaken place," the prosecutor said.

Whit agreed. "If it hadn't been for that farmer, we would have never found them."

Gil was looking in his rearview mirror. "We're really stirring up the dust. I bet that ambulance driver is cussing me out."

An apprehensive silence settled over the occupants of the car. Though all three were hardened veterans, having visited far too many death scenes, they each knew that it never got any easier. Whit had seen more of it than had either Tony or Gil. He often lay in his bed at night thinking about it.

Most people depended on the entertainment industry to educate them about violent death. As a result they enjoyed a divine naivete. Even the most graphic of the new wave of splatter films didn't come close to depicting the true outrage of a violent death. In the movies, no matter how gory they made it seem, there was always the knowledge that it didn't *really* happen, the comfort that came from knowing that the actor really walked away from his cinematic death. In their work it didn't happen that way. Homicide victims were forever dead. Take away the stench, the coagulating blood, the exposed organs. Ignore the limbs twisted into impossible positions. Disregard the skin that starts to change in both color and texture moments after the blood ceases to circulate. All those things made death ugly and revolting, but to Whit the most repulsive and yet intriguing change occurred in the eyes. He remembered someone saying that the eyes are the mirror to the soul. He wasn't a religious man, but he did believe in a divine being and felt that man does possess a soul. He believed the latter because he had seen the open eyes of so many homicide victims. There was nothing so cold and empty.

"We're almost there," Gil said. "Just around this turn, I think."

He was right. As the cruiser rounded a jagged rock outcropping, they saw the dark blue car for which a B.O.L.O. had been issued earlier that day. It was parked in a narrow graveled area.

"Look at that," Gil said.

Whit knew what the sheriff was talking about. The buzzards. The huge birds seemed to be protecting what he assumed were the bodies. For the moment the scavengers were blocking their view of the bodies.

"Stop here," Whit said. "There might be some evidence in the roadway closer to the bodies."

"What about the ambulance?" Tony asked.

"It can move up as soon as we've had a look at the scene."

Whit flung open the door. The buzzards took to the sky with a loud beating of wings. All but one, that is. The one buzzard remained, perched on a dark, glistening clump that Whit assumed was one of the boys. Its body was dusty black, its head as red as the displayed gore on which it was feeding.

"Brazen bastard, isn't he?" Tony said.

"Ugly, too," Gil said.

Whit advanced toward the body. The bird hissed at him but stood its ground.

Gil withdrew his revolver.

"Forget it," Whit said, sensing the movement behind and glancing back. "We've got enough of a mess without splat-

tering buzzard guts all over the place.'' The investigator bent
down and picked up a rock, which he hurled at the creature.
With a sharp cry it rocketed into the sky.

"Duck!" Gil cried as the animal flew straight toward
them.

It passed no more than a few feet over Whit's head.
"Gawd! Did you smell that thing?"

The others hadn't been as close to Whit, but they didn't
doubt his word. Gil kept his eyes to the sky as Tony and Whit
approached the bodies. The ridges that flanked the hollow
seemed to form a bowl that contained the steamy summer
air. Both men wiped the sweat from their faces.

The buzzards were gone, but green- and blue-bottle flies
quickly re-formed a blanket over the bloody remains.

Tony breathed deeply, trying to suppress his rising nausea.
Whit clenched his jaws as he moved within a few feet of the
bodies. "There are only two here," he said.

The ambulance crew and three deputies moved up to the
scene.

"Have you ever seen such aggressive buzzards?" Gil asked
of one of the ambulance drivers.

The man shook his head. "I haven't ever seen anything
like that. Actually, I've picked up a lot of bodies. I haven't
seen any vultures around them before, not up in Milbrook,
anyway.''

"The joys of country living," one of Gil's deputies
quipped.

Whit had been examining the area around the car. "I don't
see much to be gained by searching the ground. You guys
can bring up the ambulance.''

"You gonna wait on the local coroner?" one of the emergency medical technicians asked.

Whit looked to the prosecuting attorney for the answer.
Tony seemed speechless. "Why ask me? I don't see much
reason to haul him out here, but maybe I'm wrong.''

Whit shook his head. "I think you're right. You can start
loading them up.''

Gil was studying the bullet holes in the side of the vehicle. "Looks like an automatic weapon to me. A Mac-10, maybe."

"If so," Whit said, "he's shooting .45-caliber ammo. The holes in that car are pretty large." He worked his way between the remains of the boys and the car, trying to ignore the cloud of disturbed flies that rose from the bodies. Withdrawing a pencil from his pocket, he slipped it into the hole and allowed it to follow the bullet's shaft. The pencil came to rest at an angle of twenty or thirty degrees.

Whit looked up to the rim of the quarry. "The boys were ambushed from up there, Gil. You oughta have some of your men go up there and look for expended shells."

"Ten four," Gil said.

"Where was the third victim supposed to be?" Whit asked.

Gil pulled a small notebook from his shirt pocket. "According to the farmer, he was at the base of the cliff over there."

"Let's go see," Whit said.

"Not so quick," a voice shouted.

Whit turned. The man who had called out was Jerry Frye, an aging captain with the department. Most of the time he served civil suits and executed attachments aimed at collecting money awarded on judgments in the county's various courts.

"What's wrong?" Whit asked the older officer.

The man pushed his way toward Whit and the sheriff. He kept his eyes averted from the ravaged bodies. "I wouldn't go charging in there, Sheriff."

"Why not?"

"I got a friend who rounds up snakes and makes some money selling them to labs so they can make snakebite medicine. He comes to this here quarry an awful lot, especially in the late summer and early autumn."

"Snakes?" Whit asked.

"This here quarry's thick with copperheads. They ain't

too much good to my friend, but he says you can come across a lotta rattlesnakes here on toward the first frost. Believe it or not, they den up sometimes with the copperheads."

"We've got to go in there," Whit said.

Frye nodded. "Yeah, but you sure as shit oughta wear some high-top boots. Look at what's growing in there."

Whit looked, but he didn't see anything special. "What are you talking about, Jerry?"

"Berry bushes. Blackberries. Raspberries. That's a snake's favorite hunting ground. The berries bring the birds and the small critters and such, and the snake eats 'em."

An ambulance driver had been listening to the conversation. "We carry some boots in the ambulance. They're pretty large."

"What kinda boots?" Frye asked.

"Thick rubber boots," the EMT answered.

Frye made a face. "No good. You need leather boots. A copperhead's fangs can puncture rubber."

"I'll just have to take my chances," Whit said. "Go get the boots."

Gil had lost some of his enthusiasm. "Christ, I hate snakes."

"You stay here," Whit said. "With that knee of yours, you might be easy pickings for one of them. To be honest with you—and no offense to you, Frye—I figure it's not as bad as your friend lets on."

Frye had spent too many years as a deputy to be offended. "Think what you like, Pynchon, but it wouldn't hurt none to carry a shotgun if you're gonna go wading into that jungle."

"He's right," Gil said.

The EMT brought back two pairs of boots.

"I'll just need one," Whit said.

"I'll tag along," the ambulance crewman said.

Whit did a double take. "From what Frye says here, it might be a little risky."

"If your information's right, we're gonna have a body to get out of there. Might as well go now."

"Maybe a live one," Gil interjected. "The farmer said he was moving."

Whit pulled the boots on over his shoes. "They're a little big, but they'll do."

One of the deputies had gone to his car and was returning with a shotgun. "Take this. It's got double-ought buckshot. That oughta make mincemeat out of a snake."

Gil eyed the ambulance attendant. "You want one, too?"

The man laughed. "No thanks. I'd probably end up shooting myself or Mr. Pynchon. I'll follow him."

"It's the second man that's likely to get bit," Frye said.

Whit glanced at the veteran deputy, expecting to see him smiling. He wasn't.

"Wait a second," the other attendant said. He hurried to the ambulance and reached inside. He came out with a long metal pole and brought it back to his cohort. "You can use this to probe in front of you."

The EMT accepted it.

"What is it?" Whit asked.

"It's a support we use to hold intravenous fluids. You want me to go first with this?"

"Suits me," Whit said, "but if you see one, step aside so I can get a clear shot."

"Snakes don't bother me much," the EMT said. "If I can, I'll just shoo him away. Most of them are just as scared of us as we are of them."

Gil managed to laugh. "Like hell they are."

Dr. Paul Chandler still had six hours of his shift in front of him, and already he was bone tired. That afternoon they had treated a half a dozen cases of heat prostration, two actual heat strokes, and what seemed to be a multitude of people with chest pain. Two of the latter had been admitted with suspected myocardial infarctions. For the moment the emergency room at Milbrook Hospital was at peace. Several of the patients remained, including one of the suspected MI cases, but they were stable. Chandler, a specialist in emergency medicine and a five-year veteran of the ER, went to the small lounge just off the main emergency area for a quick glass of tea. He was just settling onto the couch when the head nurse stuck her head in.

"What is it now?" he asked.

"A phone call, Doctor. It's Dr. Atibi."

"Atibi?"

"He owns that walk-in clinic that recently opened just outside of town."

Chandler smiled. "The competition."

"You might call him that," the nurse said. "I call him a blessing."

"Can you transfer the call back here?"

"Yes, sir."

A phone hung on the wall beside the couch. When it rang, Chandler picked it up. "Chandler here."

"Sorry to bother you," the other doctor said, "but I had a patient a little earlier, and I was a bit concerned about his case."

The man spoke with a foreign dialect, but it was not so heavy that Chandler couldn't understand him. "How can I help you?"

"Well, he appeared to be the victim of a snakebite. He said a snake did bite him, and the lesions were consistent with that claim."

"What kind of snake?"

"He said a rattler snake."

"A rattlesnake," Chandler said.

"Yes. Anyway, there were two deep punctures, spaced about an inch apart. No other teeth marks. However, there appeared to be no other symptoms. I cleaned the wounds and gave him a tetanus shot. If this snake was venomous, the lack of symptoms of toxicity made me wonder."

"How much time between the attack and the time he arrived at your clinic?"

"Thirty or forty minutes, according to the patient."

"Was there evidence of edema or swelling?"

"No, sir. Just what one might anticipate with that kind of puncture wound. I suggested the man visit your ER since I have no experience with snakebite. He refused. I had trouble getting him to stay for observation."

"How long did you observe him?" Chandler asked.

"Maybe thirty minutes . . . a little longer, perhaps."

"Did the swelling or edema increase?"

"No, sir."

"Did he complain of nausea, headaches, dizziness?"

"No, sir. I tried to keep him, but he insisted on leaving. I am concerned about him. After thinking about it, I decided to call for your advice."

Chandler leaned back on the couch and took time to sip the tea. "Well, Doctor, most cases of snakebite in this area are from copperheads, not rattlers. More than likely, he was bitten by a copperhead."

"A copperhead," the doctor said, repeating the word.

"Yes, sir. In twenty-five or thirty percent of pit-viper bites, the snake doesn't actually inject venom. We don't know why, but that sounds like what happened in your case. In either a rattlesnake or a copperhead bite, obvious edema and swelling will be present within ten to twenty minutes of envenomation. I wouldn't worry about him, Doctor. If he had received a good dose of venom, you would have known it, and he wouldn't have been so quick to leave."

TWENTY-EIGHT

WHIT FOLLOWED the EMT into a narrow opening in the wall of brambles and berry bushes.

"I'll try not to let one of these things flip back in your face," the man said.

"What's your name?" Whit asked.

"Charlie, sir. Charlie Martin."

"Well, Charlie, I can handle the stickers. You just keep your eyes out for anything that slithers."

"Yes, sir. By the way, we do keep a snakebite kit aboard the ambulance."

"Fine, but I hope we won't need it." ·

The sound of buzzing bees filled the air. Whit swatted at a couple of them.

"I wouldn't do that," Martin said. "We're stirring them up enough just walking through here."

Whit tried to ignore the huge bumblebees, but he found himself keeping a wary eye above and below. "I don't know which I despise worse," he said aloud, "bees or snakes."

The ambulance attendant stopped dead in his tracks. Whit almost climbed up his back. "What is it?"

"A copperhead, sir. About three feet in front of me. He's right in our path, and he doesn't seem too anxious to move."

"So much for your theory, Charlie. If you can step aside, I can get a shot at him."

"If I move, he's going to strike. I don't know if I'm in range, but this snake sure as hell thinks so."

"What's happening?" Gil shouted. They were already out

of sight of the men back at the murder scene. Apparently they had noticed that Whit and the EMT had stopped moving.

"Take a guess," Whit shouted back.

"A snake?"

"Can you back up?" Martin asked.

Whit looked behind him, fully expecting to see another reptile blocking the path back out of the thicket. There wasn't one, just the buzzing bees. "Okay, but as soon as you're out of his range, give me a shot at him."

"Just move slowly, Mr. Pynchon."

"Don't worry." Whit took three steps backward.

Martin stood rock still.

"You coming?" Whit asked.

"In a hurry," the EMT said.

The young man almost fell back. Whit stepped out of his way and then back into the path. The snake, a deep tan banded by a lighter beige, was uncurling and heading for cover. Whit leveled the gun and squeezed the trigger. The snake vanished in an explosion of dirt and plant fibers.

"Are you all right?" Gil shouted.

"Fine," Whit said. "That's one less snake."

"Maybe you'd better go first," Martin said. "I'll be honest. I almost froze. I've seen snakes before, but never at such close quarters."

"I understand," Whit said. "If I see anything move, I'm going to shoot first and ask questions afterwards."

Whit started forward, pausing when he reached the patch of ground disrupted by the shotgun blast. The snake had been blown several feet to the left of the gap in the vegetation. Its mangled body twisted and curled on the ground.

"It's still alive," Martin said.

"But he's not gonna bother us. Let's push on."

A few minutes later the foliage thinned out. The afternoon sun had settled below the rim of the quarry, creating an area of deep, murky shadows along the base of the rock face.

Martin had moved up beside Whit as soon as they had

emerged from the squat, thick vegetation toward the front of the quarry. "This place gives me the creeps."

Whit peered into the deepening shade. "At least we can see the ground. That looks like a pool of water up ahead."

"Look there!" Martin cried.

The sharpness in his voice startled Whit. He searched the ground for the form of a snake.

"No, over there. It's someone crawling."

Whit followed the EMT's pointing finger. Finally he saw it, a figure pulling itself along the rough surface of the gutted quarry.

"We found him!" Whit shouted at the top of his voice. "Send that other EMT in here."

"No," Martin shouted. "Hold up on that."

He hurried toward the prone figure. Whit rushed to catch him. "Why hold up?" Whit asked.

"Let's see what condition he's in before we get help in here. I may need some special equipment." He dropped to his knees to examine the boy.

"Look at his hand," Whit said.

"Snakebite," the attendant said. "He's in pretty bad shape, but he isn't critical."

"What do you need?"

"A stretcher. Let's get him out of here first."

Whit stood. "Gil!"

The sheriff answered him.

"He's alive, Gil. We need a stretcher quick, but watch out for the snakes."

"Ten four."

Whit heard movement above him and to his right. He looked up and saw two deputies making their way around the rim of the quarry. They waved, and he waved back.

"Help me roll him over," Martin said.

Once the boy was on his back, he managed to open his eyes. His whole body was trembling, but he was conscious. "Who are you?"

"We're here to help you," the attendant said. "Was it a copperhead that bit you?"

The boy nodded.

"Just on your hand?"

The boy's lips moved, but no words came out.

"I think he said yes," Whit said.

"Who shot your friends?" Whit asked.

"I'd wait for later to ask him questions," the attendant said. "He's half out of his head."

"I can't wait. Besides, in his condition he probably can't speak anything but the truth. Who killed your friends, young man?"

The boy tried to answer, but again he wasn't able to produce any sounds.

"He's in shock, Mr. Pynchon."

The boy, though, continued to move his lips. He was determined to say something. Whit pressed his ears to the boy's mouth. Whatever the boy said to Whit, the investigator must have finally understood him. He just shook his head.

"What did he say?" Martin asked.

"He wants his mother."

As editor of the *Journal*, Anna found herself missing the varied excitement that was the life of a reporter. At many small newspapers the only way to earn significant salary increases was to accept promotions from news-gathering duties to news-editing duties. Newspaper management traditionally made the assumption that good reporters would make good editors. In truth, the two jobs required different skills. While her rise to the position of executive editor had been welcome, Anna had often thought that she was a better reporter than editor. When she saw an opportunity to write an occasional story, she readily jumped at it.

As she typed the last few lines of the piece, she found herself reassessing her role as an editor. Perhaps she didn't belong in a position of editorial responsibility. Kathy had no difficulty seeing the logic behind Tony Danton's arguments for withholding the piece. Anna, on the other hand, believed devoutly that the newspaper had an obligation to run the story. Was her opinion a reporter's obsession? Was that the function of an editor, to decide when the impact of a story might justify its exclusion?

Anna saved the story to the computer's main disk and then issued the command that sent it to the desk editor. Even though she was the top dog in the news division, she wanted someone to proof her story. It provided a sort of safety net.

Once the electronic wizardry had been completed, she stood and stretched. It was late afternoon, the time when she usually started her serious work. By that time, though, she had been at it for nearly two straight days. She needed some rest. Gathering up her purse, she left her office and on her way out stopped at the editorial desk. A young man was concentrating on a computer screen.

"I just sent you the piece we were talking about," she told him. "Block out a place above the fold for it, but be sure to have an alternative plan in case it gets axed."

The young man shook his head. "It's a hell of a story. It shouldn't get axed."

"I agree. I'm going home to grab a few hours of rest. I should be back after supper."

She didn't make it out of the newsroom. Barney caught her just as she was about to exit the door. "I think they've found them, Miss Tyree."

Anna didn't need to ask who he was talking about. "Where?" she asked.

"Don't know for sure. Somewhere out in the county, but I gather there's been trouble. There's been quite a bit of traffic on the police scanner, but I haven't been able to piece it together. The cops are getting real cryptic now, since so many people have scanners. I contacted one of my sources at the city police. According to him, there are some fatalities, but the ambulance was running a code three to the Milbrook Hospital. They don't do that in the case of fatalities."

"Is your source certain it's the boys?"

Barney nodded. "He says it is. The B.O.L.O. on their vehicle has been canceled. You look beat. Want me to head on over to the emergency room?"

Anna shook her head. "No way. You stay here. I'll check it out. Be sure you tell Mrs. Binder."

"Does that mean we get to go with the terrorist story?" the reporter asked.

"Yes, but it will have to be rewritten. You stay here. If I get anything, I'll phone the details to you. You can handle any follow-up that may be needed."

"Want a photog at the hospital?"

"Good idea," Anna said. "Have him meet me there."

Those in the sheriff's cruiser were eating dust as it followed the ambulance out of the hollow. In his hand Whit carried a plastic baggie containing an aluminum Coke can. It had been found by one of Gil's deputies on the roadside above the quarry. They speculated that the killer or killers had arrived at the scene first and had driven up around a bend above the quarry. While the ambulance crew had loaded the bodies and then the single survivor, Whit had followed the deputy to the place where he had found the can. Crushed grass and recent tire tracks supported their theory. The can would be forwarded to the state crime laboratory at South Charleston.

"Do we know the survivor's name?" Tony asked as the cruiser exited the hollow and started up the winding road that climbed to the plateau on which Milbrook had developed.

"I managed to pull out his wallet," Whit said. "He's the Moses kid."

Tony tried to recall the names. "So the fatalities are the Morton boy and—" The other name escaped him.

"Bert Ringwald," Whit said. "I guess his mother won't need to call that lawyer now."

Gil remained silent, concentrating on staying close to the ambulance. Strict police practice would have required that an officer remain with the surviving suspect, but by the time the two bodies and Mickey Moses had been loaded into the ambulance, there hadn't been room.

"Speaking of lawyers," Tony said, "we need to line up representation for Moses before you can talk to him."

"I know," Whit said. "How quick can we do it?"

"I'll call the juvenile officer as soon as we get to the hospital. Any idea how soon before we can talk to the kid?"

"He's pretty incoherent. Martin, that EMT, thinks it's more shock than the effect of the venom, but who knows? By the way, we oughta send a letter to the ambulance authority. Martin did a hell of a job out there."

"I'll take care of it," Tony said. "If they admit the kid to the hospital, we'll have to put a guard on him. If they don't, then we've got a real problem. We've got to find someplace to house him where we can protect him."

"Think the judge would go along with the jail?" Whit asked.

"Not if I know the judge," Tony responded.

Gil, still concentrating on the wicked curves in the road, said, "We can isolate him in the jail. I don't think we have any women incarcerated. The women's cells are segregated."

For a few moments they rode in silence. As soon as the ambulance had pulled onto the hard-surface road, its driver had flipped on its lights and siren. Gil, following closely behind, didn't bother until he reached the top of the mountain road. At that point they started encountering traffic. He hit his emergency signals.

The sudden sound seemed to jar Whit from his thoughts. He turned to Tony, who was sitting alone in the backseat. "How the hell did the killers know we were on to them?"

The prosecutor frowned. "Who says they did?"

"Why kill the kids if they didn't know?" Whit asked.

"Maybe they figured it was time to cut bait and run," Gil suggested. "Apparently that's their standard operating procedure when they decide things are getting a little too warm."

"Perhaps," Whit said, "but it strikes me as a little suspicious that this happens right at the same time that we're looking for them. I mean, we didn't even come up with names until this morning. This meeting—this ambush—had to be arranged this morning.''

"Coincidence," Tony said.

But Whit shook his head. "Yeah, a coincidence that might have saved the bastards' asses."

"You think someone tipped them?" Gil asked.

They were nearing the hospital. Whit settled back in his seat. "I think we'd better be real damned careful when it comes to protecting our witness up there. If someone did leak some information, it came from inside our ranks."

TWENTY-NINE

PERHAPS the three men hadn't been paying attention. Or maybe the ambulance had concealed the ambush that was awaiting them. Whatever the reason, neither the prosecutor, the sheriff, nor Whit Pynchon saw the welcoming committee until they stepped from the sheriff's cruiser and headed toward the rear of the ambulance. It had backed into the ER entrance to facilitate the removal of the Moses boy as well as the bodies of the other two.

The flash exploded in Whit's face as soon as he stepped around the open back door of the ambulance. "Jesus fucking Christ," he said, disconcerted by the blinding assault on his eyes.

Before his irises had time to adjust, a bright light flashed on and didn't go out. A padded microphone came up against his mouth.

"Charles Talbot, WVBE News. Can you give us a comment?"

Whit slapped the microphone out of his face.

Behind him he heard Tony saying, "No comment! No comment!"

"Get these people out of here," Whit shouted.

But other than Tony and Gil, both of whom were behind Whit, there were no other officers to enforce his command. Another mike was jammed into his face. "Will you confirm or deny reports that a right-wing militaristic group is operating in Milbrook and Raven County?"

Whit took a few steps back to assimilate the scene of pandemonium. Tony pushed up behind him. "Just get into the hospital, Whit."

"Where the hell did they come from?" Gil asked.

Whit squinted into the blinding light. He could see the ambulance crew. They were as surprised as anyone and still hadn't started to unload the victim.

"Go inside," Tony urged.

But Whit decided that something else needed to be done. He reached back and grabbed Gil. "Let's get these assholes out of here."

"Let's do it," Gil said.

While Tony looked on, still stunned by the assault of the news crews and bright lights, Whit and Gil waded into them. They pushed cameras out of their faces and grabbed people by the arms as they tried to create a tunnel through which the ambulance crew could conclude their duties.

"Clear a path," Gil was shouting.

Whit wasn't trying to communicate verbally. When one aggressive cameraman tried to stick his lens into the rear of the ambulance, Whit snagged the man by the back of his shirt and hauled him backward.

"Gawdamn," the man bawled. "Watch the camera."

"If you don't get it outta here," Whit said, "I'll shove it up your ass."

"Make room," Gil cried. "We've got an injured victim."

At some point Tony tried to bring some order to the chaos. "Let us get the victims inside," he cried. "I'll return with some kind of statement."

A newswoman with bright blond hair and heavy makeup jabbed her mike at Tony. Her shrill voice boomed out loud and clear above the clamor. "According to Chief Wallace, the burglary ring has been broken. Do you—"

Whit had heard her. "Chief Wallace?" he said.

She turned to him, her mike still held out. "He informed us—"

Whit grabbed the mike and jerked. The cord was attached to a camera that was being held by the same cameraman who had been trying to get a shot inside the ambulance. The force of Whit's tug toppled the man. The camera lens cracked against the back of the newswoman's head. "Cocksucker!" she screamed.

She tried to swing at Whit, but a tall man in a three-piece suit grabbed her from behind. "Easy, lady. Just get your people and move back out of the way."

Tears, darkened by mascara, were streaming down her face. "That bastard assaulted us. I'm going to press charges."

Whit didn't know who the man was, but he was glad he had shown up. When he spoke, his words were directed to the angry woman. "If you people don't get the hell out of this entrance now, you all will be arrested for obstructing officers in the performance of their duties."

The incident between Whit and the blonde had gotten the others' attention. Mumbling and grumbling, they started to ease back out of the entrance.

The blonde remained furious. "I want your name!" she was shouting.

The man in the suit pulled her back. She tried to yank free. "Get your fuckin' hands off me, asshole!"

That's when he flashed his badge. "Special Agent Noble, Federal Bureau of Investigation. I suggest you move out of the way."

She gaped, then seemed to recover her composure. "What are you doing here?"

Whit helped the ambulance crew extricate the stretcher bearing Mickey Moses from the ambulance. As they carried the boy into the ER, he caught sight of Anna. She was standing off to the side, a smile on her face as she shook her head at him. He smiled back and shrugged.

The man in the suit came up behind him. "I gather you're Investigator Pynchon."

"I am," Whit said, helping to guide the rolling stretcher through the double doors and into the main lobby of the Milbrook Hospital emergency room.

The man showed Whit his badge and ID. "We talked on the phone. I'm Noble with the FBI."

Whit eyed the identification. "One of the few times in my life I've been glad to see the feds."

Outside the hospital the uproar continued. Tony tried to take charge of the scene, but the assorted media people had become like sharks in a feeding frenzy. They continued to shout questions, some of them about the case and others about Whit's behavior a few minutes before. Tony answered most of them with a flat, unemotional "no comment."

"We saw body bags in the ambulance," a newsman shouted. "We want to know what's happened."

"We have an ongoing investigation," Tony shot back. "When it's appropriate, details will be made available."

"Why is the FBI here?" the blonde asked, her hair still sticking straight up as a result of the blow from the camera.

"I didn't know they were," Tony said.

The woman looked around for the man in the suit. "He was just here. He showed me his badge."

Anna had moved to the woman's side. "You're just shell-shocked."

The blonde whirled. "Who are you?"

"Anna Tyree, editor of the *Daily Journal*."

"Her boyfriend's the one that jerked your cord," someone shouted.

"Bad pun," someone else shouted.

The woman glared at Anna. "I guess you won't have any trouble getting the story."

Anna knew better, but she couldn't help herself. She shared Whit's contempt for local TV news hounds. So she said, "I've got the story already. By the way, your mascara's running."

The blonde turned to her cameraman. "Is it?"

"Yeah, all in all you look like shit, Myra."

"My purse is in the car," the woman said. "I'll be right back."

Anna smiled at the camera. "I bet it's pure hell being a celebrity."

The cameraman laughed.

The ambulance crew was coming back out with the stretcher. Tony turned to Gil, who had been standing behind them. "See if you can get them to take the bodies straight on to Charleston for the autopsies. No sense unloading them in front of these idiots."

"Will do," Gil said. He turned to head around to the front of the ambulance and out of the way of the reporters.

Tony turned back to the reporters. "Please, ladies and gentleman, we will provide you with a brief statement in a few moments. At this point we have nothing to release, but I promise not to keep you waiting."

"We gotta have something for our six o'clock newscast," a man said.

Tony had started for the door to the ER. "I'll do my best."

Anna slipped her arm into the prosecutor's as he went by her. "I'm going with you."

He shook his head. "No way. I don't want to be accused of playing favorites."

"It's a little late for that," Anna said, not intending to be denied.

A male TV reporter stepped in front of them. "If you let her go in, then you had best show the rest of us the same courtesy or else."

"Or else what?" Tony said, incensed at the threat in the man's voice.

"Or we'll scream foul," he said. "I've heard that things in this town were a little . . . well, shall we say, cozy."

"Screw you," Tony said. He guided Anna through the emergency-room door.

"I'm surprised at you," Anna said.

"I guess I've been around Whit too long. Those bastards really get under my skin. Who the hell do they think they are?"

"The electronic press," Anna said. "They prefer the image to the information."

Tony stopped, a half smile on his face. "And you're somehow above all that."

Anna went on ahead of him, glancing back over her shoulder. "I'd sure as hell like to think so."

Whit and the FBI agent waited in the ER lounge while the ER staff evaluated Moses. "Do you think the kid can finger the person behind this?" Noble asked.

"I hope so. They, meaning the higher-ups, went to a lot of trouble to be sure the kids didn't talk."

"For these groups, Pynchon, murder isn't a lot of trouble. It's one of their favored tactics. Have your lab people isolated the type of explosive that was used?"

"I have no idea. I really haven't had a chance to get back to them. It's been something of a whirlwind since yesterday. The mobile lab guys did tell us that it was a sophisticated triggering mechanism using a radio signal. They think it was plastic explosives."

"You were fortunate to have escaped. I'll bet it turns out to be C-4."

"Why?" Whit asked.

"It's the type they prefer. Small but powerful. Some of their members are in the military. They manage to smuggle it out to them. It's difficult to trace. From what I've been able to pick up, whoever designed the bomb used a little too much."

Whit worked his aching shoulder. "You can say that again. What brings you up here?"

"We heard about the explosion and thought you might be able to use our assistance. At this point it's unofficial. If this kid is able to identify someone or is willing to, then our involvement might escalate."

"If we nail the bastards, we want to try them here on murder charges."

Noble pursed his lips. "We could probably handle the case

more effectively, but we can work that out later. One thing, though.''

''What's that?'' Whit asked.

''I suspect you will discover that there's only a single individual involved. That's been their traditional method of operation. A party member either lives in a community or moves into it and rounds up locals to handle the illegal entries.''

The door to the lounge opened, and Tony stepped inside. Anna followed him.

Tony marched straight toward his investigator. ''I thought I warned you about calling the feds.''

''Whoa!'' Whit said. ''I didn't call him.''

''That's true,'' Noble said. ''Your troubles have received national attention. I'm afraid I came without an invitation.''

Tony still didn't seem convinced. ''Seems like too much of a coincidence to me.''

''I'm more interested in how those particular vultures outside knew to be here,'' Whit said.

Tony looked back to Anna for the answer.

''They were a surprise to me,'' she said. ''One of my reporters got wind that you all had located the kids and were on your way here. When I got here, they were waiting. There are three camera crews out there.''

Noble's face reflected his uncertainty. ''Is she a reporter?'' he asked of Whit.

''Oh, this is Anna Tyree, editor of the local paper. I told her the story this morning. I was hoping to apprehend the kids and then use them to lure the top men into the open. It didn't work out.''

The federal agent's face showed little relief at the explanation. He settled back in his chair, determined to say very little in front of Anna.

Whit's thoughts remained on the gathering of reporters. ''But how did they know to be here?''

''I was just about to explain,'' Anna said. ''You knew they were coming. You told me that earlier today. They arrived after lunch and went to the city hall. In case you don't know it, Chief Wallace is a little miffed because you left his people out on the discovery of the boys."

"Watkins had gone home," Whit said. "Since the call indicated an area outside of the city, we figured we'd let him get his rest."

Anna lifted her hands in a gesture of helplessness. "Hey, I'm just telling you what I got thirdhand from some of the reporters. Wallace told them that you were on your way to the hospital. He must have also let the cat out of the bag about the possible involvement by right-wing terrorists. They also knew about that before I even got here."

"The asshole," Whit said.

The lounge door opened again. Dr. Chandler walked in with a clipboard in his hand. "The patient isn't critical. In fact, I've decided against using any antivenom."

"Why?" Tony asked.

"It's rarely needed in the case of copperhead bites. Usually we only administer it to the elderly or to young children. The young man is strong, and we can treat the venom's effects other ways."

"Can we talk to him?"

"I've given him something to calm his nerves and relieve some of the pain. He's not coherent. However, he did say one thing I wanted to pass along."

"What's that?" Whit asked.

"He said his assailant was bitten, too."

Whit got to his feet. "Have you treated any other cases of snakebite?"

The doctor shook his head. "No, but I do know a doctor who has—and just this afternoon. It's rare to get one or two cases of snakebite a season, much less two in a day, so I'd wager there's a connection."

"Give us the name of the doctor," Whit said.

Chandler pulled a prescription pad from his pocket and wrote something on it. He handed it to Whit, then said, "But you may have a problem."

Whit snatched the paper. "What kind of problem?"

The ER physician scratched his head. "If it were me, I'd have to think long and hard about cooperating with you."

"For God's sakes, why?" Tony asked.

"Doctor-patient privilege, Mr. Danton."

THIRTY

WHIT FOUND the walk-in clinic with little difficulty. Dr. Atibi, its owner, had located the facility along the strip of fast-food restaurants and convenience stores on the main highway that led south toward Virginia.

Gil continued to chauffeur the investigator. Tony had remained behind at the hospital to obtain legal counsel for Mickey Moses. Whenever the boy was able to talk, they wanted to be prepared for the interview. The FBI agent went in Tony's place. The difficulty had been to get away without Anna and without another confrontation with the shark pack that was prowling outside the ER entrance.

The sheriff had solved the latter problem. He had phoned his department and arranged for an unmarked cruiser to meet them at the service entrance to the hospital. Whit had been saddled with the burden of dealing with Anna.

"We've got to go interview that doctor," Whit had told her once they were alone.

There was no mistaking the hostility displayed on her face. "You tried to use me, Whit."

"What are you talking about?"

"I should have known you had some ulterior motive in giving me that story this morning. All that crap about being fed up; you were conniving all along. It wouldn't have been so bad except you weren't going to tell me."

"I've got to go, Anna. We can discuss it later."

"You bet we will."

Whit was surprised. Usually she wanted to tag along every

chance she got. In spite of her anger, he considered himself fortunate. By the time he reached the unmarked cruiser, Gil had explained to Agent Noble the relationship between the prosecutor's investigator and the editor of the local daily.

"Let's roll," Whit said.

"Did you have to cuff her to an x-ray machine?" Gil asked.

"She didn't even want to come."

Several minutes later Gil pulled the car into a parking place in front of the clinic. "This place used to be a pizza parlor," Gil said, studying the windowed storefront.

Whit opened his door. "It probably still is."

"You'll have to forgive Whit," Gil said to the fed. "Doctors are one of the many groups of people that he doesn't like."

"I have my reasons," Whit said as they started toward the clinic. "I keep remembering the doctors' strike in Los Angeles a few years ago. The death rate dropped fifty percent."

Noble laughed.

Gil said, "That's one of his favorite stories."

The sign on the door read QUIK-CARE. Whit nodded approvingly. "I can't wait until the day when doctors really get the hang of advertising. I can see it now. Kidney transplants, two for the price of one."

Gil made a face, but Noble chuckled again. "You should come to D.C. and see what the dentists are doing for business. Replacement dentures, one-day service if you're in the office by eight."

"We've already got those here, too," Gil said.

Rarely did three men enter Quik-Care at the same time. The nurse was frowning at them even before they reached the counter. "Can I help you?"

"We'd like to see the doctor," Whit said.

"He's with a patient now."

Whit nodded back to the sign. "I'm sure he won't be too long."

The nurse didn't get the joke. "What is this in reference to? Is one of you a regular patient?"

"I've been a bit irregular," Whit said.

The nurse didn't crack a smile. "See here, if you have business—"

Whit flashed his badge. "Just get the doctor please."

Her eyes widened. "Please wait a moment." She vanished into the interior of the converted pizza parlor.

Moments later she reappeared, followed by a tall man with dark copper features. The man's foreign origins didn't surprise Gil or Whit. Most of the doctors coming to West Virginia had been educated beyond the continental boundaries of the United States.

"I'm Dr. Atibi. How may I help you?"

Whit introduced himself and Gil. He wasn't certain if he should introduce Noble, who had made a point of the unofficial status of his visit. Noble solved the problem for him. He flashed his own badge. "Agent Noble, Federal Bureau of Investigation."

The doctor's copper-colored face appeared to blanch. "My papers, I'm sure they are in order."

"We're here about a patient you treated this afternoon," Whit said.

The doctor seemed relieved. "Oh, which one?"

"A case of suspected snakebite."

"Oh, yes. But how did you know?"

"Dr. Chandler at the hospital. He told us."

"I see. What do you want to know?"

Whit fully expected to encounter the problem that Chandler had mentioned. He and Tony had discussed the issue, and they had even decided on an approach. Apparently, it wasn't going to be necessary. "If you have his name and address, we would like to have it."

"Certainly." The doctor looked back at his nurse. "We do have that information?"

"Yes, sir," she said.

The doctor smiled. "Good, please provide it to this gentleman. Is there anything else?"

Since that had gone so smoothly, Whit decided to press his luck. "Could you give us a brief description?"

Again the doctor didn't blink at the request. For the second time he turned to his nurse. "Did the patient complete the standard form?"

"Yes, Doctor."

"Then we have his description. You may have a copy of that also." The nurse went to the copier and inserted a piece of paper in it.

"You're very helpful," Whit said.

"Where I come from, we respect the authorities."

"Where is that, Doctor?"

"Panama."

The nurse handed the copy over the counter to Whit. He scanned it. "John Taylor, 301 Exeter Street, Milbrook, WV. And his description is white male, blond hair, blue eyes, five-eight, 160 pounds."

"Just a minute," the doctor said. He wheeled around to the counter. "You have given this man the wrong one."

"No, sir. No, I didn't. That was the snakebite victim."

The doctor seemed flustered. "Gentlemen, he had dark brown hair . . . brown eyes, I think. He was much taller than that and heavier, too."

Whit shrugged. "That's all right, Doctor. I doubt his name was John Taylor, and I have never heard of Exeter Street."

Noble was looking at the nurse. "Do you ever check the description given against the individual seeking treatment?"

She, too, seemed upset. "No, sir. Never. Why should I? I mean, I know what the patient looks like. He or she is usually standing here."

"Makes sense," Gil said, repressing a laugh.

Back at the hospital Tony Danton was on the phone with Pete Bainbridge, Raven County's juvenile officer. By law, the Raven County circuit judge appointed attorneys to represent juveniles, assuming, that is, that the parents couldn't afford or wouldn't consent to hire private counsel. In ninety percent of the cases, no matter how well-off the parents were, they took the freebie lawyers. After all, the courts seldom did anything serious to the juveniles, anyway. In practice, the actual mechanics of the appointments were handled through the juvenile office, which maintained a list of lawyers.

"I need someone to be ready when the boy is able to talk," Tony said.

"What about the young man's parents?" Bainbridge asked.

"We haven't talked with his mother yet. I don't think the father is in the household."

"Technically, that should be done first. Perhaps she wishes to retain private counsel."

"Dammit, Bainbridge. How often does that happen?"

"The administrative office of the supreme court insists that I follow its rules, Mr. Danton. They went to the trouble of writing them and—"

"Okay," Tony said. He gave Bainbridge the name of Mickey Moses's mother. "Call her. If she says she isn't going to retain counsel, who do you appoint?"

"Let me check the list. The next name is the Jenkins firm. They have executed an agreement with Sloan Keating through which—"

"I know about it," Tony said. "So you'll appoint Sloan?"

"Yes, if the juvenile's—"

"I understand," Tony said, cutting him off. "Can you attend to this now, Pete?"

"Yes, sir. Has the mother been made aware of her son's medical condition?"

"The hospital was to call her, Pete. That's all I know."

After hanging up he waited for ten minutes and then dialed the hospital operator. He identified himself and asked that she place an outgoing call to Sloan Keating.

The attorney's secretary answered.

"This is Tony Danton. I need to talk to Sloan."

"I'm sorry, but he has asked me to hold his calls."

"It's an emergency," Tony said.

"Just a moment."

Seconds later Keating came on the line. "What's up, Tony?"

"Has Bainbridge called you?"

"Not yet."

"You've got another case, Sloan. You might even earn a few dollars on this one."

"Great! What is it?"

"I guess you are aware of the bombing last night."

There was a moment's hesitation. "Of course."

"Well, we have a juvenile in custody who may be involved or who may know the perpetrator's name. However, he is a suspect in the recent string of burglaries. We want to talk to him."

"I haven't received a call from the juvenile office yet," Keating said. "Usually—"

"You should be getting it very soon."

"If it comes, then of course I'll be present. Is the suspect at your office?"

"He's in the hospital. He was bitten by a snake."

"A snake?"

"A copperhead."

"My goodness! How is he?"

"He's sedated right now, but he'll live. We do think someone might make an attempt on his life, though. He's gotten himself messed up in a rather sick situation."

"I will need some time alone with him, Tony, before your interview."

"No problem. I'll call when he comes around." He hung up the phone.

Whit, accompanied by the federal agent, came into the doctors' lounge. "We got a description from the doctor but nothing else," Whit said.

"Did he cooperate?"

"Hell, yes," Whit said. "He didn't bat an eye when we told him what we wanted. His patient, though, had given him a phony name and address, even a phony description. We got a good description from him and his receptionist."

"What was it?" Tony asked.

"About six feet tall, dark hair and eyes, around 190 pounds."

The prosecutor grimaced. "That fits half the men in Milbrook."

"Not quite. This guy's got two fang marks just above his ankle."

"But he isn't in the same shape as the kid," Tony said, still puzzled by it.

"Either he angered an impotent snake or maybe it was the same one that had bitten Moses, in which case it had used most of its poison on the kid."

"So what do we do now?" Tony asked. "Just wait for the kid to come around?"

Whit settled into one of the chairs in the lounge. "Noble and I were talking on the way back. We still might be able to take advantage of this situation."

Tony was shaking his head. "If you're wanting to use Moses as bait, forget it."

"We can do it safely, Tony. The kid is still here in the emergency room. When they take him up to his room, we can pull a switch. Leave Noble and I in the room where the kid's supposed to be and put him somewhere else."

"And then?" Tony asked, his interest beginning to come to life.

"Then you give a statement to that assortment of news jackals outside that leads the killers to believe the boy hasn't talked but might. It's a long shot, but they might come after the kid."

"In this hospital?" Tony countered.

"Yes," Whit said.

But Tony was again indicating his disapproval. "These maniacs have already blown up a city block. What makes you think they won't take out an entire wing of the hospital?"

"They might," Noble said, "but what's to deter them from doing that now? The culprit is going to know the juvenile is here regardless of what we do."

The federal agent had a point. "Then maybe we should get the kid out of here and tell the media that he's been spirited away to a safe place," Tony said. "I cannot endanger any more lives."

At that point Chief Hayden Wallace marched into the emergency-room lounge. "I gawdamn don't appreciate the way you've shunned my department, Pynchon. I'm buryin' an offisuh tomorrow, and you people just don't seem to give a damn."

Terry Watkins, the city's chief detective, eased in behind Wallace. He looked at Whit with apologetic eyes.

The chief had turned on Danton. "If you've got a suspect in these burglaries in custody, me and Watkins here wanna talk to him."

"He's not able to talk," Tony said.

"You take me to him, Danton. I bet he'll talk fine to me."

Pynchon glanced at Noble and winked. When he spoke, though, it was to Wallace. "Tell me, Chief, are you gonna coerce a statement out of the boy?"

"I'll do whatever I damn well need to do, Pynchon. I don't need none of this bleedin'-heart crap right now."

Pynchon's grin stretched from ear to ear. "Oh, Chief, have you met Noble here?"

The chief glared at the man in the three-piece suit. "I guess he's the kid's mouthpiece."

"No, he's with the FBI. Among their other duties, they investigate violations of civil rights by police officers."

THIRTY-ONE

THE PRESENCE of the FBI agent had subdued Hayden Wallace's enraged enthusiasm. In fact, he had left the emergency-room lounge in search of a cup of coffee. Watkins remained with Whit, Tony, and Noble.

"So what about using the kid as a decoy?" Whit asked. "If we're going to do it, we need to start making some plans."

Tony rolled his dark eyes. "The idea makes me nervous as hell. These nuts might not think twice about using another bomb. We're in a hospital, for Chrissakes."

Noble entered the debate. "I don't think that's too likely, counselor. I suspect the perpetrator might be a little gun-shy about using explosives again. He knows he botched the last one. They don't have any qualms about killing their targets, but as a rule they've managed to avoid killing too many innocent citizens. After all, they'd like to think that the average Joe is basically on their side. In the past their homicidal surgery has been rather precise. They're cold-blooded but careful."

"Can I count on that?" Tony asked.

Noble smiled. "It's not an ironclad guarantee. You know that, but it's just like Pynchon said. So long as the kid's in the hospital, you face that same danger. We can slip a ringer into the bed and surveil the room. If we give the press the right story, our guy might make a move. Frankly, I think we have another, even more serious problem."

"What's that?" Whit asked.

"Those reporters are asking about the involvement of some

far-right terroristic group. We'd be much better off if the main man didn't even think we suspected his group's involvement. If he thinks we know about him, then he might just try to slip out of town. These groups exist all over the country. They have incredible facilities for faking identifications. If he manages to get back into their fold, they can probably make him vanish even if the kid can identify him. It might appear to be less of a risk to just let the kid alone and depend upon this underground network to absorb the man.''

''At least that stops the problems in my jurisdiction,'' the prosecutor said. ''Sorry to be so self-concerned, but I was elected by the people of Raven County.''

Whit looked first at Noble and then to Watkins. ''Look, fellows, there's one thing we haven't discussed. It's my opinion that the man behind all this knew we were on to the three boys. If so, then it's because we have a leak. I think we can forget about trying to keep all these secrets. With Wallace shooting off his mouth and an informer among our troops, we'd just be wasting time.''

''That's the first I've heard about a leak,'' Noble said.

''Whit's speculating,'' Tony explained. ''It's possible that the killer simply decided it was time to do away with his henchmen.''

''More than speculation,'' Whit argued. ''I think he arranged that meeting this morning, not long after Watkins talked to his daughter.''

The detective's brow knitted. ''Are you suggesting that I'm in this?''

''God, no,'' Whit said, ''but how many people knew about it so early this morning? Not too damned many, and all of them were local cops, mostly city officers.''

''A sympathetic ear among the ranks of local police wouldn't be surprising,'' Noble said. ''We've uncovered connections between many police officers and these nuts. A lot of cops share some of the beliefs of these groups. It's frightening how deeply rooted some of these groups have become. They have members in local governments, in the state house, in Congress, even in the U.S. military.''

''So we've concluded that we might as well forget using the kid as bait,'' Tony said, much relieved.

Whit started to protest, but Noble jumped in ahead of him. ''Actually, Mr. Danton, I'd follow Whit's suggestion simply as a matter of good security. I think it highly unlikely an attempt will be made on the boy's life. On the other hand, it might be wise to put the obvious security on an empty room and try to conceal the boy somewhere else in the hospital.''

''What about manpower?'' Tony asked. ''Do we have it?''

Whit looked at Watkins. ''Can your department help?''

''Aren't you afraid the killer might be one of us?'' Watkins snapped, still miffed at the suggestion that one of his officers was in cahoots with some right-wing terrorist operation.

Whit looked at the detective for several seconds. ''I hate to say this, Terry, but you have a point.''

The detective clenched his jaws. ''Mother of God, Whit, I was being sarcastic.''

''I know that, but in doing so you raised a valid point.''

Watkins jumped up. ''Fine, I guess maybe I should go, too. I don't want to be suspected.''

''For Chrissakes,'' Tony said, ''sit down, Terry. Get off your high horse.''

''I don't like being called a traitor,'' the detective said.

''I didn't call you a traitor,'' Whit said, ''but look at the gawdamned evidence. We do have a leak.''

Tony remained unconvinced. ''That's your theory, Whit. It's a theory that fits the facts, but it's not the only theory. However, until we're certain, it's better to be safe than sorry.''

''But you don't suspect me?'' Watkins said.

''Of course not,'' Whit replied.

That seemed to satisfy the detective. He sat back down.

''Maybe we should see if Gil can give us some help,'' Whit said. ''Or maybe we can ask for some help from the state police.''

Tony actually snickered. ''That's dreaming, Whit. It's not

the state police's kind of case. If we can round up enough
guys to maintain a proper around-the-clock surveillance, I'll
go along with it. Otherwise, we'd best just secure the boy's
room the best we can and forget it. One way or another I
need to give some kind of statement to the press.''

''There's something else we need to do,'' Whit said, his
face grim. ''We need to notify the parents of the boys that
died. Any volunteers?''

There were none.

Reverend Peter Gabriel's community meeting became the
kind of event that some news reporters found more satisfying
than sex itself. The television crews were thrilled. They had
a roomful of mad and fearful people anxious to jump in front
of a camera to proclaim their anger and apprehension.

The meeting began quietly enough—in prayer, in fact. Father Gabe had spent a good part of the afternoon writing the
ten-minute invocation. As a Baptist, he could get away with
the verbosity. When people came to a Baptist church, they
expected long prayers. He didn't disappoint them. It started
out with a plea to the divine for comfort for those who had
lost loved ones and friends. It reassured the grieved that their
loved ones had gone to a better place. Of course, when he
had written it, Gabriel hadn't known about the death of the
two boys. While he doubted that either boy would find
heaven, he left his prayer unchanged for the sake of their
parents. Preachers had to do that sort of thing.

With the plight of the dead and the grief of the survivors
behind him, the preacher went on to beg for divine assistance
in returning ''some semblance of Christian sanity'' to the
streets of once heavenly Milbrook. He even dared to invoke
the name of Chief Hayden Wallace, who, he noted, was shar-
ing the podium with him. He asked God to give Wallace ''the
wisdom to bring peace back to the children of our community.'' When he was finished, Wallace was one of the loudest
to join in a collective ''Amen.''

Then all hell broke loose.

Father Gabe introduced the new police chief to the gathering and assured them that he had come to answer their questions. Those questions started even before Gabriel concluded his introduction.

"How many more folks gonna die, Chief?" That was the first question. It was shouted by a man in the front row who, though in a church, still wore a hat advertising chewing tobacco.

"Tell us that," someone else shouted.

Father Gabe tried to curb the discontent, but most of the people in attendance weren't members of his faithful following of Baptists. They hadn't come to hear excuses; they wanted to rant and rave.

"What about the boy in the hospital?" a woman screeched. "I hear tell he gunned down those friends of his. 'Cause he's a juvenile, he's gonna go free."

"We don't know that," Wallace shouted.

From the back of the room: "You gonna arrest him, Chief?"

"The murders are under investigation."

"What about the bomb?" a man cried. "I hear it was set by camel jockeys."

That made Wallace frown. "This has nothing to do with the Middle East, I can assure you."

"Terrorists," a woman screamed, not to Wallace but to the crowd. "A friend of mine's married to a cop, and that's who he said did the bombing. Terrorists! Right here in Milbrook!"

"Please," the reverend was shouting. "Please, hear the chief out. He has news."

Hayden Wallace almost wished he had a tear-gas gun. He had seen many an unruly crowd, and in his opinion the group in the church was on the verge of violence.

"Attention!" he bellowed.

The intensity of his voice managed to reach several pews deep. Those people settled down.

"Attention!" He actually pounded on the pulpit with his meaty fist.

Most of the turmoil ceased. The noise that continued came from the camera crews as they worked toward the front of the church.

"That's better," Wallace said.

"I came here to tell you that the perpetrators of the recent series of B&Es have been identified. Two of them were murdered by accomplices. However, we have no reason to believe that the third boy in our custody was the killer. In fact, he, too, was to have been killed."

A few people booed, but Wallace ignored them. "These kids were working for what I would describe as a group of organized criminals. They aren't terrorists. They're just criminals. We hope to apprehend them soon. However, I feel quite confident in telling you that you can again sleep with your windows open. The heat wave may still be with us, but the crime wave is a thing of the past."

The blond newswoman who had angered Whit earlier that day stood just below the pulpit. "What about rumors that a paramilitary right-wing group is behind the burglaries?"

Wallace glared down at her. "Just that, miss. Rumors. Speculation. As chief of police, I've seen no evidence to justify that conclusion."

"Then why the bombing?" she asked.

"The prosecutor's office is investigating the bombing," Wallace declared.

"Whit Pynchon, you mean." There was a sneer on the woman's face.

"Yes, ma'am."

"Where's Pynchon?" a man shouted.

The chief shrugged. "I can't say. He's certainly not here."

Father Gabe moved to the microphone. "Ladies and gentlemen, we came here tonight to discuss the role that we might play as private citizens in assisting our local police. I don't think that the news the chief has brought, though welcome it certainly is, lessens the need for an active community-watch program. I've talked with Chief Wallace—''

It started in the back of the church. Just one voice at first. ''We want Pynchon.''

Then it spread like a case of chicken pox in day care. Ten started chanting, then twenty.

''We want Pynchon. We want Pynchon.''

''I want that on tape,'' the newswoman cried.

The cameraman turned, his bright lighting spilling out on the crowd. The woman held her microphone high. ''Can we understand it?'' she was asking.

The cameraman cupped his ear with his hand. ''What did you say?''

Behind the pulpit the preacher sagged in frustration, but Hayden Wallace was smiling. He liked what he was hearing.

THIRTY-TWO

ANNA'S CAR was in the driveway when Whit arrived home. He hadn't expected her to be there, and when he entered the house, it was dark and quiet.

"Anna?"

She didn't answer. He went through the living room and into the kitchen. Even though it was almost seven-thirty, the evening remained quite warm. Maybe she was out on the deck. He looked, but she wasn't there. He went back into the house and down the hall to the bedroom. Anna was on the bed, curled in a fetal position, snoring lightly. The thick curtains had been drawn, and the room was twilight dark.

He went to the bed and sat down. "Anna?"

She stirred and tried to turn away from him. He put a hand on her. "If you want to sleep, that's fine, but it's almost seven-thirty."

"Too early to get up," she mumbled.

"Not in the morning. It's evening."

"Hmmm?"

"Don't you have a newspaper to get out?"

She sat straight up in bed. "Ohmigod."

"Take it easy."

"I had the alarm set for six. I must have turned it off and went back to sleep."

He put an arm around her. "You're exhausted. So am I."

Her mind was starting to work. "Oh, God. What's been happening?" She was rubbing her eyes.

"Not much. Tony released a written statement to the press

identifying the dead boys. He suggested to your buddies that
the boys were responsible for the string of housebreakings.
Your reporter was there and got it all.''

Still dressed except for her shoes, she slid over to the edge
of the bed. ''What about the terrorists?''

''He didn't mention them, but the TV people kept asking
about them.''

Anna became suspicious. ''Where does that leave my
story?''

Whit chuckled. ''Tony wants me to talk you out of using
that part of it. He thinks—''

''Fat chance.''

Whit shrugged. ''That's what I told him.''

''You aren't going to coerce me? Or try to coerce me?''

Whit stood. ''Frankly, I hope you use it. And I hope those
TV people have apoplexy.''

Anna smiled and shook her head. ''You really built a fire
under that twinkie from WWWA. God, she's such a bitch. I
must admit I enjoyed it.''

''So you're not still mad at me?''

''Too soon to say. What else is going on?''

''Are you trying to extort information?''

''Of course.''

''Well, the Moses kid is in a secure room with the FBI
agent and a deputy on guard. We have another deputy guard-
ing an empty room. It's under close surveillance.''

She looked disappointed. ''So you did decide to use the
boy as bait?''

''Actually, we didn't . . . or we aren't. It's just the best
method of security we can develop. Noble, the FBI guy,
knows the way these bastards operate. He pretty well convinced Tony and me that they were unlikely to make an attempt at the hospital.''

''Uh huh,'' she said with open suspicion. ''Is that the
party line?''

Whit crossed his heart. ''The truth as I know it.''

''You swear on your Dick Tracy watch?''

"You know I never wear a watch. I do swear, however, on my honor, and you know my reputation for truth and veracity."

"I know your reputation for being the southern end of a northbound mule."

"So are you still mad?"

She reached over and took his left hand, pulling him down to the bed.

"Watch the shoulder," he cried.

"I'm not interested in the shoulder."

He rolled on top of her. "How soon do you have to get to the paper?"

"I don't have any time at all," she said, her lips brushing his.

"None?"

"Nope."

He started to roll off, but she held him tight.

"I thought—"

"Quit thinking." She kissed him, then said, "It wastes time."

The phone rang.

Neither of them even considered not answering it. There was too much happening. Whit grabbed it. "Pynchon here."

"Hi, Daddy."

"Tressa! How's the trip?"

Anna smiled when she realized that it was Whit's daughter. She also started unbuckling his belt.

"Nashville's great, Daddy. But what's going on there? The newspaper had a story about an explosion in Milbrook."

"Nothing for you to worry about."

"Is Anna at work?"

Whit looked down at her. She was pulling down his jockey shorts. "Uh, yeah. She's at work. You know her. All work and no play."

She reached around and pinched his buttocks.

"Ouch!"

"What happened?" his daughter asked.

"I stumped my toe."

Mickey Moses started to wake up around nine P.M. Jim Noble had been sitting in the boy's third-floor room, reading a novel he had picked up in the Raleigh-Durham airport. As soon as the boy stirred, he buzzed for the nurse. Once she was in the room, Noble went to call Tony Danton. The prosecutor phoned Sloan Keating and Whit Pynchon. They all agreed to meet at the hospital at ten.

Tony arrived first. Several minutes later Whit stepped off the elevator. "Can we talk to him now?" the investigator asked.

"Keating's not here yet," Tony said. "I promised him a few minutes to confer with the boy before we attempted to interview him. The hospital phoned his mother. She's on her way, too."

"Oh, that's just what we need," Whit said. "Does she get to sit in on the interview?"

"The boy's sixteen, Whit. If the mother wants to, I can't stop her."

"Are you going to try to have him transferred to adult jurisdiction?"

"Let's see what he says, Whit. Maybe we can use that as a bargaining tool."

Whit smiled. "Always anxious to make a deal."

Before Tony could respond, the elevator door opened and Sloan Keating stepped off. The young attorney wore a bright green jogging suit and tennis shoes.

Whit blinked at the sight. "Christ, Keating, did we interrupt a tennis game or something?"

Keating brushed by Whit. "It's awfully late for this, Tony. I don't want to be here all night."

"We'll do our best," the prosecutor said. "The boy's mother is on her way, so I guess we need to wait for her."

Keating was shaking his head. "No, I want a few minutes alone with him first."

"He's down here," Tony said, starting toward the room in which the boy was housed. "Have you talked to his mother?"

"Not yet."

Agent Noble was in the room when the other three men entered. Keating eyed the agent with undisguised curiosity. "Who's this?" he asked.

Noble displayed his badge case. "We have an interest in the boy, too."

Keating's eyes flashed to Tony. "You didn't say anything about federal charges."

"There aren't any," Noble said quickly. "Not yet, anyway. If you gentlemen will excuse me, I'm going to find a cup of coffee."

"Have you talked to my client?" Keating asked.

Noble nodded. "Certainly, counselor. I'm not bound by the same restriction as state officers. We treat juveniles a little differently in federal court."

Keating wheeled on the prosecutor. "I thought we had an understanding."

"I thought we did, too," Tony said, looking to the federal agent for an explanation.

Noble grinned. "Don't worry, fellas. As soon as I advised him of his rights, he asked for a lawyer. Pretty streetwise for a sixteen-year-old. I'll be back in a few minutes."

As the agent was exiting the room, Mickey's mother eased in.

"This is Mrs. Moses," Whit said.

She nodded to the two attorneys and went straight to her son's bedside. "Oh, Mickey, how do you feel?"

"Kinda woozy," the boy said.

"What have you gotten into?"

"Trouble, I guess."

Tony used that as a chance to step forward. "A lot of trouble, young man. This is Sloan Keating. He's been appointed as your attorney."

The lawyer stepped forward so that Mickey could see him.

The boy's face seemed to drop. Whit saw the lawyer tense. "What's the matter?" Keating asked.

"You . . . you're a lawyer?"

"Sloan Keating, Mickey. I'm sorry I don't look much like a lawyer, but it's late and I was home when the prosecuting attorney called me."

"What's your name again?" Mickey asked.

"Keating, Mickey. Sloan Keating."

The boy tried to push himself up. "You were Zeke's lawyer when he got in trouble."

Keating frowned. "Zeke?"

"Ezekiel Morton," Tony said. "He was on juvenile probation, just as Mickey here is. I guess you must have represented him."

"Now I remember the name," Keating said.

Mickey's mother had moved to the head of the bed and was pushing a button to lift her son's head. "Are you hurt? Other than the snakebite, I mean."

He teared up. "I thought I was gonna die, Mom. You told me how Dad was killed. Remember?"

"Don't think about that," she said.

But the boy went on. "He was killed by a machine gun. I thought that's how I was gonna die, too. I was so scared. I kept wondering if Dad was that scared."

Keating glanced back at Whit and Tony. "Give me about ten minutes with the boy."

Tony nodded and ushered Whit from the room. "I think he'll talk to us. He sounded scared to death."

Whit wasn't as certain. "That might be a reason why he won't talk. If he does agree to roll over, what kind of protection can we offer him?"

"Maybe the feds will help us there, especially if they can use him."

"Their witness protection program?"

"That's what I was thinking," Tony said. "It beats the hell out of jail."

"Not by much."

* * *

"They did what?" Anna said, stunned by the news she was receiving from Barney.

"This community group voted to circulate a petition demanding that Whit Pynchon be fired." The reporter had a wry smile on his face. "I thought that would get a response from you."

"But why?" Anna asked. "What even got them on the subject of Whit?"

"Our new police chief," the reporter said. "He all but took credit for breaking open the burglary cases. When questions came up about the bombing of the Benning residence, the chief passed the buck to Whit. Of course, Pynchon wasn't there to defend himself. It was masterful, Anna. Here was the crowd chanting 'We want Pynchon,' and Wallace just stood up there, smiling like a cat that had swallowed a canary. He plays rough, Anna."

"That southern son of a bitch. What's he saying Whit did or didn't do about the bombing?"

"The public, and most of the press, has the impression that this kid in the hospital killed his two friends. They also think he's responsible for planting the bomb. Wallace diverted any suggestion that the kids were working for some organized group of political terrorists."

"Is that what he believes?"

"I have no idea what he believes, but I think he has it in for Whit Pynchon."

"I still don't understand why they want Whit fired. Even if they believe that, the boy is in custody. The burglars have been identified, and that part of it will stop now."

"This crowd wasn't very rational, Anna. A lot of them saw the report on the six o'clock news."

"Did you?" Anna asked.

Barney nodded.

Anna waited for him to elaborate. When he didn't, she said, "What was on it?"

"I thought you saw it."

"I fell asleep."

"They showed Whit being anything but friendly. There were shots of him shoving TV crews aside."

"Tony's statement. Didn't they read it?"

"They skimmed over it and gave the impression that it was far from satisfactory. You of all people should know, Anna, that the public acts based on what it perceives to be the truth. As far as they're concerned, Whit should have been there tonight. Because he wasn't, they think he's hiding something and deserves to be fired."

"That's stupid. It's absurd."

"It's mob mentality. Should I try to get in touch with Pynchon for a comment?"

"I'll do that," Anna said.

"One other thing. Myra Martin, that blond bombshell from WWWA, was saying that this newspaper was involved in some form of conspiracy with the prosecutor's office to withhold information from the public."

"Is that what she's going to say on the air?"

Barney held up his hands. "I have no idea. She was telling some of the other TV crews. Wallace was listening to her. So was I."

"Did you respond?"

"Not me," Barney said. "I'm just a lowly reporter. Besides, we do have a story about these Nazi groups that the others don't have."

"And we're going to use it," Anna declared. "The TV people can go screw themselves."

"Good for us, but if I were you, I wouldn't miss the eleven o'clock news."

"I'd better warn Kathy," Anna said. "This thing's getting out of control."

THIRTY-THREE

SLOAN KEATING exited the boy's room. "He's willing to co-operate to the extent that he can, Tony."

The prosecutor and Whit traded looks. "Let's try to be a little more precise than that. What do you mean?" Whit asked.

"It means he will tell you what he knows, Mr. Pynchon. You can't ask for or expect any more than that."

"In return for what?" Tony asked.

"He's not looking for a deal. The boy is contrite, Tony. I tried to get him to realize that it was in his best interests to seek certain concessions from you. Principally I wanted to request a stipulation that you will make no effort to move him to adult jurisdiction. The boy refused. He won't let me make the request. He wants it off his chest. His sincerity impressed me. I'm counting on a similar reaction on your part."

"How does his mother feel?" Tony asked.

"She's going along with her son."

Jim Noble exited the elevator, balancing a box containing five cups of coffee. "I hope I have enough for everyone," he said.

"Just what I needed," Whit said.

Noble distributed the coffee. "There are packets of sugar and cream in the box."

"The boy's going to cooperate," Tony said. "We're going in to interview him now."

The agent's face turned serious. "You understand, Tony,

that the U.S. attorney's office won't be bound by any agreements you may have made with the boy.''

"There isn't any deal, Jim. The boy says he wants to cooperate.''

The agent looked to Keating. "Is he aware that he may have some exposure under federal statutes?''

"I generally explained that to him. As I was telling the prosecutor and Mr. Pynchon, Mickey is sincerely remorseful. He only asks that you take that into consideration.''

"It's not up to me,'' Noble said.

A nurse at the third-floor station called to Whit. She was holding up the phone. "Wait on me before you start,'' Whit said.

Keating checked his watch. "It's getting late.''

"I won't be long.''

It was Anna on the phone. "I thought you might be there,'' she said.

"What's up?''

"Have you heard about the community meeting tonight?''

"No, what about it?''

"Your name came up.''

Whit glanced back at the other three men. They waited impatiently. "What do you mean?''

"They're circulating a petition requesting that you be fired.''

Whit's mouth dropped. "Me? Why, for God's sakes?''

"From what I gather, Wallace was there and made you look like an asshole. He didn't have to work very hard at it. I understand you were the raging bull on the six o'clock newscast.''

"I didn't see it,'' Whit said.

"Anyway, since we're doing a story, I'm obligated to give you a chance to respond,'' Anna said.

"No comment,'' Whit said.

"Aw, c'mon. I was hoping for something really sarcastic.''

"Such as?''

"I dunno. You're the one with the acid tongue."

"You weren't complaining about my tongue earlier, m'dear."

She laughed. "Is that all you want to say, then? Just 'no comment.' "

Tony was motioning for him to hurry up. The two other men had already gone into the boy's room. "I've gotta go, Anna. It'll have to do for now."

"Hold on. Is Tony there? I'd like a response from him."

"He's tied up. You'll have to call him later."

"Is the boy talking?"

Whit sighed. "That's what I'm trying to do, talk to him. If you'll get off the phone."

"Bye." She hung up.

"Was that Anna?" Tony asked when Whit rejoined them.

"Yeah. She says that the good people of Milbrook are mounting a major campaign because of this case."

"That community-watch thing?" Tony said.

"It started out that way. Now they're circulating a petition for you to fire me."

"You're kidding."

"She wanted a comment from you. I told her you were busy."

"Well, I can assure you that you have nothing to worry about."

"I was afraid you would say that."

While the men had been outside talking, Mickey's mother had wiped his face with a damp cloth. She had helped him comb his long brown hair and had lifted the head of his bed even higher.

"You're doing the right thing," she had said. "Your daddy would be proud of you."

"I'm sorry I got us into all this. I'm sorry most of all about Janey."

"Who's Janey?"

"Janice Benning. The one they killed with the bomb."

"But you said you didn't have anything to do with that," she had said.

"But it happened because of me."

His lawyer and the FBI agent had reentered the room. A few minutes later the other two men returned. The prosecuting attorney pulled a small voice-activated tape recorder from his pocket and placed it on the adjustable hospital table. He moved it closer to the boy.

"How do you feel?" he asked

"My arm hurts. I'm sorta dizzy, but I'm okay."

"Okay, Mickey. Before we get too far along, I've got to do a few things. First, my name is Tony Danton, and I'm the prosecuting attorney for Raven County. You understand that?"

The boy nodded that he did.

Tony went on. "Other parties present for this interview include Whit Pynchon, a special investigator in the employ of my office, your attorney, Sloan Keating, and Jim Noble, a special agent for the Federal Bureau of Investigation. Let the record indicate that your mother is also present. For the record, Mrs. Moses, may I have your full name."

She spoke loudly. "Betty Moses."

"Thank you, Mrs. Moses." Tony then gave the date and time of the interview as well as its location.

"Now, Mickey, again for the record, tell me your full name."

"It's Michael Kenneth Moses, Jr., sir."

"Your father, Mickey. I believe he is deceased."

"Yes, sir. He died in Vietnam before I was born."

Tony glanced at Mrs. Moses.

"He died just before the 1973 evacuation, she said. "I was pregnant with Mickey at the time. He never got to see his son."

Tony hadn't wanted or expected an explanation, but it was obvious that the woman had felt the need to offer it.

"Now, Mickey, before we go any farther, you have talked with your attorney, Mr. Keating?"

"Yes, sir."

"Mr. Keating advised you of your rights as a juvenile?"

"Yes, sir."

"And you understand that you don't have to talk to us unless you want to?"

The boy was nodding.

"Please answer out loud," Tony said, "so it will be on tape."

"Yes, sir. I know I don't have to talk to you."

"And you understand that what you do say can be used against you in court? You understand what that means?"

"Yes, sir."

"We haven't threatened you or made you any promises to induce you to talk to us?"

That question confused the boy. He didn't answer.

Tony repeated the question. "Have we threatened you or done anything to force you to talk to us?"

"Oh, no. No, sir. I want to."

"Have you and your mother discussed it?"

"Yes, sir. While you were outside, we talked about it. She thinks I'm doing the right thing."

Tony looked at Mrs. Moses. "Is that right, ma'am?"

"Yes, sir," she said.

The prosecutor turned back to the boy. "Just a few more of these kind of questions, Mickey. You are being treated because you were bitten by a poisonous snake, a copperhead, I believe?"

"Yes."

"Are you able to think clearly at this point?"

"Uh huh."

"Please answer yes or no."

"Yes."

"What grade are you in at school?"

"I finished the tenth grade last year."

"Make good grades?" Tony asked.

The boy shrugged. "So-so."

"But you can read and write?"

"Oh, sure."

"Mickey used to like to read all the time," his mother offered. "He coulda made better grades if he had applied himself."

Tony pulled his chair closer to the bed and adjusted the tape recorder. "Now, Mickey, we're going to get to the important part."

The boy swallowed. "I'm ready."

"Do you know two other boys by the names of Ezekiel Morton and—" Tony stopped to check his notes.

"Bert Ringwald," Whit said, standing behind the prosecutor.

"Yes, Mickey. And Bert Ringwald."

The boy lowered his head and nodded.

"Answer aloud," Tony said

"I know them. Knew them, I mean."

"You saw them killed today, I believe."

"Yes, sir." The firmness in the boy's voice wavered.

"Had the three of you been involved in certain recent illegal activities?"

"Yes."

"What had you been doing?"

"Breaking into houses and stores."

"For yourselves?" Tony asked.

"Well, yeah, but Zeke took the stuff we stole to a man. Then, after the stuff was sold or whatever, Zeke brought us money from this man."

"Who was the man?" Tony asked.

Noble, Whit, and even Keating seemed to lean forward in anticipation of the answer.

The boy, though, shrugged. "I don't know."

Tony looked back to the others, then returned his attention to Mickey. "Mickey, your lawyer indicated that you wanted to cooperate. You don't have any reason to be afraid."

"I'm not afraid," Mickey said. "I really don't know. Zeke never would tell us, and we never saw him."

Whit moaned and dropped back a few steps.

"That's what my client indicated to me," Keating said. "I told you he would tell you what he knew. He's more than willing to give you details on the B&Es, but I don't think he knows the man's identity."

"I'm being honest," Mickey said. "We were supposed to meet the man this morning . . . I mean, at noon, but it was a setup. They wanted to kill us all."

"Who's they?" Whit suddenly asked.

Tony held up a hand to stop the boy. "For the record, Investigator Pynchon posed the last question."

"I just said they. Zeke only talked about the man. That's what he called him—the man."

Tony dropped his head in his hands.

Whit moved forward to continue the interview. "Mickey, was the meeting for noon set up this morning?"

"Yes, sir. Zeke got a call."

"Do you know what time?"

"Early, maybe around ten."

"How do you know for sure?" Whit asked.

"I was at Zeke's trailer when the man called. Zeke and I were in a fight."

"A fight?" Whit said.

"I was mad. It was because of Zeke that they bombed Janey Benning's house. I had told Zeke that she thought we were involved in the break-in at her house. He musta told the man. They killed Janey and all those other people. The assholes."

His mother gasped. "Mickey!"

"That's what they are, Mom. They're worse than that."

"So what happened at the quarry?" Whit asked.

"We got there and had just got out of Mom's car. I saw something move on top of the quarry. Right after that he started shooting. I saw Zeke's head blown away. I dived for cover, but he came after me."

"When did the snake bite you?"

"I was trying to hide in the brush. The man came down from the top of the rim. When I moved, he could hear or see me, and he would start shooting with that machine. The snake got me when I was trying to get back deeper into the quarry.''

"You said the man who was trying to kill you got bitten, too.''

"Yes, sir. He kept talking to me, trying to get me to come out. Then I heard him scream. I thought maybe he had shot himself, then I realized that he'd been bitten. He didn't see the snake, though. At least he didn't know what kind it was. So I told him it was a rattlesnake. He ran.''

"Did you get a look at him?'' Whit asked.

The boy shook his head. "I was afraid to even try. He kept firing off blasts from that gun. Can I ask you something?''

"Sure.''

"How come he didn't get sick like I did?''

Whit cocked his head at the boy. "How do you know he didn't?''

"I don't know for sure.''

Whit figured he must have overhead the conversation, or at least part of it, earlier that day in the ER. "Sometimes snakes strike and don't inject venom. Perhaps it was the same snake that got you, and it had used most of its venom when it bit you.''

"Figures,'' Mickey said.

"So you can't tell us who the man was who killed your friends?'' Whit then asked.

"I think I can. It didn't make sense to me—not until now. Because I knew he got bit, too, I mean. And I don't know if it's the same man that planted the bomb or that Zeke knew.''

A jolt of shock brought a long silence to the room.

Whit took a deep breath. "Are you saying you know who the man was at the quarry?''

"Yes, sir. I'm ninety percent sure. I guess it's the same man Zeke was dealing with. Like I told you, he kept talking to me. I recognized his voice.''

"Who was it?''

"Him,'' Mickey said, pointing. "My lawyer.''

THIRTY-FOUR

THE SMALL REVOLVER came from an ankle holster Keating wore beneath the bulky pants leg of the sweat suit. He was stooping and had it in hand even before the boy finished making the accusation.

"He's armed!" Noble cried, going for his own weapon in a holster fitted to his belt. Whit's stiff shoulder prevented him from reaching for his gun.

Tony was the closest to the lawyer. He tried to move away, but the man's arm wrapped around the prosecutor's neck and jerked him backward. "You're coming with me, Danton."

Noble's gun came up.

"Don't shoot!" Whit cried.

Mrs. Moses had started to scream. Mickey still sat in the bed, his face frozen in fear.

"Shut up, lady," Keating shouted. He leveled the gun at her son.

"Please, don't shoot him," the woman said, edging around the bed to put herself between her son and the re-volver. The coal-black weapon looked like a toy, but both Whit and Noble knew better. They both recognized it as a .38 caliber, mounted on a lightweight frame and marketed as an "off-duty" special for police officers. Weighing six-teen ounces, it was often carried by women in their purses and by men in their jacket pockets.

"Don't be a fool, Keating. You can't get out of here," Whit said.

Keating's face glistened with sweat. The gun in his hand

trembled. He looked more like a scared kid than a ruthless killer. Trouble was, as frightened as Keating was, Whit realized that the young lawyer was likely to kill someone before he left the room.

Tony, a little shorter than his assailant, wasn't struggling. He leaned backward against the lawyer. His eyes were locked on Whit, as if he expected his investigator to do something.

"Danton and I are gonna back our way out this door, Pynchon. If you or the goddamn fed try anything, I'll blow his fuckin' brains all over the hospital corridor." He started inching toward the door, his arm maintaining its choke hold on Tony's neck.

"How far do you think you'll get?" Noble asked.

Keating reached the door and eased it open. "I don't have to get very far. If either one of you stick your head out that door before I get out of sight, he's dead. I don't have a damned thing to lose, and you know it."

"If you shoot him," Whit said, "I'll shoot you."

Keating grinned. "No, you won't. As soon as I shoot him, I'll drop the weapon. You won't kill an unarmed man."

"Try me," Whit said.

"You best just do as I say." He backed farther out the door.

Whit took a step toward it.

"Stop!" Keating bellowed. "I warned you."

But Whit was shaking his head. "Forget it, asshole. I'm going with you, all the way."

The lawyer's eyes flared. His gun hand came away from Tony's head.

"He's gonna shoot!" Noble screamed.

Whit dropped to the floor just before the gun went off. The explosion knifed into their eardrums.

"Jesus," Whit said, expecting to feel the pain of a gunshot wound. Instead, he felt the weight of a body, the weight of Mickey Moses's mother as she collapsed on top of him. The boy was screaming. Noble caught hold of the stricken woman and kept her from going all the way to the floor.

By the time Whit looked up, the door to the room was swinging closed. "Christ, he's gonna get away." He tried to get up, but he was tangled in the woman's legs.

"Go after him," Whit said, struggling to get free.

Noble rushed to the door but stopped before he headed out. He stood off to the side and used a single hand to push it open. Then he peeked out. Keating and Raven County's prosecutor were out of sight already, but the corridor was full of people—nurses rushing toward Mickey's room, other patients peeking out to see what was going on.

By that time Whit was on his feet. His clothing was soggy with the woman's warm blood.

Seeing the crimson on his shirt, a nurse ran up to him. "Where are you hurt?"

"Not me," Whit said. "It's her. Did you see the two men leave?"

She nodded. "He came out with Mr. Danton, waving his gun. He was pushing Mr. Danton down the hall. I think they went down the steps instead of the elevator."

Mickey Moses was out of bed, kneeling down with his mother. "For God's sake, help her. She's dying."

Whit could hear her gagging as he hurried out to join Noble. "The nurse said that they took the stairs," Whit said.

"Yeah, but where are the damned steps?"

"There, there," an excited orderly said, gesturing toward an unmarked door. "We've called hospital security, but those steps lead down to both the first floor and an outside exit."

Whit's blood turned cold. He dashed for the door. "Jesus Christ, if he gets out of the hospital—"

Noble followed. They clattered down the steps and found a hospital security guard at the bottom. "They musta went outside," the guard said. "I came down the hall, and they didn't go that way."

"Oh, Jesus," Whit said, slamming his body against the metal bar that opened the exit.

"Be careful!" Noble warned.

But Whit wasn't thinking about being careful. He was

thinking about his friend. He lunged out into the hot summer night. Noble and the security guard followed. The exit led out into a side parking area.

"You go around that way," Whit said to Noble. "I'll go around this way."

The security guard followed Whit. "You stay behind me," Whit cautioned. "You're not armed."

"The hell I'm not," the guard said, producing a small .25-caliber revolver from a pants pocket.

They moved quickly but carefully into the nearly empty parking area. They were at the closed end of the lot, and a good thirty yards separated them from the first row of vehicles. Dusk-to-dawn lights illuminated circular areas of the lot, but there were deep pockets of black between the widely spaced lamps.

"How could two men vanish so quickly?" Whit said as he scanned the lot.

"Maybe they headed straight across the lot," the guard said, pointing to a residential area that flanked the hospital parking lot. "That would be the quickest way to reach cover."

"Go back inside and call the city and the sheriff's department. Advise them what's happened and—"

"What the hell did happen?" the guard asked.

"No time to explain," Whit said. "Just tell them that Tony Danton has been taken hostage."

"We've already called the city. We do that any time we have a disturbance."

They continued to move toward the houses on the other side of the parking area. "Then go call the sheriff's department. Tell them to notify the sheriff. Go now!"

"Yes, sir."

Just as he turned to comply with Whit's request, two other security guards came running onto the lot. "Spread out, boys. Search the lot. We're looking for a man with a second man being held as a hostage."

"He's armed and very dangerous," Whit shouted.

* * *

At that instant Tony Danton was being forced into the backseat of Sloan Keating's car. The lawyer had parked in a deep shadow thrown by the hospital. Tony had just heard Whit's voice and was considering the wisdom of calling out when Keating's small gun cracked hard against the back of his head. He fell headfirst into the backseat.

Sometimes Keating's luck surprised even himself. First he was bitten by a venomous snake that didn't poison him. Then tonight, he picked just the right place to park. Maybe there was something more behind it than just luck.

Keating hoisted the prosecutor's feet into the air and jammed them into the backseat. Then, crouching low, he moved around the back of the car and slowly—quietly—opened the driver's-side door. As he eased up into the seat, he could see the party of men continuing to search for him. A security guard was walking in his direction. Another security guard followed Whit Pynchon as the prosecutor's investigator moved toward the houses on the far side of the parking lot.

Keating eased the door closed and pulled gently until it clicked. It wasn't completely closed, but it would do for the time being. He placed the gun on the seat beside him, glanced back to be certain that Tony Danton remained unconscious. Then he fished into the side pocket of the green pants for his car keys. By the time he found them, the security guard was within thirty feet of his vehicle. The man had his flashlight out and was heading toward the row of cars in which Keating's vehicle was parked.

Keating slipped the key into the ignition and prayed for the vehicle's motor to kick over on the first try.

"C'mon, baby." He flicked his wrist. The engine fired. In his mind it reinforced what he had been taught: God was an Aryan.

The security guard heard the engine and stopped. He swung the beam of his flashlight to the windshield of Keating's car. The lawyer hit his headlights, slammed the car into gear, and jammed his foot down on the gas pedal. The car roared forward. The security guard had just enough time to realize he was going to die. Keating saw it in the man's slack face just as the front of the car smashed into his midsection. At the moment of impact Keating swerved to the right. Blood and stomach juice spattered the windshield. The man's body, his arms and legs flapping like a rag doll's, sailed out of the spreading beams of the headlights. Tires squealed and the power-steering unit screeched in protest as Keating held the car in a tight circle.

"Yeah," he screamed, sensing that he was well on his way to a clean escape.

Whit heard the man cry out, then heard the soft thud as the car struck him.

"That's him!" he cried. "He's getting away." The shrill protests from the car as it made the compact circle drowned out his voice.

The investigator leveled his small .357 at the car, but he knew all along there was no way he could shoot, not with Tony in the car. Keating's vehicle completed its circle and headed for the parking lot exit.

Sirens wailed in the distance as Whit chased after the fleeing car. He ran as fast as his battered body and out-of-shape lungs allowed, but it was a vain gesture. The vehicle, easily gaining ground on Whit, bounced out of the parking lot and made a sharp turn back toward the maze of streets in the residential area of Milbrook adjacent to the hospital. Whit stopped running just as the red taillights of the vehicle vanished.

He waited for the police cars to arrive, but they never did. They had stopped at the emergency-room parking area on the other side of the hospital.

Frustrated and gasping for each breath, Whit turned back toward the building just as Noble came running back into the parking area.

"What happened?" the agent asked.

"We've lost him," Whit said, his body trembling with rage. "He got away clean."

One of the security guards carried a walkie-talkie. He used it to direct the city police units around to the parking lot. Within minutes two police cars came screaming around the hospital.

Whit hurried to the first squad car. "Issue an APB for Sloan Keating. He's a lawyer here in town. Advise your units to be careful. He has Tony Danton as a hostage. He's armed, very deadly, and wanted for murder and kidnapping."

"What kind of car?" the cop in the car asked.

"Jesus," Whit said. "I didn't get much of a look at it. Have your dispatcher run Keating's name through the Department of Motor Vehicles computer. That should give you a description of both Keating and the vehicle."

"It was a dark sedan," one of the guards said.

"Which way did it go?" the city cop asked.

"That way," Whit said, pointing toward the conglomeration of middle-class houses. "It headed straight into Milbrook. Is there any way to mount roadblocks on the various exits from the city?"

"Not in time," the cop said, "but we can try." He got on the radio at once.

The headlights from the cruisers illuminated the crumpled body of the guard on the parking lot's pavement. Whit, accompanied by Noble, walked over to the fallen security guard. His colleague was bent over him.

"How is he?" Whit asked.

The guard looked up, his eyes full of tears. "He's busted all to pieces. The bastard just ran him over."

"I'm sorry," Whit said.

"He was my brother-in-law, my little sister's husband. What the hell am I gonna tell her?"

THIRTY-FIVE

RAVEN COUNTY'S LAW enforcement brain trust organized its command center at the sheriff's department. Roadblocks had been established on all major highways leading out of the county. Whit knew, of course, that Keating had had more than enough time to reach the state line south of Milbrook before the roadblocks had been set up. As a result, the APB had been issued to all counties in West Virginia as well as the various law enforcement agencies in southwestern Virginia.

Whit sat in Gil Dickerson's office. The sheriff was plugging in a portable television that had been commandeered from one of the jail cells on the top floor.

"Are you sure you want to watch this?" Gil asked.

"Why the hell not?"

"I've heard about that meeting tonight at the church. Sounds like you became the hot topic of conversation."

"At least they haven't gotten hold of the news about the fiasco at the hospital," Whit said.

"It's probably only a matter of minutes," Gil said. "Why in the hell didn't you call me? I feel left out."

Whit dropped his head into his hands. "Christ, Gil, I didn't think it was going to be any big deal. First of all, who woulda figured that the kid would even talk? I can't get him out of my head. That boy sat there, cool as a cucumber, and fingered Keating. I don't know who was more shocked, Keating or us. Jesus, how the kid managed to confer with the bastard for ten minutes, knowing—or at least suspecting—that his lawyer was the man who had killed his friends and had tried to kill him."

"What was the word on his mother?"

"Alive but critical. The bullet entered her lung."

Gil's phone rang. He listened to the voice of his dispatcher for several minutes, then covered the receiver with the palm of his hand. "So much for peace and quiet. Anna's on the line. She's heard about the hospital incident."

"Put her on," Whit said, holding out his hand. "Anna?"

"Whit, are you all right?"

"I'm fine."

"What the hell happened at the hospital? We've got reports of a shooting, a fatality, and an abduction."

"All true," Whit said.

Gil had turned on the television. The news was just coming on.

"Are you going to give me details?" she asked.

" 'Fraid not," Whit said, watching the corny promo leading up to the newscast.

"Whit!"

"Sorry, Anna, there are lives at stake."

"Was it Tony who was abducted?" Anna asked.

"If it was," Whit said, "will you give us a little breathing space?"

"Of course."

A solemn-faced local anchorman appeared on the screen. "Hang on a second," Whit said into the phone. "I've got the eleven o'clock news on."

"So do I," Anna said.

The newscaster checked his notes. "We have just received word of a possible shooting at Milbrook Hospital. At this point in time details are sketchy, but it appears that at least one individual, a hospital security guard, is dead. We have reports that another individual, a visitor, remains in critical condition at this hour. We are attempting to contact authorities about the incident, and we hope to have a more detailed report before we go off the air."

Gil just shook his head.

"They know more than I do," Anna said.

"Let's hear the rest of the news," Whit said.

The anchorman was still talking about Milbrook. "This appears to be just the latest in a series of heart-wrenching tragedies that have afflicted Raven County's seat of government. Authorities report that two juveniles died today as a result of gunshots, and a third is being held in custody. Tony Danton, Raven County's prosecutor, refused to comment on reports that the third juvenile is a suspect in the double homicide. The killings appear to be related to a series of recent residential and commercial break-ins that have afflicted the small city. And just last night a mysterious explosion, reportedly caused by some type of bomb, claimed the lives of eight people in an exclusive section of the small city known as North Milbrook."

"Makes us sound like a war zone," Gil said.

"That much is accurate," Whit grumbled.

An off-camera individual slipped a sheet of paper onto the anchorman's desk. He scanned it, then looked back into the camera. "Late word on the violence at the Milbrook Hospital indicates that it is related to the killing of the two juveniles earlier in the day. We have managed to confirm that the shooting victim is the mother of that third juvenile, who was being held at the hospital for reasons not disclosed to the press."

Whit held the phone loosely to his ear. He barely heard Anna's voice. "Is that true, Whit?"

"Let me hear the rest of this, Anna. Then we'll talk."

The face of the anchorman was replaced by a shot of a crowd of angry people.

"Here goes," Gil said.

The anchorman continued to speak. "The citizens of Milbrook met tonight to express their anger over the close-mouthed attitude which they say is being displayed by police officials. Myra Martin has that report."

The face of the blond reporter came onto the screen.

"Brace yourself," Anna said.

Whit simply watched. "Residents of Milbrook say they

have had enough official silence, and they aren't going to stand for any more. A local Milbrook church was packed tonight by a crowd of people demanding more responsiveness from their county officials. The crowd's anger was directed toward one official in particular, a special investigator for Raven County Prosecutor Tony Danton. That man is Whitley Pynchon, shown here in a confrontation earlier today with reporters gathered outside Milbrook's hospital.''

Gil hadn't seen the six o'clock report. He gaped as he watched Whit flinging TV crews out of the way. "Jesus, they're making you look like a madman.''

"You were there, too, dammit. They just didn't have the camera aimed at you.''

"Think she'll tell the audience that they were blocking the entrance to a hospital emergency room?'' Gil asked.

"Fat fucking chance.''

The camera shifted to a view of Hayden Wallace behind the church's pulpit as Myra Martin continued with her report. "Even Milbrook's new police chief, Hayden Wallace, seemed displeased with Pynchon's handling of the investigation. Private sources indicated that Wallace believes his department should have been tapped to lead the investigation. Tonight—''

"Turn it off,'' Whit said.

"But I want to hear,'' Gil said.

"Turn the damn thing off.''

Gil hoisted himself from his chair and flipped off the switch.

"I'm still watching it,'' Anna said over the phone. "The crowd is chanting 'We want Pynchon.' ''

"Fuck 'em,'' Whit said. "If you want the story, Anna, this is your only chance.''

"I want it,'' Anna said.

Whit paused for a moment to catch his breath. Before he could launch into the complicated story, Hayden Wallace strode into Gil's office.

"Well, Pynchon, you've made a fuckin' mess of things.''

The phone hit the floor. Whit's fingers grabbed a handful

of Wallace's sports coat. He slammed the astonished chief back against the wall.

Gil got to his feet, prepared to throw himself between the two men.

"Stay the hell outta this," Whit said.

Wallace was trapped in a position in which he couldn't defend himself. "So help me God, Pynchon. You strike me and I'll have you jailed."

Whit leaned into the chief's face. "I wouldn't waste a knuckle on an asshole like you. I don't know what your game is, Wallace, but I've had all your southern drawl and your conniving bullshit I'm gonna take. I don't know who let you get up here, but you can haul your useless ass right back down to city hall. We've got things in hand."

"Like hell you do," Wallace said. His voice, though, had lost some of its fervor. "I'm pulling my men off this manhunt. See how you like that."

"You're doing nothing of the sort," Whit said, still pressing against the big man. "You can go home or you can go back to your office. Better yet, go over to that damned TV station and give 'em another interview. Do whatever the hell you like. Just stay out of my sight. And if you even act like you're gonna yank your men off the case, I'll have Gil deputize them. He's a little higher up on the totem pole than you."

"That's not legal," Wallace said.

"Maybe not down in Georgia. It is here."

Gil could hear Anna shouting over the phone. He picked it up. "Sorry, Anna."

"What in God's name is going on there?"

"Well, your boyfriend's just about ready to whip Hayden Wallace's ass."

"Tell Whit to hit him once for me."

Tony opened his eyes to discover near darkness. Nothing hurt until he tried to move. Then a hot ball of pain exploded in the back of his head. He cried out.

"No sense trying to move," a voice said.

Tony tried to think. Where the hell was he? What had happened? He knew one thing. His hands and feet were tied, and he was lying on his side on what felt like carpet. His eyes focused slowly. They detected light, but it took a few seconds for his addled mind to translate the light into an image. He was looking at two small windows. Just beyond them was a small light bulb.

A van! He was in the back of a van. The vehicle was in a building, a garage of some sort. Then, with the mounting intensity of a flash flood down a mountain hollow, the memories came back. The hospital. The boy. Whit. The gun. Keating.

"Keating!" Tony bellowed the name.

"Shut the fuck up!" the lawyer said. He was sitting in the van's front seat. Tony smelled cigarette smoke. He shifted the position of his head. For a second time the pain made him wince, but he did not cry out. He could see the lawyer's silhouette and the tiny glow from the cigarette.

"Where am I?" Tony asked.

"In a world of shit, counselor."

"Can I have something to drink?"

"Soon as I finish my smoke."

"Tell me something, Keating. Are you really a lawyer?"

The young man laughed. "Of course I am. I graduated with honors from the University of North Carolina."

"Then why the hell are you involved in something like this?"

"I don't expect you to understand, Danton, but I'm in it to save the country I love."

"You're in with a pack of rabid fanatics."

"I can assure you that they are anything but fanatics. I grew up among them. They even helped with my college tuition."

"Nice folks," Tony mumbled.

"I spent every summer in a youth camp. I killed my first nigger when I was thirteen. The movement showed me what's happened to this country. How the niggers and the Zionists are taking over. How the Mexicans and Cubans are invading us.''

Somehow the Sloan Keating Tony had known just didn't jibe with the man to whom he was talking. He had watched the attorney handling juvenile case after juvenile case with competency and compassion.

''You're a good lawyer, Keating. A sharp kid. You have a great future, and—''

''Thanks,'' the attorney said before Tony could finish. ''I was trained to operate undercover.''

''I was going to ask how in the name of God you can believe in all that Nazi bullshit.''

''Bullshit? Did you know that the Jews control the news media and the entire financial structure in this country? Did you know that? Did you know that the Christianity most people profess is nothing but a Jew scam? Did you know that we routinely knock over black drug dealers and black pimps, especially black pimps who exploit white whores? Sometimes we even eliminate them. We've been doing a lot of your work for you.''

''For God's sakes, Keating.''

''It's because of people like you that we're forced to resort to violence. You won't even listen to reason.''

''You call that hogwash you're spouting reason?''

''You're a traitor to your race,'' Keating said. Then he lapsed into silence.

Tony, ignoring the pain in the back of his head, quietly struggled with the bonds that held him. The rope was nylon. The more he worked, the tighter the knots became. He sighed in frustration.

''No sense trying to get loose,'' Keating said from the front seat of the van.

''Where are we?''

The young attorney laughed. ''You don't think I'm gonna tell you that, do you?''

"What harm can it do? I assume you plan on killing me. Dead men can't talk."

"Save your breath, Mr. Prosecutor. I made a mistake with that kid today. I'm not making another."

Tony shifted, trying to relieve the strain on his neck. "Why in God's name did you accept the appointment? You blew your cover, if that's what you call it, when he heard your voice."

"Ah! Good point, counselor. But I didn't know that. I had to find out if the kid knew who I was. I didn't know what Zeke Morton had told his friends." Keating laughed. "As it turned out, good old Zeke hadn't told them who I was at all. I could have wasted Morton and been in high cotton, as the darkies like to say."

"Still, it was mighty risky going to that hospital tonight."

Keating swiveled around in the seat. "We're trained to face up to our mistakes, Danton. If the kid had recognized me—by appearance, I mean—I would have tried to buy his silence . . . or scare the hell out of him. I don't know what I would have done about his mother. I didn't count on her being there. Of course, if he hadn't known me—which is what I thought after the interview—then that meant he'd been telling the truth out there at the quarry."

"I'm glad to see a pure-blooded Aryan warrior can screw up," Tony said. "Of course, we knew that much when you blew up a whole city block trying to kill one little girl, a white girl at that."

"We're at war, asshole. Innocent people die. Besides, that wasn't my fault. I was given bad information about the explosive."

"What happens now?" Tony asked.

"I lay low until I can be gotten out of here. Then I go in deep hiding. We've got hundreds of names of sympathizers who will provide me with a comfortable hideout. You fuckin' apologists for the race mongrels and the Jew-kikes have no idea how deeply infiltrated you are."

THIRTY-SIX

GIL AND WHIT, accompanied by Jim Noble, arrived at the small brick building that housed Sloan Keating's law office at twelve-thirty Thursday morning. An unmarked patrol car was parked across the street. A white police car, fully marked, sat directly in front of the lawyer's office. They had expected one cruiser to be at the scene. The office had been under surveillance within minutes after Keating's escape from the hospital. The presence of the second one surprised them.

The city officer in the unmarked cruiser exited his vehicle and crossed over to Gil's car. He leaned down into the driver's-side window. "Evening, fellas. The chief's already here."

"The chief?" Whit asked, bending down so he could see the officer's face.

"Yes, sir. He arrived a few minutes ago and went on inside."

"That stupid son of a bitch," Whit said. He flung open his door.

Gil, hampered by his stiff knee, hurried to extricate himself from beneath the steering wheel. "Damn, Whit. Don't go off half-cocked this time."

Whit was heading for the house. "I guess I didn't make myself very clear earlier this evening."

Both Noble and the sheriff rushed to catch Whit. Gil put a hand on his shoulder when he caught up with him. "I'm serious, Whit. Just take it easy."

"Take it easy?" Whit pulled the search warrant they had

just obtained from the pocket of his sports coat. "The son of a bitch went in without this. If he's found something, it's probably useless to us."

"Aw, surely your courts aren't that strict," Noble said.

"The hell they're not," Whit snapped. "You guys get away with murder in federal court. We have to toe the line. Even if we can get something a little shaky through a suppression hearing in the circuit court, the state supreme court eats us alive."

At that moment Hayden Wallace opened the front door to Keating's office. "Come on in, guys. I was waiting on you before I started doing anything."

"How the hell did you even know we were coming?" Whit said.

"I got a radio, Pynchon. I heard you say that you were leaving the magistrate's office with search warrants. Where's Watkins?"

Before Whit could say anything else to the chief, Gil said, "He went to Keating's apartment with some deputies."

"Let's get busy," Whit said, more anxious to search the office than continue a debate with Wallace.

The law offices of Sloan Keating were modestly furnished. The front office and waiting room contained a secretary's desk, a computer and printer, and several file cabinets.

Whit was determined to control the search. He headed for a door at the rear of the front office. "Chief, you and Gil take in here. Noble and I will handle Keating's office."

The chief grinned. "Who put you in charge?"

"Dammit, Wallace—"

"Easy, boy," Wallace drawled. "You go right ahead and handle it your way. I don't wanna get you riled twice in one night."

Whit wheeled away from the chief and headed through a door that he assumed led into the lawyer's private office. His hand searched for a light switch. When he found it, a double panel of overhead fluorescent lights flooded the room with brightness.

Noble brushed by Whit and hurried around the desk to a computer terminal. "Mind if I check this out?" the agent said.

"You'll have to. I don't know diddly shit about the things. I'll search his desk."

The federal agent settled down in front of the monitor while Whit leafed through papers on the lawyer's desk.

"He's got a modem here," the agent said. "Cross your fingers."

"Why?" Whit asked.

"These groups have established nationwide computer bulletin boards and information systems, Whit. Maybe he keeps some of the names and numbers on here. It's the kind of intelligence we'd love to get our hands on."

Whit decided that he wasn't interested. "Right now I just want to get Tony back."

"Damn it to hell," the agent said.

Whit glanced back and saw an almost entirely blank screen. At the top it read, DISK ERROR.

"What's wrong?"

The agent pounded the keys and cursed again. "It looks to me like someone fried all the data on the hard disk."

A small box of computer disks sat beside the keyboard. Noble searched through them and pulled one out. "Maybe I can get it to boot from this."

Whit just shook his head and returned his attention to the desk top.

"No luck," Noble said a moment later. "It says this disk is bad, too. Either that or he's got some sort of odd protection system."

Whit's eyes came to rest on a rectangular device affixed with a handle and an electric cord. Instead of picking it up, he withdrew a pencil from his pocket and pushed it around on top of the lawyer's desk. "This thing's heavy. Do you know what it is?"

The agent looked over his shoulder. "Yeah, I'm afraid I do. It's called a bulk eraser. You use it to reset the magnetic arrangement on magnetic recording media. It jumbles any existing data.''

''Christ, speak English.''

''It erases information on a videotape or a cassette tape or one of these.'' He was holding up one of the small plastic-encased disks.

''So Keating managed to get back here just long enough to fry the information on those disks?''

''And the information on the computer's hard disk. That thing on the desk produces a magnetic field strong enough to corrupt data within several feet. If you don't mind, I'll still have the computer and the disks shipped to our lab in Washington. Sometimes they can work miracles recovering data.''

''Be my guest,'' Whit said. He studied the filing cabinets that lined one wall of the small office. ''This is going to be a long night,'' Whit said. ''I could use some coffee.''

''Are you going through everything?''

Whit dropped down into the chair Noble had been using. ''Unless Watkins comes up with something at the asshole's apartment, it's our last hope.''

A cramp threatened to seize Tony Danton's left calf. He tried to hold rock still, hoping that it would go away, but the muscle kept twitching, teasing him with the prospect of the pain he would suffer if it did lock. His captor still occupied the passenger seat in the van. Both front seats were well padded with high backs, and Keating had lowered the upper portion so he could stretch out.

''My leg's going to cramp,'' Tony said.

''Nothing I can do about it,'' Keating said, not even turning his head to look at his hostage.

''You could cut my legs loose and secure me to the wall of the van. Or just help me shift positions.''

The young lawyer chuckled. ''Can't do that, Danton. See, there's about two pounds of plastic explosive back there, a box of six grenades, several sticks of dynamite, blasting caps, a few weapons, and lotsa ammunition. I can't have you jerking around. You can see my point."

For a moment Tony forgot about the misery in his leg and tried to look around the small compartment. On the side opposite him he could see a shelf attached to the wall, much like the design of the interior of an ambulance. It was lined with boxes.

A lighter flickered in the darkness as Keating ignited another cigarette.

"Christ," Tony said. "You shouldn't be smoking in here."

"Take it easy, Mr. Prosecutor. So long as I don't flip the butt back there, you'll be fine."

That's when the muscle in his leg decided to abandon the tenuous truce. The gripping pain made Tony cry out. The sudden scream startled Keating. He cantilevered forward. "What the fuck are you doing?"

"My leg!" Tony grimaced. "I told you it was gonna cramp."

"Lay still," the young lawyer commanded.

"Screw you," Tony said through grinding teeth. "I can't. When I get leg camps, they hurt like hell."

Keating flung open the passenger-side door and circled to the back of the van. He wrenched open the rear door and locked his hand on the short bridge of rope that laced Tony Danton's ankles together.

"Oh, Jesus," wailed Tony. "Don't pull. Please."

Keating didn't just pull. He yanked on the rope, exerting a savage traction on both of the older man's legs. Tony wailed as the cramping muscle was straightened. Then the agony vanished.

"Oh, God," Tony gasped.

"That better, counselor?"

The Raven County prosecutor was gasping his relief. "Yes. God, yes."

"I learned that as part of survival training."

"I appreciate it," Tony said, and meant it.

"Don't get the wrong idea. I've never had a chance to try it before. I was just curious to see if it worked."

A hand gently shook Whit's injured shoulder. He opened his eyes to see the gray light of the coming dawn through the sheers that covered the windows of Keating's office.

He lifted his head from the desk. "Christ, I went to sleep."

Gil Dickerson stood behind him. "I doubt you got much rest in that position, but Noble and I decided that you needed the sleep."

"What time is it?"

"A little before six." Gil placed a breakfast biscuit and a cup of coffee on the desk. "I had one of the deputies get them for us."

Whit rubbed his eyes. "How long did I sleep?"

"Three hours."

"Jesus, I've got one hell of a headache."

Dickerson went around to one of the padded plastic chairs used for the lawyer's clients. "You need more sleep. Eat something. Maybe it'll make you feel better."

"Has anyone spotted Keating's car?" Whit asked, opening the aromatic coffee.

Gil shook his head. "Not a word. Wallace is making noises that he's going to pull his men off the case. He thinks Keating made it out of town."

"I'm afraid he's right," Whit said, sipping the steaming brew.

Gil had placed that day's edition of the *Daily Journal* on the desk before awakening Whit. He pushed it across to his friend. "Anna broke the news about the right-wing group, but otherwise she treated us all right. I just got a call from the jail. The other newspeople are going crazy. They started showing up even before daylight."

Whit had taken a large bite of the biscuit. "Who the hell cares?" he mumbled.

"How much more stuff do you have to go through here?"

"Most of it," Whit said. "I shouldn't have gone to sleep. I'd also better call Anna."

"I took care of that, too. She phoned the sheriff's department around three-thirty this morning. You had just dozed off. She said to tell you she would be at home."

"Where's Noble and Wallace?"

"Noble's out in the front office. He's dozing on the sofa. Wallace left a couple of hours ago. I'd say he went home."

"I hope he stays there," Whit said. With the biscuit consumed, he started sorting through the pile of papers on the desk of the lawyer. "This stuff is out of his desk drawers. I guess I might as well finish it up before starting on the files."

"Do you really think you're going to find anything?"

Whit didn't answer immediately. He was looking at a small slip of paper he had uncovered. He lifted it. "I think maybe I have found something."

"What is it?" the sheriff asked.

"A rent receipt. It's made out to Keating. It says it's 'for warehouse space.' What the hell would he need with warehouse space?"

Gil tensed. "Does it say where?"

"Nope, but we sure as hell can check with the guy who rented it to him."

The sheriff reached for the phone book. "What's his name?"

Whit squinted at the scrawled signature. "William Shaw, I think."

Gil flipped through the pages, then ran his finger down the appropriate page. "Here's a William P. Shaw. He's the only one listed."

"Read me the number," Whit said as he grabbed the phone. He keyed it in as the sheriff relayed it.

The sleepy voice of a woman answered.

"Mrs. Shaw?"

"Yes, who is this?"

"Is your husband there?" Whit asked.

"My goodness, do you know what time it is?" she said, obviously irritated by the call.

"I certainly do," Whit said. "Please put your husband on. This is—"

Before Whit could finish the sentence, a gruff voice asked, "Who the hell is this?"

"Are you William Shaw?"

"I am. Now, who the hell are you?"

"My name is Whit Pynchon, Mr. Shaw. I'm—"

"I saw you on the news last night," the man said, his anger replaced by surprise.

"Mr. Shaw, have you rented warehouse space to a man by the name of Sloan Keating?"

"Yes, sir. Why?"

"Can you tell us where the warehouse is located?"

"He rented half a warehouse. I mean, I have one warehouse that I've divided. It's out on the highway that goes south to Virginia. Between Bert's Best Car Buys and the Dairy Queen. What's going on, anyway?"

"Did Keating say why he wanted the space?" Whit asked.

"Uh, yeah. He said he was planning to open a business and needed a place to store his inventory. Hey, c'mon, tell me what this is all about."

"What sort of business, Mr. Shaw?"

"Merchandising. That's all he told me."

"Have you checked on the property?"

The man paused for a moment. "Look, I don't wanna be a hardass or anything like that, but maybe you oughta tell me what this is all about."

"If you watched the news last night, Mr. Shaw, you know what it's about."

"But this Keating guy, he's a lawyer, ain't he? That's what he told me. I figured he was all right. If he's doing anything illegal out there, I don't know about it. I've driven by it a lot, and it didn't look to me like he was doing much at all with the building. But he pays his rent on time."

"You said it was divided in half. Who rents the other side?"

"Nobody," the man said. "I've been trying to rent the place for a year. This guy's the first one in six months to even talk to me about it."

"I appreciate the information," Whit said. "We may be back in touch with you. If we have to force our way into the building, would you be willing to open it for us?"

"Sure thing," Shaw said. "Like I said, Mr. Pynchon, if that guy's been up to no good in that building, I didn't know a damn thing about it."

"I understand," Whit said, trying to extricate himself from the call.

"One thing, Mr. Pynchon."

"What's that?"

"You really gave them pesky news reporters hell. Me and my wife both got a kick outta that. You keep up the good work."

Thirty-Seven

Sloan Keating, his car, and the prosecuting attorney of Raven County had vanished into thin air less than twelve hours before. The various roadblocks throughout the county had resulted in the arrest of three drunk drivers, but none of the participating officers had spotted Keating's car, anyone fitting Keating's description, or his hostage. The all-points bulletin issued to the surrounding counties and to Virginia officials to the south hadn't produced a single response. Given the reasonably quick response of the various departments after the violence at the hospital, Whit Pynchon believed that the subject of this search was hiding in the warehouse he had rented from William Shaw.

"It's big enough for several vehicles," Gil said as the unmarked cruiser eased by the dark metal structure and rolled down the two-lane highway.

"I think he's there," Whit said. He was driving Gil's cruiser. The sheriff sat in the back this time, his bad leg stretched out across the seat. Noble rode in the front seat.

"Any action we take is going to jeopardize Danton's life," the agent said.

Whit nodded. "Assuming, of course, that he's still alive."

"Oh, I'd bet he's alive," Noble said. "Danton's his ace in the hole."

The warehouse was just outside the city limits of Milbrook. Gil's department would provide the bulk of the manpower to surround the building, but he had insisted on notifying Terry Watkins, who in turn had phoned Wallace.

293

City officers would be on hand. The various units had been positioned in the parking area of a small department store two blocks away from the warehouse.

Whit turned the vehicle and made a second pass by the building. "There's a pretty open space around the building, and I don't see any entrance other than those double doors in front."

Gil and Noble both continued to study the structure as the cruiser headed back toward the assembly area. "I'd bet there's a back door," Gil said.

A dozen police cars were waiting in the parking lot of the department store as Whit pulled in. The three men exited the cruiser and were joined by Chief Wallace and Detective Sergeant Terry Watkins.

"You shoulda taken me with you," Wallace said. "You guys may be the detectives, but when it comes to this type of action, it's my cup of tea."

"It's also out of your jurisdiction," Whit said, not anxious to have the new chief involved at all.

"Let's brief him on the situation," Gil said. "Maybe he does know a trick or two."

"A trick or two?" Wallace said. "Jesus fucking Christ, I handled situations like these for twenty gawdamn years."

"So brief him," Whit said, "but do it in a hurry. Traffic's starting to pick up, and I want to get this over with."

Gil outlined the layout to the chief. When he was finished, Wallace shrugged. "No big deal. If you can't get inside without being seen, then you surround it. Let the bastard know he's had it and that you're not gonna make concessions."

"At which point," Whit said, "he blows away the prosecutor of this county."

"Maybe," Wallace said, "but not likely."

Whit threw up his hands. "What the hell's he got to lose, Chief? He's capable of it. How many people has he killed already? I don't think he batted an eye. He's a killing machine, pure and simple."

Wallace wasn't impressed. "Hey, pal, I've handled dozens

of these situations. Your actions are dictated by the circumstances. You got no choice. We don't know how much firepower he has. Hell, he might even have explosives in there. You start shooting first, and the whole gawdamn block might go up."

"I hadn't thought of that," Gil said.

Nor had Whit, but he wasn't about to admit it. "Okay, we surround the warehouse, then try to talk to him. I guess it's our only choice. Let's do it."

Tony Danton's stomach embarrassed him. It kept growling and gurgling loudly enough that Keating heard it.

"You hungry?" he asked.

Tony tried to shift positions. "I'm used to eating breakfast."

"With any luck, we'll be out of here today."

The prosecutor remained bound to the side of the van. After having put an end to Tony's leg cramps, Keating had left the back door of the van open and had secured Tony's legs to the rear bumper of the vehicle. At some point Tony had drifted into a fitful sleep. His protesting stomach had woken him. Keating had been standing at the rear of the van, studying a road map.

"I have to go to the bathroom," Tony said. "I don't think you want me to urinate on the carpet inside this van."

"No, I am rather proud of my van. I fully intend to get away with it. I'm leaving too much behind as it is."

"So you'd best untie me. Otherwise I am going to piss right here and now."

The younger man glared at his prisoner. He brandished an exotic assault weapon that Tony did not recognize. "I'll use this if you make any effort to escape. I trust you know that."

"I know it," Tony said. "You have my word."

At that Keating laughed. "Your word? You're a fucking politician."

"Look, it's your fancy van, Keating. Either you get me out of here, or I'm going to soil the carpet."

The barrel of the gun came around. Keating jammed it between Tony's legs. "I don't think, Mr. Prosecutor, that you are in any position to be using ultimatums."

With the hard barrel of the gun resting just below his testicles, Tony somehow managed to smile. "You pull that trigger and you'll really stain the carpet."

Keating grinned, too. "Yeah, I guess I would at that." He withdrew the gun and placed it against the bumper. He started undoing one of the knots.

"Sloan Keating!" The voice came from outside.

"Holy shit," the lawyer said, abandoning his efforts with the ropes. He snatched the rifle and ran to one of the small windows in the garage door.

"Keating!"

The lawyer saw three police cars parked a hundred feet from the front door. "Motherfuckers!" He shattered the glass with the gun's barrel and unleashed a barrage of fire. The large-caliber bullets punched holes in the sides of the police vehicles.

"Don't fire!" he heard a voice shout.

Keating abandoned the window and dashed back to the van. He bounded up inside and pulled a knife from his pocket. The blade flipped open.

"You've had it," Tony said. "You might as well give up."

Keating's fist smashed into his face. "Just shut the fuck up. I'm not dead yet."

Blood poured from Tony's nose as the younger lawyer slashed at his bindings. Within moments the prosecutor was untied, all but his hands. They remained bound.

"Out of the van," Keating ordered.

With his tied hands he tried to wipe away the blood pouring from his nose. "C'mon, Keating. I'm too damned stiff to move. Give me a minute."

With a flick of his wrist Keating sliced a gash across Tony's left cheek. "Next time it'll be your throat. Move it!"

Pins and needles surged through Tony's legs as he tried to work himself out of the van. The blood continued to ooze from his nose, augmented by a fresh torrent from the gaping wound in his cheek. Keating latched on to his arm and pulled. When Tony's feet came in contact with the greasy concrete floor of the warehouse, he collapsed.

"Keating! We want to talk." It was Whit. Tony recognized his voice.

Keating rushed to the broken window and cautiously peered out. "Fuck you," he screamed. "I've still got Danton. He's gonna die!"

"We're willing to negotiate," Whit shouted.

"Liar!" Keating bellowed.

He turned to Tony, who was using the rear bumper of the van to pull himself to his feet. Glistening blood covered the front of the prosecutor's white shirt and tan sports coat. "Get ready to die," Keating said. "They're not going to take me alive."

Whit continued to make his plea. "Keating! Just talk to me!"

The frenzied lawyer pivoted to look out the window. "I've enough explosives in here to blow up half of Milbrook, Pynchon. I'll use it. Just take your fucking cops and get the hell out of here."

"We can't do that," Whit replied. "You know that."

Anna might have not heard the phone had it rung just five or six times, but the caller wouldn't give up. On the eleventh ring she stirred. On the thirteenth she answered it.

"Anna, it's Barney. The police are involved in some kind of shoot-out just south of Milbrook. It looks like it's related to the terrorist story."

"Barney? What time is it?"

"A little after seven."

"Oh, Gawd," she drawled, drooping back on the bed.

"Did you hear what I said?"

Anna tried to get her thoughts together. "I dunno. What did you say?"

"I said that there's a shoot-out and standoff going on right now.'

She sat up in bed. "Is Whit there?"

"According to the person who tipped me, he's there. This guy they were looking for last night?"

"Keating?"

"Yeah, he's inside a warehouse with Tony Danton being held as a hostage."

Anna was already getting out of bed. "You meet me there. Oh, and call a photographer."

"I already have."

Whit, who had been standing behind Gil's cruiser, saw the barrel push forward through the broken window. "Hit the ground," he cried.

The lawyer sent another volley of gunfire at the police cruisers. Whit, down on his knees and leaning against the rear quarter panel, felt the vehicle vibrate as the bullets smashed into the other side.

Gil and Noble were also behind the car.

"Now what the fuck do we do?" Whit asked.

"Wait it out," Noble said. "If you guys have any tear gas, I might be able to lob a canister through that small window."

"Hell, no," Whit said. "If you miss, we'll be the ones breaking cover to escape it."

Noble dared to peek up over the hood. That action brought another staccato burst from inside the warehouse. The agent dropped back to the graveled ground. "It's not an impossible shot. If we get tear gas in that building, he'll come out."

"Forget it," Whit said. He leaned away from the car, looking down the line of officers gathered behind the vehicles. "Where the hell's our SWAT genius?"

Gil answered. "He and Watkins went with some of my guys around back."

At that instant Wallace's voice boomed over a bullhorn. "This is Chief Wallace, Milbrook Police Department."

"Ohmigod," Whit said, lifting his head to see.

The barrel of the gun wasn't protruding from the warehouse window. Whit couldn't see Wallace either. He was on the other side of the warehouse.

"What the fuck's he doing?" Gil asked.

The chief's voice bellowed out again. "Keating, you have no choice. Release your hostage. We guarantee you fair treatment."

"Listen to that idiot," Whit said. "Hell, he's not even inside the city limits."

"He's counting on southern charm," Gil said.

Whit peered over the hood of the car. He cupped his hands over his mouth. "Give it up, Keating. You're surrounded."

The next voice belonged to Wallace. "Can I come inside and talk to you?"

"No!" Whit roared, trying to yell loudly enough for Wallace to hear him.

Noble scooted over to Whit. "He has to be stopped. We can't let that fanatic have two hostages."

Then Keating replied. "Leave your weapon, Chief, and come inside."

Whit sprang to his feet. "Wallace!"

THIRTY-EIGHT

KEATING WENT TO Tony and hoisted him to his feet. "Either you stand or you die now, Danton."

Some of the feeling had returned to Tony's legs and feet. By leaning against the side of the van, he managed to support himself. For the first time he noticed the dark green Buick sedan parked beside the van.

Keating darted between the two vehicles and ran to the single rear door. He flipped the latch on it, then came charging back to the front.

Tony had heard Wallace's offer to come into the building. He also had heard Whit's protest. Whit was right. It was dangerous grandstanding on the part of Milbrook's new police chief. "So now you'll have two hostages," Tony said.

"Yeah," Keating said, smiling. "I guess I will."

The young lawyer kept watching the front door. "I'd sure as hell like to get a shot at the damned FBI agent. I saw him out there a minute ago. We place a high priority on killing federal dogs."

"You amaze me," Tony said. "I must admit that you frighten me, too."

"I consider that a compliment, counselor."

"Don't. It wasn't meant as one. It simply scares the hell outta me that this fanatic cause is able to recruit someone apparently as intelligent as you are."

Keating kept glancing back toward the rear of the building, waiting for Wallace to make his appearance. "Maybe you should think about that, Danton. I'm on this side because I am smart.''

''You're brainwashed.''

The back door opened with a shrill screech.

''You stay put,'' the young lawyer said.

Tony saw Wallace, his holster empty, step into the warehouse.

Whit squatted behind Gil's cruiser, staying just high enough so that he could watch the building over the hood of the vehicle. Out of the corner of his eye he caught a movement to his left. Watkins peeked around the distant corner of the warehouse. Whit raised himself up a little higher.

''The chief just went inside!'' Watkins shouted.

Whit turned to Gil and Noble. ''Cover me. I'm going to make a break for the front door.''

''That's suicide,'' Gil said.

''Maybe Wallace is diverting him. If I can get to the building without being seen, we've got a chance. Watch that window. If the barrel comes out, cut loose.''

''Dammit, Whit—''

But the prosecutor's investigator had moved around to the front of the car. He paused for an instant and then launched himself toward the warehouse. His shoulder remained tender, and he had to try to hold it stiff as he ran. He kept his eyes locked on the shattered window, ready to react if the gun's barrel appeared.

Keating held the assault rifle in both hands as Wallace approached. Tony stood between the men. ''That was a stupid thing to do,'' the prosecutor said as the chief approached.

''Like I told your investigator, I'm a veteran of these situations.''

Keating was grinning.

''What's so damned funny?'' Wallace asked. ''You really fucked this one up, boy.''

"Don't blame me. It was that damned snake."

Tony stared at Wallace. "You two are in this together?"

"Shoot him," Wallace said, his voice low enough not to be heard outside.

The smile vanished from Keating's face. "Me?"

"Shit, Keating." The chief reached out. "Give me the damned gun. Quick!"

The lawyer handed it over.

"Sorry, Keating." The lawyer still had his hand on the barrel when Wallace pulled the trigger. The impact drove his body all the way back to a wall.

"Your turn," the chief said, turning the gun on Tony. The prosecutor fell forward, knocking the weapon from the chief's hand.

"Damn you," Wallace said. He reached into his pocket and was pulling out a small automatic when the front door swung open.

Whit came rushing in. He saw Tony spread facedown on the floor. He whirled, looking for Keating. "He's there," Wallace said, pointing to the bloody body that lay twitching on the concrete floor.

"What happened?" Whit was on his knees, trying to roll his employer over onto his back. Cops came charging into the warehouse through both the front and back doors.

Tony was trying to say something as Whit struggled to turn him over, but the din of noise from the incoming officers drowned out his voice.

"Where are you shot?" Whit asked, seeing the blood as Tony managed to push himself up.

"Dammit, Whit. Get Wallace. He's in on it."

Whit frowned. "Are you shot?"

"Hell no. But don't let Wallace get away."

"Wallace?" Whit said. He looked up, expecting to see the chief standing right where he had been.

He wasn't.

"Wallace!" Whit shouted.

Noble was over at Keating's body. "He just walked out, Whit."

"He's one of them," Tony said. "Go after him."

Barney's hastily given directions had only confused Anna until he had told her that the warehouse was beside the Dairy Queen. She knew where that was. When she reached it, she turned into its parking lot. Slowly circling the ice cream stand, she saw the conglomeration of police vehicles. She also saw Chief Wallace running across the graveled lot outside the warehouse. She gunned the car and came to a stop beside him. Just as she was about to shut off the engine, the driver's door flew open.

Wallace leaned down into her face. "Get your pretty ass over the hump."

"What?"

The small gun was jammed into her face. "Get the fuck over."

She struggled to crawl over the console and gearshift. Wallace was already coming down in the seat, forcing her over.

"What's the matter with you?" she said.

He dropped the car into drive and jammed his foot down on the accelerator, wheeling the small import away from the warehouse.

Whit, exiting the warehouse, saw the white Nissan spraying gravel as it disappeared around the building. He made a dash for Gil's cruiser, hoping that none of the bullets that had drilled into its passenger side had damaged the engine.

Noble came out of the warehouse behind him.

"Where did he go?"

The ice cream stand blocked their view, but they both heard the squealing of tires from the opposite side. "He forced Anna over and took her car," Whit said as the two men climbed into the bullet-riddled cruiser.

"Another hostage situation. You people have your share of excitement down here."

Whit heaved a sigh of relief when he saw that the keys were still in the ignition. Holding his breath, he turned the key. The engine fired. "So far, so good," he said.

Whit put the transmission in reverse and left tire marks as he backed toward the highway. "The bastard headed back into town," Whit said. "Hang on."

Noble was doing more than that. He was buckling his seat belt. "Just don't kill me. I hate car chases."

"This is pretty much my first," Whit said, hitting the vehicle's lights and sirens as he peeled out onto the highway.

By that time, almost seven-thirty, the traffic on Milbrook's streets was beginning to pick up. Most of the people in front of Whit pulled over to let him pass. He hoped they weren't doing the same thing for Wallace.

"That guy up ahead isn't pulling over," Noble said, bracing his hands against the dash.

The vehicle in front of them was an old rusty truck. Its exhaust spewed a trail of blue, oily smoke. Whit laid on the horn.

"He probably can't see us," Noble said. "He's laying down a smoke screen."

"Hang on," Whit said as he swerved out into the other lane to pass the car.

He found himself staring straight into the grille of an oncoming car.

"Oh, sweet Jesus," Noble said.

Whit jerked the wheel back to the left. The front bumper of the cruiser clipped the rear bumper of the old truck. Whit braked hard as the truck started to fishtail.

"He's losing," Noble said.

The truck suddenly cut to the right and bounced over a berm. Whit emerged from the clouds of blue smoke and swerved around the truck's rear end.

"Do you see him?" Whit asked. They were heading east, driving straight into the early-morning sun. Noble used his palms to block the glare. "What the hell am I looking for?"

"A new white Nissan Sentra."

"Don't see it," the FBI man said.

"Gawdammit." Whit gave the car more gas. "If they get into town, we'll lose them for sure."

"There he is," Noble cried. "Straight ahead. The light caught him."

It turned green before Whit could reach him. Wallace must have noticed the pursuing cruiser. Whit saw the rear end of the Nissan drop as its driver floorboarded it. It swung around the car in front of him. A car was approaching from the other direction.

"Oh, Christ. He's gonna hit that car head on." Whit cringed, expecting to see the rear end of the Nissan lurch upward on impact. It didn't. Instead, the oncoming car tried to evade the accident by going off the road. It smashed into a utility pole. A woman's body crashed through the windshield right in front of Whit's eyes.

"God in heaven," Noble said.

The screaming of Whit's siren was loud enough that cars ahead of the chase were pulling off to the side.

"We'll be in the main business district in a few seconds," Whit said.

"He's slowing down," Noble cried.

Whit started to close the distance between them. "What's he doing?"

"I dunno," Noble said, "but you're gonna run up his tail pipe."

Anna couldn't stop crying. She was that scared. She had seen the face of the woman when Wallace had cut into her lane. The woman's mouth had opened in a panicked scream just before she had whipped the wheel to the left. Anna had heard the jarring crash as the vehicle had slammed right into the pole.

"You bastard!" she had screamed.

"Shut up, bitch."

Somehow he was holding the small pistol and the steering wheel at the same time. She reached for the wheel. He let go long enough to swing the gun around. The hard metal connected with her jaw, driving her head against the window on the other side.

"I oughta kill you now," he said.

That's when the car's engine seemed to heave. Wallace's eyes dropped down to the instrument panel. "What the fuck?"

He mashed the accelerator to the floor, but the car actually seemed to slow down. "Fuck you," he screamed, pounding the dash with the hand that held the gun.

Maybe he didn't know what was wrong, but Anna knew. Even though her mind remained somewhat clouded from the effects of the blow, she started to laugh. "It's out of gas," she said.

"Out of gas." He looked at the gauge.

"Sorry."

"Then you die, cunt." He lifted the pistol.

A sudden impact jolted the vehicle just as he squeezed the trigger. The bullet shattered the passenger-side window. Anna was thrown forward, but she managed to catch herself with her hands. Wallace, turned toward her, was less prepared to brace himself. His head snapped to one side and then the other. It came to rest on the steering wheel, a trickle of blood dribbling down the side of his face and into his lap.

Anna looked back over her shoulder. She saw Whit bounding out of the car that had rear-ended hers. He flung open the door and jerked Wallace's limp body from the front seat. The police chief sprawled out on the pavement, his head twisted a little more toward the side than should have been possible.

Whit peered into the car. "Are you all right?"

"What the hell did you do to my car?"

EPILOGUE

TONY AND GIL arrived at the scene of the wreck just as Hayden Wallace's body was being loaded into the ambulance. "Is he dead?" Gil asked.

Whit, standing with Anna and Jim Noble, nodded, then said, "He deserves to be."

"Did you shoot him?" Tony asked.

Whit put an arm around Anna. "No, but I was going to."

Tony, a bandage on the gash in his cheek and a plug of cotton up his swollen nose, examined the two vehicles. The sheriff's cruiser had crumpled the rear end of the smaller Nissan. "It doesn't look like that bad of a collision. What killed him?"

"A case of extreme whiplash," Anna said. "What about the woman he ran off the road?"

"We stopped to check on her," Gil said. "She didn't make it."

Tony's legs still ached. He hobbled over to one of the police cruisers and lowered himself into the front seat. Whit and Anna followed.

The prosecutor looked up at them. "What a nightmare. What's the final body count?"

"With Wallace and the lawyer and the lady back there, it's fifteen," Anna said.

"Sixteen," Whit said.

"No, fifteen. If you're counting Mickey Moses's mother, she's going to make it. I called the hospital just before the paper went to press. What happens to the boy, Tony?"

307

"I don't know yet," Tony said. "I doubt I'll try him as an adult, but he's not going to walk away scot-free."

Noble finished talking to the sheriff and came over to join them.

"I wish I could say it's been a pleasure. It hasn't, though. I'll be back in a few days. I hope you'll secure the chief's office and his lodgings for us. We want to see what we can come up with."

"Will do," Whit said.

"Now that I think back on it," the agent said, "I'll bet my pension that it was Wallace who tampered with Keating's computer system. That's why he got there ahead of us."

"And Wallace was the leak," Whit said.

Tony dropped his head. "You were right, Whit."

"I just didn't know how right." He turned back to Noble. "You're more than welcome to stay. You should consider that a compliment. As a rule I'm not so hospitable to feds."

Noble laughed. "Thanks, but no thanks. I'm going back to Washington. It's safer there—and cooler, too."

"The heat wave's supposed to end tomorrow," Anna said. "There's a Canadian cold front bearing down on us."

"Damn," Whit said.

Tony looked up at his employee. "You and Anna should take a few days. Go on down to the beach. I'm sure it's still hot down there."

"Not a good idea," Anna said. "There's a small tropical storm just off the coast of the Carolinas."

Whit threw up his hands. "Isn't she just full of good news. No wonder people read the paper and then commit suicide."

"We could drive down to Nashville and meet Tressa," Anna said. "I've never been to the Grand Ole Opry."

Gil had joined them by that time. "I've always wanted to go to the Opry. Reckon Kathy and you both could be away for a few days. We could make it a double date."

The television crew appeared out of nowhere. Whit turned at the sound of their approach and found himself staring into a camera. A microphone loomed just below his mouth. Myra

Martin was holding it. ''Mr. Pynchon, can you tell us what happened here this morning?''

Whit pulled Anna to his side. ''My press secretary, Miss Tyree, will answer all your questions.''

Whit left Anna sputtering and hurried to catch up with Gil and Noble. ''How about dropping me off at the house. I need some sleep.''

ABOUT THE AUTHOR

Dave Pedneau is a former reporter, columnist, and magistrate court judge. His novels include *A.P.B.*, *D.O.A.*, *B.O.L.O.*, and *A.K.A.*, all published by Ballantine. He lives in southern West Virginia with his wife and daughter.